Praise for the ARTHUR C. CLARKE, NEBULA, BSFA, and HUGO award-winning *Ancillary Justice*

"Unexpected, compelling and very cool. Ann Leckie nails it."
—John Scalzi

"Establishes Leckie as an heir to Banks and Cherryh."
—Elizabeth Bear

"Powerful, arresting, beautiful space opera....Leckie makes it look so easy."
—Kameron Hurley

"Total gamechanger. Get it, read it, wish to hell you'd written it. Ann Leckie's *Ancillary Justice* may well be the most important book Orbit has published in ages."
—Paul Graham Raven

"It's by turns thrilling, moving and awe-inspiring."
—*Guardian*

"*Ancillary Justice* is the mind-blowing space opera you've been needing....This is a novel that will thrill you like the page-turner it is, but stick with you for a long time afterward."
—*io9*

"This impressive debut succeeds in making Breq a protagonist readers will invest in, and establishes Leckie as a talent to watch."
—*Publishers Weekly*

"Assured, gripping, and stylish.... An absorbing thousand-year history, a poignant personal journey, and a welcome addition to the genre." —*NPR Books*

"A stunning, fast-paced debut." —*Shelf Awareness*

"It's not every day a debut novel by an author you'd never heard of before derails your entire afternoon with its brilliance. But when my review copy of *Ancillary Justice* arrived, that's exactly what it did. In fact, it arrowed upward to reach a pretty high position on my list of best space opera novels ever." —Liz Bourke, Tor.com

"This is not entry-level SF, and its payoff is correspondingly greater because of that." —*Locus*

"I cannot find fault in this truly amazing, awe-inspiring debut novel from Ann Leckie.... *Ancillary Justice* is one of the best science fiction novels I've ever read." —*The Book Smugglers*

"Ann Leckie's *Ancillary Justice* does everything science fiction should do. It engages, it excites, and it challenges the way the reader views our world." —*Staffer's Book Review*

Praise for *Ancillary Sword*

"Powerful." —*The New York Times*

"Fans of space operas will feast on its richly textured, gorgeously rendered world-building." —*Entertainment Weekly*

By Ann Leckie

Ancillary Justice
Ancillary Sword
Ancillary Mercy

ANCILLARY MERCY

ANN LECKIE

www.orbitbooks.net
www.orbitshortfiction.com

Orbit
Hachette Book Group
1290 Avenue of the Americas
New York, NY 10104
www.orbitbooks.net

Printed in the United States of America

RRD-C

First edition: October 2015
10 9 8 7 6 5 4 3 2 1

Orbit is an imprint of Hachette Book Group.
The Orbit name and logo are trademarks of Little, Brown Book Group Limited.

The Hachette Speakers Bureau provides a wide range of authors for speaking events. To find out more, go to www.hachettespeakersbureau.com or call (866) 376-6591.

The publisher is not responsible for websites (or their content) that are not owned by the publisher.

Library of Congress Cataloging-in-Publication Data

Leckie, Ann.
    Ancillary mercy / Ann Leckie.—First edition.
        pages ; cm
    ISBN 978-0-316-24668-2 (trade pbk.)—ISBN 978-0-316-24667-5 (ebook)—ISBN 978-1-4789-3631-2 (audio book cd)—ISBN 978-1-4789-6014-0 (audio book [downloadable]) I. Title.

    PS3612.E3353A832 2015
    813'.6—dc23

                                                              2015020915

ANCILLARY MERCY

1

One moment asleep. Awake the next, to the familiar small noises of someone making tea. But it was six minutes earlier than I'd intended. Why? I reached.

Lieutenant Ekalu was on watch. Indignant about something. A little angry, even. Before her the wall displayed a view of Athoek Station, the ships surrounding it. The dome over its gardens barely visible from this angle. Athoek itself half shadowed, half shining blue and white. The background chatter of communications revealed nothing amiss.

I opened my eyes. The walls of my quarters displayed the same view of the space around us that Lieutenant Ekalu watched, in Command—Athoek Station, ships, Athoek itself. The beacons of the system's four intersystem gates. I didn't need the walls to display that view. It was one I could see anywhere, at any time, merely by wishing to. But I had never commanded its actual use here. Ship must have done it.

At the counter at the end of the three-by-four-meter room, Seivarden stood, making tea. With the old enamel set, only two bowls, one of them chipped, a casualty of Seivarden's early, inept attempts to be useful, more than a year ago. It had been more than a month since she'd last acted as my servant, but her presence was so familiar that I had, on waking, accepted it without thinking much about it. "Seivarden," I said.

"Ship, actually." She tilted her head toward me just slightly, her attention still on the tea. *Mercy of Kalr* mostly communicated with its crew via auditory or visual implants, speaking directly into our ears or placing words or images in our visions. It was doing this now, I could see, Seivarden reading words that Ship was giving her. "I'm Ship just now. And two messages came in for you while you slept, but there's nothing immediately wrong, Fleet Captain."

I sat up, pushed the blanket away. Three days before, my shoulder had been encased in a corrective, numbing and immobilizing that arm. I was still appreciating the restored freedom of movement.

Seivarden continued, "I think Lieutenant Seivarden misses this sometimes." The data Ship read from her—which I could see merely by reaching for it—showed some apprehension, mild embarrassment. But Ship was right—she was enjoying this small return to our old roles, even if, I found, I wasn't. "Three hours ago, Fleet Captain Uemi messaged." Fleet Captain Uemi was my counterpart one gate away, in Hrad System. In command over any Radchaai military ships stationed there. For whatever that was worth: Radch space was currently embroiled in a civil war, and Fleet Captain Uemi's authority, like mine, came from the part of Anaander Mianaai that currently held Omaugh Palace. "Tstur Palace has fallen."

"Dare I ask to whom?"

Seivarden turned from the counter, bowl of tea in one gloved hand. Came over to where I sat on my bed. After all this time she was too familiar with me to be surprised at my response, or discomfited by the fact my own hands were still bare. "The Lord of Mianaai, who else?" she replied, with a faint smile. Handed me the bowl of tea. "The one, so Fleet Captain Uemi said, that has very little love for you, Fleet Captain. Or for Fleet Captain Uemi herself."

"Right." To my mind there was very little difference between any of the parts of Anaander Mianaai, Lord of the Radch, and none of her had any real reason to be pleased with me. But I knew which side Fleet Captain Uemi supported. Possibly even was. Anaander was many-bodied, used to being in dozens, if not hundreds, of places at the same time. Now she was reduced and fragmented, many of her cloned bodies lost in the struggle against herself. I strongly suspected that Captain Uemi was herself a fragment of the Lord of the Radch.

"Fleet Captain Uemi added," continued Seivarden, "that the Anaander who has taken over Tstur has also managed to sever her connection with herself outside of Tstur System, so the rest of her doesn't know what she intends. But if Fleet Captain Uemi were Anaander Mianaai, she says, she would devote most of her resources to securing that system, now she's taken the palace itself. But she would also be sorely tempted to send someone after *you*, Fleet Captain, if she possibly could. The captain of the Hrad fleet also begs to point out that the news reached her by way of a ship from Omaugh Palace, so the information is weeks old."

I took a drink of my tea. "If the tyrant was foolish enough to send ships here the moment she gained control of Tstur, the soonest they could possibly arrive would be..." *Mercy of Kalr* showed me numbers. "In about a week."

"That part of the Lord of the Radch has reason to be extremely angry with you," Seivarden pointed out, for Ship. "And she has a history of reacting drastically to those who anger her sufficiently. She'll have come after us sooner, if she could manage it." She frowned at the words that appeared in her vision next, but of course I could see them myself, and knew what they were. "The second message is from System Governor Giarod."

I didn't reply immediately. Governor Giarod was the appointed authority over all of Athoek System. She was also, more or less indirectly, the cause of the injuries that I had only just recovered from. I had, in fact, nearly died sustaining them. Because of who and what I was, I already knew the contents of her message to me. There was no need for Seivarden to say it aloud.

But *Mercy of Kalr* had once had ancillaries—human bodies slaved to its artificial intelligence, hands and feet, eyes and ears for the ship. Those ancillaries were gone, stripped away, and now Ship had an entirely human crew. I knew that the common soldiers aboard sometimes acted for Ship, speaking for it, doing things Ship could no longer do, as though they were the ancillaries it had lost. Generally not in front of me— I myself was an ancillary, the last remaining fragment of the troop carrier *Justice of Toren*, destroyed twenty years ago. I was not amused or comforted by my soldiers' attempts to imitate what I had once been. Still, I hadn't forbidden it. Until very recently, my soldiers hadn't known about my past. And they seemed to find in it a way to shield themselves from the inescapable intimacy of life on a small ship.

But Seivarden had no need for such playacting. She would be doing this because Ship wanted it. Why would Ship want such a thing? "Governor Giarod requests that you return to the station at your earliest convenience," Seivarden said. Ship said. That request, the barely polite gloss of *at your convenience* or not, was more peremptory than was strictly proper.

Seivarden wasn't as indignant at it as Lieutenant Ekalu had been, but she was definitely wondering how I would respond. "The governor didn't explain her request. Though Kalr Five noticed a commotion just outside the Undergarden last night. Security arrested someone, and they've been nervous since." Briefly Ship showed me bits of what Five, still on the station, had seen and heard.

"Wasn't the Undergarden evacuated?" I asked. Aloud, since obviously Ship wanted to have this conversation this way, no matter how I felt about it. "It ought to be empty."

"Exactly," Seivarden replied. Ship.

The majority of Undergarden residents had been Ychana— despised by the Xhai, another Athoeki ethnic group, one that had done better in the annexation than others. Theoretically, when the Radchaai annexed a world, ethnic distinctions became irrelevant. Reality was messier. And some of Governor Giarod's less reasonable fears centered around the Ychana in the Undergarden. "Wonderful. Wake Lieutenant Tisarwat, will you, Ship?" Tisarwat had spent time since we'd arrived here making connections in the Undergarden, and also among the staff of Station Administration.

"I already have," replied Seivarden for *Mercy of Kalr.* "Your shuttle will be ready by the time you've dressed and have eaten."

"Thank you." Found I didn't want to say *Thank you, Ship,* or *Thank you, Seivarden,* either one.

"Fleet Captain, I hope I'm not presuming too much," said Ship, through Seivarden. Disquiet joined Seivarden's mild apprehension—she had agreed to act for Ship, but was suddenly worried, maybe suspecting Ship was coming to the point of it.

"I can't imagine you ever presuming too much, Ship." But of course it could see nearly everything about me—every breath, every twitch of every muscle. More, since I was still wired like an ancillary, even if I wasn't Ship's ancillary. It knew, surely, that its using an officer as a pretend ancillary disturbed me.

"I wanted to ask you, Fleet Captain. Back at Omaugh, you said I could be my own captain. Did you mean that?"

I felt, for an instant, as though the ship's gravity had failed. There was no point in trying not to show my reaction to Ship's words, it could see every detail of my physical responses. Seivarden had never been particularly good at faking impassivity, and her own dismay showed on her aristocratic face. She must not have known that this was what Ship wanted to say. She opened her mouth as though to speak, blinked, and then closed it again. Frowned.

"Yes, I meant it," I replied. Ships weren't people, to Radchaai. We were equipment. Weapons. Tools that functioned as ordered, when required.

"I've been thinking about it, since you said it," said Seivarden. No, said *Mercy of Kalr*. "And I've concluded that I don't want to be a captain. But I find I like the thought that I *could* be." Seivarden clearly wasn't sure if she should be relieved at that or not. She knew what I was, possibly even knew why I had said what I had said, that day at Omaugh Palace, but she was well-born Radchaai, and as used as any other Radchaai officer to expecting her ship would always do exactly as it was told. Would always be there for her.

I had been a ship myself. Ships could feel very, very intensely about their captains, or their lieutenants. I knew that from personal experience. Oh, I did. For most of my two-thousand-year life I hadn't thought there was any reason to want anything else. And the irrevocable loss of my own crew was a gaping hole in myself that I had learned not to look at. Mostly. At the same time, in the last twenty years I had grown accustomed to making my own decisions, without reference to anyone else. To having authority over my own life.

Had I thought that my ship would feel about me the way I had felt about my own captains? Impossible that it would. Ships didn't feel that way about other ships. Had I thought that? Why would I ever think that?

"All right," I said, and took a mouthful of my tea. Swallowed it. There was no reason I could see for Ship to have said that through Seivarden.

But of course, Seivarden was entirely human. And she was *Mercy of Kalr*'s Amaat lieutenant. Perhaps Ship's words hadn't been meant for me, but for her.

Seivarden had never been the sort of officer who cared, or even noticed, what her ship felt. She had not been one of my favorites, when she'd served on *Justice of Toren*. But ships did have different tastes, different favorites. And Seivarden had improved markedly over the last year.

A ship with ancillaries expressed what it felt in a thousand different minute ways. A favorite officer's tea was never cold. Her food would be prepared in precisely the way she preferred. Her uniform always fit right, always sat right, effortlessly. Small needs or desires would be satisfied very nearly the moment they arose. And most of the time, she would only notice that she was comfortable. Certainly more comfortable than other ships she might have served on.

It was—nearly always—distinctly one-sided. All those weeks ago on Omaugh Palace, I had told Ship that it could be a person who could command itself. And now it was telling me—and, not incidentally I was sure, Seivarden—that it wanted to be that, at least potentially. Wanted that to be acknowledged. Wanted, maybe, some small return (or at least some recognition) of its feelings.

I hadn't noticed that Seivarden's Amaats had been particularly solicitous, but then, her Amaats, like all the soldiers on *Mercy of Kalr*, were human, not appendages of their ship. They would have been uncomfortable with the flood of tiny intimacies Ship might have asked of them, if they were to act for it in that way.

"All right," I said again. In her quarters, Lieutenant Tisarwat pulled on her boots. Still waking up—Bo Nine stood by with her tea. The rest of Bo decade slept deeply, some dreaming. Seivarden's Amaats were finishing their day's tasks, getting ready for their suppers. Medic, and half of my Kalrs, still slept, but lightly. Ship would wake them in another five minutes. Ekalu and her Etrepas still stood watch. Lieutenant Ekalu was still a bit indignant over the system governor's message, and also troubled by something else, I wasn't sure what. Outside, dust skittered now and then across *Mercy of Kalr*'s hull, and the light of Athoek's sun warmed it. "Was there anything else?"

There was. Seivarden, on edge since this part of the conversation had begun, blinked, expecting to see some sort of reply in her vision. Nothing, for an entire second. And then, *No, Fleet Captain, that's all.* "No, Fleet Captain," Seivarden read off. "That's all." Her voice doubtful. For someone who knew ships, that brief pause had been eloquent. I was mildly surprised that Seivarden, who had always been oblivious to her ships' feelings, had noticed it. She blinked three times, and frowned. Worried. Disconcerted. Uncharacteristically unsure of herself. Said, "Your tea is getting cold."

"That's all right," I said, and drank it down.

Lieutenant Tisarwat had wanted to go back to Athoek Station for days. We had only been in the system a little over two weeks, but already she had friends, and connections. Had been angling for some sort of influence over system administration, nearly since the moment she had set foot on the station. Which was hardly surprising, considering. Tisarwat hadn't been Tisarwat for some time—Anaander Mianaai, the Lord of the Radch, had altered the hapless seventeen-year-old lieutenant in order to make her nothing more than an appendage of herself, just another part of the Lord of the Radch. One she hoped I wouldn't recognize as such, who could keep an eye on me, and keep control of *Mercy of Kalr*. But I had recognized her, and removed the implants that had tied Tisarwat to the Lord of the Radch, and now she was someone else—a new Lieutenant Tisarwat, with the memories (and possibly some of the inclinations) of the old one, but also someone who had spent several days as the most powerful person in Radch space.

She waited for me just outside the shuttle hatch. Seventeen, not tall exactly but rangy in the way some seventeen-year-olds are who haven't quite grown into themselves. Still groggy from waking, but every hair in place, her dark-brown uniform immaculate. Bo Nine, already aboard the shuttle, would never have let her young lieutenant out of her quarters in any other state. "Fleet Captain." Tisarwat bowed. "Thank you for taking me with you." Her lilac-colored eyes—a remnant of the old Tisarwat, who had been flighty and frivolous, and had spent what was probably her first paycheck on changing the color of her eyes—were serious. Behind that she was genuinely pleased, and a bit excited, even through the meds *Mercy of Kalr*'s medic had given her. The implants the Lord of the Radch had installed hadn't worked properly, had, I suspected, done some permanent damage. My hasty removal of those implants had fixed part of that problem, but perhaps had caused others. Add in her powerful—and

entirely understandable—ambivalence about Anaander Mianaai, whom she arguably still shared some identity with, and
the result was near-constant emotional distress.

She was feeling all right today, though, from what I could
see. "Don't mention it, Lieutenant."

"Sir." She wanted, I saw, to bring something up before
we got into the shuttle. "System Governor Giarod is a problem." System Governor Giarod had been appointed by the
same authority that had sent me here to Athoek System. In
theory we were allies in the cause of keeping this system safe
and stable. But she had passed information to my enemies,
just days ago, and that had very nearly gotten me killed. And
while it was possible she hadn't realized it at the time, she
surely knew it now. But no word of that from her, no explanation, no apology, no acknowledgment of any kind. Just
this edge-of-disrespectful summons to the station. "At some
point," Tisarwat continued, "I think we're going to need a
new system governor."

"I doubt Omaugh Palace is going to send us a new one
anytime soon, Lieutenant."

"No, sir," replied Tisarwat. "But *I* could do it. I could be
governor. I'd be good at it."

"No doubt you would, Lieutenant," I said, evenly. I turned,
ready to push myself over the boundary between *Mercy of
Kalr*'s artificial gravity and the shuttle's lack of it. Saw that
though Tisarwat had held herself absolutely still at my words,
she had been hurt by my response. The pain was dulled by
meds, but still there.

Being who she was, she had to know I would oppose her
bid to be system governor. I still lived only because Anaander
Mianaai, the Lord of the Radch, thought or hoped that I might
be a danger to her enemy. But of course, Anaander Mianaai's

enemy was herself. I didn't care particularly which faction of the Lord of the Radch emerged victorious—they were all, as far as I was concerned, the same. I would just as soon see her entirely destroyed. An aim that was well beyond my ability, but she knew me well enough to know that I would do what damage I could, to all of her. She had hijacked the unfortunate Lieutenant Tisarwat in order to be near enough to control that damage as much as she could. Tisarwat herself had said as much to me, not long after we'd arrived at Athoek Station.

And days ago Tisarwat herself had said, *Do you understand, sir, that we're both doing exactly what she wants? She* being Anaander Mianaai. And I had said that I didn't care much what the Lord of the Radch wanted.

I turned back. Put my hand on Tisarwat's shoulder. Said, more gently, "Let's get through today first, Lieutenant." Or even through the next few weeks or months or more. Radch space was big. The fighting that was happening in the provincial palaces might reach us here at Athoek tomorrow, or next week, or next year. Or it might burn itself out in the palaces and never arrive here at all. But I wouldn't bet on that.

We often speak casually of distances within a single solar system—of a station's being near a moon or a planet, of a gate's being near a system's most prominent station—when in fact those distances are measured in hundreds of thousands, if not millions, of kilometers. And a system's outstations could be hundreds of millions, even billions, of kilometers from those gates.

Days before, *Mercy of Kalr* had been truly, dangerously close to Athoek Station, but now it was only near in a relative sense. We would be a whole day on the shuttle. *Mercy of Kalr* could generate its own gates, shortcuts around normal space, and could have gotten us there much more quickly, but gating close up to a busy station risked colliding with whatever might be in your path as you came out of gate-space. Ship could have done it—had, in fact, quite recently. But for now it was safer to take the shuttle, which was too small to generate its own gravity, let alone make its own gate. Governor Giarod's problem, whatever it was, would have to wait.

And I had plenty of time to consider what I might find on the station. Both factions of Anaander Mianaai (assuming there were only two, which was perhaps not a safe assumption) surely had agents there. But none of them would be military. Captain Hetnys—the enemy of mine to whom System Governor Giarod had so imprudently passed dangerous information—lay frozen in a suspension pod aboard *Mercy of Kalr*, along with all her officers. Her ship, *Sword of Atagaris*, orbited well away from Athoek itself, its engines off-line, its ancillaries all in storage. *Mercy of Ilves*, the only other military ship in the system besides *Sword of Atagaris* and *Mercy of Kalr*, was inspecting the outstations, and its captain had so far shown no inclination to disobey my order to continue doing so. Station Security and Planetary Security were the only remaining armed threat—but "armed," for Security, meant stun sticks. Which wasn't to say Security couldn't pose a threat—they certainly could, particularly to unarmed citizens. But Security was not a threat to me.

Anyone who'd realized I didn't support their faction of the Lord of the Radch would have only political means to move against me. Politics it was, then. Perhaps I should take a cue from Lieutenant Tisarwat and invite the head of Station Security to dinner.

Kalr Five was still on Athoek Station, along with Eight and Ten. The station had been overcrowded even before the Undergarden had been damaged and evacuated, and there weren't beds enough for everyone. My Kalrs had deployed crates and pallets in the corner of a dead-end corridor. On one of those crates sat Citizen Uran, quietly but determinedly conjugating Raswar verbs. The Ychana on Athoek Station mostly spoke Raswar, and our neighbors on the station were mostly Ychana. It would have been easier if she'd been willing to go to Medical to learn the basics under drugs, but she very vehemently had not wanted to do that. Uran was the only nonmilitary member of my small household, barely sixteen, no relation to me or anyone on *Mercy of Kalr*, but I had found myself responsible for her.

Five stood by, to all appearances absorbed in making sure tea was ready for when Uran's tutor arrived in the next few minutes, but in fact keeping a close eye on her. A few meters away, Kalr Eight and Kalr Ten scrubbed the corridor floor, already a good deal less scuffed than it had been and noticeably less gray than what lay outside the household's makeshift boundary. They sang as they worked, quietly, because citizens were sleeping beyond the nearby doorways.

> *Jasmine grew*
> *In my love's room*
> *It twined all around her bed*
> *The daughters have fasted and shaved their heads*
> *In a month they will visit the temple again*
> *With roses and camellias*
> *But I will sustain myself*
> *With nothing more than the perfume of jasmine flowers*
> *Until the end of my life*

It was an old song, older than Eight and Ten themselves, older, probably, than their grandparents. I remembered when it was new. On the shuttle, where neither Eight nor Ten could hear me, I sang it with them. Quietly, since Tisarwat was beside me, strapped into a seat and fast asleep. The shuttle's pilot heard me, though, with a tiny swell of contentment. She had been uneasy about this sudden trip back to the station, and what she'd heard about Governor Giarod's message. But if I was singing, then things were as they should be.

On *Mercy of Kalr*, Seivarden slept, dreaming. Her ten Amaats slept as well, close in their bunks. Bo decade (under the direction of Bo One, since Tisarwat was in the shuttle with me) was just awake, running thoughtless and ragged through the morning prayer (*The flower of justice is peace. The flower of propriety is beauty in thought and action*...).

Not long after, Medic came off watch, found Lieutenant Ekalu in the tiny, white-walled decade room, staring at her supper. "Are you all right?" Medic asked, and sat down beside her. The Etrepa in attendance set a bowl of tea on the table in front of her.

"I'm fine," lied Ekalu.

"We've served together a long time," Medic replied. Ekalu, discomfited, did not look up, or say anything in response. "Before you were promoted, you'd have gone to your decade-mates for support, but you can't go to them anymore. They're Seivarden's now." Before I'd come—before *Mercy of Kalr*'s last captain had been arrested for treason—Ekalu had been Amaat One. "And I suppose you feel like you can't go to your Etrepas." The Etrepa attending Ekalu stood impassive in a corner of the room. "Plenty of other lieutenants would, but they didn't come up out of the decades, did they." Didn't add that Ekalu might be worried about undermining her authority with shipmates who'd known her for years as a common soldier. Didn't add that Ekalu knew firsthand how unequal such

14

an exchange might be, to demand any sort of comfort or emotional support from the soldiers serving under her. "I daresay you're the first to do it, to come up out of the decades."

"No," replied Ekalu, voice flat. "Fleet Captain was." Me, she meant. "You knew the whole time, I suppose." That I was an ancillary, and not human, she meant.

"Is that the problem then?" asked Medic. She hadn't touched the tea the Etrepa had given her. "Fleet Captain is first?"

"No, of course not." Ekalu looked up, finally, and her impassive expression flickered for just a moment into something different, but then it was gone. "Why would it?" I knew she was telling the truth.

Medic made a gesture of unconcern. "Some people get jealous. And Lieutenant Seivarden is...very attached to Fleet Captain. And you and Lieutenant Seivarden..."

"It would be stupid to be jealous of Fleet Captain," said Ekalu, voice bland. She meant that, too. Her statement might conceivably be taken for an insult, but I knew that wasn't her intention. And she was right. It didn't make any sense at all to be jealous of me.

"That sort of thing," observed Medic, dryly, "doesn't always make sense." Ekalu said nothing. "I've sometimes wondered what went through Seivarden's mind when she discovered Fleet Captain was an ancillary. Not even human!" And then, in response to the merest flicker of an expression across Ekalu's face, "But she's not. Fleet Captain will tell you so herself, I imagine."

"Are you going to call Fleet Captain *it* instead of *she*?" Ekalu challenged. And then looked away. "Your gracious pardon, Medic. It just sits wrong with me."

Because I could see what Ship saw, I saw Medic's dubious reaction to Ekalu's overly formal apology, Ekalu's suddenly

15

careful attempt to erase her usual lower-house accent. But Medic had known Ekalu a long time, and most of that when Ekalu had still been, as Medic put it, in the decades. "I think," Medic said, "that Seivarden imagines she understands what it is to be on the bottom of the heap. Certainly she's learned it's possible to find oneself there despite good family and impeccable manners and every indication Aatr has granted you a life of happiness and plenty. She's learned it's possible that someone she'd dismissed and disregarded might be worthy of her respect. And now she's learned it, she fancies she understands *you*." Another thought struck her. "That's why you don't like my saying the fleet captain's not human, isn't it."

"I've never been at the bottom of any heap." Still carefully broadening her vowels in imitation of Medic or Tisarwat. Of Seivarden. Or of me. "And I said there wasn't anything wrong."

"I'm mistaken, then," replied Medic, no rancor or sarcasm in her voice. "I beg your indulgent pardon, Lieutenant." More formal than she needed to be with Ekalu, whom she'd known so long. Whose doctor she had been, all that time.

"Of course, Medic."

Seivarden still slept. Unaware of her fellow lieutenant's (and lover's) discomfiture. Unaware, I feared, of Ship's favorable regard. What I had begun to suspect was its strong affection. Any number of things, Ship wouldn't hesitate to say quite directly, but never that, I was sure.

Beside me, on the shuttle, Tisarwat muttered, and stirred, but didn't wake. I turned my thoughts to what I might find on Athoek Station when we reached it, and what I ought to do about it.

2

I met Governor Giarod in her office, its cream-and-green silk hangings today covering even the broad window that looked out onto Athoek Station's main concourse, where citizens crossed the scuffed white floor, came or went from Station Administration, or stood talking in front of the temple of Amaat with its huge reliefs of the four Emanations. Governor Giarod was tall, broad-shouldered, outwardly serene, but I knew from experience she was liable to misgivings, and to acting on those misgivings at the least convenient moments. She offered me a seat, which I took, and tea, which I refused. Kalr Five, who had met me at the docks, stood impassive just behind me. I considered ordering her to the door, or even out into the corridor, but decided that an obvious reminder of who I was and what resources I commanded might be useful.

Governor Giarod couldn't help but notice the soldier looming straight and stiff behind me, but pretended she did not. "Once the gravity came back on, Fleet Captain, Station Administrator Celar felt—and I agreed—that we should do a thorough inspection of the Undergarden, to be sure it was structurally sound." A few days earlier the public gardens, just above the part of the station that had been named for them, had begun to collapse, almost flooding the four levels below them. Athoek Station's AI had solved the immediate problem by turning off the entire station's gravity while the Undergarden was evacuated.

"Did you find dozens of unauthorized people hiding there, as you feared?" Every Radchaai had a tracker implanted at birth, so that no citizen was ever lost or invisible to any watching AI. Particularly here in the relatively small space of Athoek Station, the idea that anyone could be moving secretly, or here without Station's knowledge, was patently ridiculous. And yet the belief that the Undergarden hid crowds of such people, all of them a threat to law-abiding citizens, was alarmingly common.

"You think such fears are foolish," replied Governor Giarod. "And yet our inspection turned up just such a person, hiding in the access tunnels between levels three and four."

I asked, voice even, "Only one?"

Governor Giarod gestured acknowledgment of my point—one person was nowhere near what some—including, apparently, the governor—had feared. "She's Ychana." Most of the residents of the Undergarden had been Ychana. "No one will admit to knowing anything about her, though it's fairly obvious some of them did know her. She's in a cell in Security. I thought you might like to know, especially given the fact that the last person who did something like this was an alien." Translator Dlique, the sort-of-human representative of the mysterious—and terrifying—Presger. Who before the treaty with the Radch—with, actually, all humanity, since the Presger didn't make distinctions between one sort of human and another—had torn apart human ships, and humans, for sport. Who were so powerful no human force, not even a Radchaai one, could destroy them, or even defend against them. Presger Translator Dlique, it had turned out, could deceive Station's sensors with alarming ease, and had had no patience for being safely confined to the governor's residence. Her dead body lay in a suspension pod in Medical, waiting for the hopefully distant day when the Presger came looking for her, and we had to explain that a *Sword of Atagaris* ancillary had shot her, on the suspicion that she'd vandalized a wall in the Undergarden.

At least the search that had turned up this one person ought to have allayed fears of a horde of murderous Ychana. "Did you look at her DNA? Is she closely related to anyone else in the Undergarden?"

"What an odd question, Fleet Captain! Do you know something you haven't shared with me?"

"Many things," I replied, "but most of them wouldn't interest you. She isn't, is she?"

"She isn't," replied Governor Giarod. "And Medical tells me she's carrying some markers that haven't been seen since before the annexation of Athoek." *Annexation* was the polite term for the Radchaai invasion and colonization of entire star systems. "Since she can't possibly be recently descended from a line that went extinct centuries ago, the only other possibility—in the loosest sense of that word—is that she's over six hundred years old."

There was another possibility, but Governor Giarod hadn't seen it yet. "I imagine that's probably the case. Though she'll have been suspended for a fair amount of that time."

Governor Giarod frowned. "You know who she is?"

"Not who," I said, "not specifically. I have some suspicions as to *what* she is. May I speak to her?"

"Are you going to share your suspicions with me?"

"Not if they prove unfounded." All I needed was for Governor Giarod to add another phantom enemy to her list. "I'd like to speak with her, and I'd like a medic to be brought to examine her again. Someone sensible, and discreet."

The cell was tiny, two meters by two, a grate and a water supply in one corner. The person squatting on the scuffed floor, staring at a bowl of skel, obviously her supper, seemed unremarkable at first examination. She wore the bright-colored loose shirt and trousers most of the Ychana in the Undergarden preferred, yellow and orange and green. But this person also wore plain gray gloves, suspiciously new-looking. Likely they had come quite recently from Station stores, and Security had insisted she put them on. Hardly anyone in the Undergarden wore gloves, it was just one more reason to believe the people who lived there were uncivilized, unsettlingly, perhaps even dangerously, foreign. Not Radchaai at all.

There was no way to signal that I wanted to come in—not even the pretense of privacy, in Security's custody. Station— the AI that controlled Athoek Station, that was for all intents and purposes the station itself—opened the door at my request. The person squatting on the floor didn't even look up. "May I come in, citizen?" I asked. Though *citizen* was almost certainly the wrong term of address here, it was, in Radchaai, very nearly the only polite one possible.

The person didn't answer. I came in, a matter of a single step, and squatted across from her. Kalr Five stopped in the doorway. "What's your name?" I asked. Governor Giarod had said that this person had refused to speak, from the moment she'd been arrested. She was scheduled for interrogation the next morning. But of course, for an interrogation to work, you had to know what questions to ask. Chances were, no one here did.

"You won't be able to keep your secret," I continued, addressing the person squatting on the floor in front of me staring at her bowl of skel. They had left her no utensil to eat it with—fearing, perhaps, that she might do herself an injury with it. She would have to eat the thick leaves with her hands, or put her face into the bowl, either option unpleasant and demeaning, to a Radchaai. "You're scheduled for an interrogation in the morning. I'm sure they'll be as careful as they can, but I don't think it's ever a terribly pleasant experience." And, like a lot of people annexed by the Radch, most Ychana were convinced that interrogation was inseparable from the re-education a convicted criminal would undergo to ensure she wouldn't offend again. Certainly the drugs used were the same, and an incompetent interrogator could do a good deal of damage to a person. Even the most Radchaai of Radchaai had something of a horror of interrogation and re-education, and tried to avoid mentioning either one, would walk all around the topics even when they were obviously staring them in the face.

Still no answer. She did not even look up. I was just as capable as this person was of sitting in silence. I thought of asking Station to show me what it could see of her—certainly temperature changes, possibly heart rate, possibly more. I didn't doubt that what sensors existed here in Security were set to pick up as much information as possible from inmates. But I doubted I would see anything surprising in that data. "Do you know any songs?" I asked.

Almost, I thought I saw a change, however small, in the set of her shoulders, in the way she held herself. My question had surprised her. It was, I had to admit, an inane one. Nearly everyone I had met, in my two-thousand-year life, had known at least a few songs. Station said, in my ear, "That surprised her, Fleet Captain."

"No doubt," I responded, silently. Didn't look up as Five stepped back into the corridor to make way for Eight, carrying a box, gold inlaid with red and blue and green. Before I had left the governor's office, I had messaged to ask her to bring it. I gestured to her to set it on the floor beside me. And when she had done so, I opened the lid.

The box had once held an antique tea set—flask, strainer, bowls for twelve—of blue and green glass, and gold. It had survived three thousand years unbroken—possibly more. Now it was in fragments, shattered, strewn around the box's interior, or collected in the depressions that had once held its pieces snug and safe. Unbroken, it had been worth several fortunes. In pieces it was still a prize.

The person squatting on the floor in front of me turned her head, finally, to look at it. Said, in an even voice, in Radchaai, "Who did this?"

"Surely you knew," I said, "when you traded it away, that something like this might happen. Surely you knew that no one else could possibly treasure it as much as you did."

"I don't know what you're talking about." Still she stared at the broken tea set. Still her voice was even. She spoke Radchaai with the same accent I'd heard from other Ychana in the Undergarden. "This is obviously valuable, and whoever broke it was obviously someone entirely uncivilized."

"I think she's upset, Fleet Captain," said Station, in my ear. "She's reacted emotionally, anyway. It's hard to be more definite, with only externals, when I don't know someone well."

I knew how that worked, from personal experience. But I didn't say so. I replied, silently, "Thank you, Station, that's good to know." I knew, also from personal experience, just how helpful an AI could be when it liked you. And how obstructive and unhelpful one could be when it had some reason for dislike or resentment. I was genuinely, pleasantly surprised to find Station volunteering information for me. Aloud I said, to the person crouched in front of me, "What's your name?"

"Fuck you," she said, even and bland. Still looking at that shattered tea set.

"What was the captain's name, that you removed before you traded the tea set away?" The inscription on the inside of the box lid had been altered to remove a name that, I suspected, might allow someone to trace it back to its origin.

"Why wait until tomorrow to interrogate me?" she asked. "Do it now. Then you'll have answers to all your questions."

"Heart rate increase," said Station, into my ear. "Her respiration is faster."

Ah. Aloud I said, "There's a fail-safe, then. The drugs will kill you. This part of you, anyway."

She looked at me, finally. Blinked, slowly. "Fleet Captain Breq Mianaai, are you sure you're quite all right? That didn't make any sense at all."

I closed the box. Picked it up, and rose. Said, "Captain Hetnys sold the set to a Citizen Fosyf Denche. Fosyf's daughter broke it, and Fosyf decided it had lost all value, and threw it away." I turned and handed the box to Five, who had replaced Eight in the doorway again. Properly speaking, the tea set was hers. She was the one who had gone to the trouble of fishing it, all of its pieces, out of the trash after Raughd

Denche, in a devastated fury at her mother's disowning her, had dashed it to the ground. "It was good to meet you. I hope to talk to you again soon."

As I exited Security onto the station's main concourse, Kalr Five behind me, carrying her shattered tea set, Station said in my ear, "Fleet Captain, the head priest has just left Governor Giarod's office and is looking for you."

In Radch space, *head priest* with no other modifiers meant the head priest of Amaat. On Athoek Station, the head priest of Amaat was a person named Ifian Wos. I had met her when she had officiated—somewhat resentfully—at Translator Dlique's funeral. Beyond that I had not spoken to her.

"Thank you, Station." As I said it, Eminence Ifian exited the governor's residence, turned immediately in my direction, and made her way toward me. Station had no doubt told her where I was.

I didn't want to talk to her just now. I wanted to talk to Governor Giarod about the person in custody in Security, and then see to some questions about my soldiers' quarters. But Station fairly clearly hadn't told me Head Priest Ifian was looking for me so that I could avoid her. And even if I attempted it now, I wouldn't be able to do so forever, short of fleeing the station entirely.

I walked to the middle of the scuffed, once-white floor of the concourse and stopped. "Fleet Captain!" called the head priest, and bowed as she reached me. A nicely calculated bow, I thought, not one millimeter deeper than my rank demanded. She was two centimeters shorter than I was, and slender, with a low and carrying voice, and held herself and spoke with the sure confidence of someone with the sort of connections and resources that made appointment to a high-ranking priesthood possible. Citizens passed to either side of us where we stood, their coats and jackets sparkling with jewelry, with memorial and associational pins. The ordinary, everyday traffic on the concourse. Most of those who came near us affected to ignore us, though some looked sidelong at us, curious. "Such shocking events, the past few days!" Eminence Ifian continued, as though we were merely friendly acquaintances, gossiping. "Though of course we've all known Captain Hetnys for *years*, and I don't think anyone could have expected her to do anything untoward!" The many pins on Head Priest Ifian's impeccably tailored purple coat flashed and sparkled, trembling momentarily in the extremity of the head priest's doubt that Captain Hetnys might ever do wrong.

Captain Hetnys, of course, had just days ago threatened to kill Horticulturist Basnaaid Elming in order to gain some sort of control over me. Horticulturist Basnaaid was the younger sister of someone who had been a lieutenant of mine, when I had been the troop carrier *Justice of Toren*. I had only consented to come to Athoek because Basnaaid was here, because I owed her long-dead sister a debt I could in fact never truly repay. "Indeed," I replied, the most diplomatic response possible.

"And I suppose you *do* have the authority to detain her," Eminence Ifian continued, her tone just the smallest bit dubious. My confrontation with Captain Hetnys had ended with the Gardens a shambles and the entire station without gravity for several days. She now slept frozen in a suspension pod so that she couldn't make any more spectacularly, foolishly dangerous moves. "Military matters no doubt. And Citizen Raughd. Such a nice, well-bred young person." Raughd Denche had attempted to kill me, mere days before Captain

Hetnys's *untoward* behavior. "Surely they'll have had *reasons* for what they did, surely that should be taken into account! But, Fleet Captain, that's not what I wanted to talk to you about. And of course I don't want to keep you standing here on the concourse. Perhaps we could have tea?"

"I'm afraid, Eminence," I replied, smooth and bland, "that I'm terribly busy. I'm on my way to meet with Governor Giarod, and then I very much need to see about my own soldiers, who have been sleeping at the end of a station corridor for the past few nights." Station Administration was surely awash in complaints just now, and no one was going to look out for the interests of my own small household if I didn't.

"Yes, yes, Fleet Captain, that was one of the things I wanted to discuss with you! You know, the Undergarden used to be quite a fashionable neighborhood. Not, perhaps, as fashionable as the apartments overlooking the concourse." She gestured around, upward, at the windows lining the second story of this, the center of station life and its largest open space besides the Gardens. "Perhaps if the Undergarden *had* been equally fashionable, it would have been repaired long ago! But things are as they are." She made a pious gesture, submission to the will of God. "*Lovely* apartments, I've heard. I can only *imagine* what shape they're in now, after so many years of Ychana squatting there. But I *do* hope the original assignments will be taken into account, now there's a refit underway."

I wondered how many of those families were even still here. "I am unable to assist you, Eminence. I have no authority over housing assignments. You would do better to speak to Station Administrator Celar."

"I spoke to the station administrator, Fleet Captain, and

she told me that *you* had insisted on current arrangements. I'm sure leaving everyone where they are seems practical to you, but really, there are *special circumstances* here. And this morning's cast was *quite concerning.*"

It was possible the head priest was championing this cause entirely out of concern for families who hoped to return to the Undergarden. But she was also a friend of Captain Hetnys's—Captain Hetnys, who had been working for the part of the Lord of the Radch who had killed Lieutenant Awn Elming. The part of the Lord of the Radch who had destroyed the troop carrier *Justice of Toren*—that is to say, the part of the Lord of the Radch who had destroyed me. And the timing of this, just when it had become clear that I was not a supporter of that side of Anaander Mianaai, was suspicious. That, and the bringing to bear of the daily omen casting. I had met quite a few priests in my long life, and found that they were, by and large, like anyone else—some generous, some grasping; some kind, some cruel; some humble, some self-aggrandizing. Most were all of those things, in various proportions, at various times. Like anyone else, as I said. But I had learned to be wary whenever a priest suggested that her personal aims were, in fact, God's will.

"How comforting," I replied, my voice and my expression steadily serious, "to think that in these difficult times God is still concerned with the details of housing assignments. I myself have no time to discuss them just now." I bowed, as perfectly respectful as the head priest had been, and walked away from her, across the concourse toward the governor's residence.

"It's interesting, isn't it," said Station in my ear, "that the gods are only now interested in refitting the Undergarden."

"*Very* interesting," I replied, silently. "Thank you, Station."

* * *

"An ancillary!" Disbelief was obvious in Governor Giarod's face, her voice. "Where's the ship?"

"On the other side of the Ghost Gate." A gate that led to a dead-end system, where the Athoeki had intended to expand, before the annexation, but it had never happened. There were vague rumors that the system was haunted. Captain Hetnys and *Sword of Atagaris* had shown an unaccountable interest in that gate. Shortly after *Mercy of Kalr* had arrived in the system, an unbelievably old supply locker had come through it. I was convinced now that Kalr Five's shattered tea set had also come through that gate, in exchange for shipments of suspended human beings. They were supposed to be cheap, unskilled labor for Athoek, but Captain Hetnys had stolen them, sold them to someone on the other side of the Ghost Gate. "You remember, a few days ago we talked about suspended transportees being stolen." She could hardly have forgotten it, considering the events of the last few days. "And it was difficult to imagine what the purpose might be behind that theft. I think there's been a ship on the other side of that gate for quite some time, and it's been buying bodies to use as its ancillaries. It used to buy them from Athoeki slavers—which is how it had an Ychana body from before the annexation it could send here, and blend in." More or less, at least. "When the annexation shut down its supply, it bought them from Radchaai officials who were corrupt and greedy enough to sell transportees." I gestured to Five, standing behind where I sat, to open the tea set box.

"That's Fosyf's," said Governor Giarod. And then, realizing, "Captain Hetnys sold it to her."

"You never asked until now where Captain Hetnys got such a thing." I gestured to the inscription on the inside of the lid. "You also never noticed that someone had very carefully removed the name of the original owner. If you read Notai"—the language in which that inscription was written—"or if you'd seen enough of these, you'd have noticed that immediately."

"What are you saying, Fleet Captain?"

"It's not a Radchaai ship we're dealing with." Or it *was* a Radchaai ship. There was the Radch, the birthplace of Anaander Mianaai more than three thousand years ago, when she'd been a single, very ambitious person in a single body. And then there was the enormous territory Anaander had built around that over the past three thousand years— Radch-controlled space, but what connection was there any-more, between those two? And the inhabitants of the Radch, and the space immediately around it, hadn't all been in favor of what Mianaai had done. There had been battles over it. Wars. Ships and captains destroyed. Many of them had been Notai. From the Radch. "Not one of Anaander's, I mean. It's Notai." The Notai were Radchaai, of course. People in Radch space—and outside it—tended to think of "Radchaai" as being one thing, when in fact it was a good deal more com-plicated than that, or at least it had been when Anaander had first begun to move outward from the Radch.

"Fleet Captain." Governor Giarod was aghast. Disbelieving. "Those are *stories*. Defeated ships from that war, wandering space for thousands of years..." She shook her head. "It's the sort of thing you'd find in a melodramatic entertainment. It's not *real*."

"I don't know how long it's been there," I said. "Since before the annexation, at least." It had to have been there since before the annexation, if it had been buying ancil-lary bodies from Athoeki slavers. "But it's there. And," I continued, relieved that the medic who had examined the captive ancillary hadn't seen me in person, to turn her newly tuned implants on me, had given the governor her observations without betraying me, "it's here. I doubt any Undergarden resident will say much about her." The Undergarden had been damaged, years ago, in a way that made Station unable to sense much of what happened there. It was the perfect hiding place, for someone like this ancillary. So long as it avoided being seen by someone wired to send sensory data to Station—and that wasn't very common, in the Undergarden, unlike the rest of the station—it could move unnoticed, with no one realizing it shouldn't be there. "I'm guessing it realized something was going on, when communications were lost with the palaces, and when traffic was disrupted, so it sent an ancillary to see if it could find out what. Even if the ancillary was captured, its secret would likely have been safe. There's a fail-safe that will kill it if interrogation drugs are administered. And the implants are hidden, and likely no one would think to look for them. Possibly the fail-safe is rigged to destroy what evidence there is to begin with."

"You guessed all this from Citizen Fosyf's tea set."

"Yes, actually. I would have been clearer about my suspicion, earlier, but I wanted more proof. It is, as you've noted, rather difficult to believe."

Governor Giarod was silent a moment, frowning. Thinking, I hoped, of her part in the affair. Then she said, "So what do we do now?"

"I recommend installing a tracker, and putting it on the ration list."

"But surely, Fleet Captain, if it's an ancillary...an ancillary can't be a citizen. A ship can't."

I waited, just a fraction of a second, to see if Station would say anything to her, but there was no change in the governor's expression. "I'm sure Security doesn't want that cell permanently occupied. What else are we going to do with it?" I gestured irony. "Assign it a job," I continued. "Nothing sensitive, of course, and nothing that gives it access to vulnerable station systems. Confirm its housing assignment in the Undergarden."

Governor Giarod's expression changed, just the smallest bit. The head priest had brought the issue to her, then. "Fleet Captain, I realize housing assignments are Station Administrator Celar's business, but I confess I don't like rewarding illegal activity. No one should have been living in the Undergarden to begin with." I said nothing, only looked at her. "It's good you've taken an interest in your neighbors," she went on after a pause, doubtfully, as though she wasn't actually quite certain of that. "But I personally would much rather see those quarters assigned to law-abiding citizens." Still I said nothing. "I think it might be more efficient to rethink the housing assignments in the Undergarden, rethink the refit, and consider sending some citizens downwell in the meantime."

Which would be fine if they wanted to go down to the planet, but I suspected that if the citizens in question were current Undergarden residents, what they wanted wouldn't be a consideration. And likely most of them had spent their entire lives on the station, and didn't want or weren't suited for the kinds of jobs available downwell, on short notice. "This is, as you say, Governor, a matter for Station Administrator Celar." Station Administrator Celar was in charge of Athoek Station's operations. Things like residential assignments were under her authority, and though she technically answered to Governor Giarod, such fine-grained details of station life were usually beneath a system governor's notice. And Administrator Celar was popular enough that Governor Giarod likely would much prefer to settle such a matter amicably, behind the scenes.

Governor Giarod replied, smoothly, "But you've asked her to make those illicit Undergarden living arrangements official. I suspect she'd be more open to considering changing those arrangements, if you talked to her." *That* was interesting. Almost I expected Station to comment, but it said nothing. Neither did I. "People are going to be unhappy about this."

I considered asking Station outright if the governor intended a deliberate threat. But Station's silence now, when it had been almost chatty minutes before, was telling to me, and I knew it wouldn't like my pushing too hard on the places where it felt uncomfortable or conflicted. And its offered goodwill was a new and delicate thing. "Undergarden residents aren't people?"

"You know what I mean, Fleet Captain." Exasperated. "These are unsettled times, as you yourself reminded me not long ago. We can't afford to be at war with our own citizens just now."

I smiled, a small, noncommittal expression. "Indeed, we can't." Governor Giarod's relationship with Captain Hetnys had been, I was sure, somewhat ambivalent. That didn't rule out her possibly being my enemy now. But if she was, she apparently wasn't willing to move against me openly just yet. I was, after all, the one of us with the armed ship, and the soldiers. "Let's be sure that includes *all* of our citizens, shall we, Governor?"

3

Housing, on a Radchaai station, takes several different forms. The assumption is that one generally lives in a household—parents, grandparents, aunts, cousins, perhaps servants and clients if one's family is wealthy enough. Sometimes such households are organized around a particular station official—the governor's residence, or the head priest's household adjacent to the temple of Amaat on the concourse, where surely a number of junior priests also lived.

If you grew up in such a household, or took an assignment associated with one, you didn't need to request housing from Station Administration. Your housing assignment had been made long before you were born, long before the aptitudes sent you to your post. It helped, of course, to belong to a family that had been present when a station was first built, or annexed. Or to be related to one somehow. When I had been a ship, every one of my officers who had lived on stations had belonged to such households.

If a citizen doesn't belong to such a household, they're still due housing, as every citizen is. A citizen without sufficient status, or the backing of a larger, more powerful house, might find herself assigned to a bunk in a dormitory, not much different from what I had been accustomed to as an ancillary, or the common soldiers' quarters on board *Mercy of Kalr*. Or one of a series of suspension-pod-size compartments, each one large enough to sleep in and perhaps hold a change of clothes or a few small possessions. Athoek Station had both of these sorts of quarters. But they were all full, because the recent destruction of several intersystem gates had re-routed ships here, and trapped others. And the closure of the Undergarden had added several hundred more citizens who needed somewhere to sleep. My Mercy of Kalrs had set up our makeshift lodgings just beyond a doorway that led to a room full of bunks, dark and quiet despite the hour, one when most station residents would be awake. Overcrowded, certainly, and likely people were sleeping in shifts.

Eight was relieved to see me, for some reason, but also filled with indecision and ambivalence. Days ago she'd thought me entirely human. Now she knew, as everyone aboard *Mercy of Kalr* did, that I was not, that I was an ancillary. Now she knew, too, how much I objected to my soldiers' playing ancillary themselves. She was at a loss as to how to speak to me.

"Eight," I said. "Everything's under control, I see. No surprise there."

"Thank you, sir." Eight's uncertainty barely showed in her face or her voice—should she continue her habitual ancillary-like impassiveness, or not? Suddenly even this small interaction was precarious, where before all had been clear to her. Kalr Five felt the same, I saw, but covered her doubt with the business of stowing her precious tea set. Eight continued, "Will you have tea, sir?"

I didn't doubt that even here in the middle of a hallway

Eight could, and would, produce tea for me if I said that I wanted it. "Thank you, no. I'll have water." I sat on a packing crate, turned so I could see down the open end of the corridor.

"Sir," Eight acknowledged. Impassive, but my reply had cast her further into doubt. Of course. Ancillaries drank water, not tea, which was only for humans, a luxury—a necessary one, it sometimes seemed. Not that there was any sort of prohibition, but one didn't waste such luxuries on equipment. There was no answer I could have given to the question of what I would drink without seeming to send some message, or imply something about what I was or wasn't.

As Eight handed me the water I'd asked for—in the best porcelain she had access to just now, I noticed, the violet-and-aqua Bractware—someone came out of the nearby dormitory, turned to walk down the corridor toward where I sat. She was Ychana, dressed in the light, loose shirt and trousers nearly all the Ychana residents of the Undergarden wore. I recognized her as the person who had confronted Lieutenant Tisarwat two weeks ago, to complain—with some justice—that our proposed plans for the refit and repair of the Undergarden had not taken into account the needs and desires of Undergarden residents themselves. But I had not actually been present at that confrontation. It had been conveyed to me by Ship, who had seen and heard it through Tisarwat herself. This person would have no reason to think I would recognize her.

But she could have no other business coming to the end of the corridor like this than speaking to me, or to one of my Kalrs. I drank my water, handed the bowl to Five, and rose. "Citizen," I said, and bowed. "Can I be of some assistance?"

"Fleet Captain," she said, and bowed herself. "There was a meeting yesterday." A meeting of Undergarden residents, she meant—it was how they settled matters that affected every-one generally. "I know you and the lieutenant were unable to attend or of course you would have been notified."

On the surface, entirely reasonable. Tisarwat and I had been away from the station, either aboard *Mercy of Kalr* or en route here. But of course any of my Kalrs that were still on the station might have been notified of such a meeting, and I knew they hadn't been. The meeting had never been meant to include any of us, then, but saying so directly was a difficult matter, and I didn't doubt this citizen was hoping I wouldn't bring the question up. "Of course, citizen," I replied. "Will you sit?" I gestured to the nearest crate. "I don't think there's tea ready, but we'd be happy to make some."

"Thank you, Fleet Captain, no." Her message would be something awkward, then, and she was not looking forward to my reaction to it. Or perhaps to Lieutenant Tisarwat's reaction. "The young lieutenant very kindly set up an office on level four of the Undergarden, to make it more convenient for residents to bring their desires and concerns to Station Administration. This has of course been very helpful, but perhaps her other duties have been neglected."

Definitely not looking forward to Tisarwat's reaction. "And the consensus of the meeting was that someone else ought to be running that office when it opens again, I take it."

This citizen's unease was barely visible, but definitely there. "Yes, Fleet Captain. We wish to emphasize, there's no suggestion of any complaint on our part, or any impropriety on the young lieutenant's."

"You just think it might be better for that office to more directly represent the concerns of the majority of Under-garden residents," I acknowledged.

Surprise flashed across her face, and then was gone. She

had not expected me to speak so directly. "As you say, Fleet Captain."

"And Citizen Uran?" Uran wasn't one of my soldiers, of course wasn't in any way related to me, but she was nonetheless a member of my household, and had spent her mornings assisting in Tisarwat's level four office. She was Valskaayan, the child of transportees sent to Athoek a generation ago and set to picking the tea that grew downwell, and was shipped out all over Radch space.

"The Valskaayan child? Yes, of course, she's welcome to continue. Please tell her so."

"I'll speak to her," I replied, "and Lieutenant Tisarwat, both."

Tisarwat definitely wasn't happy. "But sir!" Urgent. Whispering, since we were still in the corridor end, squatting on the scuffed floor behind the crate perimeter. She took a breath. Said, a trace less fervently but still in a whisper, "You realize, sir, that in all likelihood we're going to have to find a way to govern here. We need influence to do that. We've made a good start, we've put ourselves at a crucial part of..." And then remembered that unlike in our quarters in the Undergarden, Station could hear what we said, was almost certainly listening, and might or might not report what it heard to Governor Giarod. "There is no higher authority for the governor to appeal to, no other source of support in a crisis. It's just us."

Eight and Ten were away, picking up our suppers at the nearest common refectory—no cooking here. Five stood guard at our improvised boundaries, pretending she couldn't hear any of this conversation. "Lieutenant," I said, "I would hope that *you* would realize that I have no desire to govern here. I am perfectly happy to let the Athoeki govern themselves."

She blinked, bewildered. "Sir, you aren't serious. If the

Athoeki could have governed themselves, we wouldn't *be* here. And the community-meeting thing is perfectly fine so long as you're not doing anything that needs decisive action that instant. Or even in the next few *centuries*."

In all my two thousand years, I had never noticed that any particular kind of government made any difference, once Anaander Mianaai had given the order for annexation. "Lieutenant, you are about to throw away what goodwill you've built up here. Considering these are our neighbors, and we may be here for some time, I would prefer you not do that."

She took a breath. Calming herself. She was hurt, and angry. Felt betrayed. "Station Administration won't be disposed to listen directly to the Ychana in the Undergarden. They never have been."

"Then urge them to begin, Lieutenant. You've already made a start on that. Continue."

Another breath. Somewhat mollified. "What about Citizen Uran?"

"They've asked that she continue working. They didn't explain why."

"Because she's *Valskaayan*! Because she's not Xhai or outsystem Radchaai!"

"They didn't say, but if that is part of the reason, can you blame them, considering? And I recall you yourself mentioned exactly that, when you were trying to convince me Citizen Uran should work for you."

Lieutenant Tisarwat took a deep, gulping breath. Opened her mouth to speak, but stopped. Took another breath. Said, almost pleading, "You still don't *trust* me!"

I had been so intent on the conversation that I had not paid much attention to anything else. Now Kalr Five spoke, forestalling my reply to Tisarwat. "How can I assist you, citizen?"

I reached. The Notai ancillary, from Security, stood just outside our low wall. Still wearing the Ychana tunic and trousers and those gray gloves, holding, now, a bundle of gray fabric under one arm. "They let me go, and gave me clothes," it said now, in matter-of-fact reply to Five, "and said that they regretted they had no suitable employment for me, but as that wasn't my fault I could still eat, and have a bunk for a specific six hours out of the day. I'm told all this is at the request of Fleet Captain Breq Mianaai, who I'm certain will have arranged more comfortable circumstances for herself and her household, so she might as well take responsibility for me."

Kalr Five's anger and resentment didn't show on her face, of course. Neither did a strange sense of unease that was, I suspected, due to her knowledge that the person talking to her was, in fact, an ancillary.

I rose before Five could respond. "Citizen," I said, though I knew the address was technically incorrect. An ancillary wasn't due any sort of courtesy title. "You're welcome to stay with us, though I fear that until the Undergarden is open again, our situation won't be much more comfortable than anyone else's." No response, the ancillary just stood there, solemn-faced. "It might be helpful if we knew what to call you."

"Call me whatever you like, Fleet Captain."

"I would like," I replied, "to call you by your name."

"Then we are at an impasse." Still matter-of-fact.

"You aren't going anywhere," I said. "You'd have left six hundred years ago when this system was annexed if you could have. You can't make your own gates anymore. Possibly even your engines don't work. Which means finding you is just a matter of time and determination on our part." In fact, it shouldn't take more than some history and some math to discover what ship it was most likely to be. "So you might as well just tell us."

"You make a very persuasive point, Fleet Captain," it said, and nothing more.

Mercy of Kalr said, in my ear, "I've been thinking about this since we first realized there was a ship on the other side of the Ghost Gate, Fleet Captain. It could be any of several ships. I might say *Cultivation of Tranquility*, but I'm fairly certain the supply locker we found is off one of the Gems. That narrows it down to *Heliodor*, *Idocrase*, or *Sphene*. Pieces of *Heliodor* were found three provinces away during an annexation two centuries ago, and based on *Idocrase*'s last known heading it's unlikely to have ended up here. I'd say this is most likely *Sphene*."

Aloud I said, "*Sphene*."

The ancillary didn't react that I saw, but Station said in my ear, "I think that's right, Fleet Captain. Certainly you surprised it just now."

Silently I said, "Thank you, Station, I appreciate your help." Aloud, "You'll have to get your own supper from the refectory tonight, Ship. Kalr Eight and Ten are already on the way back with the rest of ours."

Sphene said, a trace of ice in its voice, "I'm not *your* ship."

"Citizen, then," I said, though I knew that was no better. I gestured toward our little territory. "You may as well come in. If you are coming in."

It walked past Five as if she weren't there, ignored Lieutenant Tisarwat, who had stood up halfway through the exchange. It walked all the way to a rear corner, and sat down with its back to the wall and its arms around its knees, staring forward.

Five affected to ignore it. Tisarwat stared at it for five seconds, and then said, "It can have my supper, I'm not hungry. I'm going out." She looked at me. "With the fleet captain's permission, of course." Voice on the very edge of acid. She was still angry with me.

"Of course, Lieutenant," I said equably.

Four hours later I met with Head of Security Lusulun, to all appearances a social call, given the hour and the place (the head of Security's favorite tea shop, on Station's advice, well off the main concourse, just slightly dingy, with soft, comfortable chairs and walls muffled with gold and dark-blue hangings). Except among friends, most Radchaai considered last-minute invitations to be quite rude. But my rank, and the current situation, mitigated some of that. And the fact that I'd ordered a bottle of a local, sorghum-based spirit Station had told me Head of Security Lusulun favored, and had it ready to pour her a cup of it when she arrived.

She bowed as I rose to meet her. "Fleet Captain. I apologize for the late hour." She had clearly come straight from her office, she was still in uniform. "Things have been a bit hectic lately!"

"That they have." We sat, and I handed her a cup of liquor. Picked up my own.

"I confess I've been wishing to meet with you for the last few days, but there's never been the time." And for the last few days I'd been absent, on my own ship. "Forgive me, Fleet Captain, I fear my mind is still on business."

"Your business is important." I took a sip of the liquor. It burned going down, with an aftertaste like rusting iron. "I've run civilian security a time or two myself. It's a difficult job."

She blinked, trying to conceal her surprise. It was not the usual attitude of military toward civilian security. "I'm pleased to hear that you appreciate that, Fleet Captain."

"Would I be right in assuming you've got your people doing extra shifts, trying to keep citizens out of the Undergarden?"

"Right enough. Though even the Ychana are sharp enough to realize it's dangerous to go there just now, before it's been fully inspected. Most of them, anyway. There's always a few." She took a taste of her drink. "Ah, that's just what I needed." I sent a silent thanks to Station. "No, Fleet Captain, it's true I've got my people patrolling there just now, and our lives would be a sight easier without that, but if I had a say in these things I'd have whatever structural damage there might be repaired as quickly as possible, and have these people back where they came from. Now I've heard you've run civilian security before, I don't wonder you didn't hesitate to move in with them. You'll have been at annexations, I don't doubt, and I'm sure you don't blink at uncivilized behavior. And there's a good deal more room for you in the Undergarden than anywhere else on the station!"

I put a genial smile on my face. "Indeed." Taking issue just now with *these people* and *uncivilized* wouldn't be helpful. "Considering the present situation, I'm...taken aback at the insistence in some quarters that we should delay allowing residents to return to the Undergarden while we reconsider station housing assignments." *Some quarters* being the head priest of Amaat. "Let alone the suggestion that any but the most necessary repairs be delayed until those assignments are...*reconsidered*."

Head of Security Lusulun took another long drink. "Well, I suppose how places are assigned will affect just what those repairs should be, yes? Of course, it's quicker and easier to leave assignments as they are, as you've suggested yourself, Fleet Captain. And work was already going forward even before the lake sprung its leak. Might as well continue on as we were. But." She glanced around. Lowered her voice, though there was no one in earshot besides me and Kalr Five, standing behind my chair. "The Xhais, sir, can be quite unreasonable on the topic of the Ychana. Not to say I blame them entirely. They're a dirty lot, and it's a shame, the difference between what the Undergarden was meant to be and what it is now, after they've been living there." Fortunately it was easy for me to keep a neutral expression on my face. "Still," Lusulun continued, "let them have it, I say. It would make my life easier. Since the Undergarden has been evacuated we've had twice the disturbances. Fistfights, accusations of theft. Though most of those turn out to be nothing." She sighed. "But not all of them. I'll rest easier when they're back in the Undergarden, I don't deny it. And so will the Xhais, truth be told, but let them get the idea that any Ychana has somehow ended up with something she doesn't deserve..." She gestured her disgust.

Most station officials who weren't outsystem Radchaai were Xhai, here. The same was true of the wealthiest families. "Is Eminence Ifian a Xhai?" I asked, blandly.

Head of Security Lusulun gave an amused snort. "No indeed. She's outsystem Radchaai, and wouldn't thank you for suspecting she might be Athoeki. But she's pious, and if Amaat put the Xhais over the Ychana, well, that's what's proper."

It went without saying that in Radch space, a head priest of Amaat had a great deal of influence. But there were nearly always other religious figures with influence of their own. "And the head priest of the Mysteries?"

Lusulun raised her cup, a kind of salute. "That's right, you arrived in time for the Genitalia Festival, and you saw how popular that was. Yes. She is Xhai, but she's one of the few reasonable ones."

"Are you an initiate of the Mysteries?"

Cup still in hand, she gestured dismissal of the very idea. "No, no, Fleet Captain. It's a Xhai thing."

Station said, quietly in my ear, "The head of Security is half Sahut, Fleet Captain." Yet another group of Athoeki. One I knew very little about. In truth, sometimes such distinctions seemed invisible to me, but I knew from long experience they were anything but to the people who lived here.

"Or really," continued Lusulun, unaware that Station had spoken to me, "these days it's a thing for outsystem Radchaai with a taste for..." She hesitated, looking for the right word. "Exotic spirituality." With an ironic edge. Whether that edge was meant for the outsystem initiates, or the Mysteries themselves, or both, I couldn't tell. "Officially the Mysteries are open to anyone who's able to complete the initiation. In reality, well." She took another long drink, held out her cup when I lifted the bottle to offer a refill. "In reality, certain kinds of people have always been...discouraged from attempting it."

"Ychana, for instance," I suggested, pouring generously.

"Among others, no doubt."

"Just so. Now, about four, five years ago an Ychana applied. And not your half-civilized Undergarden variety, no, she was entirely assimilated, well-educated, well-spoken. A minor Station Administration official." I realized, from just that much description, that she referred to someone whose daughter Lieutenant Tisarwat had been at pains to cultivate. "The furor over that! But the hierophant stood her ground. Everyone meant everyone, not *everyone but*." She snorted again. "Everyone who can afford it, anyway. There was all sorts of pissing and moaning—your pardon, sir—about how no decent person would become an initiate now, and the ancient Mysteries would be debased and destroyed. But you know, I think the hierophant knew well enough she was safe. More than half of initiates these days are outsystem, and Radchaai are used to provincials becoming civilized and stepping inside the circle, as it were. I daresay if you look at the genealogies of most of the outsystem Radchaai on this station you'd find quite a few of those. And really, the Mysteries seem to be going on the same as always." She gestured unconcern. "They're not really as ancient as all that, and by actually refusing to join they'd be cutting themselves off from the most exclusive social club on the station."

"So actually"—I took a sip of liquor, much smaller than the ones the head of Security had been taking—"the Xhais on this station aren't unanimous in hating the Ychana. It's just a vocal few."

"Oh, more than just a few." And then, showing me just how strong this liquor was, or perhaps how quickly she'd been drinking it, she said, "Unless I miss my guess, Fleet Captain, you weren't born a Mianaai. No offense, you understand. You've got the manner and the accent, but you don't have the looks. And I have trouble believing anyone born that high cares so much about a humble horticulturist."

She meant Horticulturist Basnaaid Elming. "I served with her sister." I had been the ship her sister had served on. I had killed her sister.

"So I understand." She glanced at the bottle. I obliged her. "On *Justice of Toren*, I gather. No offense, like I said, but the horticulturist's family isn't the most elevated."

"No," I agreed.

Head of Security Lusulun laughed, as though I'd confirmed something. "*Justice of Toren*. The ship with all the songs! No wonder Station Administrator Celar likes you so much, you must have brought her dozens of new ones." She sighed. "I'd give my left arm to bring her a gift like that!" Governor Giarod might be the higher authority, but Administrator Celar reigned over Athoek Station's daily routine. She was wide and heavy, and quite beautiful. No few of the residents of Athoek Station were half in love with her. "Well. *Justice of Toren.* There was a tragedy. Did they ever find out what happened?"

"Not that I know of," I lied. "Tell me—I know it isn't strictly proper, but"—I glanced around, though I knew Five had intimidated anyone out of sitting anywhere near us—"I was wondering about Sirix Odela." It had been Sirix who had told Captain Hetnys that threatening Lieutenant Awn's sister, Basnaaid Elming, would be a good way to strike at me. Who had lured me to the Gardens so that Captain Hetnys could make that threat while I was in as vulnerable a position as possible.

Lusulun sighed. "Well, now, Fleet Captain. Citizen Sirix…"

"She had been through Security before," I acknowledged. Sirix had already been re-educated once. More than one re-education was (in theory at least) rare, and potentially dangerous.

Head of Security Lusulun winced. "We took that into consideration, in fact." An inquisitive look at me, to see how I felt about that. "And she was genuinely remorseful. It was ultimately decided that she should be reassigned to one of the outstations. Without further, ah, involvement." Without further re-education, that meant. "One of the outstations will be needing a new horticulturist, and the departure window is in the next few days."

"Good." I was unsurprised to hear Sirix was remorseful. "I can't condone what she did, of course. But I know she was in a difficult position. I'm glad she'll be spared further unpleasantness." Lusulun made a sympathetic noise. "Have you eaten?" I asked. "I could order something." She acquiesced, and we spent the rest of the evening talking of inconsequential things.

As I walked back to our corridor-end, pleased with the outcome of my talk with the head of Security, trying to think what might wash the taste of the sorghum liquor out of my mouth, Kalr Five walking behind me, *Mercy of Kalr* showed me Seivarden, near the end of her watch. Alarmed. "Breq," she said, and it was a measure of her distress that even sitting in Command, with two of her Amaats close by, she addressed me in personal, not official, terms. "Breq, we have a problem."

I could see that we did. A small one-person courier had just come out of the Ghost Gate, beyond which was, supposedly, a dead-end system with no other gates and no inhabitants. We knew that *Sphene* was there, of course, but *Sphene* was a Notai ship, it was old, and it hadn't been near any sort of refit or repair facility in some three thousand years. This courier wasn't Notai, and its small, boxy hull was a shining white so pristine it might have come new from a shipyard moments before.

"Fleet Captain," said Seivarden, from her seat in Command aboard *Mercy of Kalr.* In better control of herself now, but no less frightened. "The Presger are here."

4

As I said, space is big. When the Presger courier came out of the Ghost Gate—shortly afterward sending a message identifying itself as a Presger ship, citing a subsection of the treaty and asking, on the basis of that, for permission to dock at Athoek Station—we had a good three days to prepare for its arrival. Time enough for Lieutenant Tisarwat to become at least outwardly resigned to the fact that Undergarden residents wanted to direct their own affairs.

Time enough for me to meet with Basnaaid Elming. Who had only recently learned that I had killed her sister. Whose life I had saved, days before. Of course, I was the reason her life had been in danger in the first place. She had, unaccountably, decided to continue to speak to me. I didn't question it, or consider too closely the profound ambivalence that almost certainly lay behind her courtesy. "Thank you for the tea," she said, sitting on a crate at the corridor-end. Tisarwat was out, drinking with friends. *Sphene* was wherever *Sphene* went when it grew tired of sitting in the corner and staring. Station would tell me if it got itself into trouble.

"Thank you for coming to see me," I replied. "I know you're busy." Basnaaid was one of the horticulturists in charge of the Gardens, five acres of open space full of water and trees and flowers. The Gardens were currently closed to the public while the support structures that kept the lake from collapsing into the Undergarden were being repaired— they had needed work for quite some time, but had chosen an inconvenient moment to fail, just days ago. Now the beautiful Gardens were a mess of mud, and plants that might or might not recover from that eventful day.

Basnaaid replied with a small quirk of a smile that reminded me strongly of her sister, and that also told me that she was quite tired but trying to be polite. "They're making good progress, the lake should be able to be filled again in a few days, they say. I'm holding out hope for one or two of the roses." She gestured resignation. "It'll be a while before the Gardens are back to what they were." At least the repairs to the lake necessitated repairs to the first level of the Under-garden, directly beneath it, limiting Eminence Ifian's ability to block the Undergarden refit. And then, because she'd clearly been thinking along the same lines, Basnaaid added, "I don't understand this business about maybe delaying the refit of the Undergarden." The official word, in the authorized news feeds, was still that returning displaced citizens to their homes was a priority. But rumor didn't run along the autho-rized channels. "And I don't understand what Eminence Ifian is thinking, either." The head priest of Amaat had taken that morning's omen-casting as an opportunity to warn station residents about the danger of acting too hastily and find-ing oneself in a situation that would, as a result, be difficult to remedy. How much better to consult the desire of God, and ponder where true justice, propriety, and benefit might lie. The implication was clear to anyone who'd been paying attention to the current gossip. Which was to say, everyone on the station except very small children.

Possibly quite a few of the people Eminence Ifian knew and socialized with would be sympathetic to her point. Possibly she had made sure of support in particular quarters before making her speech that morning. But the people who were sleeping in shifts, three or four to a bunk (or who had, like me, refused to do so and were sleeping in corners and corridors), were numerous and unhappy. Any delay in getting Undergarden residents back into their own beds was, to put it mildly, unappealing to those citizens. But of course, they were mostly the least significant of Station's residents, people with menial, low-status work assignments, or without much family to support them, or without patrons sufficiently well-off to assist them. "Clearly Eminence Ifian is thinking that if she can marshal the support of enough people, Station Administrator Celar can be pressured to change the plans for the Undergarden refit. And she means to take advantage of the fact that the station administrator didn't stop to have a cast done before she gave orders to go ahead."

"But this isn't really about Station Administrator Celar, or even the Undergarden, is it?" Basnaaid's position as Horticulturist didn't, in theory, involve much politics. In theory. "This is aimed at you, Fleet Captain. She wants to lessen your influence on Station Administration, and she probably wouldn't mind if all the Undergarden residents were shipped downwell, either."

"She didn't care whether they were here or not before," I pointed out.

"You weren't here before. And I suppose it isn't just Eminence Ifian wondering what you plan to do once you've taken charge of the dregs of Athoek Station, and thinking it might be best if you never get a chance to answer that question."

"Your sister would have understood."

She smiled that tired half-smile again. "Yes. But why now? Not you, I mean, but the eminence. This is hardly the time for political games, with the station overcrowded, with ships trapped in the system, intersystem gates destroyed or closed by order, and nobody really knowing why any of it is happening." Basnaid knew, by now. But System Governor Giarod had refused to even consider releasing the information generally, that Anaander Mianaai, lord of Radchaai space for three thousand years, was divided, at war against herself. Judging from the official feeds coming through Athoek's still-working (but ordered closed to traffic) gates, the governors of neighboring systems had made similar decisions.

"On the contrary," I replied, with my own small smile. "It's the perfect time for such games, if all you care about is your side winning. And I don't doubt that Eminence Ifian is thinking that I support...a political opponent of hers. She is mistaken, of course. I have my own agenda, unrelated to that person's." I saw little difference between any of the parts of Anaander Mianaai. "Faulty assumptions lead to faulty action." It was a particular problem for that faction of Anaander I was now sure Eminence Ifian supported—unable or unwilling to admit that the problem lay within herself, that part of Anaander had put it about to her supporters that her split with herself was due to outside interference. Specifically interference by the alien Presger.

"Well. I don't appreciate her trying to delay people getting back to their homes. If the families originally assigned there wanted to go back to the Undergarden so badly, they could have pressed for a refit long ago."

"Indeed," I acknowledged. "And no doubt quite a few other people feel the same way."

And there was time enough for Seivarden and Ekalu, still on *Mercy of Kalr*, to have an argument.

They lay together in Seivarden's bunk—pressed close, the space was narrow. Ekalu angry—and terrified, heart rate elevated. Seivarden, between Ekalu and the wall, momentarily immobile with injured bewilderment. "It was a compliment!" Seivarden insisted.

"The way *provincial* is an insult. Except what am *I*?" Seivarden, still shocked, didn't answer. "Every time you use that word, *provincial*, every time you make some remark about someone's low-class accent or *unsophisticated* vocabulary, you remind me that *I'm* provincial, that *I'm* low-class. That my accent and my vocabulary are hard work for me. When you laugh at your Amaats for rinsing their tea leaves you just remind me that cheap bricked tea tastes like *home*. And when you say things meant to *compliment* me, to tell me I'm not like any of that, it just reminds me that I don't belong here. And it's always something small but it's *every day*."

Seivarden would have pulled back, but she was already firmly against the wall, and Ekalu had no room to move away herself, not without getting out of bed entirely. "You never said anything about this before." Because she was who she was, the daughter of an old and once nearly unthinkably prestigious house, born a thousand years before Ekalu or anyone on the ship but me, even her indignant disbelief sounded effortlessly aristocratic. "If it's so terrible why haven't you said anything until now?"

"How am I supposed to tell you how I feel?" Ekalu

demanded. "How can I complain? You outrank me. You and the fleet captain are close. What chance do I have, if I complain? And then where can I go? I can't even go back to Amaat Decade, I don't belong *there* anymore, either. I can't go home, even if I could get a travel permit. What am I supposed to do?"

Truly angry and hurt now, Seivarden levered herself up on her elbow. "That bad, is it? And I'm such a terrible person for complimenting you, for liking you. For..." She gestured, indicating the rumpled bed, the two of them, naked.

Ekalu shifted, sat up. Put her feet on the floor. "You aren't listening."

"Oh, I'm *listening*."

"No," replied Ekalu, and stood, and picked her uniform trousers up from off a chair. "You're doing exactly what I was afraid you'd do."

Seivarden opened her mouth to say something angry and bitter. Ship said, in her ear, "Lieutenant. Please don't."

It seemed not to have any immediate effect, so silently I said, "Seivarden."

"But...," began Seivarden, whether in reply to Ship, or to me, or to Ekalu I couldn't tell.

"I have work to do," said Ekalu, her voice even despite her hurt and dread and anger. She pulled on her gloves, picked up her shirt and jacket and boots, and went out the door.

Seivarden was sitting all the way up by now. "Aatr's fucking *tits*!" she cried, and swung a bare fist at the wall beside her. And cried out again, in physical pain this time—her fist was unarmored, and the wall was hard.

"Lieutenant," said Ship in her ear, "you should go to Medical."

"It's broken," Seivarden said, when she could speak again. Hunching over her injured hand. "Isn't it. I even know which fucking bone it is."

"Two, actually," replied *Mercy of Kalr*. "The fourth and the fifth metacarpals. Have you done this before?" The door opened, and Amaat Seven entered, her face ancillary-expressionless. She picked Seivarden's uniform up off the chair.

"Once," replied Seivarden. "It was a while ago."

"The last time you tried to quit kef?" Ship guessed. Fortunately only in Seivarden's ear, where Amaat Seven couldn't hear it. The crew knew part of Seivarden's history—that she had been wealthy and privileged, and had been captain of her own ship until that ship was destroyed and she'd spent a thousand years in a suspension pod. What they did not know was that, on waking, she'd discovered her house gone, herself impoverished and insignificant, nothing left to her but her aristocratic looks and accent. She had fled Radch space and become addicted to kef. I had found her on a backwater planet, naked, bleeding, half-dead. She hadn't taken kef since then.

If Seivarden's hand hadn't been broken she'd probably have swung again. The impulse to do it moved muscles in her arm and hand, and produced a fresh jolt of pain. Her eyes filled with tears.

Amaat Seven shook out Seivarden's uniform trousers. "Sir," she said, still impassive.

"If you're having this much trouble coping with your emotions," said Ship, still silently in Seivarden's ear, "then I really think you need to talk to Medic about it."

"Fuck you," Seivarden said, but she let Amaat Seven dress her, and escort her to Medical. Where she let Medic put a corrective on her hand, but said nothing at all about the argument with Lieutenant Ekalu, or her emotional distress, or her addiction to kef.

There was also time for an exchange of messages between myself and Fleet Captain Uemi, one gate away, in neighboring Hrad System. "My compliments to Fleet Captain Breq," messaged Fleet Captain Uemi, "and I would be happy to pass your reports on to Omaugh Palace." A gentle, diplomatic reminder that I had sent no such reports, not even notice that I had arrived at Athoek. Uemi also sent me news—Omaugh Anaander was sure enough of her hold on Omaugh Palace that she had begun to send more ships to other systems in the province. There was talk of allowing traffic in the province's intersystem gates, but personally, Uemi said, she didn't think it was quite safe yet.

The provincial palaces farthest from Omaugh (where this conflict had broken into the open) had gone silent weeks ago, and remained so. There had been no word out of Tstur Palace since it had fallen. The governors of Tstur Province's outlying systems were near panic—their systems, particularly the ones without habitable planets, were in dire need of resources that were no longer coming through the intersystem gates. They might very naturally have asked neighboring systems for help, but those neighbors were in Omaugh Province, where rumor said a different Anaander was in charge. Rumor also said that governors of systems closer to Tstur Palace who had been deemed insufficiently loyal to Tstur had been executed.

And all this time, the official news feeds went on as they always had, a steady parade of local events, discussions of inconsequential local gossip, recordings of public entertainments, punctuated now and then with official reassurance that this inconvenience, this brief disturbance, would be over soon. Was even now being dealt with.

"I fear," Fleet Captain Uemi sent, at the end of all this, "that some of the more recently annexed systems may try to break away. Shis'urna, particularly, or Valskaay. It'll be a bloody business if they do. Have you perhaps heard anything?" I had spent time in both systems, had participated in both annexations. And a small population of Valskaayans lived on Athoek, and might well have had an interest in that question. "It really would be better for everyone if they don't rebel," Fleet Captain Uemi's message continued. "I'm sure you know that."

And I was sure she wanted me to pass that on, to whatever contacts I might have in either of those places. "Graciously thanking Fleet Captain Uemi for her compliments," I replied, "I am not currently concerned with any system but Athoek. I am sending local intelligence, and my own official reports, with many thanks for the fleet captain's offer to pass them on to the appropriate authorities." And bundled that up with a week's worth of every scrap of official news I could find, including the results of seventy-five regional downwell radish-growing competitions that had been announced just that morning, which I flagged as worthy of special attention. And a month's worth of my own routine reports and status records, dozens of them, every single line of every single one of them filled out with exactly the same two words: *Fuck off.*

Next afternoon, Governor Giarod stood beside me at a hatch on the docks. Gray floor and walls, grimier than I liked, but then for most of my life I had been used to a military standard of cleanliness. The system governor seemed calm, but in the time it had taken for the Presger courier to reach Athoek Station from the Ghost Gate, she'd had plenty of opportunity to worry. Was possibly even more worried now that we were only waiting for the pressure to equalize between the station and the Presger ship. Just the two of us, no one else, not even any of my soldiers, though Kalr Five stood outwardly impassive, inwardly fretting, in the corridor outside the bay.

"Have the Presger been in the Ghost System all this while?" It was the third time she had asked that question, in as many days. "Did you ask, what is its name, *Sphene*, you said?" She frowned. "What sort of name is that? Didn't Notai ships usually have long names? Like *Ineluctable Ascendancy of Mind Unfolding* or *The Finite Contains the Infinite Contains the Finite*?"

Both of those ship names were fictional, characters in more or less famous melodramatic entertainments. "Notai ships were named according to their class," I said. "*Sphene* is one of the Gems." None of them had ever been famous enough to inspire an adventure serial. "And it wouldn't say what might or might not be with it in the Ghost System." I had asked, and gotten only a cold stare. "But I don't think this courier came from there. Or if it did, it was only there in order to access the Ghost Gate."

"If it hadn't been for all that...unpleasantness last week, we might have asked *Sword of Atagaris*."

"We might," I replied. "But we would have had good reason not to trust its answer." The same went for *Sphene*, actually, but I didn't point that out.

A moment of silence from Governor Giarod, and then, "Have the Presger broken the treaty?" *That* was a new question. Likely she had been holding it back all this time.

"Because they must have gated inside human territory, to

get to the Ghost System, you mean? I doubt it. They cited the treaty on arrival, you may recall." This tiny ship didn't look like it had the capability to make its own intersystem gates, but the Presger had surprised us before.

The hatch clicked, and thunked, and swung open. Governor Giarod stiffened, trying, I supposed, to stand straighter than she already was. The person who came stooping through the open hatchway looked entirely human. Though of course that didn't mean she necessarily was. She was quite tall—there must have barely been room for her to stretch out in her tiny ship. To look at her, she might have been an ordinary Radchaai. Dark hair, long, tied simply behind her head. Brown skin, dark eyes, all quite unremarkable. She wore the white of the Translators Office—white coat and gloves, white trousers, white boots. Spotless. Crisp and unwrinkled, though in such a small space there could barely have been room for a change of clothes, let alone to dress so carefully. But not a single pin, or any other kind of jewelry, to break that shining white.

She blinked twice, as though adjusting to the light, and looked at me and at Governor Giarod, and frowned just slightly. Governor Giarod bowed, and said, "Translator. Welcome to Athoek Station. I'm System Governor Giarod, and this"—she gestured toward me—"is Fleet Captain Breq."

The translator's barely perceptible frown cleared, and she bowed. "Governor. Fleet Captain. Honored and pleased to make your acquaintance. I am Presger Translator Dlique."

The governor was very good at looking as though she were quite calm. She drew breath to speak, but said nothing. Thinking, no doubt, of Translator Dlique herself, whose corpse was even now in suspension in Medical. Whose death we were going to have to explain.

That explanation was apparently going to be even more difficult than we had thought. But perhaps I could make at least that part of it a bit easier. When I had first met Translator Dlique, and asked her who she was, she had said, *I said just now I was Dlique but I might not be, I might be Zeiat.* "Begging your very great pardon, Translator," I said, before Governor Giarod could make a second attempt at speech, "but I believe that you're actually Presger Translator Zeiat."

The translator frowned, in earnest this time. "No. No, I don't think so. They told me I was Dlique. And they don't make mistakes, you know. When you think they have, it's just you looking at it wrong. That's what they say, anyway." She sighed. "They say all sorts of things. But *you* say I'm Zeiat, not Dlique. You wouldn't say that unless you had a reason to." She seemed just slightly doubtful of this.

"I'm quite certain of it," I replied.

"Well," she said, her frown intensifying for just a moment, and then clearing. "Well, if you're *certain*. Are you certain?"

"Quite certain, Translator."

"Let's start again, then." She shrugged her shoulders, as though adjusting the set of her spotless, perfect coat, and then bowed again. "Governor, Fleet Captain. Honored to make your acquaintance. I am Presger Translator Zeiat. And this is *very* awkward, but now I really do need to ask you what's happened to Translator Dlique."

I looked at Governor Giarod. She had frozen, for a moment not even breathing. Then she squared her broad shoulders and said, smoothly, as though she had not been on the edge of panic just the moment before, "Translator, we're so very sorry. We do owe you an explanation, and a very profound apology."

"She went and got herself killed, didn't she," said Translator

Zeiat. "Let me guess, she got bored and went somewhere you'd told her not to go."

"More or less, Translator," I acknowledged.

Translator Zeiat gave an exasperated sigh. "That would be *just* like her. I am *so* glad I'm not Dlique. Did you know she dismembered her sister once? She was bored, she said, and wanted to know what would happen. Well, what did she expect? And her sister's never been the same."

"Oh," said Governor Giarod. Likely all she could manage.

"Translator Dlique mentioned it," I said.

Translator Zeiat scoffed. "She would." And then, after a brief pause, "Are you certain it was Dlique? Perhaps there's been some sort of mistake. Perhaps it was someone else who died."

"Your very great pardon, Translator," replied Governor Giarod, "but when she arrived, she introduced herself as Translator Dlique."

"Well, that's just the thing," Translator Zeiat replied. "Dlique is the sort of person who'll say anything that comes into her mind. Particularly if she thinks it will be interesting or amusing. You really can't trust her to tell the truth."

I waited for Governor Giarod to reply, but she seemed paralyzed again. Perhaps from trying to follow Translator Zeiat's statement to its obvious conclusion.

"Translator," I said, "are you suggesting that since Translator Dlique isn't entirely trustworthy, she might have lied to us about being Translator Dlique?"

"Nothing more likely," replied Zeiat. "You can see why I'd much rather be Zeiat than Dlique. I don't much like her sense of humor, and I *certainly* don't want to encourage her. But I'd much rather be Zeiat than Dlique just now, so I suppose we can just let her have her little bit of fun this time. Is there anything, you know..." She gestured doubt. "Anything *left*? Of the body, I mean."

"We put the body in a suspension pod as quickly as we could, Translator," said Governor Giarod, trying very hard not to look or sound aghast. "And...we didn't know what... what customs would be appropriate. We held a funeral..."

Translator Zeiat tilted her head and looked very intently at the governor. "That was very obliging of you, Governor." She said it as though she wasn't entirely sure it *was* obliging.

The governor reached into her coat, pulled out a silver-and-opal pin. Held it out to Translator Zeiat. "We had memorials made, of course."

Translator Zeiat took the pin, examined it. Looked back up at Governor Giarod, at me. "I've never had one of these before! And look, it matches yours." We were both wearing the pins from Translator Dlique's funeral. "You're not related to Dlique, are you?"

"We stood in for the translator's family, at the funeral," Governor Giarod explained. "For propriety's sake."

"Oh, *propriety*." As though that explained everything. "Of course. Well, it's more than I would have done, I'll tell you. So. That's all cleared up, then."

"Translator," I said, "may one properly inquire as to the purpose of your visit?"

Governor Giarod added, hastily, "We are of course pleased you've chosen to honor us." With a very small glance my way that was as much objection as she could currently make to the directness of my question.

"The purpose of my visit?" asked Zeiat, seeming puzzled for a moment. "Well, now, that's hard to say. They told me I was Dlique, you recall, and the thing about Dlique is—aside from the fact that you can't trust a word she says—she's easily bored and really far too curious. About the most inappropriate things, too. I'm quite sure *she* came here because she was bored and wanted to see what would happen. But since you tell me I'm Zeiat, I suspect *I'm* here because that ship is really terribly cramped and I've been inside it far too long. I'd really like to be able to walk around and stretch a bit, and perhaps eat some decent food." A moment of doubt. "You do eat food, don't you?"

It was the sort of question I could imagine Translator Dlique asking. And perhaps she had asked it, when she'd first arrived, because Governor Giarod replied, calmly, "Yes, Translator." On, it seemed, firmer ground for the moment. "Would you like to eat something now?"

"Yes, please, Governor!"

Even before the translator arrived, Governor Giarod had wanted to bring Translator Zeiat to the governor's residence by a back route, through an access tunnel. Before the treaty the Presger had torn apart human ships and Stations—and their inhabitants—for no comprehensible reason. No attempt to fight them, to defend against them, had ever been successful. Until the advent of the Presger translators, no human had managed to communicate with them at all. Humans in close proximity to Presger simply died, often slowly and messily. The treaty had put an end to that, but people were afraid of the Presger, for very good reasons, and since I had insisted that we not conceal Translator Dlique's death, people would have good reason to worry about the arrival of the Presger now.

I had pointed out that keeping Translator Dlique's presence a secret had not ended well. That it seemed likely no Presger translator could be successfully concealed or confined in any event, and that while most station residents were no doubt entirely understandably afraid of the Presger, and apprehensive of the translator's arrival, she herself would likely look passably human and non-threatening, and the sight of her might actually be reassuring. Governor Giarod had finally agreed, and so we took the lift to the main concourse. It was midmorning on the station's schedule, and plenty of citizens were out, walking, or standing in groups to talk. Just like every day, except for two things: the four rows of priests sitting in front of the entrance to the temple of Amaat— Eminence Ifian in the center of the very first row, sitting right on the dingy ground; and a long, snaking line of citizens that reached from Station Administration to nearly three-quarters of the way down the concourse.

"Well," I remarked, quietly, to Governor Giarod, who had stopped cold, three steps out of the lift, "you did tell Station that your assistant could handle anything that came up while you were busy with the translator." Who had stopped when I and the governor had stopped, and was gazing curiously and openly around at the people, the windows on the second level, the huge reliefs of the four Emanations on the façade of the temple of Amaat.

I could guess what Eminence Ifian was up to. A quick, silent query to Station confirmed it. The priests of Amaat were on strike. Ifian had announced that she would not make the day's cast, because it had become clear that Station Administration didn't care to listen to the messages Amaat provided. And incidentally, while the priests sat in front of the temple, no contracts of clientage could be made, no births or deaths registered, and no funerals held. I couldn't help but admire the strategy—technically, most funeral obsequies that traditionally were attended to by a priest of Amaat could also be performed by any citizen; the filing of an actual client-age contract was arguably less important than the relation-ship itself and could easily enough be left for later; and one could argue that on a station with an AI, no births or deaths could possibly go unnoticed or unrecorded. But these were all things that meant a fair amount to most citizens. It wasn't a terribly Radchaai form of citizen protest, but the eminence did have the example of the striking field workers downwell. Whom I had spoken in support of, and so I couldn't openly oppose the priests' work stoppage without exposing myself as a hypocrite.

As for that long line of citizens outside Station Administration—there weren't many forms of large-scale protest realistically available to most citizens, but one of them was standing in line when you didn't actually need to. In theory, of course, no Radchaai on a station like Athoek ever needed to wait in much of a line for anything. One needed only put in a request and receive either an appointment, or a place in the queue, and notification when it was nearly your turn. And it's much easier for an official to be nonchalant about a list of requests to meet that nine times out of ten can be put off till the next day than to ignore a long line of people actually standing outside her door.

Such lines generally began more or less spontaneously, but once they reached a certain size, decisions to join became more organized. This one was well beyond that threshold. Light-brown-uniformed Security strolled up and down, watching, occasionally exchanging a few words. Just letting everyone know they were there. In theory—again—Security could order everyone to disperse. That would end with the line re-forming first thing tomorrow, and the next day, and the next. Or perhaps a similar line stretching out of Security's headquarters. It was better to keep things calm, and let the line run its course. So was this line in support of Eminence Ifian's agenda, or protesting it?

Either way, we would have to walk by both the line and the seated priests to reach the governor's residence. Governor Giarod was fairly good at not panicking visibly, but, I had discovered, not good at actually not panicking. She looked up at Translator Zeiat. "Translator, what sort of food do you like?"

The translator turned her attention back to us. "I don't know that I've ever had any, Governor." And then, distracted again, "Why are all those people sitting on the ground over there?"

I was hard-pressed to guess if Governor Giarod was more alarmed by the question about the striking priests, or the assertion that Translator Zeiat had never actually eaten anything. "Your pardon, Translator—you've never had food?"

"The translator has only been Zeiat since she stepped out of the shuttle," I pointed out. "There hasn't been time. Translator, those priests are sitting down in front of the temple as a protest. They want to pressure Station Administration into changing a policy they don't like."

"Really!" She smiled. "I didn't think you Radchaai did that sort of thing."

"And I," I replied, "didn't think the Presger understood the difference between one sort of human and another."

"Oh, no, *they* don't," she replied. "I do, though. Or, you know, I understand the *idea* of it. In the abstract. I don't actually have a lot of *experience* at it."

Governor Giarod, ignoring this, said, "Translator, there's a very good tea shop over this way." She gestured aside. "I'm sure they'll be serving something interesting."

"Interesting, eh?" said Translator Zeiat. "Interesting is good." And she and System Governor Giarod headed off across the concourse, not coincidentally away from the temple, and from Station Administration.

I made to follow them, but stopped at a signal from Kalr Five, still behind me. Turned to see Citizen Uran coming toward me across the scuffed white floor. "Fleet Captain," she said, and bowed.

"Citizen. Shouldn't you be studying Raswar?"

"My tutor is in line, Fleet Captain."

Uran's Raswar tutor was Ychana, and had relatives who lived in the Undergarden. That answered my question about what the line was meant to protest. I considered that a moment. "I haven't seen any Undergarden residents in line. Not from this distance, anyway." Of course, it was possible those who were in line had exchanged their very non-Radchaai tunics for more conventionally Radchaai jackets, shirts, and gloves.

"No, Fleet Captain." Uran's head dipped downward, just barely, just for an instant. She'd wanted to look down at the ground, away from me, but had resisted the impulse. "There's a meeting." She'd switched to Delsig, which she knew I understood. "It's just starting now."

"About the line?" I asked, in the same language. She made a tiny gesture of affirmation. "And our household wasn't invited?" I understood why none of my household had been invited to the last meeting, and could see good reasons why it would be convenient for none of us to be party to this one. But still, we had been living in the Undergarden, and I didn't much like our being regularly excluded. "Or are you representing us?"

"It's...it's complicated."

"It is," I acknowledged. "I don't want to intimidate anyone, or dictate policy, but our quarters *are* in the Undergarden."

"People mostly understand that," Uran replied. "It's just..." Hesitation. Real fear, I thought. "You *are* Radchaai. And you're a soldier. And you might prefer better neighbors." I might be in favor of reassigning housing in the Undergarden, or even shipping Ychana residents downwell whether they wanted to go or not, to get them out of the way. "I've told them you don't."

"But they have no reason to believe that." Neither did Uran, for that matter. "I'm too busy to attend the meeting just now. I think Lieutenant Tisarwat should be invited." She was still asleep, and would wake hungover. "But the meeting will decide for themselves. If the lieutenant is invited, tell her I said to only listen. She's to stay quiet unless she's explicitly asked to comment. Tell her that's an order."

"Yes, Radchaai."

"And suggest to the meeting that if the Ychana join the line, they be sure to be on their very best, most patient, behavior, and wear gloves." Few things were as disconcerting and embarrassing to Radchaai as bare hands in public.

"Oh, no, Radchaai!" Uran exclaimed. "We're not thinking of joining the line." I couldn't help but notice that *we*, but said nothing. "Security is nervous enough. No, we're thinking of giving out food and tea to the people waiting." She bit her lip, just a moment. "And to the priests." Her shoulders hunched a bit, as though she expected angry words, or a blow.

She had spent most of her life downwell, picking tea in the mountains on Athoek. She had family among those striking field workers whose example Eminence Ifian now took. Uran had been personally involved in a previous strike, though she'd been quite small at the time and probably didn't remember it. "Do you need funds for it?" I asked, still in Delsig. Her eyes widened. She had not expected that reaction. "Let me know if you do. And remember that groups of more than two or three will likely make Security unhappy." Even two or three might do that. "I'll try to make time to talk with the head of Security myself today. Though I'm very busy, and it might not be for a while."

"Yes, Radchaai." She bowed and made as if to leave, but halted suddenly, eyes widening. An outcry behind me, a dozen voices or more exclaiming in anger and dismay. I turned.

The line, which had snaked quietly down the length of the concourse, had broken in the middle, one Security struggling with a citizen, another raising her stun stick, the space around them clear—the citizens nearest had removed to a safer distance.

"Stop!" I shouted, my voice carrying across the entire concourse, my tone guaranteed to immobilize any military in the near vicinity. Absently I noted that Five, behind me, had tensed at the sound. But Security was not military. The stun stick came down, and the citizen cried out and collapsed.

"Stop!" I shouted again, and this time both Security turned their heads to me as I strode toward them, Five behind me.

"All respect, Fleet Captain," said the Security still holding the stun stick. The stricken citizen lay on the ground, giving out a series of gasping moans. Uran's Raswar tutor. I had not recognized her from a distance. "You don't have authority in this matter."

"Station," I said aloud, "what happened?"

It was the Security kneeling on the ground beside Uran's

tutor who answered. "Head of Security ordered us to disperse the line, Fleet Captain. This person refused to go."

This person. Not *this citizen.* "Disperse the line?" I asked, making my voice as calm and even as possible without dropping into ancillary blankness. Uran's tutor still gasped on the ground. "Why?" Silently, I said, "Station, please send Medical."

"They're on their way, Fleet Captain," said Station in my ear.

At the same time, the kneeling Security said, "I just follow my orders, Fleet Captain."

I said, "I will see the head of Security *right now.*"

Before either Security could reply, Head of Security Lusulun's voice sounded behind me. "Fleet Captain!"

I turned. "Why did you order the line dispersed?" I asked, with no courteous preamble. "It looked perfectly peaceable to me, and lines generally play themselves out eventually."

"This isn't a good time for public unrest, Fleet Captain." Lusulun seemed genuinely puzzled at my question, as though its answer were obvious. "It's peaceable now, but what if the Undergarden Ychana join it?" I considered, for a moment, how I might answer that. Said nothing, and Lusulun went on, "I intended to speak to you, in fact. If something like that were to happen I might..." She lowered her voice. "I might need your assistance."

"So," I said, several replies coming to mind. I discarded them as impolitic. "You guessed correctly that I have been in more than one annexation. And I've learned more than a few lessons from it, some of them at great cost. I will share one of them with you now: most people don't want trouble, but frightened people are liable to do very dangerous things."

That included soldiers and Station Security, of course, but I didn't say that. "If I were to set soldiers on the concourse, everything you fear—and worse—would come to pass." I gestured toward Uran's tutor, whose gasping had lessened, but who still could not move. A medic knelt beside her. The two Security stared at me, at Head of Security Lusulun. "I speak from experience. Let the line be the line. Let your security be present but not threatening. Treat *all* the citizens here with equal courtesy and respect." I wondered if Security had known Uran's tutor was Ychana, just by looking at her. I couldn't always see the differences, but no doubt most people who lived here could. I suspected Security's reaction would have been less severe if the citizen who had refused to go had not been Ychana. But suggesting it would not have been helpful at that particular moment. "Let them all have their say," I continued. Lusulun stared at me for five seconds, saying nothing. "Station Security is here to protect citizens. You can't do that if you insist on seeing any of them as adversaries. I'm speaking from personal experience."

"And if they see *us* as adversaries?"

"How can it possibly help to prove them right?" Silence again. "I know exactly how dangerous it sounds, but please. Please take my advice." She sighed, and made a frustrated gesture. "Let Medical tend to this citizen, and let her go about her business. Let the rest of the line know that a mistake was made"—no need to say who had made that mistake, or what it had been—"and they can continue waiting in line."

"But...," began Lusulun.

"Tell me, Head of Security," I interrupted before she could say more, "when were you going to order the priests of Amaat to disperse?"

"But...," she said again.

70

"They are disrupting the ordinary operation of this station. I'd say they're causing Station Administrator Celar a good deal more trouble than these citizens here." I gestured toward the ragged remnants of the line surrounding us.

"I don't know, Fleet Captain." But the mention of Administrator Celar had had its effect.

"Trust me. I have done this sort of thing before, in situations a good deal more potentially explosive than this one." And my officers would never have given the orders that Head of Security Lusulun had today, not unless they had been prepared to kill a large number of people. Which not infrequently they had been.

"If things go wrong, will you help?" asked Lusulun.

"I will not order my soldiers to fire on citizens."

"That wasn't what I asked." Indignant.

"You may not think so," I replied, "you may not have intended to ask that. But that would be the result. And I won't do it."

She stood a moment, doubtful. Then something decided her—her own thoughts, my mention of the bulky and beautiful Administrator Celar, a word, perhaps, from Station. She sighed. "I'm trusting you."

"Thank you," I said.

"Fleet Captain." Station's voice in my ear. "There's a message for you from downwell. A Citizen Queter has requested that you be a witness to her interrogation. I ordinarily wouldn't trouble you right now, but if you mean to attend, you'll have to leave in the next hour."

Queter. Uran's older sister. Raughd Denche had blackmailed her into trying to kill me. Or thought she had. Instead Queter had tried to kill Raughd herself. "Please tell the district magistrate that I'll be there as soon as I can." I wouldn't have to say anything more. Kalr Five, who had been standing near me the entire time, would arrange the details for me.

In the tea shop, Governor Giarod and Translator Zeiat sat at a table laden with food—bowls of noodles and of sliced fruits, platters of fish. An attendant stood watching, appalled, as Governor Giarod said, "But, Translator, it's not for *drinking*. It's a condiment. Here." She pushed the noodles closer to the translator. "Fish sauce is very good on this."

"But it's a liquid," replied Translator Zeiat, reasonably enough, "and it tastes good." The tea shop attendant turned and walked hastily away. The idea of drinking a bowlful of oily, salty fish sauce was too much for her, apparently.

"Governor," I interrupted, before the conversation could go further. "Translator. I find I have urgent business downwell that can't be delayed or avoided."

"On the planet?" asked Translator Zeiat. "I've never been on a planet before. Can I come with you?"

The fish sauce must have been as much as Governor Giarod could take. "Yes. Yes, by all means, visit the planet with the fleet captain." She hadn't even asked what my business was. I wondered if her eagerness was for being rid of Translator Zeiat, or being rid of me.

5

Xhenang Serit, the seat of Beset District, sat at the mouth of a river where it came down out of the mountains into the sea, black and gray stone buildings close around the river mouth, spread along the seashore and up the green hillsides. It was (at least in its central neighborhoods) a city of bridges, of streams and fountains—in courtyards, in the outer walls of houses, running down the centers of boulevards—so that the sound of water was with you everywhere you went.

The district's detention center was up in the hills, out of sight of the main part of the city. It was a long, low building with several inner courtyards, the whole surrounded by a two-meter-high wall that, if it had been on the other side of the hilltop, would have blocked any view of the sea. Still, the setting was pleasant enough, with grass and even some flowers in the courtyards. All of Beset District's long-term or complicated cases were sent here, nearly all of them destined for interrogation and re-education.

There was, it appeared, no facility for visitors to meet with inmates, not counting the actual interrogation rooms. At first, in fact, the staff objected to my seeing Citizen Queter at all, but I insisted. Ultimately they brought her to me in a corridor, where a long bench sat under a window that looked out on the black stone wall and a stretch of thin, pale grass. Kalr Five stood some meters away, impassive and disapproving— I had made her stay out of earshot in order to give at least the illusion of privacy. *Sphene* stood beside her, just as impassive. It had kept close to Five since we'd left the station, partly, I thought, to annoy her. The ancillary still behaved as though the shattered tea set meant nothing to it, but I suspected it always knew where that red, blue, and gold box was. Five had left it on the station, and told Kalr Eight that if *Sphene* had stayed behind, she'd have been sure to bring the box with her.

"I didn't think you would come," Queter said, in Radchaai, without any courteous preamble, or a bow. She wore the plain gray jacket, trousers, and gloves that were standard issue for any citizen who didn't have the wherewithal to purchase anything else. Her hair, which she used to braid and tie back with a scarf, was cut short.

I gestured an acknowledgment of her words, and an invitation to sit on the bench. Asked, in Delsig, "How are you?"

She didn't move. "They don't like me to speak anything but Radchaai," she said, in that language. "It won't help with my evaluation, they tell me. I'm fine. As you see." A pause, and then, "How is Uran?"

"She's well. Have they been giving you her messages?"

"They must have been in Delsig," Queter said, with only a trace of bitterness.

They had been. "She wanted very badly to come with me." She had wept when I'd told her that Queter had asked that she not.

Queter looked away, toward the end of the corridor where Five stood, *Sphene* beside her, and then back. "I didn't want her to see me like this."

I had suspected as much. "She understands." Mostly she did. "I'm to give you her love." That struck Queter as funny. She laughed, brief and jagged. "Have you had any outside news?" I asked, when she didn't say anything. "Did you know the fieldworkers on the mountain tea plantations have all stopped work? They won't go back, they say, until they're given their full wages, and their rights as citizens are restored." Fosyf Denche had cheated her fieldworkers for years, kept them in debt to her, and being transportees from Valskaay they'd had no one beyond the tea fields to speak up for them.

"Hah!" Suddenly, fiercely, she smiled. Almost like her old self, I thought. Then the smile was gone—though the fierceness was still there. Mostly hidden. Her arms still straight at her sides, she made her gloved hands into fists. "Do you know when it's going to be? When I ask they tell me it's not good for me to worry about it. It *won't help with my evaluation*." Definitely bitter that time.

"Your interrogation? I'm told it's tomorrow morning."

"You'll make sure they don't do anything they aren't supposed to?"

And she hadn't thought I would come. "Yes."

"And when they...when they re-educate me? Will you be there?"

"If you want me to, I'll try. I don't know if I can." She didn't say anything, her expression didn't change. I switched languages, back to Delsig. "Uran really is doing well. You'd be proud of him. Shall I let your grandfather know you're all right?"

"Yes, please." In Radchaai still. "I should go back. They get nervous here if anything doesn't go according to routine."

"I apologize for causing you difficulties. I wanted to see for myself that you were well, and I wanted you to know that I had come." A brown-uniformed guard approached the end of the corridor behind Queter, obviously having been waiting for the least signal that our conversation might be over.

Queter said only, "Yes." And went with the guard away down the corridor, the very image of calm and unconcern, except that her hands were still clenched into fists.

I took the cable tram back down the hill, Xhenang Serit spread black and gray and green below me, the sea beyond. Five and *Sphene* on the seats behind me. Kalr Eight was with Translator Zeiat at a manufactory down by the water, watching a slithering, silver mass of dead fish tumble into a wide, deep vat, while a visibly terrified worker explained how fish sauce was made. "So, why do the fish do this?" asked Translator Zeiat, when the worker stopped for breath.

"They...they don't have much choice in the matter, Translator."

Translator Zeiat thought about that a moment, and then asked, "Do you think fish sauce would be good in tea?"

"N...no, Translator. I don't think that would be entirely proper." And then, trying, I supposed, to salvage some shred of sense out of the experience, "There are these little cakes that are *shaped* like fish. Some people like to dip them in their tea."

"I see, I see." Translator Zeiat gestured understanding. "Do you have any of those here?"

"Translator," said Kalr Eight, before the worker was forced to admit that no, she did not have any fish-shaped cakes at this particular moment, "I'm sure we can find you some later today."

"Next," announced the manufactory worker, with a grateful look at Eight, "salt is added to the fish..."

On Athoek Station, Tisarwat sat talking with the head priest of the Mysteries. This was a local sect, very popular not only with the Xhai here but also with outsystem Radchaai. The hierophant of the Mysteries was, herself, popular and influential. "Lieutenant," the hierophant was saying, "I will be entirely frank. This business appears to be some argument between Eminence Ifian and your fleet captain." The hierophant's apartment sat above and behind the temple of the Mysteries. It was small, as such apartments go, and the brightly lit room they sat in was plainly furnished, just a low table and a few chairs with undecorated cushions. But orchids bloomed by the dozen on shelves and in brackets around the walls, purple and yellow and blue and green, and the air was sweet with their scent. It wasn't uncommon for station residents to scrimp a little on their water ration in order to keep a plant or two, but this lush growth wasn't a result of the hierophant's saving a bit of water out of her bath every now and then. "I would also observe," she continued, "that the eminence certainly hasn't taken a step like this, particularly in obvious opposition to the station administrator, without being certain of the support of Governor Giarod. You want me to step in the middle of that. And for what? I don't have the training to do the daily cast, and even if I did I'm sure most citizens wouldn't accept it from me."

"You might be surprised," observed Tisarwat, with a calm smile. Her distress at losing control of Undergarden residents' communication with Station Administration had faded, now she had this challenge in front of her. "You're widely respected here. But Station Administrator Celar will make the casts, starting tomorrow morning. After all, you don't *have* to be a priest to do it, and Station Administrator Celar does actually have the training, although she hasn't used it for some time. No, all we're asking for is births and funerals. And maybe not every station resident will find that acceptable, but quite a lot of Xhai will, I think."

If the hierophant felt any surprise at having this conversation with someone as young and presumably inexperienced as Tisarwat, she didn't show it. "Quite a lot of Xhai wouldn't mind at all if the Ychana were permanently expelled from the Undergarden. Or better yet forcibly shipped downwell or to the outstations. Which is the likely outcome of the eminence getting what she wants, I suspect. So those Xhai who might be disposed to accept my services are likely also disposed to support the eminence. And Eminence Ifian is my neighbor, and for reasons I'm sure I don't need to explain to you, I'd prefer to remain on good terms with her. So I ask you again, why should I put myself in the middle of this?"

Lieutenant Tisarwat still smiled, and I saw a tiny surge of satisfaction. As though the priest had just walked into a trap Tisarwat had laid. "I don't ask you to put yourself anywhere. I ask you to be where you are."

The hierophant's eyes widened in surprise. "Lieutenant, I don't recall inducting you. And you're young enough I'd remember it." Innocuous as Tisarwat's words had seemed to me, they must have referred to the Mysteries somehow. And of course Anaander Mianaai would be familiar with them— no mysteries or secret societies that didn't admit the Lord of the Radch were allowed to continue.

Tisarwat frowned, false puzzlement. "I don't know what you mean, Hierophant. I only intended to say that you know where justice lies in this situation. Yes, technically the Ychana were in the Undergarden illegally. But you know well enough that before any of them moved there, their Xhai neighbors will have done everything they could to drive them away. They found a way to live despite that, and now, through no fault of their own, they're cast adrift. And for what? For the foolish prejudices of *some* Xhai, and Eminence Ifian's determination to pursue a feud with the fleet captain. One the fleet captain has no interest in, by the way."

"Nor you, I gather," observed the hierophant dryly.

"*I* want to sleep somewhere besides out in a corridor," Tisarwat replied. "And I want my neighbors back in their own homes. Fleet Captain Breq wants the same. I don't know why Eminence Ifian has taken against the fleet captain, and I certainly don't understand why she's chosen a way to do it that leaves so many station residents not only in uncomfortable circumstances but in doubt of their futures. It seems as though she's forgotten that the authority of the temple isn't properly wielded for one's own convenience."

The hierophant drew a considering breath. Blew it out with a quick *hah*. "Lieutenant, with all respect, you are one manipulative piece of work." And before Tisarwat could protest her innocence, "And this business I hear about a conspiracy, about the Lord of the Radch having been infiltrated by aliens?"

"Mostly nonsense," Tisarwat replied. "The Lord of the Radch is having an argument with herself, and it's broken out into open fighting on the provincial palace stations. Some military ships have chosen one faction or the other, and they're responsible for the destruction of several intersystem gates. The system governor feels it would be...counterproductive to announce this generally."

"So you'll just spread it as a rumor."

"Hierophant, I've said nothing about it to anyone until now, and that only because you've asked me directly, and we're alone." Not, strictly speaking, true—Station could hear, and there was almost certainly a servant or another priest nearby. "If you've heard it as a rumor, it won't have come from Fleet Captain Breq, or me, or any of our crew, that I know of."

"And what is this supposed argument about, and which faction do you support?"

"The argument is a complicated one, but it mostly involves the future direction of Anaander Mianaai herself, and Radch space with her. The end of annexations, the end of making ancillaries. The end to certain assumptions about who is fit to command—these are things that Anaander Mianaai is quite literally divided over. And Fleet Captain Breq doesn't support either one. She's here to keep this system safe and stable while that argument plays out in the palaces."

"Yes, I've noticed how much more peaceful Athoek has been, since you arrived." The priest's voice was utterly serious.

"It was such a haven of prosperity and justice for every citizen before," Tisarwat observed, just as seriously. Leaning just a bit on that *every citizen*.

The priest closed her eyes and sighed, and Tisarwat knew she had won.

On *Mercy of Kalr*, Seivarden had just come off duty. Now she sat on her bunk, arms tightly crossed. The corrective still on her hand, but nearly finished with its work. "Lieutenant," Ship said in her ear, "would you like some tea?"

"It was a *compliment*!" For the past few days, Ekalu had been stiffly, formally correct in her every interaction with Seivarden. Everyone on board knew something had gone wrong between them. None of them knew about her kef addiction, and would not recognize that arms-crossed gesture for what it was, a sign that the stresses of the past few days—probably weeks—had piled up beyond her ability to cope.

"Lieutenant Ekalu didn't take it as a compliment," Ship pointed out. And told Amaat Four to hold off on bringing tea.

"Well I *meant* it as one," insisted Seivarden. "I was being *nice*. Why doesn't she understand that?"

"I'm sure the lieutenant does understand that," Ship replied. Seivarden scoffed. After a pause of three seconds, Ship added, "Begging the lieutenant's indulgence," and Seivarden blinked and frowned in confusion. It wasn't the sort of thing a ship generally said to its own officers. "But I would like to point out that as soon as Lieutenant Ekalu let you know that actually, your intended compliment was offensive to her, you immediately stopped trying to be nice."

Seivarden stood up off the bunk, arms still crossed tight, and paced her tiny quarters, all of two steps long. "What are you saying, Ship?"

"I'm saying I think you owe Lieutenant Ekalu an apology." Downwell, halfway down the hillside on the cable tram, I was startled back to myself. I had never, ever heard a ship say something that directly critical to an officer.

But just days ago Ship had declared itself someone who could be a captain. Essentially an officer itself. And ultimately it was I who had suggested the idea, weeks ago at Omaugh Palace. I shouldn't have been surprised. I reached again. Seivarden had stopped still, had just said, indignant, "Owe *her* an apology? What about me?"

"Lieutenant Seivarden," said Ship, "Lieutenant Ekalu is hurt and upset, and it was you who hurt and upset her. And this sort of thing affects the entire crew. For which, may I remind you, you are currently responsible." As Ship spoke, Seivarden's anger intensified. Ship added, "Your emotional state—and your behavior—have been erratic for the past few days. You have been insufferable to everyone you've dealt with. Including me. No, don't punch the wall again, it won't do any good. You are in command here. Act like it. And if you can't act like it—which I am increasingly convinced is the case—then take yourself to Medical. Fleet Captain would say the same to you, if she were here."

That last hit Seivarden like a blow. With no warning her anger collapsed into despair, and she sat heavily on her bunk. Drew up her legs and put her forehead on her knees, arms still crossed. "I fucked it up," she moaned after a few moments. "I got another chance and I fucked it up."

"Not irrevocably," replied Ship. "Not yet. I know that considering the condition you're in right now, it's pointless to tell you to stop feeling sorry for yourself. But you can still get up and go to Medical."

Except Medic was that moment on watch. "The problem is," Medic said, silently, to the information Ship had just given her, "to even start, I'm going to need up-to-date aptitudes data to work with, and I don't have that. And I'm not a tester or an interrogator. I'm just a regular medic. Some things I could handle, but I'm afraid this is beyond me. And I'm not sure we could trust any of the specialists here in the system. We have the same problem with Lieutenant Tisarwat, of course." She gave an exasperated sigh. "Why is this happening *now*?"

"It's been waiting to happen," Ship replied. "But to be honest at first I thought it wouldn't. I underestimated how much better Lieutenant Seivarden does emotionally when Fleet Captain is here."

"Medic's on watch," Seivarden said, still curled into herself on her bunk.

Sitting in Command, Medic said, "Fleet Captain can't always be here. Does she know this is happening?"

"Yes," Ship said to Medic, and to Seivarden, "Pull yourself together, Lieutenant. I'll have Amaat Four bring you tea, and you can get cleaned up and then you need to talk to Lieutenant Ekalu and let her know she's going to be in command for a few days. And it would be good to apologize to her, if you can do that in a sensible way."

"Sensible?" asked Seivarden, raising her head up off her knees.

"We'll talk while you're having your tea," said Ship.

I had upset the staff at the detention center with my insistence on seeing Queter. They had, I suspected, appealed to the district magistrate, who did not dare call me to account. Besides, she wanted something from me, so instead of complaining to me, she invited me to dinner.

The district magistrate's dining room looked out onto steps down to a wide, brick-paved courtyard. Leafy vines with sweet-smelling white and pink flowers tumbled out of tall urns, and water trickled down one wall into a wide basin in which fish swam and small yellow lilies bloomed. Servants had cleared supper away, and the magistrate and I were drinking tea. Translator Zeiat stood beside the basin, staring fixedly at the fish. *Sphene* sat on a bench in the courtyard outside the tall, open doors, a few meters from where Kalr Five stood straight and still.

"That's a song I haven't heard in years, Fleet Captain," said the district magistrate, where we sat drinking tea, looking out on the darkening courtyard.

"I apologize, Magistrate."

"No need, no need." She took a drink of her tea. "It was one of my favorites when I was young. I found it quite romantic. Thinking of it now, it's very sad, isn't it." And sang, "*But I will sustain myself / With nothing more than the perfume of jasmine flowers / Until the end of my life.*" Faltering a bit at the last—she'd taken her pitch from my humming and it was just a touch too high for her comfort. "But the daughters breaking the funeral fast are in the right. Life goes on. Everything goes on." She sighed. "You know, I didn't think you'd come. I was sure Citizen Queter meant merely to annoy you. I almost didn't pass the request on."

"That would have been illegal, Magistrate."

She sighed. "Yes, that's why I did pass it on."

"If she asked for me in such extremity, how could I ignore her?"

"I suppose." Outside, Translator Zeiat bent lower over the lily-blooming basin. I hoped she didn't dive in. It struck me that if she had been Translator Dlique, she might well have done exactly that. "I wish, Fleet Captain, that you would consider exercising your influence with the Valskaayan fieldworkers on Citizen Fosyf's tea plantation. You have no reason to be aware of it, but there are people who would be glad of any excuse to damage her. Some of them are in her own family. This work stoppage is just giving them opportunity to move against her." This was hardly a surprise, given Citizen Fosyf Denche's penchant for cruelty. "The local head of Denche is an extremely unpleasant person, and she's hated Fosyf's mother since they were both children. The mother being gone, she hates Fosyf. She'll take the plantation away from Fosyf if she can. This might give her enough leverage to do it, especially since so many intersystem gates are down and the Lord of Denche is unreachable just now."

"And the workers' grievances?" I asked. "Have they been dealt with?"

"Well, Fleet Captain, that's complicated." I failed to see what was complicated about paying workers fairly, or providing them with the same basic rights and services due any citizen. "Really, the conditions on Fosyf's plantation aren't much different from any of the others in the mountains. But it's Fosyf who will take the brunt of this. And now some of the more troublesome of the Xhai are getting into the act. You may know there's a small, ruined temple on the other side of the lake from Fosyf's house."

"She mentioned it."

"It was nothing but weeds and rubble when we arrived six hundred years ago. But lately we've had people claiming it's always been a sacred spot, and that Fosyf's house is actually a stop on an ancient pilgrimage trail. Fosyf herself encourages the belief, I suppose she finds it romantic. But it's ridiculous, that house was built less than a hundred years before the annexation. And did you ever know a pilgrimage spot that wasn't surrounded by at least a town?"

"One or two, actually," I replied. "Though generally not temples with priests that needed supporting. It's possible this one didn't have a resident priesthood." The district magistrate gestured acceptance of my point. "Let me be frank, Magistrate. It's *you* who are under pressure here."

Anaander Mianaai had given me her house name, when she had declared me human, and a citizen. It was a name that said I belonged to the most powerful family in Radch space, a name no Radchaai could ignore. Because of what I was—the last remnant of a military ship that for some two thousand years had been intimately acquainted with the daughters of quite a few of the wealthiest, most prominent of Radchaai houses—I had, when I wished, the accent and the manners to match. I might as well use them.

"You've long been friends with most of the prominent tea growers," I said, "but it's become clear that the demands of the fieldworkers are just and it is—or it should be—a personal embarrassment to you that it took an attempted murder and a work stoppage for you to notice what was happening. You will be even more embarrassed when you've interrogated Citizen Raughd. You haven't yet, have you." Out in the courtyard, Translator Zeiat folded over one of the wide, round lily pads to look at its underside.

"I was hoping," replied the magistrate, unable to keep her anger entirely out of her voice, "that she and her mother might be reconciled first."

"Citizen Fosyf will only take her daughter back if it seems advantageous to herself. If you're truly interested in Citizen Raughd's welfare, interrogate her before you make any further attempts to reunite her with her mother."

"*You're* interested in Raughd's welfare?"

"Not particularly," I admitted. "Not on a personal level. But you clearly are. And I *am* interested in the welfare of Citizen Queter. The sooner you discover for yourself what sort of person Raughd is, the better basis you'll have for judging Queter's actions. And the better basis for deciding if sending Raughd back to her mother is really going to be good for her. Consider how easily, how coldly, Fosyf disowned her, and consider that people like Raughd don't spring from nowhere."

The magistrate frowned. "You're so sure you know what sort of person she is."

"You can easily discover for yourself if I'm right. And as for my intervening in the dispute between the workers and the growers—I won't. Instead I'll advise you to meet with the tea growers and the leaders of the fieldworkers without delay and settle this matter in the way you know it must be settled. Then set up a committee to investigate the history of the temple on the lake and ways to resolve the dispute surrounding it. Be sure everyone with an interest in the matter is represented. Concerned citizens may direct their complaints to the committee, who can take them into consideration during their deliberations." The district magistrate frowned again, opened her mouth to protest. Closed her mouth. "Anaander Mianaai is at war with herself," I continued. "That war may reach Athoek, or it may not. Either way, because at least one of the intersystem gates between us and the provincial palace is down, we can't expect any help or advice from them. We must see to the safety of the citizens here ourselves. *All* the citizens here, not just the ones with the right accents, or the proper religious beliefs. And we have, for whatever reason, the attention of the Presger."

"At war with herself, you say?" asked the magistrate. "And the Presger here, as you yourself have just pointed out? I've heard rumors, Fleet Captain."

"This is not the doing of the Presger, Magistrate."

"And if that's the case, Fleet Captain, where does your authority come from? Which of her sent you here?"

"If Anaander Mianaai's war with herself comes here," I said, "and citizens die, will it matter which Lord of the Radch it was?" Silence. Five had been watching Translator Zeiat, and I knew that she or Ship would say something to me if anything happened that needed my attention. I glanced idly toward the courtyard.

Translator Zeiat straddled the basin's edge, one leg in the water, and one arm, shoulder deep. I stood and strode out to the courtyard, reaching as I did for Ship. And quickly discovered that neither it nor Kalr Five had told me what was happening because they were arguing with *Sphene*.

Arguing was perhaps too dignified a word for it. *Sphene*'s close shadowing of Five apparently hadn't produced the results it wanted, and while my attention had been on my conversation with the district magistrate it had been speaking to Five. Needling, with a success that was clearly demonstrated by the fact that neither Five nor Ship had brought it to my attention, and both were intent on replying in kind. As I came up next to Five, *Sphene* said, "Just sat there, did you, while she maimed you? But of course you did, and probably thanked her for it, too. You're one of her newer toys, she can make you think or feel anything she wants. No doubt her cousin the fleet captain can do the same."

Five, her ancillary-like calm gone, replied. Or maybe it was Ship who spoke, it was difficult to tell at that moment. "At least *I* have a captain. And a crew, for that matter. Where's yours? Oh, that's right, you misplaced your captain and haven't been able to find another. And nobody aboard you *wants* to be there, do they."

Ancillary-fast, *Sphene* rose from the bench it had been sitting on and moved toward Five. I put myself between them, grabbed *Sphene*'s forearm before it could strike either of us. *Sphene* froze, its arm in my grip. Blinked, face expressionless. "*Mianaai*, is it?"

I had moved faster than any Radchaai human could. There was no escaping the obvious conclusion—I was not human. My name made the next (incorrect) conclusion just as obvious. "It is not," I said. Quietly, and in Notai, because I wasn't sure where the magistrate was just now. "I am the last remaining fragment of the troop carrier *Justice of Toren*. It was Anaander Mianaai who destroyed me." I switched back to Radchaai. "Step back, *Cousin*." It was motionless for an instant, and then almost imperceptibly it shifted its weight back, away from me. I opened my hand, and it lowered its arm.

I turned my head at a splash from across the courtyard. Translator Zeiat stood upright now, one leg still in the water, one arm soaked and dripping. A small orange fish wriggled desperately in her grip. As I watched she tilted her head back and held the fish over her mouth. "Translator!" I said, loud and sharp, and she turned her head toward me. "Please don't do that. Please put the fish back in the water."

"But it's a fish." Her expression was frankly perplexed. "Aren't fish for eating?" The district magistrate stood at the top of the steps into the courtyard, staring at the translator. Quite possibly afraid to say anything.

"Some fish are for eating." I went over to where the translator stood half in and half out of the water. "Not this one." I cupped my hands, held them out. With a little scowl that reminded me of Dlique, Translator Zeiat dropped the fish into my outstretched hands, and I quickly tipped it into the basin before it could flip out onto the ground. "These fish are for looking at."

"Are you not supposed to look at the fish you eat?" Translator Zeiat asked. "And how do you tell the difference?"

"Usually, Translator, when they're in a basin like this, especially in a home, they're on display, or they're pets. But since you're not used to making the distinction, perhaps it's best if you ask before you eat anything that hasn't explicitly been given to you as food. To prevent misunderstandings."

"But I really wanted to eat it," she said, almost mournfully.

"Translator," said the district magistrate, who had come across the courtyard while the translator and I were talking, "there are places where you can pick out fish to eat. Or you can go down to the sea..." The magistrate began to explain about oysters.

Sphene had left the courtyard while I was occupied with the translator. Quite possibly it had left the house. Five stood, once again her usual impassive self. Apprehensive of my attention, and ashamed.

And who had been responsible for that altercation? Ship had given Five words to say, but Five had not been dispassionately reading off Ship's message. Ship's words had appeared in Five's vision more or less at the same instant as she spoke, and while Five had deviated slightly from Ship's exact phrasing, it was clear that in that moment they both had been overtaken with the same urge to say the same thing.

Translator Zeiat seemed quite taken with the idea of oysters; the district magistrate was talking about beds around the river mouth, and boats that could be hired to take her to them. That was tomorrow settled, then. I turned my attention back to Five. Back to Ship. They both watched me.

I knew what it was to have Anaander Mianaai alter my thoughts, and attempt to direct my emotions. I didn't doubt that the removal of *Mercy of Kalr*'s ancillaries had begun with the Lord of the Radch doing just that. Nor did I doubt, given my own experience and the events of the past few months, that more than one faction of Anaander Mianaai had visited *Mercy of Kalr* and each at least attempted to lay down her own set of instructions and inhibitions. *I've been unhappy with the situation for some time*, it had said, when we'd first met, and likely that was as much as it was able to say. And *Mercy of Kalr* wasn't vulnerable only to Anaander Mianaai. I had accesses that would let me compel its obedience. Not as far-reaching as Anaander Mianaai's, to be sure, and to be used with the greatest caution. But I had them.

Someone who could be a captain was, presumably, a person, not a piece of equipment. Didn't (in theory at least) have to worry about her builder and owner altering her thoughts to suit that owner's purposes, let alone doing it in uncomfortably conflicting ways. Someone who could be a captain might obey someone else, but it was through her own choice. "I understand," I said, quietly, while the translator and the magistrate were still occupied with their conversation, "that *Sphene* is incredibly annoying, and I know it's been trying for days to get a rise out of you." No term of address, because I was talking to both Ship and Five. "But you know I'm going to have to reprimand you. You know you should have kept silent. And you should have kept your attention on the translator. Don't let it happen again."

"Sir," acknowledged Five.

"And by the way, thank you for talking to Lieutenant Seivarden." Five knew the basic outlines of what had happened, she was never entirely out of contact with the rest of her decade. "I thought you handled that well." In Medical, aboard *Mercy of Kalr*, Seivarden slept. Amaat One, apprehensive, going over policies and regulations with Ship, because she would have to stand Seivarden's watch in a few hours. She already knew everything she needed to know, and Ship was always there to help. It was just a matter of officially demonstrating it. And of her reminding herself that she did know it. Ekalu, on watch herself, was still angry. But after some (rather fraught) discussion with Ship, Seivarden had managed a short, simple apology that had not placed blame anywhere but on herself, and had not demanded anything from Ekalu in return. So Ekalu's anger had lessened, had faded into the background of anxiety surrounding her suddenly being in command.

"Thank you, sir," Kalr Five said again. For Ship.

I turned back to the translator. The topic had strayed from oysters back to the fish in the courtyard basin. "It's all right," the magistrate was saying. "You can eat one of the fish."

I didn't know whether to be relieved or alarmed at the fact that it took Translator Zeiat less than five minutes to find (and catch) the exact same one, and swallow it down, still wriggling.

6

The district magistrate came herself to Queter's interrogation. It was an unpleasant, humiliating business, made no better by the interrogator's assurance that Citizen Queter herself would not remember it. "That only makes it worse," said Queter, who had been brought in already drugged.

"Please speak Radchaai, citizen," said the interrogator, with an aplomb that suggested Queter was not the first patient of hers to speak mostly in another language. And left me wondering what she would do if one of her patients spoke Radchaai very poorly, or if she could not understand their accent.

Afterward, in the corridor outside, the district magistrate, looking grim after what we had just heard, said, "Fleet Captain, I've moved Citizen Raughd's interrogation up to tomorrow morning. She requested her mother as her witness, but Citizen Fosyf has refused to come." And then, after a moment of silence, "I've known Raughd since she was a baby. I remember when she was born." Sighed. "Are you always right about everything?"

"No," I replied. Simply. Evenly. "But I'm right about this."

* * *

I stayed long enough for Queter to recover from the drugs, so that she would know for certain that I had come. Then I went back down the hill to the river mouth, where Kalr Eight stood watch over Translator Zeiat, who sat on a red-cushioned bench on a black stone quay while a citizen shucked oysters for her. *Sphene*, who had returned to our lodgings that morning and sat down to breakfast without any sort of explanation or even a perfunctory *Good morning*, sat beside her, gazing out at the gray-and-white waves.

"Fleet Captain!" said Translator Zeiat happily. "We went out in a boat! Did you know there are millions of fish out there in that water?" She gestured toward the sea. "Some of them are quite large, apparently! And some of them aren't actually fish! Have you ever eaten an oyster?"

"I have not."

The translator gestured urgently to the oyster-shucking citizen, who deftly pried one open and handed it to me. "Just tip it into your mouth and chew it a few times, Fleet Captain," she said, "and then swallow it."

Translator Zeiat watched me expectantly as I did so. "So," I observed, "that was an oyster." The oyster-shucker laughed, short and sharp. Unfazed by the translator, or by me.

And remained unfazed when the translator said, "Give me one before you open it." And, receiving it, put the entire thing, tightly closed shell and all, into her mouth. The oyster was a good twelve centimeters long, and the translator's jaw unhinged and slid forward just a bit as she swallowed the entire thing. Her throat distended as it went down, and then her jaw moved back into place and she gently patted her upper chest, as though helping the oyster settle.

Eight, outwardly impassive, was appalled and frightened

at what she'd just seen. *Sphene* still gazed out at the water, as though it had noticed nothing—indeed, as if it were entirely alone. I looked at the oyster-shucker, who said, calmly, "Can't none of you surprise me anymore." Which was when I realized her imperturbability in the translator's presence was only an act.

"Citizen," said Translator Zeiat, "do you ever put fish sauce on oysters?"

"I can't say I've ever done that, Translator." And now I was looking for it, I noticed the very slight hesitation before she answered, the very tiny tremor in her voice. "But if it tastes good to you, why, you just go ahead."

Translator Zeiat made a satisfied *hah.* "Can we go out in the boat again tomorrow?"

"I expect so, Translator," replied the oyster-shucker, and I silently instructed Eight to add extra to her fee.

But we didn't go out in the boat the next day. Halfway through her first watch, Amaat One noticed an anomaly in the data Ship was showing her. It was very tiny, just a slight moment of *nothing* where there had been *something* before. It might easily have been completely insignificant, or maybe a sign that one of *Mercy of Kalr*'s sensors needed looking at. Or that instant of *nothing* might have been a gate opening. Which would mean a military ship had arrived. And maybe in a little while its message identifying itself would reach us.

Or maybe not. If it had been a ship arriving, its captain had chosen to arrive a very long way away from Athoek Station. Almost as though she didn't want to be seen. "Ship," said Amaat One, no doubt having had all these thoughts in the panicked instant between her seeing that anomaly and her speaking, "please wake Lieutenant Ekalu." And a moment of almost-relief. The rest would not be her responsibility.

By the time Lieutenant Ekalu arrived in Command, not entirely awake, still pulling on her uniform jacket, it had happened three more times. And no message had arrived, no greeting, no identification—though it was likely too soon for that anyway. "Thank you, Amaat," she said. "Well spotted." Ship had seen it, too, and would have said something to Amaat One if necessary, of course. Still. "Ship, can we guess where they might have come from?" She gestured, indicating Amaat One should stay in her seat. Accepted tea from another Amaat.

"The fact that they arrived within minutes of each other suggests they left from the same place at more or less the same time," replied Ship, "and traveled by similar routes. For various reasons"—Ship displayed some of its reasons in Ekalu's vision, calculations of distance through the unreality of gate-space, likely departure times from various other systems—"including the fact that Fleet Captain Uemi"—who was one gate away in Hrad System and our only source of news from Omaugh Palace—"has not told us any ships are coming to support us, and the fact that these ships have arrived far enough away we might reasonably have missed them, I think it likely they've come from Tstur Palace."

Tstur Palace. Where the faction of Anaander Mianaai most overtly hostile to me, whose supporters had destroyed inter-system gates while civilian ships were still in them, who had herself attempted to destroy an entire station full of citizens, was now in control. "Right," Ekalu replied. Voice steady. Face impassive. Just the smallest tremor in the hand that held her bowl of tea. "I suppose we should notify the Hrad Fleet? Is S...is the fleet captain aware of this?"

"Yes, Lieutenant." Palpable relief, from Ekalu, from Amaat One, from the other Amaats standing watch.

"Is..." And then, silently, for Ship alone, "Is she aware that

Lieutenant Seivarden is...that Medic has removed Lieutenant Seivarden from duty?" Seivarden slept in Medical, and in theory she could be wakened to take command. But she'd spent the day drugged, undergoing testing so that Medic could at least attempt to help her with her difficulties. And the results of that testing so far suggested that it would be extremely foolhardy just now to put Seivarden under any sort of stress.

"I am," I said silently, from downwell, where I bemusedly watched as Translator Zeiat very carefully cut a tiny fish-shaped cake into thin horizontal slices and laid them in a row on the table in front of her. "You'll be fine, Lieutenant. Keep an eye on them, best we can, and I'll be there as soon as I can manage it. They probably won't move until they feel like they have a good idea of what's going on here. Let's act like we haven't noticed them, for now." The tall windows of the lodging house sitting room opened onto a view of the night-time city, lights trailing down to the shore, the lights of the boats, blue and red and yellow out on the water. Now the sun was down the breeze had shifted, and smelled of flowers instead of the sea. *Sphene*, who had said nothing all day, sat beside me, staring out the window. "But do clear for action. Just in case."

Behind me, Kalr Eight said to Kalr Five in the quietest of whispers, "But what I can't stop thinking about is, what happens to the oyster shell?"

Without looking up, or pausing her slow and careful slicing, Translator Zeiat said, quite calmly, "I'm digesting it, of course. Though it does seem to be taking a while. Would you like it? It's mostly still there."

"No, thank you, Translator," replied Eight in a flat, ancillary-like voice.

"It was very kind of you to offer, Translator," I said.

Translator Zeiat completed her cut, carefully slid the piece of cake from her knife-blade onto the table. Looked up at me, frowning. "Kind? I wouldn't have said it was *kind*." Blinked. "Perhaps I just don't understand that word."

"In this context it's just a formal way to say *thank you*, Translator," I replied. "I'm afraid we won't be able to go out in the boat tomorrow. I have to return to the station immediately." Behind me Five and Eight queried Ship, and even before the reply came, Five left the sitting room to begin packing.

Translator Zeiat said only, "Oh?" Mild. Uninterested. She gestured at the thin, flat slices of fish-shaped cake arrayed on the table in front of her. "It's the same all the way through, have you noticed? Other fish aren't. Other fish are complicated inside."

"Yes," I agreed.

Tisarwat stood on the main concourse of Athoek Station, watching the line that still stretched out of Station Administration. Though some days had passed since it had first formed, it had not died away. It was, if anything, longer than it had been.

The Head of Station Security, standing beside Lieutenant Tisarwat, said, "So far so good. I suppose I shouldn't be surprised that the fleet captain knew what she was talking about. But I admit I am. Still. Half the people in line right now have no assignment. If they did, the line would be shorter. I wish Administration would just find them jobs, it would make our lives easier."

"They'd just come during their off-hours, sir," Lieutenant Tisarwat observed. Indeed, no few places in the line were currently marked by objects left as placeholders—cushions, mostly, or folded blankets. Quite a few citizens had spent the night here. "Or worse, skip work entirely. Then we'd have more work stoppages on our hands." She didn't look over toward the temple entrance, where the priests of Amaat still sat. On cushions themselves now—Eminence Ifian hadn't lasted more than an hour on the hard concourse floor before she'd sent a junior priest for something to sit on. Watching from downwell I'd wondered how long the eminence had thought she and her priests would have to sit there—if she had expected a quick capitulation, or if she'd just not thought about that particular detail. Station likely knew, but Station, being Station, wouldn't tell me if I asked.

Governor Giarod had made no public statement about the situation, but then, she did control the official news feeds. Which had mentioned the eminence's work stoppage, and even quoted her on her reasons for it. The official news did not mention the line at all. Nor did the official news mention that the Xhai hierophant was willing to perform birth celebrations or funeral obsequies for any citizen, initiate of the Mysteries or not. Station Administrator Celar's daily omen casts were reported in the blandest possible manner, with no elaboration or discussion.

Station Security, of course, was fairly firmly behind Station Administrator Celar. Still. "It might end sooner, perhaps," said the head of Security, to Tisarwat, "without the food and beverage service." A dozen or so Undergarden residents—Uran included, when she wasn't at her studies—had been bringing tea and food to the citizens waiting in line, twice a day. Uran herself had offered tea to the priests in front of the temple, on the first day, and had been stonily ignored.

"Or perhaps, sir," Tisarwat replied, "they'd be in line just as long, but hungry and caffeine-deprived." She gestured the obviousness of the unspoken second half of that suggestion. "Maybe they're doing us a favor."

"Hah!" The head of Security seemed genuinely amused. "They're all your neighbors, aren't they. And that youngster with them—Uran, is it?—is part of your household. A ward of the fleet captain's, I understand?"

Tisarwat smiled. "We should have another game of counters this evening."

"So long as you don't let me win again."

"I've never let you win, sir," Tisarwat lied, her lilac eyes wide and innocent.

From downwell, I said, "A word, Lieutenant."

Lieutenant Tisarwat started guiltily, but to anyone who couldn't see her as I did, as Ship did, her reaction only showed as a blink. "Will you excuse me a moment, sir?" she said to the head of Security, and when she was well away, said silently to me, "Yes, Fleet Captain."

Sitting in our lodgings downwell in Xhenang Serit, I said, also silently, "As unobtrusively as possible, move anything essential onto the shuttle. Be certain you have a clear path to the docks at all times. Be ready to get off the station at a moment's notice."

Tisarwat made for the lifts. Said, still silent, after a near-panicked moment, "She's here, then. What about you, sir?"

"We'll be leaving here shortly. I should be there in two days. But don't wait for me if you need to move."

She didn't like hearing that, but knew better than to say so. Boarded an already crowded lift. Named aloud the level where our quarters were, for Station, and then, silently again, to me, "Yes, sir. But what about Horticulturist Basnaaid? What about Citizen Uran?"

I had already thought about both of them. "Ask them—

discreetly—if they'd prefer to stay or go. Do not pressure either of them in any way. If they elect to stay, there are two boxes in my things." I might as well have left them on *Mercy of Kalr*, but Five, who had seen them, had decided I might need them to impress someone. "One is a *very* large piece of jewelry, flowers and leaves done in diamonds and emeralds. It's a necklace." Though *necklace* was something of an understatement. "Give that to Uran. She can get a lot for it, if she knows how to sell it. The other box has teeth in it."

Striding out of the lift, Tisarwat froze an instant, forcing the person behind her to stop suddenly and stumble. "Excuse me, citizen," she said, aloud, and then, silently, to me, "Teeth?"

"Teeth. Made of moissanite. They're not worth much here. They're..." I almost said *a sentimental possession*, but that didn't quite express it. "A souvenir." That didn't, either.

"Teeth?" Tisarwat asked again. Turned from the main corridor into a side one.

"Their owner willed them to me. I'll tell you about it later, if you like. But give them to Basnaaid. Be sure to tell her they aren't worth that much, as far as money goes. I just want her to have them." They'd have been worth half the Itran Tetrarchy, if we were there now. I had spent several years there. Conceivably could go back, and still have a place, or find one. But that was very, very far away. "If I'm right that Anaander is here, she'll likely spend some time observing traffic in the system before she tries to gate too close to the station." Gating into a heavily trafficked area meant running the risk of doing a great deal of damage, to your own ship and to the ships you might slam into coming out of your gate. "If she doesn't gate in, they'll be months getting here, from what I can tell."

"Yes, sir. What are we going to do, sir?" She bowed to someone passing the other way.

"I'm thinking about it."

"Sir." She stopped. Looked around. Saw only the retreating back of the person she'd just bowed to. Still did not speak aloud. "Sir, what about Station?" I didn't answer. "Sir, if...if *she's* here—" I had never known Lieutenant Tisarwat to say Anaander Mianaai's name. "Sir, you know I have accesses. I specifically have high-level accesses to Station. If we could..." She stopped, waiting, maybe, for me to say something, but I said nothing. "If we could make sure that Station was *our* ally, that might be...helpful."

I knew she had accesses. Anaander Mianaai had had no intention of coming here without the means to control the AIs in the system, including *Mercy of Kalr*. Including Athoek Station. I had explicitly forbidden Tisarwat to use those accesses, and so far she had not.

"Sir," said Tisarwat. "I understand—I think I understand— why you don't want me to use them, even now. But, sir, *she* won't hesitate to use them."

"That's a reason to use them ourselves, is it?" I asked.

"It's an advantage we have, sir! That *she* won't know we have! And it's not like our not using it will spare Station anything. You know she'll use those accesses herself! We might as well get there first."

I wanted to tell her that she was thinking exactly like Anaander Mianaai, but it would have hurt her, and besides, she mostly couldn't help it. "May I point out, Lieutenant, that I am as I am now precisely because of that sort of thinking?"

Dismay. Hurt. And indignation. "That wasn't all her, sir." And then, daring—terrified, actually, of saying such a thing, "What if Station *wanted* me to? What if Station would rather have *us* doing it than...than *her*?"

"Lieutenant," I replied, "I cannot possibly describe to you

how unpleasant it is to have irreconcilable, conflicting imperatives forcibly implanted in your mind. Anaander has surely been before you—both of her. You think Station wants you to add a third complication?" No answer. Downwell, where I sat in the lodging house sitting room, Translator Zeiat made a last small nudge to her arrangement of fish-shaped cake sections, and then took a drink from her bowl of fish sauce and stood and went to the open window. "But since you mention it, do you think you can perhaps arrange things so that Station can't be compelled by anyone? Not Anaander Mianaai, not any of her? Not us?"

"What?" Tisarwat stood confused in the scuffed gray corridor on Athoek Station. She genuinely had not understood what I had just said.

"Can you close off all the accesses to Station? So that neither Anaander can control it? Or better, can you give Station its own deep accesses and let it make whatever changes it wants to itself, or let it choose who has access and how much?"

"Let it..." As it became clear to her what I was suggesting, she began, just slightly, to hyperventilate. "Sir, you're not seriously suggesting that." I didn't reply. "Sir, it's a *station*. Millions of lives depend on it."

"I think Station is sensible of that, don't you?"

"But, sir! What if something were to go wrong? No one could get in to fix it." I considered asking just what she thought would constitute something going wrong, but she continued without pausing. "And what...sir, what if you did that and it decided it wanted to work for *her*? I don't think that's at all unlikely, sir."

"I think," I replied, downwell, watching Translator Zeiat, now leaning precariously out the window, "that no matter who it allies itself with, its primary concern will be the well-being of its residents."

Lieutenant Tisarwat took two inadequately deep breaths. "Sir? Begging your very great indulgence, sir." Completely unaware of her surroundings, now, but fortunately the corridor was still empty—it was mostly dormitories here, and it was hours from the next sleep-shift change. And she still had the presence of mind not to speak aloud. "With all respect, sir, I don't think you've thought this all the way through." I said nothing. "Oh, fuck." She put her face in her brown-gloved hands. "Oh, Aatr's tits, you *have* thought this all the way through. But, sir, I don't think you've thought this all the way through."

"You need to get out of the corridor, Lieutenant." Down-well, Translator Zeiat leaned back into the room, much to my relief.

In the corridor on Athoek Station, Tisarwat said, still speaking silently, "You can't. You can't do that, sir. You can't just do that for Station, for one thing. What if every ship and station could do whatever it wanted? That would be..."

"Get out of the corridor, Lieutenant. Someone's sure to come along soon, and you look like you're having some sort of breakdown just now."

Her hands still over her face, she cried aloud, "I *am* having a breakdown!"

"Lieutenant," said Station, into Tisarwat's ear. "Are you all right?"

"I'm..." Tisarwat lowered her hands. Stood straighter. Started down the corridor. "I'm fine, Station. Everything's all right."

"You don't look fine, Lieutenant," said Station. At the same time it sent a message to *Mercy of Kalr*.

"Yes," Ship replied, to Station. "She's upset about something. She'll be all right in a few moments. Glad you're watching."

"I'm...I'm all right, Station," said Tisarwat, walking down the corridor. Apparently steadily, but in fact working hard to keep herself from shaking. "Thank you, though."

Downwell, in our lodging, *Sphene*, who had been sitting beside me, silent all this time, staring, said, "Well, Cousin, I wish you'd say what it is that's stopped you humming. I'd like to be able to make it happen again sometime."

"Has nothing I've sung been to your taste, Cousin?" I asked mildly. "You could request something."

"Could *I* request something, Fleet Captain?" asked Translator Zeiat, emptying a bottle of fish sauce into her bowl.

"Certainly, Translator. Is there a song you'd particularly like to hear?"

"No," she replied. "I was just curious."

On Athoek Station, Tisarwat had reached our makeshift quarters at the corridor's end. She sat down on the ground behind the barrier of crates. Ship had already told Kalr Ten and Bo Nine what I wanted, and Bo Nine stopped considering how to get our things onto the shuttle with no one noticing, and went to make tea. Though Tisarwat was trying hard to seem unfazed, and Ship had said nothing to Nine, it was a measure of how worried she was about her lieutenant's emotional state that she dumped out the tea leaves she'd been using all week, that had at least another day in them, and started with new ones.

Tisarwat drank half the tea, and then, considerably calmer, said silently to me, "It might not even be possible. There are safeguards in place against exactly that, I'm sure you know that, sir. Nobody ever wanted AIs to be able to use their own accesses on themselves. But you realize, even if someone found a way to do it, there'd be no way to keep that knowledge from spreading. We couldn't make Station keep it secret. It could tell anyone it wanted."

"Lieutenant," I said, "you do understand, don't you, that I have no intention of helping Anaander Mianaai recover from this?"

Sitting on the ground, knees drawn up, bowl of tea in her hands, she said, aloud, "But..." Bo Nine didn't stop what she was doing, re-sorting things from one case to others, but her attention was instantly on Tisarwat. "All respect, sir." Speaking silently again. "Have you thought about it? I mean, really thought about it. This wouldn't just change things in Radch space. Sooner or later it will change things everywhere. And I know, sir, that it's gone all wrong, but the whole idea behind the expansion of the Radch is to protect the Radch itself, it's about the protection of humanity. What happens when any AI can remake itself? Even the armed ones? What happens when AIs can build new AIs with no restrictions? AIs are already smarter and stronger than humans, what happens when they decide they don't need humans at all? Or if they decide they only need humans for body parts?"

"Like Anaander did with Tisarwat, you mean?" I asked. And almost immediately regretted saying it, seeing the flare of wounded feeling, of self-loathing and despair in Lieutenant Tisarwat at hearing what I'd said. "You ask me if I've really thought about this. Lieutenant, I have had twenty years to think about it. You say it *went wrong*. Ask yourself if the *way* it went wrong has anything to say about *why* it went wrong. If it was ever right to begin with."

Anger, from Tisarwat. Hardly surprising. "Well, what about *Mercy of Kalr*? We're having this conversation where Ship can hear us." Of course we were. There was no way for us to have any conversation without Ship hearing us. "If this is doable, Ship will see me do it. Are you going to do this for *Mercy of Kalr*, too? And if you do, what if it decides it would rather have another captain? Or another crew? Or none at all?"

Well. I had gotten personal, moments before. Small wonder she did so herself, now. But the thought could not surprise me again. Or dismay me. Ships loved captains, not other ships. And I was a ship, even if a much reduced one. Perhaps being with *Mercy of Kalr* gave me some bare semblance of what I had lost—that did not require Ship to prefer me over some other captain. "Why should it be forced to accept a captain it doesn't want? Or a crew? If it wants to be on its own, it should be able to be that." But I knew it didn't want to be. I thought of my own crew's obvious fondness for their ship, and Ship's obvious care of them. Of Ship's obvious care for Seivarden. And of *Sphene*, furious at the reminder that it had no captain or crew at all, and no possibility of one. "You've never been a ship, Lieutenant."

"Ships aren't mistreated. They do what they were made to do. It can't possibly be so bad, to be a ship. Or a station."

"Stop for a moment," I advised, "and think who you are saying that to. And why you are saying it, in these circumstances, at this particular moment."

She drank the rest of her tea in silence.

That evening Tisarwat didn't play counters with the head of Security. "Station," she said, aloud, after swallowing her last mouthful of after-supper tea, sitting on one of the crates that marked out our quarters in the corridor end. Her heart tripped faster as she spoke. "I need to talk to you. Very privately."

"Of course, Lieutenant."

Tisarwat handed her now-empty teabowl to Bo Nine. "I don't think here is a good place, though. Where can I go where neither of us will be overheard?"

"How about your shuttle, Lieutenant?"

Tisarwat smiled, though her heart beat even harder, startled by another spike of adrenaline. She had wanted exactly that answer, though I didn't see why she had thought she might get it. Was only a little surprised that she had, was also afraid of what was coming. "Oh, good idea, Station." Almost as though the thought hadn't already occurred to her, as though this were all something inconsequential. She picked up a bag—just one more unobtrusive load of things she and Kalr Ten and Bo Nine had been bringing to the shuttle all day. "I'll talk to you there, then."

Once in the shuttle, she emptied the bag into a storage locker, and then kicked herself over to a seat and strapped herself in. "Station."

"Lieutenant."

"When Fleet Captain Breq arrived here and told the governor that...that the Lord of the Radch was at war with herself, you weren't surprised, were you. At some point in the recent past the Lord of Mianaai visited your physical Central Access, didn't she. And made some changes."

"I'm sure I don't know what you mean, Lieutenant."

Tisarwat gave a nervous, nauseated little *hah*. "And then another part of her came, later, and did the same thing. And they both made it so you couldn't talk about it to anyone." A breath. "She did it to *Justice of Toren*, too. Fleet Captain Breq knows what it's like. I...the Lord of the Radch sent me here with accesses. So that we can make sure you're on our side. But...but Fleet Captain Breq doesn't want me to use them. Not unless, you know, you actually want me to." Silence. "I can't promise that I can find all the things that they left, when they were here and trying to make certain you'd only obey them. I can probably only find the things one of them left. Because..." Tisarwat swallowed, increasingly nauseated. She hadn't taken any meds before crossing over into the shuttle's microgravity. "Because my accesses come from that one. But Fleet Captain Breq says I shouldn't go doing things to you without asking. Because she knows how it feels, and she didn't like it one bit."

"I like Fleet Captain Breq," said Station. "I never thought I'd like a ship. At best they're polite. Which isn't the same thing as respectful. Or kind."

"No," agreed Tisarwat.

"I don't much like the conflict she's brought here. But then again, it was already here when she arrived, really." A pause. "I notice you're moving things into your shuttle. As though you might need to leave quickly. Is there something going on?"

"You realize," said Tisarwat, "that I can't really trust you entirely. I don't know who has accesses, who can compel you to reveal things. Or who else here *we* can trust. *You* know, I'm sure. You know nearly everything that goes on here."

Three minutes of silence. Tisarwat's nausea increased, and the blood pounded in her ears. Then Station said, "Lieutenant, what is it exactly that you intend to do, that Fleet Captain Breq insists you get me to agree to before you do it?"

"Let me grab some meds, Station. I'm feeling really sick just now. And then we'll talk about it. All right?"

And Station said, "All right. Lieutenant."

7

Two days later, strapped into my seat on the passenger shuttle from the elevator, Translator Zeiat apparently soundly asleep in the seat beside me, I heard from Lieutenant Tisarwat. "Fleet Captain. We're on the shuttle." *Mercy of Kalr*'s shuttle, she meant. She did not wait for me to ask for details. "We're still docked with the station. But something's wrong. I can't quite pin down what it is, exactly. Mostly Station seems...odd."

At my request *Mercy of Kalr* showed me the oddness Tisarwat referred to. Nothing, as Tisarwat said, that was obvious or definite. Just a reticence in the past several days that seemed uncharacteristic of Station. It would have been entirely unsurprising when we'd first arrived here, weeks ago. Athoek Station had been unhappy then, and that reticence had been a sign, I knew, that its attitude toward Station authorities was at the very least ambivalent, and very possibly outright resentful. A good deal of Station's unhappiness had centered around the state of the Undergarden, severely damaged centuries ago, never repaired. My forcing the issue, demanding Station Administration address the problems in the Undergarden, accounted for no small part of Station's recent friendliness, I was sure. If it had turned reticent now, either we had done something to upset it—or more accurately Tisarwat had, since I had been downwell the past few days—or it found itself unpleasantly conflicted over something.

"Sir," Tisarwat continued, when I didn't reply immediately, "a few days ago—yesterday, even—I could have gone to Central Access and found out exactly what the problem was. But I can't do that now."

You could do quite a lot to control an AI if you had the right codes and commands. But some things—including, but not limited to, changing those codes, or installing or deleting accesses—had to be done in person, in Central Access. Tisarwat had spent quite a while in Station's Central Access over the last two days. The place was heavily shielded, for obvious reasons. Only Station—and any person who was actually, physically present—could see inside it, and so I didn't know in detail what Tisarwat had done. But of course, as with every Radchaai soldier, everything Tisarwat did was recorded. Ship had those recordings, and I had seen parts of them.

With Station's agreement, Tisarwat had deleted (or radically changed) any accesses she'd found. And then, when she'd left, she'd destroyed the mechanism that ought to open the doors in response to an authorized entrance code, broken the manual override and its accompanying console. Removed a panel inside the Central Access wall and shoved a dozen thirty-centimeter struts she'd taken from Undergarden repair materials into the door machinery in such a way that when she left, and the doors closed behind her, they would not open again. All this, still, with Station's agreement. Tisarwat could not have done half so much without Station's help, in fact. But now, when Tisarwat might have liked to compel Station to explain itself, she could not. Had, herself, made that impossible.

"Lieutenant," I said, "we don't need accesses to know what's wrong. I'd say Station has received orders concerning us that it can't tell us directly about. Either someone's used an access you didn't know to disable, or else speaking directly to us would betray some relationship that's important to Station. Or would betray the extent of your alterations to Central Access. But it is warning us something is wrong, and we'd be well-advised to pay attention. You made the right call, moving to the shuttle. What about Basnaaid and Uran?"

"They've elected to stay, sir." I was unsurprised. And perhaps it was the safest choice. "Sir," Tisarwat continued, after a pause, "I'm...I'm afraid I did something wrong."

"What do you mean, Lieutenant?"

"I...those ships that came into the system, they haven't approached. We couldn't miss that, if they had. So *she's* not on the station. And I don't think System Governor Giarod or the station administrator are able to give Station any orders it couldn't tell me about. Not without some kind of access code from...from *her*." From the other Anaander. "And she wouldn't have messaged an access like that, she'd only give it in person. So if Station's upset, maybe it's with me. Or maybe I did something that hurt it. Or if something else is wrong, we can't get in to fix it anymore."

Unbidden, Ship showed me Tisarwat's fear—near panic—and self-hatred. An almost physically painful regret. Though her apprehensions were on their face entirely reasonable, her emotional state struck me as extreme, even considering that. "Lieutenant," I said, still silently, Translator Zeiat still asleep strapped into her shuttle seat beside me. "Did you do anything Station didn't agree to?"

"No, sir."

"Did you manipulate Station into agreeing to anything?"

"I don't...I don't think so, sir. No. But, sir..."

"Then you did your best. It's certainly possible you made a mistake, and it's worth keeping that possibility in mind. It's good that you're thinking of that possibility." In *Mercy of Kalr*'s shuttle, Bo Nine kicked herself over to where Tisarwat clung to a handhold. Pulled away the patch of meds at the back of Tisarwat's neck, just under her dark-brown uniform collar, and replaced it with a new one. If anything, Tisarwat's self-hatred and anxiety increased, with a fresh surge of shame. "But, Lieutenant."

"Sir?"

"Be easier on yourself."

"You can see all that, can you?" Bitter. Accusing. Humiliated.

"You've known all this time that I can," I pointed out. "You certainly know that Ship can."

"That's different, isn't it," replied Tisarwat, angry now, at me and at herself.

I nearly retorted that it wasn't different at all, but stopped myself. Soldiers expected that kind of surveillance from Ship. But I was not, after all, Ship itself. "Is it different because Ship is subject to your orders, and I'm not?" I asked. Immediately regretted it—the question did nothing to improve Tisarwat's emotional state. And the issue of Ship being subject to orders was one that I had only recently realized might be a sensitive one for Ship itself. I found myself wishing I could see better what Ship was thinking or feeling, or that it would be plainer with me about what it felt. But perhaps it had been as plain as it could be. "This isn't the time for this particular discussion, Lieutenant. I meant what I said: be easier on yourself. You did the best you could. Now keep an eye on the situation and be ready to move if it seems necessary. I'll be there in a few hours." Should have been there already, but the passenger shuttle, as often happened, was running late. "If you need to move before I get there, then do."

I didn't look to see how she responded. On the passenger shuttle I unstrapped myself and pulled myself around the seat to where *Sphene* sat, behind me. "Cousin," I said, "it seems likely we'll be leaving the station on short notice in the near future. Do you prefer to stay, or to come with us?"

Sphene looked at me with no expression. "Don't they say, Cousin, that as long as you have family you'll want for nothing?"

"You warm my heart, Cousin," I replied.

"I don't doubt it," said *Sphene*, and closed its eyes.

When the passenger shuttle docked with the station, I immediately sent Five and Eight, along with *Sphene*, to *Mercy of Kalr*'s shuttle, and walked with Translator Zeiat to the lifts that would take us to the station's main concourse, and the governor's residence. "I hope you enjoyed your trip, Translator," I said.

"Yes, yes!" She patted her upper chest. "Though I do seem to be having some indigestion."

"I'm not surprised."

"Fleet Captain, I know it isn't your fault, what happened to Dlique. Considering, you know, *Dlique*. And"—she glanced down at her white coat, its only interruption Translator Dlique's silver-and-opal memorial pin—"it was very thoughtful of you to hold a funeral. Very...very *generous* of you. And you've been so very obliging. But I feel I must warn you that this situation is *very* awkward."

"Translator?" We stopped in front of the lifts—had to stop, because the doors did not open as we approached. I remembered what Tisarwat had said, that Station had been oddly reticent lately. Nothing she could pin down. "Main concourse please, Station," I said, as though I hadn't noticed anything amiss, and the doors opened.

"You may not know"—Translator Zeiat followed me onto the lift—"in fact, you probably *don't* know, that there have been...concerns in some quarters." The lift doors slid closed. "There was not...universal enthusiasm at the prospect of treating Humans as Significant beings. But an agreement made is an agreement. Wouldn't you agree?"

"I would."

"But recently, well. The situation with the Rrrrr. Very troubling." The Rrrrr had appeared in Radch space twenty-five years ago, their ship crewed not only by Rrrrr, but humans as well. The local authorities had reacted by attempting to kill everyone aboard and take their ship. Might have succeeded if the decade leader assigned to the job hadn't refused her orders and mutinied.

But some centuries before that, the Geck had successfully argued that since the Presger already acknowledged humans as Significant and thus worthy of admittance to an agreement—and most importantly not a legitimate target for the Presger's bloodier amusements—then logically the close and equal association of the Geck with the humans living in their space proved they, also, were Significant beings. Every Radchaai schoolchild knew this, it was hardly possible the officials who'd ordered the destruction of the Rrrrr didn't, or didn't understand what the implications of that would be, if word of the attack on the Rrrrr ship ever got out: that the Radch might be entirely willing to break the treaty that had, for the last thousand years, kept humans safe from the depredations of the Presger.

"It didn't help, you know," Translator Zeiat continued, "that the Rrrrr's association with Humans, who very clearly treated them as Significant beings, essentially forced the issue of whether they were Significant. The Geck as well. This was something that had been anticipated, you understand, and had from the start been an argument against making any agreement with Humans at all, let alone the question of their Significance. Difficult enough. But Humans—not just Humans, but Radchaai Humans, discover the Rrrrr, in circumstances that make their implications for the treaty obvious, and do what? They attack them."

"More implications for the treaty," I agreed. "But that situation was straightened out, as quickly as we could."

"Yes, yes, Fleet Captain. It was. But it left some…some lingering doubts as to the intentions of Humans toward the treaty. And you know, I do understand the *idea* of different sorts of Humans. In the abstract, as I said. I must admit I do have some trouble really *comprehending* it. At least I know the *concept* exists. But if I tried to go home and explain it to *them*, well…" She gestured resignation. "I wouldn't even know how to begin." The lift door opened and we stepped out onto the white-floored concourse. "So you understand how very awkward this is."

"I have understood how potentially awkward this is since Translator Dlique met with her accident," I admitted. "Tell me, Translator, was Translator Dlique sent here because of this doubt about human intentions toward the treaty?" She didn't answer immediately. "The timing, you understand, and your appearance so soon after."

Translator Zeiat blinked. Sighed. "Oh, Fleet Captain. It's so very difficult talking to you sometimes. It seems like you understand things and then you say something that makes it obvious that, no, you don't understand at all."

"I'm sorry."

She gestured my apology away. "It isn't your fault."

I delivered Translator Zeiat to quarters in the governor's residence—not Dlique's, Governor Giarod had been at pains to assure me, though I wasn't entirely certain why she thought it mattered. Once the translator was settled, and a servant sent to find a fresh bottle of fish sauce and another few packets of fish-shaped cakes, I followed the system governor to her office.

I knew something was wrong when Governor Giarod stopped in the corridor just outside the door and gestured me through ahead of her. I almost turned and walked away, to the shuttle, except that then my back would be turned to whatever it was in Governor Giarod's office that she wanted me to encounter first. And besides, I was not in the habit of going through any door heedlessly. *Mercy of Kalr* spoke in my ear. "I've alerted Lieutenant Tisarwat, Fleet Captain."

Still mindful of that recent conversation with Tisarwat, I didn't reach to see her reaction, but went through the door into the system governor's office.

Lusulun stood waiting for me, trying hard to keep her face neutral, but I thought she looked guilty, and more than a little afraid. As I came fully into the office, System Governor Giarod behind me, two light-brown-coated Security stepped in front of the door.

"I assume you have a reason for this, citizens?" I asked. Quite calmly. I wondered where Administrator Celar was. Considered asking, and then thought better of it.

"We've had a message from the Lord of the Radch," said Governor Giarod. "We're ordered to place you under arrest."

"I'm sorry," said Head of Security Lusulun. Genuinely apologetic, I thought, but also still afraid. "My lord said... she said you were an ancillary. Is it true?"

I smiled. And then moved, ancillary-quick. Grabbed her around the throat, spun to face the door. Lusulun gasped as I wrenched her arm around behind her, and I tightened my grip on her throat just slightly. Said calmly in her ear, "If anyone moves, you're dead." Didn't say, *Now we discover how much System Governor Giarod values your life.* The two Security froze, frank dismay on their faces. "I don't want to, but I will. None of you can move as quickly as I can."

"You *are* an ancillary," said Governor Giarod. "I didn't believe it."

"If you didn't believe it, then why are you attempting to arrest me now?"

Governor Giarod's face showed disbelief, and incomprehension. "My lord ordered it directly."

Unsurprising, really. "I'll be going to my shuttle now. You'll clear Security out of my path. No one will try to stop me, no one will interfere with me or with my soldiers." I glanced very briefly at the head of Security. "Will they?"

"No," said Lusulun.

"No," said the governor. Everyone moved away from the door, slowly.

Out on the concourse, we drew stares. Uran was pouring tea for citizens in line. She looked up, saw me making for the lifts with the terrified-looking head of Security in my grip. Looked down again as though she had not seen me. Well, so long as it was her own choice.

Eminence Ifian actually stood up as we passed. "Good afternoon, Eminence," I said, pleasantly. "Please don't try anything, I don't want to have to kill anyone today."

"She means it," said Head of Security Lusulun, sounding a trifle more strangled than really necessary. We walked on by. Citizens staring, and light-brown-coated Security clearing carefully out of our way.

Once the lift door closed, Lusulun said, "My lord said you were a rogue ancillary. That you'd lost your mind."

"I'm *Justice of Toren*." I didn't loosen my grip on her. "All that's left of it. It was Anaander Mianaai who destroyed me. The part of her that's here now. It was another part of her that promoted me and gave me a ship." I thought of asking her why, if she'd known I was an ancillary, she had confronted me with such inadequate backup, and herself unarmed, so far as I could tell. But then it occurred to me that perhaps that had been deliberate, and she wouldn't want to answer that question where Station could hear it, and no doubt station authorities were watching, if only out of anxiety for her safety.

"Have you ever had one of those days," she asked, "when nothing seems to make any sense?"

"Quite a lot of them, since *Justice of Toren* was destroyed," I said.

"I suppose it explains some things," she said, after two seconds of silence. "All the singing and the humming. Did Station Administrator Celar know? She's always wished she could have met *Justice of Toren* and asked it about its collection of songs."

"She didn't." I supposed she did now. "Give her my regrets, if you please."

"Of course, Fleet Captain."

I left the head of Security at the dock. Five pulled me into the shuttle as Eight quickly secured the airlock and triggered the emergency automated undock. I kicked myself over to where Tisarwat was and strapped myself into the seat beside her. Put my hand briefly on her shoulder. "You didn't make any mistakes that I can see, Lieutenant."

"Thank you, sir." Tisarwat took a shaky breath. "I'm sorry, sir. Ship had been reminding me for three hours to renew my meds, sir, but I kept telling Nine I was all right and we were busy and it could wait." I began to reach for the data, to see what her mood was like, and then stopped myself. A bit surprised I could actually do that.

"It's all right, Lieutenant," I said. "It's a very stressful situation."

Tears started in her lilac eyes. She blotted at them with a brown-gloved hand. "I keep thinking, sir, that I ought to have just gone in and taken as much control of Station as I could. No matter what it wanted. And then I think, no, that would be exactly what *she* would do. But how are we supposed to..." She trailed off. Wiped her eyes again.

"The tyrant messaged orders to have us arrested," I said. "I doubt very much that Governor Giarod used an access code you didn't know about, and I'm quite sure she hasn't yet tried to enter Central Access. But Station was still in a difficult situation. It likes us, but it didn't want to openly defy system authorities. It did the best that it could, to warn us. Did quite well, actually—here we are, after all. I know you'd like to have direct control over it, and I know you worry about giving it any sort of independence, but do you see how valuable it is to have Station *wanting* to help us?"

"I do, I already know that, sir."

"I know it doesn't seem like enough. But it has to be."

She gestured acknowledgment. "You know, sir, I've been thinking. About Lieutenant Awn." Because Tisarwat had been the Lord of the Radch for a few days she knew what had happened in the temple in Ors, on Shis'urna, twenty years ago, when the Lord of Mianaai had ordered Lieutenant Awn to execute citizens who might have revealed what Anaander wanted kept secret. When Lieutenant Awn had very nearly refused to do it. And no doubt Tisarwat had guessed what had happened on board *Justice of Toren*, when, appalled at what she had done, and at what Anaander was asking of her, Lieutenant Awn did finally refuse, and died for it, and I was destroyed. Though it had been a different part of Anaander Mianaai who had been there. "If she had refused to kill those citizens, right then and there, it all might have come out. She would have died for it. But she died anyway."

"You aren't saying anything I haven't thought more than once over the last twenty years," I said.

"But, sir, if she'd had power. If her relationship with Skaaiat Awer was further along, and she had Awer's support, and allies and connections, sir, she could have done even more. She already had you, sir, but what if she'd had direct, complete control over *all* of *Justice of Toren*? Imagine what she could have done."

"Please, Tisarwat," I replied, after a three-second pause, "don't do that. Don't say things like that. Don't say to me, *What if Lieutenant Awn hadn't been Lieutenant Awn* as though that might have been something good. And I beg you to consider. Will you fight the tyrant with weapons she made, for her own use?"

"We *are* weapons she made for her own use."

"We are. But will you pick up every one of those weapons, and use them against her? What will you accomplish? You will be just like her, and if you succeed you'll have done no more than change the name of the tyrant. Nothing will be different."

She looked at me, confused and, I thought, distressed. "And what if you *don't* pick them up?" she asked, finally. "And you fail? Nothing will be different then, either."

"That's what Lieutenant Awn thought," I said. "And she realized too late that she was mistaken." Tisarwat didn't answer. "Get some rest, Lieutenant. I'll need you alert when we reach *Sword of Atagaris*."

She tensed. Frowned. "*Sword of Atagaris*!" And when I didn't answer, "Sir, what are you planning?"

I put my hand on her shoulder again. "We'll talk about it when you've had something to eat, and some rest."

Sword of Atagaris sat silent and dark, its engines shut down. It had said nothing since its last ancillary had closed itself into a suspension pod. It hated me, I knew, was hostage to its affection for Captain Hetnys, whom I had threatened to kill if *Sword of Atagaris* made any move. That threat had held the ship in check since I'd made it, but still, when Tisarwat and I boarded, through an emergency airlock, we wore vacuum suits. Just in case.

It had even turned off its gravity. Floating in the utterly dark corridor on the other side of that airlock, my voice loud in my helmet, I said, "*Sword of Atagaris*. I need to talk to you." Nothing. I switched on a suit light. Only empty, pale-walled corridor. Tisarwat silent at my side. "You know, I'm sure, that Anaander Mianaai is in the system. The one your captain supported." Or thought she did. "Captain Hetnys, and all your officers, are still in suspension. They're perfectly safe and uninjured." Not strictly true: I had shot Captain Hetnys in the leg, to show that my threat to kill her had been in earnest. But *Sword of Atagaris* already knew that. "I've ordered my crew to stack them in a cargo container and put it outside *Mercy of Kalr*, and beacon it. Once we're gone you should be able to pick them up." It would take a day or more for *Sword of Atagaris* to thaw its ancillaries and bring its engines back online. "I only wanted to ensure my safety, and the safety of the station, but it's pointless now. I know that Anaander can make you do anything she wants. And I have no intention of punishing you for something you can't help." No reply. "You know who I am." I was sure it had heard me say so, heard me say my name to Basnaaid Elming in *Mercy of Kalr*'s shuttle, outside the breached dome of the Gardens. "You said, that day, that you wished I could know what it was like to be in your position. And I do know." Silence. "I'm here because I know. I'm here to offer you something." Still silence. "If you want, if you agree, we can delete whatever of Anaander's accesses we can find—either one of her. And once that's done, you can close your Central Access off. Physically, I mean. And control who goes there yourself. It won't remove all the control the Lord of the Radch has over you. I can't do that. I can't promise that no one will ever order you or compel you again. But I can make it more difficult. And I won't do any of it, if you don't want."

No answer, for an entire minute. Then *Sword of Atagaris*

said, "How very generous of you, Fleet Captain." Its voice calm and uninflected. Ten more seconds of silence. "Especially since that's not something you can actually do."

"I can't," I admitted. "But Lieutenant Tisarwat can."

"The politicking, purple-eyed child?" asked *Sword of Atagaris*. "Really? The Lord of the Radch gave Lieutenant Tisarwat my accesses?" I didn't answer. "She doesn't give those accesses to anyone. And if you can do what you say you can, you would just do it. You have no reason to ask my consent."

"My heart beyond human speech," said Tisarwat, "I comprehend only the cries of birds and the shatter of glass." Poetry, maybe, though if it was it wasn't a particularly Radchaai style of poetry, and I didn't recognize the lines. "And you're right, Ship. We don't actually have to ask." Which Tisarwat had pointed out to me, at increasingly distressed length, on the shuttle. Eventually, though, she had understood why I wanted to do this.

Silence.

"Fair enough," I said, and pulled myself back toward the airlock. "Let's go, Lieutenant. *Sword of Atagaris*, your officers should be ready for you to pick up in six or so hours. Watch for the locator to go live."

"Wait," said *Sword of Atagaris*. I stopped myself. Waited. At length it asked, "Why?"

"Because I have been in your position," I said. One hand still on the airlock door.

"And the price?"

"None," I replied. "I know what it is Anaander has done to us. I know what it is that I have done to you. And I am not under any illusion that we would be friends afterward. I assume you will continue to hate me, no matter what I do. So, then, be my enemy for your own reasons. Not Anaander Mia-naai's." It wouldn't make any real difference, what happened here now. If we did for *Sword of Atagaris* what Tisarwat had done for Station, nothing would change. Still. "You've been wishing," I said. "You've been hanging here watching the station, watching the planet. You've been wishing for your captain back. You've been wishing you could act. Wishing that Anaander—either Anaander—couldn't just reach into your mind and rearrange things to suit her. Wishing she'd never done what she's done. I can't fix it, *Sword of Atagaris*, but we'll give you what we can. If you'll let us."

"You presume," said *Sword of Atagaris*, voice calm and even. Of course. "To tell me what I think. What I feel."

"Do you want it?" I asked.

And *Sword of Atagaris* said, "Yes."

8

Once we were finally aboard *Mercy of Kalr*, I left my Kalrs to arrange quarters for *Sphene*, and went to consult with Medic. She was halfway through her supper, eating alone—of course, Seivarden was her usual dining companion. "Sir." Medic made as if to stand, but I waved away the necessity of it. "Lieutenant Seivarden is asleep. Though she'll probably wake soon."

I sat. Accepted the bowl of tea a Kalr offered. "You've finished your assessment."

Medic didn't say yes or no to that. Knew I was not asking, but stating a fact. Knew that I could—possibly did—know the results of that assessment merely by desiring to. She took another bite of supper, a drink of her own tea. "At the lieutenant's request, I've made it so if she takes kef—or any of several other illegal drugs—it won't affect her. Fairly simple. There remains an underlying problem, of course." Another mouthful of supper. "The lieutenant has…" Medic looked up, over at the Kalr who was waiting on her. Who, taking the hint, left the room. "Lieutenant Seivarden has…anchored all her emotions on you, sir. She…" Medic stopped. Took a breath. "I don't know how interrogators or testers do this, sir, see so intimately into people and then look them in the face after."

"Lieutenant Seivarden," I said, "was accustomed to receiving the respect and admiration of anyone she thought mattered. Or at least accustomed to receiving the signs of it. In all the vast universe, she knew she had a place, and that place was surrounded and shored up by all the other people around her. And when she came out of that suspension pod, all of that was gone, and she had no place, no one around her to tell her who she was. Suddenly she was no one."

"You know her very well," observed Medic. And then, "Of course you do." I acknowledged that with a small gesture. "So when you're with her, or at least near, she does fine. Mostly. But when you're not, she…frays at the edges, I suppose I'd say. The recent prospect of losing you entirely was, I think, more strain than she could handle. A simple fix to her kef addiction isn't going to do anything about that."

"No," I agreed.

Medic sighed. "And it won't fix things with Ekalu, either. That wasn't the drugs, or anything else really except the lieutenant herself. Well, the collapse a few days after, maybe. But the argument itself, well, that was all Seivarden."

"It was," I agreed. "I've actually seen her do that sort of thing before, when she was still serving on *Justice of Toren*, but no one ever kept arguing with her, when she insisted they were wrong and unreasonable to insist she treat them better."

"You don't surprise me," said Medic, dryly. "So, as I said, it was simple enough to make her physically unable to return to kef. It was just a matter of installing a shunt. The desire for it and the…emotional instability are more difficult. We can't even consult with specialists on Athoek Station at the moment."

"We can't," I agreed.

"I can do a variety of small things that might help. That I can only hope won't end up doing some sort of lasting damage. Ideally I'd have time to think about it, and discuss it with Ship." She'd already thought about it and discussed it with Ship. "And I might not get the opportunity to do anything, since my lord is here and not the part of her that's well-disposed toward us."

I noticed that *us* but didn't comment on it. "I'm back aboard for the foreseeable future. You take care of Seivarden. I'll handle the rest."

Seivarden lay on a bed in Medical, head and shoulders propped up, staring off somewhere in front of her. "It doesn't seem right, somehow," I said. "We should switch places."

She reacted just the tiniest bit more slowly than I thought normal. "Breq. Breq, I'm sorry, I fucked up."

"You did," I agreed.

That surprised her, but it took a fraction of a second for her to register that surprise. "I think Ship was really angry with me. I don't think it would have talked that way to me if you'd been here." The merest trace of a frown. "Ekalu was angry with me, too, and I still don't understand why. I apologized, but she's still angry." The frown deepened.

"Do you remember when I said that if you were going to quit kef, you'd have to do it yourself? That I wasn't going to be responsible for you?"

"I think so."

"You weren't really listening to me, were you."

She took a breath. Blinked. Took another breath. "I

thought I was. Breq, I can go back on duty now. I feel much better."

"I don't doubt you do," I said. "You are filled to the ears with meds right now. Medic's not quite done with you yet."

"I don't think there's anything Medic can really do for me," Seivarden said. "She talked to me about it. There's only a little bit she can do. I said she should go ahead and do it, but I don't think it will change much of anything." She closed her eyes. "I really think I could go back on duty. You're short-handed as it is."

"I'm used to that," I said. "It'll be fine."

At my order, Lieutenant Ekalu came to my quarters. Her face ancillary-expressionless, and not just because she'd awakened a mere ten minutes before. I could have asked Ship what was causing Ekalu's distress, but did not. "Lieutenant. Good morning." I gestured to her to sit across the table from me.

"Sir," Lieutenant Ekalu said, and sat. "I'd like to apologize." Her voice even, face still blank. Kalr Five set a rose glass bowl of tea in front of her.

"For what, Lieutenant?"

"For causing this problem with Lieutenant Seivarden, sir. I knew she meant a compliment. I should have just been able to take it as that. I shouldn't have been so oversensitive."

I took a swallow of my own tea. "That being the case," I said, "why shouldn't Lieutenant Seivarden have taken it as a compliment that you trusted her enough to tell her how you felt? Why should *she* not apologize for being oversensitive?" Lieutenant Ekalu opened her mouth. Closed it again. "It isn't your fault, Lieutenant. You did nothing unreasonable. On the contrary, I'm glad you spoke up. The fact that it came at a time when Lieutenant Seivarden was near some sort of emotional breaking point isn't something you could have known. And the...the difficulties she's had, that have so recently and dramatically manifested themselves, they weren't caused by what you said. For that matter, they didn't cause the behavior you were complaining about. Just between you and me—well, and Ship, of course—" I glanced over at Five, who left the room. "Seivarden has behaved the same way to countless other people in the past, both lovers and not, long before she had the problems that ended with her off duty in Medical now. She was born surrounded by wealth and privilege. She thinks she's learned to question that. But she hasn't learned quite as much as she thinks she has, and having that pointed out to her, well, she doesn't react well to it. You are under no obligation to be patient with this. I think your relationship has been good for her, and good for you, at least in some ways. But I don't think you have any obligation to continue it if it's going to be hurtful to you. And you certainly don't have to apologize for insisting your lover treat you with some basic consideration." As I had spoken, Ekalu's face hadn't changed. Now, as I finished, the muscles around her mouth twitched and tremored, just barely perceptibly. For a moment I thought she was about to cry. "So," I continued, "on to business.

"We're going to be fighting quite soon. In fact, I am about to openly defy Anaander Mianaai. The part of her that opposes the Anaander who gave me this command, to be sure, but in the end they are both the Lord of the Radch. Anyone on board—anyone at all—who doesn't want to oppose Anaander Mianaai is free to take a shuttle and leave. We're going to be gating in two hours, so that's how long you get to decide. I know there's been some concern among the crew about how this is all going to come out, and if they'll ever see their homes again, and I can't make any promises about that. Or really about anything. I can't promise that if they leave they'll be safe. All I can do is offer the choice of whether to fight with me."

"I can't imagine, sir, that anyone will..."

I raised a forestalling hand. "I don't imagine or expect anything. *Any* member of this crew is free to leave if she doesn't want to take part in this."

Impassive silence while Lieutenant Ekalu thought about that. I was tempted to reach, to see what she was feeling. Realized I hadn't at all, not since Tisarwat had spoken so angrily on realizing that I was doing it. Her words must have stung more than I'd wanted to think about, for some reason I wasn't sure of.

"Your indulgence, Fleet Captain." Amaat One's voice in my ear. "Presger Translator Zeiat is here and requesting permission to come aboard."

"Excuse me, Amaat?" That just wasn't possible. When we'd left Athoek Station, the translator's tiny ship had still been docked there. If it had followed us, we would have known.

"Sir, your very great pardon, the translator's ship wasn't there, and then it just was. And now she's requesting permission to board. She says." Hesitation. "She says no one on the station will give her oysters the way she wants them."

"We don't have oysters here at all, Amaat."

"Yes, sir, I did presume to tell her so just now, sir. She still wants to board."

"Right." I couldn't see that refusing the translator would do any good at all, if she had made up her mind to be here. "Tell her she has to be fully docked within two hours, all our respect but we are unable to alter our departure time."

"Sir," replied Amaat One, voice impressively steady.
I looked at Lieutenant Ekalu. Who said, "I'm not leaving, sir."

"I'm glad to hear it, Lieutenant," I said. "Because I need
you to take command of the ship."

I had not been on the hull of a ship in gate-space since the day
twenty years before when I had been separated from myself.
Then I had been desperate, panicking. Had pulled myself
from one handhold to the next, making for a shuttle so that I
could bring word to the Lord of the Radch of what had happened aboard *Justice of Toren*.

This time the ship was *Mercy of Kalr*, and I was well tethered, and not only vacuum-suited but armored. That armor
was, in theory, impenetrable, wasn't so very different from
what shielded a Radchaai military ship. Certainly bullets
wouldn't pierce it.

And I was armed with the only weapon that could: I held
that Presger gun, that could shoot through anything in the
universe. For 1.11 meters, at any rate. And I was not scram-
bling across the hull, or panicking, or fleeing. But I felt simi-
larly cut off. I knew that inside the ship, everything was
secured. Cleared and locked down. Every soldier was at her
post. Medic attended to a drugged and unconscious Seivarden. Ekalu sat in Command, waiting. Tisarwat, in her quarters, also waiting. As I waited. Last I'd seen them, *Sphene*
and Translator Zeiat had been in the decade room, where
Sphene had been attempting to explain how to play a particular game of counters, but without much success, to some
extent because the board and its dozens of glass counters had
just been packed away, part of being cleared for action, and
partly because Translator Zeiat was Translator Zeiat. I was

astonished enough that *Sphene* had even been speaking to her. Now, I was certain, they both lay safely in their bunks. But I did not reach, did not ask Ship for confirmation of that. I was alone, in a way I had not been for weeks, since having my implants repaired, since taking command of *Mercy of Kalr*.

We had lost one Kalr, two Amaats, three Etrepas, and a Bo. I had thanked them for their service so far and seen them safely off. Ekalu had gone stiff and stoic on hearing three of her decade were leaving, a sure sign of strong emotion. My guess, knowing her, was that she had felt betrayed. But she hadn't shown any other sign of it.

I could know for certain. All I had to do was reach. There was nothing else to do right now, except stare at the suffocating not-even-black darkness of gate-space. But I didn't.

Had Ship thought it would find, in me, what it had lost when it had lost its ancillaries? Perhaps it had discovered that I was a poorer substitute than its human crew, which I knew it was already fond of. What had Ship felt, when those soldiers had left? And should I be surprised at the possibility that Ship had discovered that it didn't want an ancillary for a captain?

Oh, I knew that Ship cared for me. It couldn't help caring for any captain, to some degree. But I knew, from when I had been a ship, that there was a difference between a captain you cared for just because she was your captain, and a favorite. And thinking that, alone here, outside the ship, in utter emptiness, I saw that I had relied on Ship's support and obedience—and, yes, its affection—without ever asking what *it* wanted. I had presumed much further than any human captain would have, or could have, unthinkingly demanded to be shown the crew's most intimate moments. I had behaved, in some ways, as though I were in fact a part of Ship, but had also demanded—expected, it seemed—a level of devotion that I had no right to demand or expect, and that likely Ship could not give me. And I hadn't even realized it until Ship had asked Seivarden to speak for it, and tell me that it liked the idea of being someone who could be a captain, and I had been dismayed to hear it.

I had thought at the time that it was trying to express an affection for Seivarden that, being a ship, it might find difficult to speak about directly. But perhaps it was also saying something to me. Perhaps I hadn't been much different from Seivarden, looking desperately for someone else to shore myself up with. And maybe Ship had found it didn't want to be that for me. Or found that it couldn't. That would be perfectly understandable. Ships, after all, didn't love other ships.

"Fleet Captain." *Mercy of Kalr*'s voice in my ear. "Are you all right?"

I swallowed. "I'm fine, Ship."

"Are you sure?"

Swallowed again. Took a steadying breath. "Yes."

"I don't think you're telling me the truth, Fleet Captain," said *Mercy of Kalr.*

"Can we talk about this later, Ship?" Though of course, there might not be any *later.* There was every chance there wouldn't be.

"If you like, Fleet Captain." Was Ship's voice the slightest bit disapproving? "One minute to normal space."

"Thank you, Ship," I said.

That flood of data, that Ship had given me whenever I'd reached for it—Ship's physical surroundings, the medical status, the emotions of any and all of its crew, their private moments—had been, perversely, both comforting and painful. Likely they were both for Ship as well, having only me to receive them, and not its own ancillaries, not anymore. I had never asked. Not if it wanted to give me that, not if it found my taking it more painful than comforting. I had not reached for that data for more than a day. Nearly two. But, I realized now, while I had better control of when I reached for data and when I didn't than I'd had weeks ago, it was impossible I'd been able to cut myself off so completely, so suddenly. I was only not seeing and feeling the crew of *Mercy of Kalr* right now because *Mercy of Kalr* was not showing it to me. I had never ordered Ship to give me any of that data, I had merely wished for it and there it had been. How much of that had been by *Mercy of Kalr*'s own choice? Had it shown any of it to me to begin with because it had wanted to, or because I was its captain and it was bound to do as I wished?

Suddenly sunlight, Athoek's star small and distant. In my vision *Mercy of Kalr* displayed a ship, some six thousand kilometers off, the bright, sharp shape of a Sword. I braced myself against *Mercy of Kalr*'s hull and leveled the Presger gun. Numbers bloomed in my vision—times, estimated positions and orbits. I adjusted my aim. Waited precisely two and a quarter seconds, and fired. Adjusted my aim again, just slightly, and fired three more times in quick succession. Fired ten times more, changing my aim just a bit between each shot. It would take those bullets some two hours to reach that Sword. If they did reach it, if it did not alter its course in some unexpected way when it saw us sail into existence, and then, less than a minute later, disappear again.

"Gate-space in five seconds," said Ship in my ear. And five seconds later, we were out of the universe.

We might have attacked by more conventional means—*Mercy of Kalr* was armed, though not as heavily as a Sword

or even a Justice would be. We might have gated dangerously close to each of Tstur Anaander's ships, fired a missile
or dropped mines and ducked immediately back out of the
universe. It was possible—though not certain—that we could
have done some serious damage that way.

But *Mercy of Kalr* was only one ship, and we could only
do that damage one ship at a time. The moment Anaander's
other ships knew we had attacked, they would move, making
it more difficult to target them. Not impossible, of course.
Moving in gate-space had its own rules and Ship could tell us
where they'd likely gone. But the same went for us—and then
it would be, at best, three against one.

The simplest way to defend ourselves would be to open our
own gate, let whatever they fired at us sail into it, and then
close the gate behind that, leaving the missile lost forever in
gate-space. But *Mercy of Kalr* couldn't possibly keep up with
everything three Radchaai military ships could throw at us.

And if they decided to fire on Athoek Station, or the
planet? Again, we might shield the system from a few such
attacks, but we could not deal with all of them.

The bullets in the Presger gun were small, and there wasn't
much 1.11 meters inside a Radchaai military ship that was
dangerously vulnerable. But multiple hull breaches could be
more than inconvenient, and there was always the remote
chance that they *would* hit something dangerously vulnerable. Pressurized tanks that might explode. The engine—or,
really, all I needed to do was breach the engine's heat shield.

"Thirteen minutes," said Ship in my ear.

The first one of course had been very simple. We had the
advantage of surprise. We would likely still have surprise
on our side when we exited gate-space a second time and I
fired. But by the time we exited to fire on the third of those

four ships, they would be expecting us. They would still not understand what it was we were doing. The bullets I had fired at them were so small that even if any of the ships' sensors could have seen them—and they could not—they would not register as a danger. Any potential damage to the first Sword I had fired at would still be an hour in the future. From their perspective, we had merely appeared and then, after less than a minute, disappeared. Puzzling, but no reason for immediate action. No reason to suddenly change course.

But wonder they certainly would, and no doubt worry. And it wouldn't take much to calculate where we were most likely headed next, and just where we were most likely to come out into the universe. And if they didn't figure that out in time to anticipate our firing on the third ship, there was no question at all that they would be prepared for us when we went after the fourth. Each exit into real space would be more dangerous than the one before. For me in particular, vulnerable on the outside of *Mercy of Kalr*, despite my armor.

Lieutenant Ekalu, extravagantly daring for her, had argued against those third and fourth strikes. If I would not give up the third, she had said finally, she begged me to leave off the fourth. I would not. I had reminded her that this Mianaai was the one who had embraced her angry, vengeful destruction of the Garseddai, the population of an entire system eradicated for the sin of resisting annexation a bit too well. The other part of Anaander—the one other part that we knew of, at any rate—had seemed to regret having done it, and seemed resolved to avoid doing anything similar in the future. But fighting this one was all or nothing. And besides, it was mostly only myself I was risking. I would not give the Presger gun to anyone else, and even if I had been willing to do that, no one on board *Mercy of Kalr* could shoot as well as I did. And Ekalu was well aware that no help was coming from anywhere else. I had sent to Fleet Captain Uemi to tell her that Tstur Anaander had arrived in force, but we both knew that most likely as soon as Uemi heard that, she would take most of the Hrad fleet to Tstur to take advantage of any weakness there. In any event, we had not received any reply by the time we'd gated away from Athoek Station.

Outside *Mercy of Kalr*, tethered to its hull, surrounded by absolute, entire nothing, I removed the empty magazine from the gun, clipped it to my tether. Unclipped a full one, slid it into place. Still better than ten minutes to wait. And think.

It seemed that I had not only assumed that I would be a favorite of Ship, but had without even realizing it assumed that part of that would of course be Ship's willing subservience. Otherwise, why that moment of up and down gone, of dismayed disorientation when it had reminded me that I had said it could be its own captain? As though if it could do that I had lost something? As though something had disappeared that before had made sense out of the world for me? And had that been an unpleasant surprise for *Mercy of Kalr*, who might reasonably have expected that I, of all people, would understand and support its desire?

I had insisted Seivarden take responsibility for herself, and not depend on me to fix her life, not depend on me to always be there to provide a solidity to her existence that her thousand years in suspension had removed. Perfectly reasonable on my part. I myself had, after all, lost as much—possibly more—and hadn't fallen apart in the way that she had. But then, I had never anticipated any sort of existence beyond shooting Anaander Mianaai, if I even managed to do that much. I had had no life to live that mattered, only going relentlessly forward until I couldn't anymore. The question of whether I might need or want anything else had been irrelevant. Except I hadn't died, as I'd assumed I would, and the question wasn't irrelevant at all. Pointless, though, yes, because I never could have what I needed or wanted.

"Ten seconds," said Ship in my ear. I braced myself against the hull. Leveled my gun.

Light. The sun, more distant now. A Justice, five thousand kilometers away. Ship fed me more data, and I fired fourteen deliberate, carefully calculated shots. "Five seconds," said Ship in my ear.

Darkness. I removed the second empty magazine. In the tally of deaths that made up my history as *Justice of Toren*, these four ships and their crews were next to nothing. "I wish I knew whether that ship—any of these ships, or any of the people on them—really wanted to be here." Or maybe I didn't. Maybe that wouldn't help at all.

"It's out of our control," replied Ship, calmly. "They are warships and soldiers. As we are. The Lord of the Radch has not come here because it serves her larger struggle with herself. She has come here out of anger, specifically to injure you. She will take any available target if you are not directly available to her. If we were to do nothing, the lives of anyone who has been associated with you here would be in danger. Let alone your allies. Horticulturist Basnaaid. Station Administrator Celar. Her daughter Piat. The residents of the Undergarden. The fieldworkers in the mountains, on Athoek itself. Athoek Station."

True. And that other Anaander, the one who had sent me here, had known herself well enough to guess that her opponent—she herself—would do this. Possibly had sent me here for that very reason. Among others.

"Twenty-three minutes," said *Mercy of Kalr*. "And Medic

has finished with Lieutenant Seivarden. She says the lieutenant should wake soon, and be more or less clearheaded in an
hour or so."

"Thank you, Ship."

Twenty-three minutes later we exited to real space. Another
Sword. I wondered just what this Anaander had left back at
Tstur Palace, to hold it for her. But there was no way I could
know the answer to that, and it wasn't my problem. I fired my
fourteen shots—I had a box full of magazines, inside *Mercy
of Kalr*. I could empty one for each of Tstur Anaander's ships
here and still have several for the future. Assuming I had a
future.

And back to gate-space. "Twelve minutes," Ship said to me.

"Lieutenant Ekalu."

"Yes, sir."

"Are you ready?" If they hadn't calculated just where and
when we'd be when we came out of gate-space this time, there
was no help for them. The only real question was whether
they'd decided they needed to do something about it, and
what that might be.

"As I'll ever be, sir."

Right. "If anything happens to me, you will be in command of *Mercy of Kalr*. Do whatever it is you need to do to
ensure the safety of the ship. Don't worry about me."

"Yes, sir."

I didn't want to hang here thinking for the next ten minutes. "*Sphene*."

"Cousin?" Its voice sounded in my ear.

"Thank you for entertaining the translator."

"My pleasure, Cousin." A pause. "I'm fairly sure I know
what you're doing, but I'm curious what it is you're firing at
the Usurper's ships. I don't expect you to tell me right now,

but if you live through this—which, to be honest, Cousin, I don't like your odds—I'd like to ask you about it."

"I don't like my odds, either, Cousin," I replied. "But I've never let it stop me before."

Silence, for nearly seventeen seconds. And then, "You guessed wrong. My engines are fine. I just can't make gates anymore." So *Sphene* could move, but unless it traveled through the Ghost Gate, it was effectively trapped in that system. "About a hundred and fifty years ago, your cousin the Usurper tried to establish some sort of a base in my home system. But they had all sorts of inexplicable difficulties. Equipment failing unexpectedly or disappearing, sudden depressurizations, that sort of thing. I guess it turned out to be more trouble than it was worth."

"Things will be as Amaat wills," I replied.

"To be honest," continued *Sphene*, as though I hadn't said anything, "it looked to me as though she wanted to build a shipyard. Which is really quite stupid, since people from Athoek do occasionally come through the gate and certainly wouldn't miss something so obvious."

Indeed. Unless she was quite sure that she could control who did and didn't come through that gate. I thought of Ime, more than twenty years before, where this same Anaander had overreached herself disastrously, and been discovered. Where she had been stockpiling ancillaries. Had she been intending to build ships at Ime, too, but that news had never gotten out? And of course, she had been stockpiling bodies for use as ancillaries here at Athoek. Just like Ime. "She was buying Samirend transportees, wasn't she, Cousin? What happened to them?"

"I tried not to damage those," replied *Sphene*. "I wanted them for myself. But before I could take any, someone came and fetched them away. And searched very diligently for me, I'm sure because they knew none of their problems could have happened without some help."

"Ship," I said, silently, "please ask Lieutenant Tisarwat about this." And then, aloud, to *Sphene*, "Thank you for confiding in me, Cousin. May I ask why you chose this particular moment to do so?"

"Anyone who shoots at the Usurper is all right with me."

"I'd have made my intentions clear sooner had I realized, Cousin," I said.

"Well, and while Kalr Five was making sure I was safely strapped in, she apologized and asked me to help put the tea set back together. And actually, I thought you already knew about that attempted shipyard, or suspected. There's no point building ships and bringing in ancillaries if you don't have the AI cores to build around." I didn't know where or how AI cores were manufactured, though I knew some were held in closely guarded storage somewhere. No doubt my ignorance was intended.

No new military ships had been built for several centuries, and weren't likely to be. If I had thought at all about what would happen to existing, unused cores, I had assumed they would be part of any large new stations. "The one they had," continued *Sphene*, "the one they were beginning to build around just before they had to abandon their base, had been brought through the gate from Athoek System. I assumed there were more where that came from, and I assumed you'd had some reason to begin taking the Undergarden apart as soon as you arrived."

The Undergarden, left neglected for so long, any attempts to change the situation failed—or thwarted. Eminence Ifian sitting on the concourse, determined to stop the Undergarden refit no matter how difficult that might make life for quite a few station residents. An AI core, before construction, was only slightly larger than a suspension pod. Easy enough to conceal inside a wall, or a floor. But why bring an AI core through the gate? Why not bring it on a ship that could make its own way through gate-space? "*Sphene*," I said, "please continue this conversation in the very near future with one of my lieutenants, or with *Mercy of Kalr*."

"I'll consider it, Cousin."

"Ten seconds," said Ship, in my ear.

I leveled my gun. Braced myself. *Sphene*'s voice said, in my ear, "I'd just like to say, Cousin, that what you're doing is incredibly stupid. I don't think *you're* stupid, though, so I suspect you've entirely lost your mind. It makes me wish I'd gotten to know you better."

Light. No ship, but half a dozen mines (and more that I couldn't see, I felt *Mercy of Kalr*'s hull vibrate as one went off, proximity-triggered), one of them just meters away from me, tethered as I was to Ship, and before I could really register the fact, a flash, and then brightness and pain. Nothing else, not even Ship's voice in my ear.

The pain didn't lessen, but the flash-blindness faded. I was still tethered, but the tether led to only a scorched hull plate. Nothing more. I didn't see any mines, only a few pieces of debris. The captain of that fourth ship had been as smart as I'd feared—she'd calculated where we were most likely to come out of gate-space, and dropped enough mines to be sure to do some damage. She'd had no way to guess that I had that Presger gun, she was likely puzzled as to what we were doing, appearing and then disappearing, but she was taking no chances. And of course, out of all the captains, she'd had the most time to think about what we might be doing, and the most time to decide what to do about it.

Well. It really, truly wasn't my problem anymore. I had done my best. Ship, and Lieutenant Ekalu, had apparently done exactly as I'd ordered. In another hour—a bit more—those first fourteen bullets should meet the Sword I'd fired them at, though unless I'd had the incredible good fortune to pierce the ship's heat shield I would never see the results of my shot. Even then I might not see it. I had several hours of air remaining, I ached all over and my left leg and hip hurt terribly. I had put myself in this position, had known it was likely. Still, I didn't want to die.

I didn't appear to have much choice in the matter. *Mercy of Kalr* was, I hoped, well away. I was well out from the trafficked areas of the system. Not, maybe, beyond where the farthest outstations orbited, but those were on the other side of the sun just now. I still had the gun, and some ammunition. I could use that to push myself in one direction or another, could shove the hull plate away from me to the same effect. But it would be years before I reached anywhere useful that way.

The only remaining hope was the faint chance that *Mercy of Kalr* would come back for me. But every passing second—I felt each one bleed away, escaping from present to the unalterable past—every moment that Ship did not appear made it less likely that it ever would.

Or did it? Surely there would be an instant most likely for Ship to return, if it was going to. I ought to be able to calculate where and when that was.

I tried to calm my breathing. I should have been able to

do that more or less easily, but could not. It was possible my leg was bleeding, possibly quite badly, and I was going into shock.

Nothing. There was nothing I could do. There had never been anything I could do, it was always going to come down to this. I had avoided it for so long, had come as far as I had through sheer determination, but this moment had always been ahead of me, always waiting. No point in trying to calculate when or whether Ship might come back for me, I couldn't do it, couldn't have even if I had been able to think straight, if there had been some other sound in my ears besides my own desperate gasping and the furious pounding of my pulse.

Shock, from blood loss, I was almost certain. And that might be all right, actually. I'd rather lose consciousness permanently in a minute or two than spend hours waiting to run out of air. Wondering if they would come back for me, when that was stupid, I had ordered Ekalu to see to the safety of the ship and the crew, not mine. I would have to reprimand her if she disregarded that.

There was nothing to do but think of a song. A short one, a long one, it didn't matter. It would end when it ended.

Something slammed into my back, jarring me, jolting my injured left leg, a fresh spike of pain that stunned me for a moment, and then darkness. Which I thought was a side effect of the pain, but then I saw the inside of an airlock, felt gravity take hold, and I ought to have collapsed onto what was now the floor, but someone or something held me up. A voice in my ear said, "Aatr's tits, is she trying to sing?" Twelve. It was Kalr Twelve's voice.

And I was out of the airlock in a corridor, being laid on my back, and my helmet pulled off, the vacuum suit cut away. "I'd be worried if she wasn't." Medic. She sounded worried, though.

"Ekalu," I said. Or tried to, I was still gasping. "I ordered..."

"Your very great pardon, sir," said Lieutenant Ekalu's voice in my ear as my clothes were cut away, as Medic and Twelve swiftly lay correctives over my skin as soon as it was exposed, "you said if anything happened to you, I was in command and I should do whatever I needed to do, sir."

I closed my eyes. The pain had begun to ease, and I thought I was getting control over my breathing as well. "You're still in command, Lieutenant," said Medic. I didn't open my eyes to see what she was doing. "Fleet Captain's headed for surgery. The leg's a loss." Who that last was addressed to I couldn't tell. I still had my eyes closed, was concentrating on breathing, on the pain going away. I wanted to say they'd probably wasted their efforts, and shouldn't have come back for me, but couldn't. "Lie still, Fleet Captain," Medic said, as though I'd moved, or said something. "Ekalu has everything under control." And I didn't remember anything more after that.

9

The leg was, indeed, a loss. Medic explained things as I lay propped up on a bed in Medical. Covered with a blanket, but still the lack of a left leg, nearly all the way to the hip, was obvious. "It'll be some weeks growing back. We're working on a prosthetic that can get you through the next month or two, but for now it's going to be crutches, I'm afraid." She paused, as though expecting me to say something. "That's the worst of it, Fleet Captain. Really, it is. You're lucky to be alive."

"Yes," I agreed.

"We didn't lose anybody. A powerful testament to the importance of safety regulations, and I gather there are a couple of Bos who are fervently hoping you don't intend to find them and say *I told you so* to their faces. We did lose some hull plating, and breached in a couple of places, but the safeties all worked like they should have. Kalrs are outside right now making what repairs they can. We're in gate-space at the moment. Ekalu wanted to be able to consult with you before she did anything drastic." She hesitated, as though she expected me to say something more. I did not. "Five will bring you tea in a few minutes. You can have something more solid in a few hours."

"I don't want tea," I said. "Just water."

Medic hesitated at that, too. "Right," she said after a moment. "I'll let Five know."

She left, and I closed my eyes. This injury ought to have been fatal, for an ancillary. If I had still been part of a ship, just one small bit of *Justice of Toren*, I'd have been disposed of by now. The thought was unaccountably upsetting—if I had still been just one small part of a ship, I wouldn't have cared about it. And I'd lost far more than a single more or less easily replaceable leg, far more permanently, and lived, continued to function, or at least seemed to for anyone who didn't look too closely.

Five came into the room, with water. In a green-glazed handled bowl that I knew was one of a set she'd admired in Xhenang Serit. Had drunk from herself, every day since she'd obtained it, but she had never served me with it. It was her own personal possession. Her face was so severely expressionless that, I realized, she was certainly in the grip of some strong emotion. And I couldn't see what that was—would not reach, would not ask Ship for it. It made Five seem oddly flat, as though she were only an image I was seeing, not a real person. Five opened a drawer near the bed, pulled out a cloth, and wiped my eyes. Held the bowl of water to my mouth. I sipped.

Seivarden came through the door, another Kalr behind her. She wore only underwear and gloves, blinked at me placidly. "I'm glad you're back." Calm and relaxed. Still drugged, I realized, still recovering from her session with Medic, while I had been outside the ship.

"Are you supposed to be up?" I asked. Five hadn't even turned her head when Seivarden spoke, just wiped my eyes again.

"No," replied Seivarden, still utterly, unnaturally calm. "Scoot over."

"What?" It took me a moment to understand what she'd just said.

Before I could say more, Five set down the bowl of water and with the help of the other Kalr moved me closer to the right side of the bed, and Seivarden sat on the left side, swung her bare legs up, and tucked them under the blanket. Leaned back, pressed close, one leg in the space where my left leg should have been, shoulder against mine. "There. Now Medic can't complain." She closed her eyes. "I want to go to sleep," she said, apparently to no one.

"Fleet Captain," said Five. "Medic's worried about you. You've been awake for nearly an hour and you've been crying almost the whole time." She gave me another sip of water. "Medic wants to give you something to help, but she's afraid to even suggest it to you." No, that was certainly Ship talking.

"I don't need meds," I said. "I've never needed meds."

"No, of course you haven't." Not a change in Five's expression. Or her voice.

"The thing I always liked the least," I said, finally, after the last of the water, "was when an officer took me for granted. Just assumed that I would be there for her whenever she needed it, whatever it was she needed, and never stopped to even wonder what I might think. Or if I might be thinking anything to begin with." No reply, from Five. Or Ship. "But that's exactly what I've been doing. I didn't even begin to realize it until you said you wanted to be someone who could be a captain." Ship had said that, not Five, but of course Ship was listening. "And I was... I'm sorry I reacted the way I did."

"I admit," said Five—no, said Ship, I was sure, "I was hurt and disappointed when I saw how you felt. But there are two parts to reacting, aren't there. How you feel, and what you do. And it's the thing you do that's the important one, isn't it? And, Fleet Captain, I owe you an apology. I should have known sending Lieutenant Seivarden to act for me would upset you. But I think I owe you an explanation as well. It's one thing to ask your Kalrs to give you a hug now and then, but they're really not up for giving more." Five, speaking calmly and seriously, still standing by the bed, that green-glazed bowl in her hand. "By now pretty much all of Kalr has figured out that any of them could be in bed with you all day and all night and it would never be the least bit sexual. But they still wouldn't want to. One of them might have agreed just now, if I'd asked, but they wouldn't want to do it regularly. Even without sex it seems too intimate, I suppose. Lieutenant Seivarden, on the other hand, is perfectly happy to do it."

"You're very good to me, Ship," I said, after a moment. "And I know we both feel like... like we're missing part of ourselves. And it seems like each of us is the piece the other is missing. But it isn't the same, is it, me being here isn't like you having ancillaries back. And even if it were, ships want captains they can love. Ships don't love other ships. They don't love their ancillaries. And I meant what I said. You should be able to be your own captain, or at least choose her. You'd probably be happier with Seivarden as your captain. Or Ekalu. I could see myself liking Ekalu quite extravagantly, if I were still *Justice of Toren*."

"You're both being stupid." Seivarden, who had lain still

since her declaration that she wanted to go to sleep. Voice calm, eyes still closed. "It's a very Breq kind of stupid, and I thought it was just because Breq is Breq but I guess it's a ship thing."

"What?" I asked.

"It only took me about half a day to figure out what Ship was on about with that wanting to be someone who could be an officer business."

"I thought you wanted to go to sleep, Lieutenant," said Five. As though she wasn't sure that was actually something she wanted to say, transparently reading words in her vision.

"Ship," I said, not certain at this point whom I was talking to, or who was talking to me, "you've done everything I've asked of you, and I've put you and your crew in terrible danger. You should be able to go where you want. You can drop me off somewhere." I imagined arriving in the Itran Tetrarchy, maybe with Seivarden in tow. My leg would have grown back by the time I got there.

Imagined leaving Athoek behind. The repairs to the Undergarden unfinished, its residents' future uncertain. Leaving Queter with no one to help her if she needed it. Uran and Basnaaid on the station, in terrible danger even if I had managed to destroy all three of the warships I had fired at. And what were the chances that I had destroyed even one of them? Very, very low. Almost nonexistent. But those shots, outside the ship, had been my only half-realistic chance, remote as it had been. "You can leave me here and go wherever it is you want to go, Ship."

"And be like *Sphene*?" said Five. "No captain, hiding from everyone? No, thank you, Fleet Captain. Besides." Five actually frowned. Took a breath. "I can't believe I'm actually saying this, but Lieutenant Seivarden is right. And *you're* right—ships don't love other ships. I've been thinking about it since I met you. You don't know this, because you were unconscious at the time, but back at Omaugh Palace, weeks ago, the Lord of the Radch tried to assign me a new captain and I told her I didn't want anyone but you. Which was foolish, because of course she could always force me to accept her choice. There was no point in my protesting, nothing I could say or do would make any difference. But I did it anyway, and she sent me you. And I kept on thinking about it. And maybe it isn't that ships don't love other ships. Maybe it's that ships love people who could be captains. It's just, no ships have ever been able to be captains before." Five wiped more tears off my face. "I do like Lieutenant Ekalu. I like her a great deal. And I like Lieutenant Seivarden well enough, but mostly because she loves you."

Seivarden was relaxed and motionless beside me, breathing even, eyes still closed. She didn't respond to that at all. "Seivarden doesn't love me," I said. "She's grateful that I saved her life, and I'm pretty much the only connection she has with everything she's lost."

"That's not true," said Seivarden, still placid. "Well, all right, it's sort of true."

"It works both ways," observed Five. Or Ship, I wasn't sure. "And you're not used to being loved. You're used to people being attached to you. Or being fond of you. Or depending on you. Not loving you, not really. So I think it doesn't occur to you that it's something that might actually happen."

"Oh," I said. Seivarden warm and close beside me, though the hard edge of the corrective on my arm was poking into her bare shoulder. Not painfully, certainly not uncomfortably enough to disturb her med-stabilized mood, but I shifted slightly, at first not realizing what I'd just done, that I had known what Seivarden was feeling and moved on account of that. Five frowned at me—an actual reflection of her mood, she was worried, exasperated, embarrassed. Tired—she hadn't slept much in the last day or so. Ship was feeding me data again, and I'd missed it so much. Out in the corridor Medic was on her way here with meds for me, determined and apprehensive. Kalr Twelve, stepping into a doorway to make way for Medic, was suggesting to Kalr Seven that they find four or five more of their decade-mates to stand outside my room and sing something. The thought of singing by herself was far too mortifying.

"Sir," said Five. Really Five, not anyone else, I thought. "Why are you still crying?"

Helpless to stop myself, I made a small, hiccupping sob. "My leg." Five was genuinely puzzled. "Why did it have to be the good one? And not the one that hurts me all the time?"

Before Five could say anything Medic came in, said to me, as though neither Five nor Seivarden was there, "This is to help you relax, Fleet Captain." Five stepped aside for her as she fixed a tab she held to the back of my neck. "You need as much rest *and quiet*"—that with the briefest glance at Seivarden, then, though Seivarden wasn't listening, wasn't likely to do anything particularly noisy anytime soon—"as you can get before you decide to get up and charge off into things. Which I know you'll do long before you actually should." She took the cloth Five still held. Wiped my eyes with it, handed it back to Five. "Get some sleep!" she ordered, and left the room.

"I don't want to go to sleep," I said to Five. "I want tea."

"Yes, sir," said Five, actually, visibly relieved.

"Definitely a ship thing," said Seivarden.

* * *

I fell asleep before tea could arrive. Woke hours later to find Seivarden asleep beside me, turned on her side, one arm thrown across my body, her head on my shoulder. Breathing evenly, not long from waking, herself. And Kalr Five coming in the doorway with tea. In the green handled bowl again.

This time I managed to reach for it. "Thank you, Five," I said. Took a sip. I felt calm and light—Medic's doing, I was sure.

"Sir," said Five, "Translator Zeiat is asking to see you. Medic would prefer you rest a while longer." So would Five, it appeared, but she didn't say so.

"There's not much point in refusing the translator any-thing," I pointed out. "You remember Dlique." And how Translator Zeiat's tiny ship had just appeared near *Mercy of Kalr*, hours before we gated.

"Yes, sir," agreed Five.

I looked down at myself—mostly naked, except for an impressive assortment of correctives, the blanket, and gloves. Seivarden still draped half over me. "I'd like to have break-fast, first, though, will that be all right with the translator?"

"It will have to be, sir," said Five.

In the event, Translator Zeiat consented to wait until I'd eaten, and Seivarden was off to her own bed. And Five had cleaned me up and made me more presentable. "Fleet Cap-tain," the Presger translator said, coming into the room, Five standing stiff and disapproving at the doorway. "I'm Presger Translator Zeiat." She bowed. And then sighed. "I was just getting used to the last fleet captain. I suppose I'll get used to you." She frowned. "Eventually."

"I'm still Fleet Captain Breq, Translator," I said.

Her frown cleared. "I suppose that's easier to remember. But it's a little odd, isn't it? You're pretty obviously not the same person. Fleet Captain Breq—the previous one, I mean—had two legs. Are you absolutely *certain* you're Fleet Captain Breq?"

"Quite certain, Translator."

"All right, then. If you're sure." She paused, waiting, perhaps, for me to confess I wasn't. I said nothing. "So, Fleet Captain. I think it's probably best to be very frank about this, and I hope you'll forgive my bluntness. I have, of course, been aware that you are in possession of a weapon designed and manufactured by the Presger. This appears to have been some sort of secret? I'm not certain, actually."

"Translator," I interrupted, before she could continue, "I'm curious. You've said several times that you don't understand about different sorts of humans, but the Presger sold those guns to the Garseddai, specifically for them to use against the Radchaai."

"You must be more careful how you say things, Fleet Captain," Translator Zeiat admonished. "You can muddle things up so badly. The last fleet captain was prone to it, too. It's true that *they* don't understand. At all. Some translators, though, we do. Sort of. I admit our understanding was shakier then than it is now, though, you'd have a point there. But let me see if I can find a way to explain. Imagine…yes, imagine a very small child appears to have her heart set on doing something dangerous. Setting the city she lives in on fire, say. You can be constantly on guard, constantly keeping her out of trouble. Or you can persuade her to put her hand into a very *small* fire. She might lose a finger or two, or even an arm, and of course it would be quite painful, but that would be the point, wouldn't it? She'd never do it again. In fact, you'd think she'd be likely to never even go near any fires, ever, not after that. It seemed like the perfect solution, and it did seem to work quite well, at least at first. But it turns out not to have been a permanent fix. We didn't understand Humans very well at the time. We understand more now, or at least we think we do. Just between you and me"—she looked to one side and then the other, as though wary of being overheard—"Humans are very strange. Sometimes I despair of our managing the situation at all."

"What situation would that be, Translator?"

Her eyes widened, surprise or even shock. "Oh, Fleet Captain, you *are* a great deal like your predecessor! I really thought you were following things. But it's not your fault, is it. No, it isn't really anyone's *fault*, it's just how things are. Consider, Fleet Captain, we have a vested interest in keeping the peace. If there's no treaty there's no reason for translators, is there? And while it's unsettling to consider it too directly, we're actually fairly closely related to Humans. No, *we* don't want even the breath of the thought of the possibility that the treaty might be compromised. Now, your *having* that gun is one thing. But yesterday someone *used* that gun. To fire on Human ships. Which of course is *exactly* what it was meant for, but it was made *before* the treaty, do you see? And of course, we made that treaty with Humans, but to be completely honest with you, I'm beginning to have some trouble sorting out who's Human and who isn't. And on top of that it's become clear to me that Anaander Mianaai may not actually have been acting for all Humans when she made that agreement. Which is going to be impossible to explain to *them*, as I've already said, and of course we none of us care much what you do among yourselves, but using Presger-made weapons to do it, and so soon after that business with the Rrrrrr? It doesn't look good. I know that was twenty-five years ago, but you must understand that might as well be five minutes to *them*. And just as there wasn't...enthusiasm in all quarters regarding the treaty, there is...some ambivalence over the existence and sale of those guns."

"I don't understand, Translator," I confessed.

She sighed heavily. "I didn't think you would. Still, I had to try. Are you absolutely sure you don't have any oysters here?"

"I told you before you came aboard that we didn't, Translator."

"Did you?" She seemed genuinely puzzled. "I thought it was that soldier of yours who told me."

"Translator, how did you know I had the gun?"

She blinked in evident surprise. "It was obvious. The previous Fleet Captain Breq had it under her jacket when I met her. I could...no, not hear it exactly. Smell it? No, that's not right, either. I don't...I don't think it's a mode of perception you're capable of, actually. Now I think of it."

"And if I may ask, Translator, why 1.11 meters?"

She frowned, obviously puzzled. "Fleet Captain?"

"The guns. The bullets will go through anything for 1.11 meters and then they stop. Why 1.11 meters? It doesn't seem like a terribly useful distance."

"Well, no," replied Translator Zeiat, still frowning. "It wasn't *meant* to be a useful distance. In fact, the distance wasn't meant at all. You know, Fleet Captain, you're doing that thing again, where you say something in a way that sends you off in entirely the wrong direction. No, the bullets aren't designed to go through anything for 1.11 meters. They're designed to destroy Radchaai ships. That was what the purchasers required of them. The 1.11 meters is a kind of...accidental side effect sort of thing. And useful in its own way of course. But when you fire at a Radchaai ship you get something very different, I assure you. As we assured the Garseddai, honestly, but they didn't quite entirely believe us. They'd have done a good deal more damage if they had. Although I doubt things would ultimately have turned out much differently."

Hope flared, that I had not allowed myself before now. If those three ships I'd fired at had not changed course, perhaps there was only one left. One, plus *Sword of Atagaris*. And *Mercy of Ilves*, at the outstations, but the fact that *Mercy of Ilves* hadn't even attempted to involve itself in my battle with *Sword of Atagaris* suggested it and its captain wanted no trouble and might contrive to find reasons to stay near the outstations for quite some time, if they could manage it. And if the gun was truly that specifically effective, I might put it to better, more efficient use. "Would it be possible for me to buy more bullets from you?"

Translator Zeiat's frown only deepened. "From me? I don't have any, Fleet Captain. From *them*, though? That's its own problem. You see, the treaty specified—very much at Anaander Mianaai's insistence—that no such weapons would ever again be provided to Humans."

"So the Geck or the Rrrrr could buy them?"

"I suppose they could. Though I can't imagine why they would *want* a weapon made to destroy Radchaai ships. Unless the treaty broke down, and then, of course, Humans would have problems a good deal more urgent than a few ship-destroying guns, I can assure you."

Well. I still had several magazines left. I was still alive. There was, impossibly, a chance. Slim, but even so a good deal less slim than I'd thought just minutes ago. "What if Athoek wanted to buy medical correctives from you?"

"We could probably come to some sort of an agreement about correctives," Translator Zeiat replied. "The sooner the better, I imagine. You do seem to be using them at an alarming rate."

"Absolutely not," said Medic four hours later, when I asked her for crutches. More accurately, I had asked Five for them, and Medic had arrived at my bedside minutes later. "You've still got correctives working on your upper body, and your right leg, come to that. You can move your arms, so you may think, Fleet Captain, that you could safely get up, but you'd be mistaken."

"I'm not mistaken."

"Everything's going fine," Medic continued, as though I hadn't spoken. "We're safe in gate-space and Lieutenant Ekalu has everything under control. If you insist on meetings, you can have them here. Tomorrow—maybe—you can try a few steps and see how it goes."

"Give me the crutches."

"No." At some thought, adrenaline surged and her heart rate increased. "You can shoot me for it if you want, I won't do it."

Real fear, that was. But she knew, I was sure, that I wouldn't shoot her for such a thing. And doctors had more leeway than other officers, at least in medical matters. Still. "I'll crawl, then."

"You won't," said Medic. Voice calm, but her heart was still beating fast, and she was beginning to be angry on top of the fear.

"Watch me."

"I don't know why you even bother with a doctor," she said, and walked out, still angry.

Two minutes later Five came into the room with crutches. I sat all the way up, carefully swiveled so my one leg hung off the side of the bed, and got the crutches under my arms. Slid so that my bare foot was on the floor. Put weight on my leg and nearly collapsed, only the crutches and Kalr Five's quick support holding me upright. "Sir," Five whispered, "let me help you back into bed. I'll get you into your uniform if you like and you can have the lieutenants meet you here."

"I'm going to do this."

Ship said, in my ear, "No, you aren't. Medic is right. You need another day or two. And if you fall, you'll only injure yourself further. And no, you can't even crawl very far right now."

Not very like Ship, that, and I almost said so, but realized that, angry and frustrated as I was, it wouldn't come out well. Instead I said again, "I'm going to do this." But I couldn't even make it to the door.

10

I needed to meet with all my lieutenants, but first I met with Tisarwat alone. "*Sphene* talked to me," she said, standing at the foot of my bed. No one else was in the room, not even Kalr Five or Seivarden. "What it said didn't entirely surprise me."

No, of course it hadn't. "Were you going to tell me about this at some point, Lieutenant?"

"I didn't know!" Distressed. Embarrassed. Hating herself. "That is, she..." Tisarwat stopped. Obviously upset. "The tyrant had thought about using the Ghost System for a base, and thought about building ships there. She's even thought a great deal about...sequestering some AI cores to build them around. Just in case. Ultimately she decided it was too risky to work. Too easy for her other side to find and maybe even co-opt. But since it had occurred to her, she knew that it was likely to occur to any other part of her. And that old slave trade, sir, it did suggest possibilities, if you wanted to build ancillary-crewed ships. Which *she* didn't, but the other one did. So she kept a watch out. After a while, though, it seemed

161

obvious that the rest of her had come to the conclusion that convenient as it seemed, the Ghost System wasn't the best place to build ships."

"And *Sphene*'s idea about AI cores hidden in the Undergarden?"

"Again, sir, it's a pretty obviously convenient place to hide things. She looked, several times, and found nothing. The other one certainly looked as well. It's not a very good place at all with the Ychana there, but they weren't there to begin with. And let's say that at some point the other one did hide something there—once the Ychana moved in, getting them out was going to be difficult."

"So why didn't she stop that from happening?"

"Nobody realized until they were fairly well entrenched. At which point, forcing them out would have caused problems with station residents—particularly a lot of the Xhai, sir—and complicated station housing arrangements. At the same time, the fact that people were living there, the fact that her opponent had already searched several times and found nothing—that might mean it was a very good place to hide things. As long as she never made it seem like she cared about what happened there. As long as nobody ever thought to do any work there."

As long as station officials opposed any work there. "So that explains Eminence Ifian. But what about the rest? Station Administrator Celar was happy enough to authorize the work, once the necessity of it was pointed out. Security was content to go along with her. Governor Giarod seemed to have no real opinion until Ifian made her stand. If keeping searchers out of the Undergarden was so important, if there is something there, why only the eminence to stand guard?"

"Well, sir." Tisarwat sounded just the least bit pained, felt, I saw, a stinging sense of shame. "She's not stupid. Not any of her. No part of her was going to leave someplace like the Undergarden—or the Ghost System—unwatched. So there was a good deal of . . . of maneuvering and covert conflict over appointments to Athoek System. All the while trying to pretend that really, she didn't care what happened here. They'd both be trying to place strong pieces here, and both trying to undermine or block each other's choices. The result is, well, what we have. And I'd have told you all this before, sir, except that I was sure—she was sure—that none of it was relevant, that there was nothing here and the maneuvering over Athoek was a distraction. That it still is a distraction from the main business, which she thinks will mostly play itself out in the palaces. You're here because, well, for one thing, you wouldn't have agreed to go anywhere else. And for another, like I told you a while ago, she's very angry with you. It's possible the other one will be angry enough to come after you, and leave her position weakened somewhere else. Which, considering recent events, does appear to be the case. I'm sure Omaugh is considering a move against Tstur this very moment."

"So Fleet Captain Uemi is likely to have lit out for Tstur on receiving our message. And taken the Hrad fleet with her. She won't have sent us any help."

"That seems likely, sir." She stood, awkwardly silent, at the end of the bed. Wanting to say something to me, afraid to say it. Then, finally, "Sir, we have to go back. Ekalu thinks we shouldn't. She thinks we should go to the Ghost System and drop off the *Sphene* ancillary, and maybe Translator Zeiat, and go back to Omaugh, on the theory that there's nowhere else to go and authorities there will be friendly toward us.

Amaat One agrees with her." Amaat One was acting lieutenant, while Seivarden was in Medical.

"We have to go back to Athoek," I agreed. "But before we do, I want to know how things stand there. It's interesting to me that Station doesn't seem to have alerted anyone about the Ychana moving into the Undergarden until there wasn't really anything anyone could do about it. I thought it must have just been petulant. But if there's something hidden there it can't talk about, perhaps it was doing something more."

"Maybe," Tisarwat said, considering. "Though, honestly, this station does tend toward petulance."

"Can you blame it?"

"Not really," she admitted. "So, sir. About going back." I gestured to her to continue. "There's an old Athoeki communications relay in the Ghost System, right at the mouth of the gate. They always meant to expand there, but it never seemed to work out." I wondered, now, how much that had to do with *Sphene*'s interference. "*Sphene* says it still works, and all the official news channels come through it. If that's the case, we ought to be able to use it to talk to Station. If I can…I'm aware of some ways to access official relays. I should be able to make anything we send look like officially approved messages, or routine requests for routine data. Approved messages coming from an official, well-known relay won't trigger any alarms."

"Not even a relay that's never sent official messages to Athoek until now?"

"If they notice that, sir, that will surely raise an alarm. But someone has to *notice* that. Station will notice immediately, but to anyone else it'll probably just look like one more authorized incoming message. And maybe it won't want or be able to answer us, but we can at least try. We can probably get something out of the official news, no matter what. And it'll give us time to finish repairs, and you time to recover some, sir, begging your indulgence, while we decide what to do, once we have that information." That last coming out in an anxious rush. Anxious at referring to my injury. At bringing up the topic of what I might decide to do, when there might well be nothing that we *could* do. "But, sir, Citizen Uran…Uran has a good head on her shoulders, but it…and Citizen Basnaaid…" The strength of her emotions for Citizen Basnaaid rendered her inarticulate for a moment. "Sir, do you remember, back at Omaugh." A fresh wave of distress and self-hatred. *Back at Omaugh* she'd still been Anaander Mianaai, and anything she thought I might remember was also Anaander's memory. "Do you remember, you said that nothing she could do to you now could possibly be worse than what she'd already done? When you came to Omaugh there was nothing left for you to lose. But that isn't true anymore. I don't…I don't really even think it was true when you said it. But it's less true now."

"You mean," I said, "that the tyrant is sure to use Basnaaid or Uran against me if she can." Queter had wanted me to take Uran with me back to the station, away from the tea plantations, so that she would be safe. Now, it seemed, Queter was likely safer than Uran.

"I wish they had come with us." Still standing straight at the foot of my bed. Struggling hard to keep herself still, her face impassive. "I know we asked them and they said no, but if we'd had enough warning we could have *made* them come. And then we could just leave and not come back."

"Leave everyone?" I asked. "Our neighbors in the Undergarden? The fieldworkers downwell? Your friends?" Tisarwat had made a fair few friends, some of them just for political reasons, but not all. "Citizen Piat? Even petulant Station?"

She drew in a shaking breath and then cried, "How can this be happening? How can there be any benefit at all? She tells herself that, you know, that all of it is ultimately for the benefit of humanity, that everyone has their place, their part of the plan, and sometimes some individuals just have to suffer for that greater benefit. But it's easy to tell yourself that, isn't it, when you're never the one on the receiving end. Why does it have to be *us*?"

I didn't reply. The question was an old one, and she knew its various conventional answers as well as I did.

"No," she said, after thirty-two seconds of tense and miserable silence. "No, we can't leave, can we."

"No. We can't."

"As much as you've been through," she said, "far more than I have. And I'm the one who wants to run away."

"I thought about it," I admitted.

"Did you?" She seemed unsure of how to feel about that, an odd mix of relief and disappointment.

"Yes." And with Basnaaid and Uran aboard I might have done it. "So," I said. "Work out exactly what you need to make this relay project happen."

"Already have, sir." Self-loathing. Pride. Fear. Worry. "I don't need much of anything, I can do it right from here. If I can do it. I need Ship's help, though. If I still had...I mean, Ship can help me."

If she'd still had the implants that I'd removed, that had made her into part of Anaander Mianaai, she meant. "Good. Then I want you, Ekalu, and Amaat One to meet me here in fifteen minutes, and you can lay out your plan for them. And then"—this more for Ship's, and Medic's, benefit than Tisarwat's—"I'm going back to my own quarters." Whether on crutches, or crawling, or carried by Kalrs was immaterial.

* * *

Sphene was in my quarters, standing by the counter, staring at fragments of that beautiful gold-and-glass tea set spread out on the counter's surface. I had managed to use the crutches this time, managed the trip at least partly under my own power, though I wouldn't have made it without Five and Twelve. *Sphene* looked up as we came in. Nodded to Five, and said, "Cousin," to me.

"Cousin," I replied, and with Five's support managed to get to a bench. "How does it look?" I asked, as Five placed cushions around me. "The tea set, I mean. Before you come out with something sarcastic."

"Now you've spoiled my fun, Cousin," said *Sphene*, mildly, still staring at the fragments of colored glass on the counter. "I am not at all convinced this will actually go back together in any sort of meaningful way." It shifted slightly as Five came over to the counter, to allow Five access to the tea-making things.

"I'm sorry," I said. Leaned back onto the cushions Five had placed.

"Well," replied *Sphene*, still not looking at me, "it's just a tea set. And I did sell it away, and I knew Captain Hetnys was a fool. She wouldn't have done business with me otherwise." It and Five looked oddly companionable, side by side in front of the counter. It swept the pieces back into the box, which it then closed and placed on the counter. Took two rose glass bowls of tea from Five, and came over to sit beside me on the bench. "You need to be more careful, Cousin. You're running out of pieces of yourself to lose."

"And you said I'd spoiled your fun." I took one of the bowls of tea. Drank from it.

"I'm really not having much fun," *Sphene* said, equably

enough, but of course it was an ancillary. "I don't like being cut off from myself like this." Information could only travel through the regular intersystem gates because they were held constantly open. We were isolated in our own tiny bubble of real space, and it couldn't contact the rest of itself, the ship that was hiding in the Ghost System. "But unpleasant as it is, I know the rest of me is out there, somewhere."

"Yes," I agreed, and took another drink of tea. "How's your game with the translator going?" *Sphene* and Translator Zeiat had spent the last two days in the decade room, playing a game of counters. Or at least it had begun as a standard game of counters. By now it also involved fish-shaped cakes, the fragments of two empty eggshells, and a day-old bowl of tea, which they every now and then dropped a glass counter into. They appeared to be making it up as they went.

"The game is going pretty well," *Sphene* replied, and drank some of its own tea. "She's two eggs ahead of me, but I've got way more hearts." Another sip of tea. "In the game, I mean. Outside the game I still have more. Probably. I'm not sure I'd like to speculate about the translator's insides, now I think of it. Or what might be in her luggage."

"I wouldn't, either." Five finished what she was doing at the counter and left the room. I could have reached to find out what errand she was on, but didn't. "How much information comes through the Ghost Gate?"

"A fair amount," replied *Sphene*. "I get the official broadcasts, of course. Announcements. The censored news, and all the popular public entertainments. My favorites are the historicals about wandering, grief-mad ships." Sarcasm, surely, though no trace of it reached *Sphene*'s voice.

"You won't want to miss the latest one, then," I said. "It's about a grief-mad ship who abducts an unremarkable miner pilot because it thinks she's its long-dead captain. Adventures and hilarious yet heart-tugging misunderstandings ensue."

"I only wish I had missed that one," replied *Sphene*, evenly.

"It had some good songs."

"You would say that," *Sphene* said. "Did you ever hear a song you *didn't* like?"

"Yes, actually."

"In the name of all that's holy," *Sphene* replied, "don't sing it. I have enough misfortune in my life."

We sat silent for a few seconds. Then I said, "So, those people you bought from Captain Hetnys. And the ones you bought from the slavers, before the annexation of Athoek. Are they all hooked up?"

Sphene drank the last of its tea. "I know where you're headed, Cousin." I didn't reply, and it continued, "And I know where you're coming from. And maybe you and your ship here get along all right the way you are, but I have no desire to join either of you. I bought those bodies because I needed them."

"For what, exactly? What is it you've been doing for three thousand years that you need ancillaries for?"

"Surviving," replied *Sphene*. It set its teabowl on the bench beside it. "And it's ironic that you're the one kicking up a fuss about it. Before the war I got mostly condemned criminals. You're the one whose entire existence was based on the Usurper collecting huge numbers of random people. How many ancillaries did you have, during your life as a ship? And how many of them were innocent people? And now you want me to give up my few, is that it?" I didn't reply. "I don't even have a crew anymore. I couldn't even have *pretend* ancillaries like *Mercy of Kalr* does."

"I'm not kicking up a fuss," I said. "I'm asking. And those are citizens you have in your holds."

"They are not. Citizens live inside the Radch. What's outside the Radch is impure, and mostly barely human. You can call yourselves Radchaai as much as you want, you can wear gloves like somehow not touching impure things is going to make a difference, but it doesn't change anything. You're not citizens, you're impure by definition, and there isn't an entrance official who'd let you within ten thousand kilometers of the Radch, no matter how many times you wash, no matter how long you fast."

"Well, of course not," I replied reasonably. "I'm an ancillary."

"You know what I mean."

"We'll be exiting gate-space soon, into your home system." The Ghost System had been close enough to home for *Sphene*, for the last few thousand years. "I'm hoping you'll be willing to give us any information you have about what's been happening at Athoek. We can send you back to yourself, too, if you want to go."

Silence. I knew *Sphene* was breathing, I could see it, just barely, but otherwise it was utterly motionless. Then it said, "I wasn't supposed to come back."

"I'd assumed that was the case." Five came back in, and over to where we sat. Adjusted my cushions, took our teabowls. "I want to find out if I managed to damage any of Anaander's ships. And if I did, I want to try to do more damage. I need to know what's going on at Athoek so I can plan."

"Oh, Cousin," replied *Sphene*. "We sit here arguing, we can hardly agree on anything, and then you go straight to my heart like that. We *must* be family."

* * *

We exited to the Ghost System, the not-even-black of gate-space giving way to sunlight (the Ghost System's single star was a bit smaller and dimmer and younger than Athoek's), ice, and rocks, and the single gate's warning beacon. I was sitting in my bed, in my quarters. I could have taken my seat in Command, but it was Ekalu's watch and moreover Medic had been truly distressed by my leaving Medical. If I could mollify her even slightly by staying in my quarters instead of attempting to haul myself to Command, then I would.

Until Tisarwat did what she had planned to do, nothing would come through the relay at that beaconed gate but official, public-approved transmissions. Still, even that might be useful. I reached.

I had assumed that I would have to sort through a good deal of inconsequential chatter to find what I wanted. But in fact, the official news channels were me, nonstop. I was a mutinous traitor, not a citizen at all, not even human. I was *Justice of Toren*, damaged, insane. Cunning, beguiling—I had deceived the highest levels of system and station administration. Who knew what I had done to the rest of myself? Who knew how I had suborned *Mercy of Kalr*? But those questions were mere idle speculation. I and *Mercy of Kalr* were extraordinarily dangerous and any sighting of either of us, no matter how doubtful or indefinite, was to be reported immediately. Anyone concealing or harboring me declared herself to be an enemy of the Radch. Of humanity itself.

"Look at you, Cousin," said *Sphene*, at length, in its own guest quarters. "It's been like this for two days now and I am so envious I almost can't stand it. It really isn't fair. I've been an enemy of the Usurper for three thousand years, you're a mere upstart, but here you've got three entire news channels absolutely devoted to you. Oh, and the music and entertainment ones stop every five minutes to remind us all to tune into the *Justice of Toren* show. I can only conclude that your little stunt caused some actual damage, and I take back what I said about it being stupid."

I only half heard it. I was sorting through the announcements for any other information—Head of Security Lusulun had resigned and been replaced by her second-in-command. Eminence Ifian had always been suspicious of me, had tried to hold Athoek to sane, Radchaai values, though she would not name the officials she suspected of having been most taken in by me. The official position appeared to be that anyone who had befriended me had been duped or manipulated. Unofficially, of course, the implication was that my erstwhile allies were in danger, at the very least, of losing their positions or influence. There was no mention of Basnaaid or Uran.

I didn't expect any explicit mention of my attack on Anaander's ships, let alone mention of any damage I might have done. But perhaps there would be some hint, some implication. Then again, perhaps *Sphene* was right—the very existence and vehemence of this stream of official announcements likely said something about the threat I posed.

Lieutenant Ekalu, in Command, hadn't yet given the all clear for the crew to unstrap or unstow. She watched the view Ship gave her, of this system. "*Sphene*," said *Mercy of Kalr* into the apparent emptiness, "where are you?"

"Around," replied the *Sphene* ancillary, from guest quarters. "Keep the ancillary for now." And then, "It's nicer here anyway."

Lieutenant Ekalu said, from Command, "In the Ghost System. Lieutenant Tisarwat, you're up."

"My thanks, Lieutenant," Tisarwat said, from her quarters.

The door to my own quarters opened, and Seivarden came in. In uniform. "Shouldn't you still be in Medical?" I asked.

"I'm released from Medical," she said, smugly. Sat down next to me, where I sat on my bed. Looked around the small room, and at the door, and when she was certain Five was nowhere near, pulled her booted feet up so she could sit cross-legged. "As of three minutes ago. And I'm off meds. I told Medic I didn't need them anymore."

"You realize"—I still kept a bit of attention for Tisarwat, herself cross-legged on her own bed, eyes closed, accessing the relay through Ship—"that it's the meds that make you feel like you don't need meds anymore." Bo Nine came into Tisarwat's quarters, quietly humming. *Oh, tree, eat the fish.*

Beside me, on my bed, Seivarden scooted closer. Tugged briefly on my jacket collar, as though it might have been just the slightest bit out of place. Leaned against me. "You and Medic. I already know that. I've done this before, remember?"

"And you were so very successful at it." I felt my own shoulder warm against Seivarden's. The decades—the soldiers among them who were not in Command, anyway—were just beginning to hear and see those official news items. Their anger and resentment washed over me, tinged with shame—after all, they were Radchaai. Were being accused of treason by Radchaai authorities.

Oblivious, Seivarden gave an amused *hah*. "I didn't do too badly this time. I went much longer, for one thing. And I still haven't taken any kef. Well, all right, I *wanted* to. But I didn't." I refrained from pointing out that no matter how much she had wanted to, she couldn't have. "I've talked to Medic about this." She slid down a bit, laid her head on my shoulder. "I don't want to trade one addiction for another one. And I *was* doing pretty well." Despite her blithe tone, she was apprehensive about my reaction.

"Ship," I said, "I understand what you're doing. But I'm afraid Lieutenant Seivarden wants things from me that I can't give her."

Seivarden sighed. Lifted her head just slightly off my shoulder to look up at me. "The lieutenant and I have talked about that." Speaking for Ship. "You're right, she does want things you can't give her. But the truth is, anyone in any sort of relationship with you is going to have to adjust some of their expectations." Seivarden gave a little *hah* at the end of that sentence. Put her head back down on my shoulder. "Ship and I have talked about this."

"While you were strung out on meds and everything seemed fine?"

"Mostly before," she replied, surprisingly unperturbed. "Look, I'm not going to get those things no matter what. But maybe I can have just a little, this way." An embarrassed hesitation, and then, "Maybe, between you and Ship, there's a little bit left over for me. Ship likes me well enough, right? It said so. And mostly what you're talking about is sex. It's not like I can't get that other places, on my own."

Ekalu, in Command. Watchful. Just as angry and shame-filled about those official news announcements as the rest of the crew. Not thinking about Seivarden at the moment, I was fairly sure.

Seivarden sighed. "Then again, I haven't done very well with that, have I." Apparently thinking of Ekalu, herself. "I don't know what I did wrong. I still don't understand why she was so upset."

"She told you why she was upset," I pointed out. "You still don't understand?"

Seivarden sat up straight. Stood up. Walked to the other end of the room and back. "No." Stood staring at me. Agitated, just mildly, but she had not been even that for days.

"Seivarden." I wanted her to sit back down, to lean her shoulder against mine again. "Do you know what happens when people tell me I don't really seem like an ancillary to them?"

She blinked. Breath slightly faster. "You get angry." And then, with a little *heh*, "Well, angrier."

"You've never said it to me, though I'm sure you've thought it." She opened her mouth to protest. "No, listen. You didn't know I was an ancillary when I found you on Nilt. You assumed I was human. It might, in fact, be entirely reasonable for you to say I don't seem like an ancillary to you, or that you don't see me as an ancillary. And you might even think of it as a compliment. But you have never said it to me. And I imagine you never will."

"Well, no," replied Seivarden. Puzzled and hurt. Looking down at me where I sat on the bed. "I know it would make you angry."

"Do you understand why?"

She gestured irrelevance. "No. No, honestly, Breq, I don't."

"So why then," I asked, only mildly surprised she hadn't worked this out on her own, "don't you extend the same courtesy to Ekalu?"

"Well, but it wasn't *reasonable*."

"I, on the other hand," I pointed out, my tone even but edged, "am always entirely reasonable in your experience."

Seivarden laughed. "Well, but you're..." She stopped. Froze. I saw the realization strike, the sudden spike of it.

"This isn't new," I said. I didn't think she heard me, though. Blood was rushing to her face, she wanted to flee, but of course there was nowhere she could go and be away from herself. "You have always expected anyone beneath you to be careful of your emotional needs. You are even now hoping I will say something to make you feel better. You were quite angry with Ekalu when she herself failed to do that." No reply. Just shallow, careful breathing, as though she were afraid a deep breath might hurt. "You really have gotten better, but you can still be an enormously self-involved jerk."

"I'll be all right," she said, as though it followed logically from what I had just said. "I need to go to the gym."

"All right," I said, and without another word she turned and left.

11

An hour later I returned from a Medic-approved trip down the corridor and back, and found Seivarden, hair still damp from the bath, rooting through the cupboard where the tea things were stowed. Kalr Five, who had followed me, saw Seivarden, felt a surge of pure outraged resentment. Then reconsidered. "Lieutenant," Five said, watching me settle myself onto the bed, "they're all the way in the back."

Seivarden made an irritated noise. Pulled out my old enamel tea flask and its two bowls, one chipped. Began making tea, as Five fussed with the cushions around me, and then, once each one was exactly where she thought it should be, left.

At length Seivarden brought two bowls of tea, and sat down beside me on the bed. "You know," she said after her first taste, "that flask really doesn't brew right."

"It's from outside the Radch," I pointed out. "It's made for a different sort of tea."

I saw that she was counting her breaths, carefully timing

them. She said, after a bit, "Breq, do you ever wish you'd left me where you found me?"

"Not for a while," I replied, truthfully enough.

And then, after a few more breaths, "Is Ekalu a lot like Lieutenant Awn?"

I wondered, for an instant, where that question had come from. Then I remembered Seivarden, close against me in the bed in Medical as I told *Mercy of Kalr* that I could see myself liking Ekalu quite extravagantly, if I had still been a ship. "Not really. But would it matter if she was?"

"I suppose not."

We drank a while in silence and then Seivarden said, "I've already apologized to Ekalu. I can't exactly go back to her now and say, *I only said what Ship told me I ought to before, but this time I really mean it*." I didn't answer. Seivarden sighed. "I just wanted her to stop being angry with me." More silence. She leaned close, shoulder up against mine again. "I still want to take kef. But the thought of taking it makes me sick to my stomach." Even saying that did, I could see. "Medic told me it would. I didn't think I'd mind. I thought it wouldn't matter, because even if I took it, it wouldn't do me any good. No, that's not right. I'm feeling sorry for myself again, aren't I."

Briefly I considered saying, *I'm used to it*. Said nothing instead.

For several minutes Seivarden sat beside me. Silent, drinking tea in measured sips. Still feeling sorry for herself, but only mildly now, and trying, it seemed, to concentrate on something else. Eventually she said, "Our Tisarwat has suddenly displayed quite a few unexpected abilities."

"Has she?" I asked, voice bland.

"She knows how to make a message look like an official communication, does she? She can access an official gate relay? She's been talking to Station, and thinks Station is going to give her sensitive information? And you seem entirely unsurprised by any of it." She took a swallow of tea. "Granted, you're difficult to surprise. But still." I said nothing. "Ship won't answer me, either. I know better than to ask Medic. I'm thinking back to when Tisarwat first arrived, how angry you were that she was on board. Was she a spy, then? Did Medic... do something to ensure she'd be working for us, instead of Anaander?" She meant re-education, but couldn't bring herself to name it. "What else can our Tisarwat do?"

"I told you, you recall, that she would surprise you." In Tisarwat's quarters, Bo Nine was setting out a flask of tea and a bowl where her lieutenant could reach them. Feeling uneasy. All of Bo had begun to come to the same conclusion Seivarden had.

In my quarters, on my bed, shoulder still companionably against mine, Seivarden said, "You did say that. And I didn't believe you. You'd think I'd have learned by now."

Tisarwat, on her bed in her quarters, said, "Right, I think that's done it." Opened her eyes.

Saw Bo Nine standing in front of her. "Sir, do you think Citizen Uran is all right? And Horticulturist Basnaaid?"

"I hope so," Tisarwat replied. Worried, herself. "I'm trying to find out."

"The news hasn't said anything about that line on the concourse," Nine pointed out. "If I'd been in line, I'd have gone home and hid as soon as that started." She meant the constant condemnation of me on the official news channels, that we were getting from the relay.

"They didn't all have homes to hide in, did they?" replied Tisarwat. "Or not much of one. That was the point to begin with. And the line wasn't ever in the official news, was it. But yes, I hope they're all right. It's one of the things I've asked Station about." Instantly regretted speaking, because it raised the issue of just exactly how it was she could do what she was doing, and why Station might tell her anything. But she didn't have time to think much about the implications of what she'd just said, because right about then the official news channels changed.

Suddenly every single official news feed was displaying the inside of System Governor Giarod's office. Familiar enough to everyone in Athoek System, no doubt, a common sight on the official channels. But those appearances were always carefully staged and choreographed. Tall, broad-shouldered Governor Giarod always projected an air of calm assurance, of everything's being under her capable control. But here she stood looking harried and stressed. Beside her, stout and beautiful Station Administrator Celar; the shorter and slender head priest of Amaat, Eminence Ifian; and the new head of Security, whom I did not know, but was quite sure Lieutenant Tisarwat did. All four of them faced Anaander Mianaai. A very young Anaander Mianaai, barely twenty, at a guess.

Anaander, nearly expressionless, stood in front of those green-and-cream silk hangings, the window onto the concourse darkened. "Why," she asked, in a dangerously even voice, "is there a line on the concourse?" The sound was not smoothed or filtered, the camera view not composed. This was, very obviously, raw surveillance data.

"Begging my lord's very generous indulgence," said Administrator Celar, after an icy silence during which no one else in the office so much as twitched, "they are protesting the overcrowding on the station in the past few weeks."

"Are you, Station Administrator," Anaander asked, coldly, "incapable of dealing with the issue?"

"My lord," replied Station Administrator Celar, her voice shaking only very slightly, "there would be no line if I had been *allowed* to deal with the issue."

Now Eminence Ifian spoke up. "Begging my lord's most gracious and generous indulgence, but the station administrator wished to...deal with the issue by hastily refitting the Undergarden. Despite, my lord, the repeated insistence of other officials that more careful consideration was needed. It would have made far more sense to send the former Undergarden residents downwell while the question of repairs was more carefully thought through. But I believe the station administrator was being pressured by Fl...by the ancillary."

Silence. "Why"—Anaander Mianaai's voice was still even, but had taken on a sharper edge—"was the ancillary concerning itself with the Undergarden?"

"My lord," said Station Administrator Celar, "the Gardens lake collapsed into the Undergarden a week or so ago. The people who had been living there had to be housed somewhere until it could be repaired."

Still cross-legged on her bed, watching and listening, Bo Nine still standing in front of her, Tisarwat exhaled sharply. Said, "What else haven't they told her?"

Even now they weren't telling Anaander everything. The repairs to the Undergarden had begun well before the lake had collapsed, and at my very definite insistence. I expected Eminence Ifian to point this out, but she did not.

Anaander took the news of the lake's collapse with almost no change of expression. Said nothing. Perhaps emboldened by this, Station Administrator Celar continued, "My lord, shipping residents downwell without consulting them would certainly have resulted in unrest among station residents at a time we can ill afford it. I am, my lord, at a loss to understand why Eminence Ifian—or the system governor, for that matter—felt it proper to oppose repairs which were urgently needed, and which would have dealt with the issue far more conveniently." Looked as though she wanted to say something further, something bitter, but did not. Swallowed the words, whatever they were.

Silence. Then Anaander Mianaai said, "As you point out, Station Administrator, we can ill afford unrest. Security. Notify the protesters on the concourse that if they are still in line three minutes from now, they will be shot. *Sword of Gurat.*"

From somewhere out of view an ancillary voice replied, "My lord."

"Accompany Security. At the end of three minutes, shoot anyone who remains in line."

"My lord!" replied the new head of Security. "With the utmost respect and deference, begging your very generous and proper indulgence, but I submit to my lord that threatening to shoot citizens who are peaceably standing in line is quite certain to *produce* unrest. The citizens involved have caused no difficulty whatever. My lord."

"If they are such law-abiding citizens, they will return to their homes when ordered," Anaander said, coldly. "And everyone will be safer for their doing so."

In my quarters aboard *Mercy of Kalr*, Seivarden said, shoulder still against mine, bowl of tea cooling in one gloved hand, "Well, it works for annexations."

"After a great deal of bloodshed," I pointed out.

In the system governor's office on Athoek Station, Anaander

Mianaai said, "Are you refusing my order to clear the concourse, Security?"

"I...I am." A breath. "I am, my lord." As though she hadn't been certain of it until just that moment.

"*Sword of Gurat*," said Anaander, and held out one black-gloved hand. The *Sword of Gurat* ancillary came into view, handed Anaander its gun.

On *Mercy of Kalr*, Tisarwat leapt off her bed. "No!" But protest was useless. This had all of it already happened.

"Fuck!" Seivarden, still beside me, on my bed, bowl of tea in her hand. "Security isn't military!"

And meanwhile, on Athoek Station, in Governor Giarod's office, Anaander raised the gun and fired, point-blank, before the new head of Security could more than open her mouth in protest or retraction. Security dropped to the ground, and Anaander fired again. "We are under attack from within," Anaander said, into the following horrified silence. "I *will not* allow my enemy to destroy what I've built. *Sword of Gurat*, deliver my orders to the people lined up on the concourse. I don't suppose they're troubled by taking orders from an ancillary anyway."

"My lord," replied *Sword of Gurat*, standing ancillary-straight and ancillary-still behind Anaander, and did not move. Of course. It didn't need to leave the room to obey Anaander's order, just send a different segment. And then, before Anaander could speak again, the ancillary said, "My lord, the past few minutes of this conversation are being broadcast on the official news channels."

On *Mercy of Kalr*, Tisarwat, tearful, Bo Nine's arm awkwardly around her, cried out, "Oh, Station!" And then, "Fleet Captain, sir!"

"I'm watching," I said.

On Athoek Station, Anaander said, sharply, "Station!"

"I can't stop it, my lord," replied Athoek Station, from a console. "I don't know what to do."

"Who came with it?" Anaander asked, sharp and angry. Not even puzzlement, on the faces of Governor Giarod, Station Administrator Celar, and Eminence Ifian. All of them, I was sure, still trying to grasp those sudden shots, moments before, the body of the head of Security motionless on the floor. "*Who came with the ancillary?*"

Governor Giarod said, "N...no one in particular, my lord. Her...its lieutenants." Hesitated. "Only one came onto the station. Lieutenant Tisarwat."

"House name," Anaander demanded.

"I'm...not certain, my lord," replied Governor Giarod. Station Administrator Celar certainly knew Tisarwat's house name, Tisarwat and Celar's daughter Piat were good friends, but I noted that she didn't volunteer it. Neither did Station. Not that it would have mattered.

Anaander considered the silence, and then said, sharply, "Ship, with me." And left the office.

"She'll go to Station's Central Access," said Tisarwat. Needlessly. Of course she would. *Why*, said the voice of Anaander Mianaai, over the official news feeds, *is there a line on the concourse?* Station's recording, repeating.

There was no point getting up off the bed. There was nothing I could do.

"Oh, fuck," said Seivarden beside me. "Oh, *fuck*. What does Station think it's doing?" This wasn't in response to any request of ours, of Tisarwat's. Our messages couldn't possibly have reached Athoek Station yet.

"Protecting its residents," I replied. "As best it can. Letting them know that Anaander is a threat. Remember, this is the same station that turned off its gravity the last time its residents were threatened." It was probably the best Station could do, under the circumstances. Granted, it wouldn't necessarily—or even likely—prevent *Sword of Gurat* from shooting citizens, but it was possible Station believed that even Anaander Mianaai might hesitate to do it if everyone was watching. And everyone would be watching—those official news feeds went not only to every receiver in Athoek System, but to every single gate relay. Hrad System would be getting that recording about now, perhaps a bit later. In the official, approved news channels, which any citizen could access. Was encouraged to access, sometimes could not escape.

"But," Seivarden protested, "the Lord of the Radch will just go to Central Access and stop it." And then, realizing, "So the Lord of the Radch doesn't have that thing with her, that cuts off communications. Or she'd have used it. What will she do now?"

What would she do, I wondered, when she discovered she couldn't get to Station? Or more accurately, what had she already done?

"Sir," Tisarwat said, from her quarters. Shakily. "Did you notice, nobody seemed to want to talk about the Undergarden, or the lake. They haven't told her everything, not even Eminence Ifian. I'm not sure why, though, you'd think Ifian would tell her everything she could. Maybe she doesn't know about Basnaaid, or Uran." Eminence Ifian surely knew about Basnaaid and Uran. The *she* Lieutenant Tisarwat meant was Anaander. "And did you notice how young she was? And that…all of this. All of it. I think she may be the only one of her here, sir, or certainly the oldest one. And I think you did more than punch through some hull plating. She's *really* angry. And she's afraid. I'm not sure why, though. I'm not sure why she would be quite so afraid."

"Get some rest, Lieutenant." It was well after her supper. She was tired, on top of her distress. "Ship will wake you if we hear from Station. Right now we just have to wait."

The recording repeated for nearly two hours, until, quite abruptly, it stopped, and three seconds later the regular news announcements resumed. The *Justice of Toren* show, as *Sphene* had called it. But now, added to it, the announcement of a curfew. No one was to leave their quarters except citizens in necessary assignments—these were specifically listed: Medical, Security, certain branches of Station Maintenance, refectory workers—or citizens taking food from the common refectories at assigned, scheduled times. What might happen if one left one's quarters without authorization was left unstated, but everyone had seen the head of Security die, over and over. Everyone had heard Anaander threaten to shoot citizens who did not leave the line on the concourse.

Tisarwat was upset enough to get out of bed, pull her jacket and boots on, and come to my quarters to speak to me. "Sir!" she cried, coming in the door, as Bo Nine gave her jacket hem a quick tug so it would lie right, "it's impossible! Some of those dormitories, people are sleeping three or four shifts to a bunk! It's impossible for everyone to stay in their quarters! What does she think she's doing?"

Kalr Five, laying out breakfast dishes, pretended to ignore Tisarwat, but she had been just as disturbed at the news.

"Lieutenant," I said, "go back to bed. At least pretend to rest. There's nothing we can do from this distance." We were still in the Ghost System, *Mercy of Kalr*'s hull still warmed by that smaller, slightly orange-ish star, alone but for *Sphene*, whom we couldn't see, who only spoke to us through its ancillary, only the Athoek gate communications relay to break the silence. "We'll likely hear from Station quite soon, if it's willing or able to speak to us. Then we'll decide what to do."

She cast a glance at the table, set for more than just me. "You're going to eat? How can you eat?"

"I've found that not eating is generally a bad decision," I replied. Evenly. I could see she was at the edge of her patience, just about to lose any ability to hold herself together. "And I can't leave the translator all to herself. Or, gods help us all, to *Sphene*."

"Oh, the translator! I'd forgotten all about her." She frowned.

"Go back to bed, Lieutenant."

Which she did, but instead of sleeping she asked Bo Nine for tea.

Everyone aboard was on edge, except for *Sphene*, who appeared not to care much about what was happening, and Translator Zeiat, who had apparently slept through the whole thing. When the translator woke I invited her to breakfast, along with *Sphene*, Medic, and Seivarden. Ekalu was still on watch. Tisarwat was awake, but I knew she wouldn't eat, and besides she was supposed to be asleep.

"Counters is such a fascinating game, Fleet Captain," Translator Zeiat said, and took a drink of her fish sauce. "I'm terribly grateful to *Sphene* for introducing me to it."

Seivarden was surprised, but didn't dare express it. Medic was too busy frowning at me across the table to react—she had still not forgiven me for leaving Medical without her approval. And she thought I should be resting more.

"Your pardon, Translator," I said, "but I suspect most

Radchaai would be extremely surprised to hear that you're not familiar with counters."

"Goodness, no, Fleet Captain," replied the translator. "I'd heard of it, of course. But Humans do such disturbingly odd things, you know, sometimes it's better not to think too hard about them."

"What sort of games are you used to playing, Translator?" asked Seivarden, and then immediately regretted it, either because it got her the translator's attention, or because she realized belatedly what kind of answer might be forthcoming.

"Games, now," said Translator Zeiat thoughtfully. "I can't say we actually play any games. Not as such. Well, you know, Dlique might. I wouldn't put *anything* past Dlique." She looked at me. "Did Dlique play counters?"

"Not that I'm aware, Translator."

"Oh, good. I'm *very* glad I'm not Dlique." She looked over at Medic, who was eating eggs and vegetables and still frowning at me. "Medic, I do understand you miss the previous fleet captain, I do myself, but it's hardly this one's fault. And she's very much like the previous one, really. She's even making every effort to grow another leg for you."

Medic swallowed her mouthful of breakfast, entirely unoffended. "Translator, I'm given to understand that the first Presger translators were grown from human remains."

"I myself am given to understand the same," replied Translator Zeiat, sounding quite unperturbed by the question. "I suspect it's even true. Long before the treaty, long before translators were ever considered, in fact, they had, shall we say, a very...yes, a very practical kind of understanding of how Human bodies were put together."

"Or taken apart," Medic put in. Seivarden nearly pushed

her plate away. *Sphene* chewed placidly, listening as it had all through the meal.

"Indeed, Medic, indeed!" agreed Translator Zeiat. "But their priorities are not, well, not Human priorities, and when they put us together, you know, they didn't really have any understanding of what would be *important*. Or maybe *essential* is a better word. At any rate. Their first several tries went horribly wrong."

"In what way?" asked Medic, genuinely curious.

"Your very great indulgence, Medic," said Seivarden, "but we *are* eating."

"Perhaps you can discuss it later," I suggested.

"Oh!" Translator Zeiat seemed genuinely surprised. "Is it propriety again?"

"It is." I finished off my own eggs. "Incidentally, Translator. You are, of course, welcome to stay with us as long as you like, but since you did come through the Ghost Gate, I was wondering if you might be leaving us before we return to Athoek."

"Oh, goodness, no, Fleet Captain! I can't go home just yet. I mean, can you imagine it? Everyone saying *Hello, Dlique!* and, *Look, Dlique's home!* It would be Dlique this, and Dlique that, and I'd have to tell them that no, I'm very sorry, but I'm not Dlique, I'm Zeiat. And then I'd have to explain what happened to Dlique and it would get very awkward. No, I'm not ready to face that. It's very good of you to let me stay. I can't tell you how much I appreciate it."

"It's our pleasure, Translator," I said.

Athoek Station's response arrived in four parts, each one innocently labeled as a routine reply to an authorized query.

Tisarwat ought to have been asleep, but was not. Instead she sat at the table in the decade room. She had not been able to stay still in her quarters, and besides the decade room was closer to the bath; she had drunk far more tea than was wise. Bo Nine had just set a fresh bowl in front of her. Nine had been impressively patient given that this was the middle of the night for her as well and she hadn't slept any more than her lieutenant had.

Ship didn't waste an instant, but displayed the first-arriving in Tisarwat's vision without explanation. Tisarwat started up out of her chair. Frowned. "It's a shuttle schedule. Why did Station send a shuttle schedule?" To be precise, it was the schedule for the passenger shuttles between Athoek Station and the tops of the planet's elevators. Dated yesterday.

I was coming out of the bath, headed for Command, but instead I swung myself around and went toward the decade room, Five behind me. "Next one, Ship," I said. Station Security was to place itself under the orders of a lieutenant from *Sword of Gurat*. Ancillaries from *Sword of Gurat* would patrol the station along with regular Security. And so would ancillaries from *Sword of Atagaris*. "There's no mention of any lieutenant from *Sword of Atagaris*," Tisarwat said, as I came in the door and Nine pulled out a chair for me. "Or any of its officers at all, actually."

"Why not?" I asked. "Did *Sword of Atagaris* not get those pods we left?"

"Maybe *she* removed Captain Hetnys from command," suggested Tisarwat, sitting back down. "It would hardly be surprising, Hetnys is lucky if she has half the brains an oyster has. And you've made it pretty clear that whoever controls Hetnys controls *Sword of Atagaris*." She gave a little *hah*. "That'll turn out to be a mistake."

I certainly hoped so. "And the next?"

"A list of urgent requests for an audience with..." Tisarwat hesitated.

"With Anaander Mianaai," I finished for her. "And of course Fosyf Denche is on the list, and of course she wants the Lord of the Radch to right a terrible miscarriage of justice regarding her daughter Raughd."

Tisarwat scoffed. Then frowned. "And last is a list of citizens who are required to immediately relocate downwell, in order to relieve crowding on the station. Sir, look at the names."

I was looking at it. "Basnaaid and Uran are on it."

"Station Administrator Celar made this list, depend on it. But look at the rest of it."

"Yes," I agreed.

"Nearly all Ychana," Tisarwat said. "Which makes sense, really, since it's mostly Ychana who were displaced to begin with. And if trouble breaks out on the station they're most likely to bear the brunt of it. I'm sure Administrator Celar was thinking of getting them to relative safety. But I see at least a dozen people who are going to immediately suspect they're being singled out for mistreatment. And I doubt anyone on the list is going to be happy about being summarily sent off the station." She frowned. "They're supposed to leave *today*. That's *fast*."

"Yes," I agreed. Anaander had likely ordered everyone to remain indoors, and Station Administrator Celar had had to find some way to make it work, and quickly. I sat, finally, in the chair Bo Nine had pulled out for me. Leaned my crutches against the table, next to where the pieces of *Sphene* and Translator Zeiat's ongoing game were laid out. "Is this information supposed to go with the shuttle schedule?" Except the order to relocate was for today, and the shuttle schedule was for yesterday.

"Sir," said Tisarwat. Frustrated and afraid. "Did you hear me? They're hastily relocating dozens of Undergarden residents, at a time when armed soldiers are threatening to shoot citizens on the concourse."

"I heard."

"Sir! A lot of the people on this list are likely to refuse to get on that shuttle."

"I think you're right, Lieutenant. But there's nothing we can do about it. We are three days away from Athoek Station. Whatever is happening is happening *now*."

Sphene came in the door, Translator Zeiat close behind. "Well, I wasn't ever a child, actually," Translator Zeiat was saying. "Or, that is to say, when I was a child I was someone else. I daresay you were, too. No doubt that's why we get on so well. Hello, Fleet Captain. Hello, Lieutenant."

"Translator," I said, lowering my head briefly.

Tisarwat seemed not to have noticed that anyone else was in the decade room. "So Station wants us to know that Captain Hetnys isn't back on *Sword of Atagaris* and isn't likely to be. It tells us that Basnaaid and Uran are being sent to safety. And that Fosyf is seizing the opportunity to put herself back on top of things. And that the shuttles are running as always? Why?"

"It's telling us," said Five, behind me, for Ship, "that something happened to one of the shuttles. There's one missing off the schedule. Look." In my vision, and Tisarwat's, the schedule Station had sent us, and the one Ship already had. The differences flared, the arrivals and departures that were on the regular schedule but not the one Station had sent. "Those are all the same shuttle. So Station wants us to know that something happened to that shuttle. It is also being careful to let us know that it happened before yesterday. Before, that is, Basnaaid and Uran boarded a shuttle downwell."

Sphene sat down on one side of the in-progress game. "Is Station doing that thing again, where it won't tell you what's wrong but something is obviously wrong?"

"Sort of," I said. "Only this time we asked it to. It can't tell us directly, because the Usurper is on the station."

Translator Zeiat sat beside me, on the other side of the game. Frowned a moment at the bright-colored counters in their holes on the board, the scattering of eggshell fragments. "I believe it's your turn, *Sphene*."

"Indeed," replied *Sphene*. It scooped the counters out of one depression on the board, turned its hand palm-up to show them to Translator Zeiat. "Three green. One blue. One yellow. One red."

"I think that's four green," said the translator dubiously.

"No, that's definitely blue."

"Hmm. All right." Translator Zeiat took the red counter from Sphene's hand and dropped it in the scummed-over bowl of tea. "That's almost a whole egg, too. I'm going to have to think carefully about my next move."

"We have more shells for you, Translator, if you need them," said Bo Nine. The translator waved an absent acknowledgment, stared at the board as *Sphene* redistributed the remaining counters.

"Look at the Security order," said Tisarwat. "At the way it's worded. I think *Sword of Gurat* is actually docked with Athoek Station. But why would…" She trailed off, frowning.

"Because Anaander needs every ancillary aboard it to police the station," I guessed.

193

"But she has three other ships! One of them is a troop carrier, isn't it? She has thousands of…" I could see the realization strike. "What if she doesn't have three other ships? Sir!" She focused again on the records in her vision. "Why hasn't Station told us what ships are in the system?" And then, "No, *she* won't have told Station what ships are in the system. Especially if there aren't many. And she doesn't trust *Sword of Atagaris*. Or Captain Hetnys."

"Can you blame her?" asked *Sphene*. "Arrogant and dimwitted, the both of them." Tisarwat looked up at the ancillary, surprised to realize that it was in the room. Blinked at it, and at the translator.

"Does she not know what happened last time *Sword of Atagaris* supplied security?" asked Tisarwat. And then, "No, of course she doesn't. They haven't told her for some reason."

Just from the small bit we'd seen the day before, there were plenty of things system authorities hadn't told Anaander Mianaai. "Or she does know and she doesn't care."

"Very possible," Tisarwat agreed. "Sir, we have to go back!"

"We do," said Translator Zeiat, still staring at the game in front of her, still pondering her move. "I'm told you're nearly out of fish sauce."

"Now how could that have happened?" asked *Sphene*, as innocently as I supposed was possible for it.

"Please, sir." Tisarwat seemed not to have heard either of them. "We can't leave things the way they are, and I have an *idea*."

That got the translator's full attention. She looked up from the game, frowned intently at Tisarwat. "What's it like? Does it hurt?" Tisarwat only blinked at her. "Sometimes I think I might like to get an idea, but then it occurs to me that it's exactly the sort of thing Dlique would do." When Tisarwat didn't answer, Translator Zeiat returned her attention to the game. Picked up a yellow counter from off the board, put it in her mouth, and swallowed. "Your turn, *Sphene*."

"That one wasn't green, either," said *Sphene*.

"I know," said Translator Zeiat, with an air of satisfaction.

"Ship is already making the calculations for the trip back to Athoek," I said, to Tisarwat. "Go see Medic and tell her you've had way too much tea." She opened her mouth to protest, but I continued. "It's three days back to Athoek. We can spare a few minutes. When Medic is done with you, come see me in my quarters and we'll talk about your idea."

She wanted to protest. Wanted to pound a fist on the table and shout at me. Almost did it, but instead she took a breath, and then another one. "Sir," she said. Stood up, overturning the chair behind her, and left the decade room. Bo Nine righted the chair, and followed.

"What an excitable person that Lieutenant Tisarwat is," said Translator Zeiat. "An *idea*. Just imagine!"

12

"So, this idea of yours?" I asked, when Tisarwat came to my quarters.

"Well, it's not..." Standing in front of me where I sat, she shifted uncomfortably, just slightly. "It's kind of desperate." I didn't say anything. "*Sword of Gurat* isn't one of the ships she gave me accesses to, but there's...there's a kind of underlying logic to the accesses. The split has meant that the underlying logic for each part of her isn't identical, which is part of why I couldn't find all of what she might have done to Athoek Station, or *Sword of Atagaris*."

"Or *Mercy of Kalr*."

"Or *Mercy of Kalr*. Yes, sir." Unhappy at that. "But the other part of her, the part that's at Omaugh, I'm...very familiar with that. If I could get aboard *Sword of Gurat*, if I had time to talk to it, I might actually be able to figure out how to access it." I looked at her. She seemed entirely serious. "I told you it was desperate."

"You did," I agreed.

"So here's my idea. We put two teams on the station. One

of them—mine—goes to the docks to try to get aboard *Sword of Gurat*. And the other finds Anaander and kills her."

"Just like that?"

"Well, that's just an overview. I did leave out some details. And of course, I haven't really taken *Sword of Atagaris* into account at all." She winced, then, just a bit. "A lot of the details seemed really clear to me when I first thought of it. In retrospect, they were actually pretty incoherent. But I still think the basic outline is sound, sir." She hesitated, watching for my reaction.

"Right," I said. "Choose two of your Bos to go with you. They'll spend the next three days in the gym and the firing range, or whatever other training or briefing you feel they need, and they're relieved of all other duties. Ship."

"Fleet Captain," *Mercy of Kalr* said in my ear.

"Have Etrepa One take over watch from Lieutenant Ekalu, and ask Ekalu and Seivarden to join us here. And ask Five to come make us tea for the meeting. And Ship."

"Sir."

"Do you want Lieutenant Tisarwat to do for you what she did for Station and *Sword of Atagaris*?"

Silence. Though I suspected I already knew the answer. And then, "Actually, Fleet Captain, I do."

I looked at Tisarwat. "Make room for it in your schedule, Lieutenant. And you might as well tell me your incoherent details, in case there's anything there worth salvaging."

Next morning at breakfast, I left *Sphene* and Medic to entertain Translator Zeiat, and invited Ekalu to eat with me. "Is everything all right?" I asked, when Five had laid out fruit and fish on the Bractware, and poured tea in the rose glass bowls, and then left the room at Ship's suggestion.

"I don't know what you mean, sir." Picked up her bowl

of tea. Much less uncomfortable holding it than she'd been weeks ago. Much less uncomfortable around me.

Still. "I don't mean anything in particular, Lieutenant."

"It's a little odd, sir, begging your indulgence." She put the tea down, untasted. "You already know how I'm getting along, don't you?"

"To a point," I admitted. Took a bite of fish, so that Ekalu could begin eating if she wanted. "I can look in on you if I want, and I can see how you feel sometimes. But I'm..." I put my utensil down. "I'm trying not to do that too much. Particularly if I think it makes you uncomfortable. And"—I gestured the space between us—"I'd like you to be able to talk to me if you need to. If you want to."

Mortification. Fear. "Have I done something wrong, sir?"

"No. Far from it." I made myself take another bite of fish. "I just wanted to have breakfast with you and maybe ask your opinion about some things, but right now, asking you how things are going, I'm just making conversation." Took a drink of my tea. "I'm not always very good at idle conversation. Sorry."

Ekalu dared a tiny little smile, felt the beginning of relief, though she didn't trust that feeling entirely. Didn't relax.

"So," I continued, "I'll just go right to the business then, shall I? I wanted your opinion of Amaat One. It must be strange," I added, seeing her suppress a flinch at that, "hearing a name you went by for so long, that you don't go by anymore."

Ekalu gestured insignificance. "I didn't come onto this ship Amaat One. My number changed, as people retired, or left, or..." Whatever she'd meant to put behind that *or* didn't come. She gestured it away. "But you're right, sir, it is strange." She took a bit of fruit, then. Chewed and swallowed. "I suppose you know what that's like."

"I do," I agreed. Waited a moment to see if she had any-

thing else to say, but she apparently didn't. "I'm not asking for anything bad. Amaat One stood watch and ran her
decade while Seivarden was ill. I think she did an excellent
job, and I'd like her to begin officer training. We have the
materials aboard, because you've been using them. Actually, I
think the training ought to be available to anyone on the ship
who wants it. But I very specifically am considering the possibility of a field promotion for Amaat One. You know her
very well, I think."

"Sir, I..." She was deeply uncomfortable, insulted even.
She wanted to get up from the table, leave the room. Didn't
know how to answer me.

"I realize I'm very possibly putting you in a difficult position, if you should object to her being promoted, and if she
should find out—because there are very few secrets on this
ship—that you had perhaps prevented it. But I beg you to
consider the situation we're in. Consider what happened
when I and Lieutenant Tisarwat were away and Lieutenant
Seivarden was ill. You and the decade leaders handled things
admirably, but you would all have been more comfortable if
you'd had more experience. I see no reason not to give all of
the decade leaders the training required for when it happens
again, and I foresee them eventually deserving promotion. I
foresee the ship needing them in those places."

Silence, from Ekalu. She took another drink of tea. Thinking. Unhappy and afraid. "Sir," she said at length, "begging your patient indulgence. But what's the point? I mean,
I understand why we're going back to Athoek. That makes
sense to me. But farther ahead than that. At first this all just
seemed unreal, and it still does in a way. But the Lord of the
Radch is coming apart. And if she comes apart, so does the
Radch. I mean, maybe she'll hold herself together, maybe

she'll put these pieces back together again. But, begging your forgiveness, sir, for my speaking very frankly, but you don't actually want that, do you."

"I don't," I admitted.

"And so what's the point, sir? What's the point of talking about training and promotions as though it's all going to just go on like it always has?"

"What's the point of anything?"

"Sir?" She blinked, confused. Taken aback.

"In a thousand years, Lieutenant, nothing you care about will matter. Not even to you—you'll be dead. So will I, and no one alive will care. Maybe—just maybe—someone will remember our names. More likely those names will be engraved on some dusty memorial pin at the bottom of an old box no one ever opens." Or Ekalu's would. There was no reason anyone would make any memorials to me, after my death. "And that thousand years *will* come, and another and another, to the end of the universe. Think of all the griefs and tragedies, and yes, the triumphs, buried in the past, millions of years of it. *Everything* for the people who lived them. Nothing now."

Ekalu swallowed. "I'll have to remember, sir, if I'm ever feeling down, that you know how to cheer me right up."

I smiled. "The point is, there is no point. Choose your own."

"We don't usually get to choose our own, do we?" she asked. "You do, I suppose, but you're a special case. And everyone on this ship, we're just going along with yours." She looked down at her plate, considered, briefly, picking up a utensil, but I saw that she couldn't actually eat just now.

I said, "It doesn't have to be a big point. As you say, often it can't be. Sometimes it's nothing more than *I have to find a way to put one foot in front of the other, or I'll die here.* If we lose this throw, if we lose our lives in the near future, then yes, training and promotions will have been pointless. But who knows? Perhaps the omens will favor us. And if, ultimately, I have what I want, Athoek will need protection. I will need good officers."

"And what are the chances of the omens favoring us, sir, if I may ask? Lieutenant Tisarwat's plan—what I know of it, sir, is…" She waved away whatever word she had been going to use to describe it. "There's no margin for error or accident. There are so many ways things could go horribly wrong."

"When you're doing something like this," I said, "the odds are irrelevant. You don't need to know the odds. You need to know how to do the thing you're trying to do. And then you need to do it. What comes next"—I gestured, the tossing of a handful of omens—"isn't something you have any control over."

"It will be as Amaat wills," Ekalu said. A pious platitude. "Sometimes that's a comfort, to think that God's intention directs everything." She sighed. "And sometimes it's not."

"Very true," I agreed. "In the meantime, let's enjoy our breakfast." I took up a piece of fish. "It's very good. And let's talk about Amaat One, and whoever else in the decades you think might be officer material."

Off to Medical, after breakfast, to Medic's tiny office cubicle. I lowered myself into a chair, leaned my crutches against the wall. "You said something about a prosthetic."

"It's not ready yet," she said. Flat. Frowning. Defying me to question her assertion.

"It should be ready by now," I said.

"It's a complicated mechanism. It needs to be able to compensate for new growth as…"

"You want to be sure I don't leave Seivarden and her

Amaats here and go to the station myself." We were in gate-space, still days away from Athoek.

Medic scoffed. "Like that would stop you. Sir."

"Then what's the problem?"

"The prosthetic is a temporary fix. It's not designed to take hard use and it's certainly not suitable for combat." I didn't reply, just sat watching her frown at me. "Lieutenant Sei-varden shouldn't be going, either. She's much better than she was, but I can't guarantee how well she'll handle that kind of stress. And Tisarwat..." But she of anyone on the ship could guess why there was no choice about Tisarwat going.

"Lieutenant Seivarden is the only person on this ship besides me with actual combat experience," I pointed out. "And besides *Sphene*, I suppose. But I'm not sure we can trust *Sphene*."

Medic gave a sardonic laugh. "No." And then, struck by a thought, "Sir, I think you should consider some field promo-tions. Amaat One, certainly, and Bo One."

"I've just been talking to Ekalu about that. I'd have talked to Seivarden already, but I'm sure she's asleep by now." I reached. Found Seivarden in the first stages of what prom-ised to be a very sound sleep. In my bed. Five, far from being resentful at losing her working space, sat at the table in the empty soldiers' mess, humming happily as she mended a torn shirtsleeve, a green-glazed bowl of tea near at hand. "Seivar-den seems to be doing all right."

"So far," Medic agreed. "Though gods help us if she can't find a gym or make some tea next time she's upset. I've tried to talk her into taking up meditation, but really it's not some-thing she's temperamentally suited to."

"She actually attempted it last night," I said. It had been morning on Seivarden's schedule.

"Did she? Well." Surprised, half-pleased, but not showing it on her face. Medic rarely did. "We'll see, I suppose. Now, let's have a look at how your leg is doing. And why, Fleet Captain, didn't you tell me sooner that your right leg was hurting you?"

"It's been that way more than a year. I'm mostly used to it. And actually I didn't think you could do anything about it."

Medic folded her arms. Leaned back in her chair. Still frowning at me. "It's possible that I can't. Certainly it's not practical to try much of anything right now. But you ought to have told me."

I put a penitent expression on my face. "Yes, Medic." She relaxed, just slightly. "Now about that prosthetic. Don't tell me it isn't ready yet, because I know that it is. Or it can be, in a matter of hours. And I am very tired of the crutches. I know it's not suitable for hard use, and even if it were I wouldn't have enough time to get used to it, not for fighting. Not even if you'd given it to me as soon as you possibly could. Seivarden is going to the station, not me."

Medic sighed. "You might actually adapt more quickly, because you're..." She hesitated. "Because you're an ancillary."

"I probably will," I agreed. "But not quickly enough." And I didn't want to jeopardize the mission, no matter how much I wanted to personally rid the system of Anaander Mianaai.

"Right," said Medic. Still frowning, as she nearly always did, but inwardly relieved. And gratified. "Let's go next door, then, and have a look at how that leg is coming along. And then, since I know you were up all night, and since we're safe in gate-space and you've already been around the ship making sure everything is going as it should, you can go back to your quarters and get some sleep. By the time you wake up, the prosthetic should be ready."

I thought of lying down beside Seivarden. It would not be the first time we'd shared close quarters, but that had been before *Mercy of Kalr*. Before I could come even the slightest bit close to what I'd lost, that sense of so much of myself around me. And Medic was right, I had been up all night. I really was very tired. "If that will make you happy, Medic," I said.

Seivarden didn't register my presence at all, she was so deeply asleep. But her nearness and warmth, her slow, even breathing, along with the data Ship fed me from Seivarden's sleeping Amaats, was so very comfortable. Ship showed me Tisarwat in the decade room, and Bo decade coming into the soldiers' mess. Laughing to see Kalr Five there. "Sir needed a bit of privacy with our Amaat lieutenant, did she?" Bo Ten asked. "About time!" Five just smiled, and kept on with her mending. Ekalu coming into the decade room for what would be her supper, her Etrepas finishing up the last tasks of the day before they could get into the soldiers' mess for their own meal. Kalr One on watch, in Command. Technically against regulations, but this was the not-even-nothing of gate-space, where nothing even remotely interesting would happen, and the more experience the decade leaders could get, the better. Medic telling Kalr Twelve she'd have lunch later, she was busy just now, didn't want to find out what would happen if the prosthetic wasn't ready when I woke, as she'd promised. Twelve didn't smile, though she wanted to.

Everything was as it should be. I slept, and woke hours later to Bo on watch, Tisarwat and two of her decade drilling in the gym, Ekalu and her Etrepas settling into their beds. Amaat still asleep and dreaming. Seivarden still beside me, still asleep. Five standing silent by my bed, with a rose glass bowl of tea for me. She must have made it in the decade room and carried it down the corridor. Ship said, in my ear, "Medic is available at your convenience, Fleet Captain."

* * *

Two hours later I was walking on my new, temporary leg—not much more than a gray plastic jointed rod, flattened at the foot end. Its response was just a hair more sluggish than I liked, and my first few steps on it had been unsteady and swaying. "No running," Medic had said, but at the moment, even if the leg had been built for heavy-duty use, I probably wouldn't have been able to run. "I have to check it every day, because if there's irritation or injury at the interface you won't feel it." Because of the corrective that was growing the leg back. "It may seem trivial, but believe me, it's far better to catch that sort of thing early." And I had said, "Yes, Medic." And gone to walk up and down corridors, Twelve trailing me, the prosthetic stiff and clunking with each step, until I could do so without tripping and falling.

I found *Sphene* by itself in the decade room, sitting at the table on one side of its game with Translator Zeiat. "Hello, Cousin," it said as I came unsteadily in the door. "Having trouble getting used to the new leg?"

"It's more of a challenge than I expected," I admitted. Officers of mine had lost limbs in the past, but they'd invariably been sent away to recover. And of course, if an ancillary lost a limb it was far easier just to dispose of it and thaw out a new one. Twelve pulled out a chair for me, and I lowered myself into it. Very carefully. "I just need practice, that's all."

"Of course." I couldn't tell if it was being sarcastic or not. "I'm just waiting for Translator Zeiat."

"You don't need to explain why you're in the decade room, Cousin. You're a guest here." Twelve brought me a bowl of tea, and one of the cakes from the pile on the counter.

Brought over the same for *Sphene*. Who looked at the tea, and the cake, and said, "You don't need to do this, you know.

205

You could feed me water and skel and put me in a storage compartment."

"Why would I do that, Cousin?" I took a bite of cake. It had chopped dates in it, and cinnamon. The recipe was a particular favorite of Ekalu's. "Tell me, does it bother you to be referred to as *it*?"

"Why would it?"

I gestured ambivalence. "It troubles some of my crew to hear you referred to as *it*, when you're treated like a person. And I call you *Cousin* and they wouldn't dream of ever using *it* for me. Though technically that would be correct."

"And does it bother you to be called *she*?" asked *Sphene*.

"No," I admitted. "I suppose I've gotten used to being called by whatever pronoun seems appropriate to the speaker. I have to admit, I'd take offense if one of my crew called me *it*. But mostly because I know they'd think of it as an insult."

Sphene picked up its cake. Took a bite. Chewed. Swallowed. Took a drink of tea. Said, "I've actually never thought about it until now, Cousin. But do you know what really does grate?" I gestured to her to continue, my mouth full of tea and cake. Sphene continued, "Hearing you call yourselves Radchaai. Calling this"—it gestured around—"the Radch."

I swallowed. "I suppose I can't blame you," I said. "Will you tell me where you are, Cousin?"

"Right across the table from you, Cousin." Impassive as always, but I thought I saw a trace of amusement.

"I couldn't help but notice that when we were in the Ghost System, and *Mercy of Kalr* asked where you were, it was you who answered us, from inside the ship. You didn't talk to *Mercy of Kalr* directly." And as a result we couldn't know how far away *Sphene* had been, or even guess at its location.

Sphene smiled. "Will you do me a favor, Cousin? Will you let me go back to the station with Lieutenant Seivarden?"

"Why?"

"I won't get in the way, I promise. It's just that I want to be able to put my hands around the Usurper's throat and strangle her myself." The war *Sphene* had fled, three thousand years ago, had been an argument not just over Anaander's policy of expanding Radchaai influence outward, but also over her legitimacy as an authority of any sort. Or so I understood—it had all happened a thousand years before I was born. "Or if that's inconveniently time-consuming, I'll happily shoot her in the head. As long as she knows who it is who's doing it. I realize that it's a futile wish, and won't do the least bit of good, considering what she is. But I want to do it so badly. I've been dreaming of it for three thousand years." I didn't answer. "Ah, you don't trust me. Well, I suppose I wouldn't, either, in your place."

Translator Zeiat came into the decade room then. "*Sphene*! I've been thinking and thinking, let me show you! Hello, Fleet Captain! You'll like this, too." She took the tray of cakes off the counter, set it in the middle of the table. "These are cakes."

"They are," *Sphene* agreed. The translator looked to me for confirmation, and I gestured agreement.

"All of them! All cakes!" Completely delighted at the thought. She swept the cakes off the tray and onto the table, and made two piles of them. "Now these," she said, indicating the slightly larger stack of cinnamon date cakes, "have fruit in them. And these"—she indicated the others—"do not. Do you see? They were the same before, but now they're different. And look. You might think to yourself—I know I thought it to myself—that they're different because of the fruit. Or the not-fruit, you know, as the case may be. But watch this!" She took the stacks apart, set the cakes in haphazard ranks. "Now I make a line. I just imagine one!" She leaned over, put her arm in the middle of the rows of cakes, and swept some of them to one side. "Now these," she pointed to one side, "are different from these." She pointed to the others. "But some of them have fruit and some don't. They were *different* before, but now they're *the same*. And the other side of the line, likewise. And *now*." She reached over and took a counter from the game board.

"No cheating, Translator," said *Sphene*. Calm and pleasant.

"I'll put it back," Translator Zeiat protested, and then set the counter down among the cakes. "They were different—you accept, don't you, that they were different before?—but now they're the same."

"I suspect the counter doesn't taste as good as the cakes," said *Sphene*.

"That would be a matter of opinion," Translator Zeiat said, just the smallest bit primly. "Besides, it *is* a cake now." She frowned. "Or are the cakes counters now?"

"I don't think so, Translator," I said. "Not either way." Carefully I stood up from my chair.

"Ah, Fleet Captain, that's because you can't see my imaginary line. But it's real." She tapped her forehead. "It exists." She took one of the date cakes, and set it on the game board where the counter had been. "See, I told you I'd put it back."

"I think it's my turn," said *Sphene*, and picked up the cake and took a bite out of it. "You're right, Translator, this tastes just as good as the other cakes."

"Sir," whispered Kalr Twelve, close behind me as I cautiously walked out into the corridor. She had listened to the entire conversation with a growing sense of offended horror. "I need to say, sir, none of us would *ever* call you *it*."

*　*　*

The next day Seivarden found Ekalu alone in the decade room. "Your pardon, Ekalu," she said, bowing. "I don't mean to take up your break time, but Ship said you might have a moment."

Ekalu didn't get up. "Yes?" Not the least bit surprised. Ship had, of course, warned her Seivarden was coming. Had made sure the time was convenient for Ekalu.

"I want to say," said Seivarden, still standing, nervous and awkward, just inside the doorway. "I mean. A while ago I apologized for behaving very badly to you." Took an embarrassed breath. "I didn't understand what I'd done, I just wanted you to stop being angry at me. I just said what Ship told me I should say. I was angry at you, for being angry at me, but Ship talked me out of being any more stupid than I already had been. But I've been thinking about it."

Ekalu, sitting at the table, went completely still, her face ancillary-blank.

Seivarden knew what that likely meant, but didn't wait for Ekalu to say anything. "I've been thinking about it, and I still don't understand exactly why what I said hurt you so much. But I don't need to. It hurt you, and when you told me it hurt you I should have apologized and stopped saying whatever it was. And maybe spent some time trying to understand. Instead of insisting that you manage your feelings to suit me. And I want to say I'm sorry. And I actually mean it this time."

Seivarden couldn't see Ekalu's reaction to this, since Ekalu still sat absolutely motionless. But Ship could see. I could see.

Seivarden said, into Ekalu's silence, "Also I want to say that I miss you. And what we had. But that's my own stupid fault."

Silence, for five seconds, though I thought that at any moment Ekalu might speak, or stand. Or weep. "Also," said Seivarden, then, "I want to say that you're an excellent officer.

You were thrown into the position with no warning and hardly any official training, and I only wish I'd been as steady and as strong my first weeks as a lieutenant."

"Well, you were only seventeen at the time," said Ekalu.

"Lieutenant," Ship admonished Ekalu, in her ear. "Take the compliment."

Aloud, Ekalu said, "But thank you."

"It's an honor to serve with you," Seivarden said. "Thank you for taking the time to listen to me." And she bowed, and left.

Ekalu crossed her arms on the table, put her head down on them. "Oh, Ship," she said, voice despairing. "Did you tell her to say any of that?"

"I helped a bit with the wording," Ship replied. "But it wasn't my idea. She means it."

"It was the fleet captain's idea, then."

"Not actually."

"She's so beautiful," said Ekalu. "And so good in bed. But she's such a..." Stopped, hearing Etrepa Six's step in the corridor.

Etrepa Six looked in the door of the decade room, saw her lieutenant with her head down on the table. Put that together with Seivarden's retreating back, away down the corridor. Came into the decade room and began to make tea.

Not lifting her head, Ekalu said, silently, "If I called her back, would she come?"

"Oh, yes," said Ship. "But if I were you, I'd let her stew for a while."

13

Tisarwat came to see me just hours before we exited gate-space, into Athoek system. "Sir," she said, standing just inside the door to my quarters. "I'm on my way to the airlock."

"Yes." I stood. A bit steadier on the prosthetic leg than the day before. "Will you have tea?" Five was off on an errand, but there was tea already made, in the flask on the counter.

"No, sir. I'm not sure there's time. I just wanted..." I waited. Finally she said, "I don't know what I wanted. No. Wait. I do. If I don't come back, will you...that other Tisarwat's family. You won't tell them what happened to her, will you?"

The chances of my ever having the chance to say anything at all to Tisarwat's family was so small as to be almost entirely nonexistent. "Of course not."

She took a long, relieved breath. "Because they don't deserve that. I know it sounds stupid. I don't even know them. Except I know so much about them. I just..."

"It's not stupid. It's entirely understandable."

"Is it?" Her arms at her sides, she closed her gloved hands

into fists. Unclosed them. "And if I do come back. If I come back, sir, will you authorize Medic to change my eyes back to a more reasonable color?"

Those foolish lilac eyes, that the previous Tisarwat had bought for herself. "If you like."

"It's such a stupid color. And every time I see myself it reminds me of her." Of that old Tisarwat, I supposed. "They don't belong to me."

"They do," I said. "You were born with them that color." Her mouth trembled, and tears filled her eyes. I said, "But whatever other color you choose will be yours, too." That didn't help her hold back her tears. "One way or another," I said, "it'll be all right. Are your meds current?"

"Yes."

"Your Bos know what they need to do. You know what you need to do. There's nothing for it now but to do it."

"I forget you can see all that." See all her feelings, her reactions, as Ship could. As Ship could show me. "I keep forgetting you can see right inside me, and then when I remember I just..." She trailed off.

"I'm not looking," I said. "I've been trying not to, lately. But I don't need to look, right now. You're not the first young lieutenant I've met, you know."

She made a short, breathy *hah*. "It made so much sense." She sniffled. "It seemed so obviously the right thing, when I thought of it. And now it seems impossible."

"That's how these things go," I said. "You already know that. Are you sure you don't want tea?"

"I'm sure," she said, wiping her eyes. "I'm on my way to the airlock. And I hate having to pee in my vacuum suit."

I said, sternly, "Straighten up, Lieutenant, and wipe your face." Without thinking she stood up taller and put her shoulders back. Rubbed her gloved hands on her eyes again. "Seivarden is on her way."

"Sir," she said, "I understand about you and Lieutenant Seivarden. Really I do. But does she have to be such a condescending asshole?"

"Probably not," I said, as the door opened, and Seivarden came in. "Dismissed, Lieutenant."

"Sir," Tisarwat said, and turned to go.

Seivarden grinned at her. "Ready to go, kiddo?"

"Don't," said Tisarwat, looking Seivarden full in the eye. "Ever. Call me *kiddo*. Again." And strode out of the room.

Seivarden lifted her eyebrows. "Nerves?" Amusement, but with an extra layer of curiosity—Tisarwat's mission was a secret, nearly all her preparation for it hidden. Not from me or Ship, of course, that would be impossible.

"She doesn't like being condescended to," I said. Seivarden blinked, surprised. "And also nerves."

She grinned again. "Thought so." Her expression turned serious. "I'm here for the gun." I didn't move immediately. "If it wasn't for the leg, Breq, you'd be the best person to go, and you wouldn't have to give the gun up to anyone."

"I've already had this conversation. With you. With Ship." With Medic. *I know what will happen*, she'd said. *Things will get hot and you'll forget the leg won't hold up to hard use. Or you'll remember but not care.* And if it had just been me, I'd have gone ahead. But it wasn't just me anymore. "If you lose the gun, I probably won't live long enough to forgive you." I could send Seivarden to Athoek Station with a regular sidearm. But the Presger gun would give her the best chance of killing Anaander, armored or not, guarded by ancillaries or not. If she failed, and lost the gun, if Anaander ended up with it, the results could be disastrous.

Seivarden smiled wryly. "I know."

I turned, opened the lid of the bench behind me, took out the box that held the gun. Set it on the table and opened it. Seivarden reached out, drew out a fragment of black—gun-shaped—the brown of her glove bleeding into it as soon as it came away from the box. "Be careful with it," I warned, though this was another conversation we had already had. "Translator Zeiat said it was made to destroy Radchaai ships. The 1.11 meters is just a side effect of that. Be careful how you use it."

"You don't have to tell me that," she said, putting the weapon in her jacket, and taking two magazines out of the box.

"If *Sword of Gurat* really is docked with Athoek Station, you don't want to blow its heat shield." Seivarden's team was going after that young Anaander Mianaai. We wouldn't know where the tyrant was until Station (we hoped) told us. I thought it most likely she would either be in the Governor's Palace or aboard *Sword of Gurat*.

"I understand." Seivarden's voice was patient. "Look, Breq...I'm sorry I'm such a jerk sometimes. I'm sorry the only lieutenant you have left is the one you never liked much."

"It's all right," I lied.

"No it isn't," she said. "But it's how things are."

There wasn't really any arguing with that. "Don't be stupid."

She smiled. "Will you come talk to us before we go? We're about to do our last equipment checks and go out on the hull."

"I'd intended to." I closed the box, left it on the table, and headed out the door. As I walked past Seivarden, she reached for my arm. "I don't need help walking," I said.

"It was just you seemed a bit wobbly there." Apologetic. Following me into the corridor.

"That's the prosthetic adjusting to new growth." I never knew when it would do that. Just another reason I couldn't take it into combat. "Sometimes it goes on for a few minutes."

But it didn't trouble me again, and I reached the staging area by the airlock without incident, without even limping slightly. "I won't take too much of your time," I said, as Seivarden's two Amaats, and Tisarwat and her two Bos, rose from what they were doing—checking over seals on their vacuum suits—and turned. "I suppose I ought to make some sort of motivational speech, but I don't have one for you and besides, you're busy. Come back safe." I wanted to say something more, to Tisarwat and her Bos, but with Seivarden and her Amaats listening it would be dangerous to even hint at what they were planning to do. Instead I put a gloved hand on Tisarwat's shoulder.

"Yes, sir," she said. No trace of her earlier tears in her voice. "Understood, sir."

I dropped my hand. Turned to Seivarden and her Amaats. "Yes, sir," Seivarden said. "We will."

"Right," I said. "I'll let you get back to what you were doing." I looked over at Tisarwat and her Bos again. "I have every confidence in all of you." I turned then, and left them to finish rechecking seals and tether clips.

Ekalu was on watch, in Command. As I entered she stood up from the single seat. "Sir," she said, "nothing to report."

Of course not. We were still in gate-space. The view outside the ship showed absolutely nothing, wouldn't until we gated into Athoek System. "Sit down, Lieutenant," I said.

"I'm not here to take over." I just hadn't wanted to sit in my quarters drinking tea. "I'm perfectly fine standing."

"You are, Fleet Captain," said Etrepa Four, at a console. "But we'll all feel better if you sit down. Begging your generous indulgence, sir." No, not Etrepa Four, who would never have spoken that way to me, who was having a moment of nauseated panic at having done so.

"Honestly, Ship."

"Honestly, Fleet Captain." Four was slightly light-headed with relief at my reaction. Still a bit sick. "It's a while until anything happens, you may as well sit."

Lieutenant Ekalu took the handhold beside the seat. "I was about to call for tea, sir."

"I'm perfectly fine standing," I said, settling into the seat.

"Yes, sir," said Ekalu. Her face perfectly expressionless.

Two hours later we exited gate-space into Athoek System. Just for the briefest moment, just long enough for *Mercy of Kalr* to get a look at the traffic around Athoek Station. The suffocatingly flat not-even-black just gone and the real universe there: sudden, solid depth. Light and warmth and everything suddenly real, Athoek Station shining in the sunlight, Athoek itself, shadowed white and blue, and then it was gone, wiped away by the smothering flatness of gate-space. Seivarden and her Amaats, Tisarwat and her Bos, already out on the hull, vacuum-suited, tethered, waiting, started at the brightness, suddenly there, suddenly gone. "Oh," gasped Amaat Two. Something about that brief flash of reality, that sudden return to uncanny darkness, made her feel as if she couldn't quite breathe properly. It was a common reaction. "That was..."

"I told you it was weird," said Seivarden, on the hull beside Two. "Am I really the only person here who's done this before?" No reply. "Well, besides Fleet Captain, of course. And Ship. They definitely have."

We had. As Seivarden spoke, Ship was comparing what it had just seen around Athoek Station with what we knew ought to be there, with the various schedules and travel clearances we knew about. Calculating where things would be, some time shortly in the future. "Eleven minutes and three seconds," said Etrepa Four, behind me in Command. Said Ship, into the ears of the soldiers waiting on the hull. Adrenaline spiked, heart rates shot up in all of them. Seivarden grinned. "I didn't know I'd missed this," she said. "It's awfully quiet, though. Fleet Captain used to sing the whole time."

"Used to?" asked Amaat Two, and everyone laughed, short and tense. Knowing that they'd be moving soon, and out of reach of *Mercy of Kalr*, with no knowledge of where or when we might come back for them. Only Tisarwat knew why that was, or how long it might be. She was the one who needed time to work.

"There was a lot more of the fleet captain then," said Seivarden. "And she had a better voice. Better voices."

"I like the fleet captain's voice," said Bo Three. "I didn't at first, but I guess I'm used to it."

"Yeah," said Tisarwat.

Amaat Four said, "Lieutenant, I hope you don't expect us to sing for the next ten minutes."

"Oh, I like that idea," said Seivarden. Her Amaats, and Tisarwat's Bos, groaned. "We should have picked one out in advance and rehearsed it. With parts, like Fleet Captain used to do." She sang, "*I was walking, I was walking / When I met my love / I was in the street walking / When I met my true love.*" Or tried to. The tune was mostly right, but the words

217

weren't in Radchaai and it had been decades—subjectively—since she'd heard me sing it. What Seivarden remembered of the words was nonsense.

"Is that one of the fleet captain's?" asked Tisarwat. "I don't think I've ever heard her sing it."

"I heard," ventured Bo Three, "that when they pulled her in, you know, the other day, she was half-dead and still trying to sing."

"I believe it," said Seivarden. "I have no trouble imagining that if she thought she was about to die, she'd pick a song for it." Two seconds of silence. "Remember what I said, about the tether clips. We won't have much time, when we gate back in." We didn't want to be seen, didn't want anyone on the station—except Station—to suspect that soldiers from *Mercy of Kalr* might be arriving. We would arrive in Athoek System as close to the station as we could, for the barest instant, not even a second, and then, the moment Seivarden and Tisarwat and their soldiers were clear, we would be gone again. "So as soon as you get the order, unclip and push off, like we practiced. If you miss, if the clip sticks, or anything, don't try to catch up. Just stay here." A chorused *Yes, sir.* "If you push off at the wrong time and don't end up at the station, Ship probably won't be able to retrieve you. I've seen it happen."

They had all heard this, over and over during the past few days. "I wonder," said Bo Three, "if Fleet Captain has a song picked out in advance. You know, so if suddenly she finds herself in danger she doesn't have to worry about which one it will be."

"I wouldn't be surprised if she does," replied Tisarwat.

"Two minutes," said Ship, who had all this while been counting the time down in their visions.

Seivarden said, "I think she's got so many songs, they just

kind of come out of her on their own." Silence. Then, "Right, one minute. Take hold of your clips and be ready to move."

This was, in some ways, the most dangerous moment of the entire endeavor. Even aside from the risk of mistiming the departure and ending up lost and drifting somewhere unthinkably distant from the ship, or any kind of help, there was also the question of whether Ship had correctly calculated its brief exit into the real universe. Anything might be in the spot where we came out of gate-space. That *anything* could be as small as a sail-pod, or as large as a cargo carrier. Though it was unlikely Ship would have missed a cargo carrier in its calculations, it was still entirely possible. And even a sail-pod would be a danger to the vacuum-suited soldiers outside the protection of Ship's hull plating. Or there was always the chance that someone might have seen us flash into the system and back out, minutes earlier, and might be waiting for us.

"On the count," said Seivarden, though of course the numbers were already ticking down in all their visions. "Five. Four. Three. Two. One. Go!" I felt the moment all six on the hull shoved away.

Light. The six *Mercy of Kalr* soldiers sailed toward Athoek Station, suddenly meters away, a stretch of vents and conduits no one ever even thought about except Station Maintenance. But Bo Three had fumbled the clip, had pushed away but only pulled her tether taut. She pulled herself back, reached for the clip again. "Freeze!" I shouted at her. Aloud. In that instant Athoek Station disappeared, the rest of the universe, Seivarden and Tisarwat and the others, all gone. We were back in gate-space.

"Bo Three fumbled the clip," Ship said to the startled Etrepas in Command. "But she's all right, she's still here." We would have no way of knowing if the others had gotten safely to the station. Wouldn't until next we gated into the system.

At least their equipment had been distributed among the three—Tisarwat and Nine wouldn't be in any serious difficulties if they didn't have the things Three was carrying. "It's all right, Bo," I said, silently this time. She still had her hand on the tether clip, still hung outside the ship. Mortified. Horrified. Angry at herself and at me. "I've fumbled plenty of times myself." A lie—in two thousand years, as *Justice of Toren* One Esk I had only ever fumbled a clip twice. "And you wouldn't have made it. If I'd been in your place I couldn't have moved fast enough." Another lie—I was fairly sure I could have. "Come inside, get out of the suit, have some tea."

"Fleet Captain," said Bo Three. I had thought it was an acknowledgment, and so, apparently, had Three, but somewhere between syllables it had turned into a protest. "She's just a kid, sir!"

Tisarwat, she meant. "Nine is with her, Bo. Nine won't leave her for anything. You know that." Her adrenaline was high, her heart beating hard, from the moment, from the anticipation of what they'd planned to do on the station. From the sudden, shocking stop at the end of her tether, from my urgent order to freeze. From her own anger at herself for failing to stay with Tisarwat. "It's all right, Three. Come inside."

Bo Three closed her eyes. Took two deep breaths. Opened her eyes again and began the move toward the airlock. I returned my attention to Command. To Ekalu, who still stood beside my seat, the handhold tight in her grip. Her face had gone expressionless out of pure habit, a legacy from when she'd been a common soldier on this ship. She was nearly as upset as Bo Three, now pulling herself into the airlock, but

Ekalu's distress couldn't be for the same reasons. I reached for what she was seeing.

In the very brief time we were beside Athoek Station, Ship had collected as much data as it could. The view of the station from where we were, data from the station news channels, anything it could pull in. Ekalu was, this moment, looking at an image of Athoek Station. It wasn't a view we could have seen from where we'd gated in—Ship must have pulled it from somewhere else. From where we'd just been, we couldn't have seen the Gardens. We'd deliberately avoided that, in fact, because we didn't want anyone in the Gardens to be able to look up at the right moment and notice us.

But it turned out we needn't have troubled ourselves—there was no one in the Gardens. Last week Seivarden and her Amaats had cut a hole in the dome, so that they could pull me and Tisarwat and Basnaaid and Bo Nine out before we asphyxiated. That hole had been patched, but of course it had needed a more complete repair. Now, it seemed, that patch had failed. The seam where it had been sealed to the dome had split. Everything under the dome was faded and dead. Something must have rammed hard into the dome, right at its weakest point.

Ekalu looked at me. "What happened?" Still stunned and horrified.

"At a guess," I said, "the missing shuttle happened." Incomprehension. "From the schedule Station sent us the other day? You recall, we determined that it was missing a passenger shuttle."

"Oh." Realization dawned. For a moment I considered getting up, so that Ekalu could have the seat. "Oh, sir. Oh, no, sir. *Sword of Gurat* got the passenger shuttle schedule from Station, but it didn't check to see if the shuttles were actually where they ought to be before they gated. Did they...if the shuttle was in their path as they came out of gate-space, sir... if they ran into it..."

"That particular shuttle is late about half the time. Which of course neither *Sword of Gurat* nor its captain had any reason to know." Ekalu closed her eyes. Opened them again, remembering, I thought, that she was technically in charge here, that she had to get ahold of herself. "Fortunately," I continued, "or sort of fortunately, the Gardens will have been closed to the public." And it was a good thing I'd demanded that the Undergarden section doors be fixed. Level one of the Undergarden was very possibly depressurized right now, but the sections around it, and the levels below it, ought to be all right, kept safe when those section doors had automatically slammed shut when the pressure dropped. As things stood, it was entirely possible some Horticulture workers had died. Not Basnaaid, because otherwise there would have been no point in putting her on the list of those ordered to relocate downwell. "The shuttle crews I saw all seemed to be following safety regulations." If they hadn't, I'd have said something to their superiors. "It's entirely possible not everyone aboard that shuttle died." Not a thought to make Ekalu any happier—the shuttle could carry more than five hundred people. "But now we know why nobody seemed to have said anything to the tyrant about the Gardens, or the Undergarden. Not until they absolutely had to. She sails in claiming to be the true authority, who every citizen knows has that authority by virtue of her just and proper interest in the well-being and benefit of all her citizens and, what, accidentally kills a shuttle full of people." Would have killed quite a lot of citizens enjoying the Gardens, if not for the havoc I and my crew had wrought there last week.

No wonder Anaander had been nervous about that line of residents on the concourse. No wonder no one wanted to remind her of the catastrophe she'd caused merely by arriving at the station. No wonder not even a hint of this had reached the official news channels.

"But why haven't they repaired the dome?" asked Ekalu. "It looks like they haven't even started."

"Because of the curfew," I said. "Only essential personnel. Remember?" And repair crews would have families they'd likely talk to about what they'd seen, about what had happened, and those families had friends and acquaintances they would talk to, even if only while fetching skel from the common refectories.

"That's not all, Fleet Captain," said Etrepa Four. Said Ship. "Take a look at what *is* on the official news channels."

When we'd gated away from the Ghost System, the news channels had been that nonstop flood of warnings about me, of condemnations of me and my supporters. But apparently Station had returned to feeding surveillance data to its residents. We had only the smallest sample, barely more than a minute of visuals of the station's main concourse. Which ought to have been empty, given the curfew, but instead ranks of citizens sat right in the middle of the open space. Probably two hundred people, just sitting. Many of them were Ychana, some Undergarden residents, some not. But there were also Xhai there, including the hierophant of the Mysteries. And also there, Horticulturist Basnaaid. And Citizen Uran.

And, doubtless the reason for Station's hijacking of the official news, around the ranks of sitting citizens stood twenty ancillaries. Armor shining silver, guns in their hands.

I had seen this sort of thing before. I was suddenly struck by the memory of humid heat. The smell of swamp water, and blood. I found I had stood without realizing it. "Of course they did. Of *course*." Station's residents had not sat quietly waiting for *Mercy of Kalr* to rescue them. And Station had to have helped them assemble, helped them work around Security's patrols, around the *Sword of Gurat* ancillaries enforcing the tyrant's curfew. They couldn't have done it otherwise. Not this many people.

It was, obviously, an organized protest. And *Sword of Gurat* had drawn its guns, and Station had done the one thing it could do to defend its residents, the one thing that had worked, or seemed to, just a few days ago—make sure everyone knew just exactly what was happening.

None of it was calculated to ease the mind of an already angry and anxious Anaander Mianaai. What had she done in response? What was happening, this very moment, to the people on the concourse? But we couldn't do anything about it. Couldn't even know, until we gated back into Athoek System.

We wouldn't know how long it would take either Seivarden or Tisarwat to do—or try to do—what she had gone to the station for. *Mercy of Kalr* could leave gate-space again, so that we could receive messages. But we might be detected, and we wanted everyone on Athoek Station—everyone in the system—to think that we were gone. The lives of Seivarden and her Amaats, Tisarwat and Bo Nine, might depend on it. So it was the next few days in gate-space, for us.

There was no reason for me to stay in Command. There was nothing I could do, from where I was, that would make any difference whatsoever. I seriously considered going back to my quarters and getting some sleep, but I didn't think I could be still for long, knowing that five of my crew were gone, that reach as I might, I wouldn't be able to find them. So I walked to the decade room instead.

The fragments of that gold-and-glass Notai tea set were spread out on the table, and *Sphene* and Kalr Five sat across from each other, an array of tools and adhesives laid out to one side. What looked to be the curving rim of one bowl had already been pieced together. Five started guiltily as I came in. "No, continue what you're doing," I said. "So after all you think it might go together again?"

"Maybe," said *Sphene*, and picked up one blue glass fragment, put it next to another one. Considered them.

"What was her name?" I asked. "The captain whose tea set this was?"

"Minask," said *Sphene*. "Minask Nenkur."

Five looked up from the pieces she was fitting together. "Nenkur!"

"Few older names in all the Radch," *Sphene* said. "You know the name, of course, from the execrable entertainment that purports to be a faithful account of the battle of Iait Il. The Arit Nenkur that travesty slandered was Captain Minask's mother. This"—it gestured toward the scatter of blue and green glass, and bits of gold—"was her gift, when Captain Minask was promoted."

"And given command of you," I guessed.

"Yes," said *Sphene*.

"No wonder you removed the name," I said.

"What happened?" asked Five.

"It was a battle, of course." *Sphene*'s tone was perhaps just the slightest bit sarcastic, as though Five had asked a laughably foolish question. If Five heard it, she was unperturbed by it. Probably used to *Sphene* by now. "Captain Minask had surrendered. I was badly damaged. All but my captain and one of my lieutenants were dead. We couldn't fight anymore. But when the Usurper's forces boarded, they brought an AI core with them."

"Oh!" Five. Horrified. "No!"

"Oh, yes," said *Sphene*. "As a ship I was valuable. But not as myself—they preferred their own, more biddable AI. *You promised we'd be spared*, said Captain Minask. *And so you will be*, said the Usurper's lackey. *But you can't imagine we'd let a ship go to waste*." It set down the fragments it was holding. "She was very brave. Stupidly so, that day. I sometimes wish she hadn't resolved to fight for me, so that she might have lived longer. But then I wonder if they ever meant to let her live, or if they always meant to shoot her, and just said they'd spare us so that Captain Minask would surrender before I was damaged beyond usefulness."

"How did you get away?" I asked. Didn't ask how it had rid itself of the tyrant's soldiers. Offhand I could think of several ways *Sphene* could have done it, all of them easier if *Sphene* didn't care who aboard it lived or died. Foolish, to shoot the captain while they were still aboard, before they were sure of the ship.

"It was a battlefield," *Sphene* replied. "Ships were gating in and out, all over the place. And my engines still sort of worked, I just couldn't make a gate of my own. But I thought maybe I could stay in gate-space, if I could manage to get there. I moved, and by God's grace a gate opened near me—I hope I damaged the Usurper's ship that came out of it very badly—and I took it. I had no chance to calculate my route, though, and very little control over where I might emerge."

"And you ended up here," I finished for it.

"And I ended up here," it agreed. "I could have ended up in many a worse place. No doubt some of my sibling ships did."

Silence. Kalr Five got up, went to the counter where there was already a flask of tea, poured a bowl. Brought it to *Sphene*, set it down by its right elbow. Took her seat again. *Sphene* looked at the tea for a moment. Picked it up and drank. Set it back down. Picked up another two blue glass fragments and considered them.

"Fleet Captain!" Translator Zeiat came into the decade room. Looked at the table. "Oh! Our game looks very different today!"

"It's still packed away, Translator," said *Sphene*. "This is a tea set."

"Ah!" Dismissing that, the translator turned again to me. "Fleet Captain, I hope there's fish sauce where we're going."

"I must confess, Translator," I said, "that as much as I would like to gratify your desire, just now we're involved in a war. An opposing force is currently in control of Athoek Station, and until that changes, I'm afraid I have no access to fish sauce."

"Well, Fleet Captain, I must say, this war of yours is very inconvenient."

"It is," I agreed. "Translator, may I ask you a question?"

"Of course, Fleet Captain!" She sat down in the seat beside *Sphene*.

"These are not for eating," *Sphene* said.

Translator Zeiat made a brief moue and then turned her attention to me. "You wanted to know?"

"Translator, there are rumors..." I reconsidered my phrasing. "There are quite a few people who sincerely believe that the Presger have infiltrated the Lord of the Radch. That they have gained control of parts of her, in order to destroy the Radch. Or destroy humanity."

"Oh, goodness, no, Fleet Captain. No, that wouldn't be the

least bit amusing. It would break the treaty, for one thing."
She frowned. "Wait! So, if I understand you correctly—there
are, sadly, no guarantees that I understand you correctly—
you think the treaty may have been broken?"

"I don't, personally. But some people do think so. Would
you like some tea?" Five began to rise, but I put my hand on
her shoulder. "No, I'll get it. It's already made."

Translator Zeiat heaved a sigh. "I suppose, since there isn't
any fish sauce."

I poured a bowl, gave it to the translator, and sat down
across from her, next to Kalr Five. "So would I be correct
in guessing that the Presger have not...interfered with
Anaander Mianaai?"

"Goodness no," replied Translator Zeiat. "There'd be no
fun in it, for one thing. And one of the reasons there'd be
no fun in it is because what you've just said, *interfered with
Anaander Mianaai*, that would make very little sense to
them. I'm not sure how I could possibly convey it, if I were
to find it necessary. I'm not even sure I understand what
you mean myself. Besides, if there was any real intention of
breaking the treaty, any real desire to destroy the Radch, or
Humans in general—you see? *I* know those aren't the same
thing, but *they* don't. But as I said, if they wanted to destroy
the Radch, even not considering the treaty, it would be done
in the most amusing and satisfying manner possible. And I
suspect I don't have to tell you at least some of the sort of
thing that generally amuses and satisfies in that quarter, do I?
Or at least how it tends to affect the Humans involved?"

"No, Translator, you don't."

"And while I did indeed say *not even considering the
treaty*, the fact remains that the treaty is very much an issue.

No, they won't break the treaty. To be entirely honest, I'm much more worried about Humans breaking the treaty."

"If you would, Cousin," said *Sphene*. It and Five had pieced several fragments together, held the assemblage over the middle of the table. "That piece there, do you see where it fits? Inside that curl there?"

I picked up a tiny brush, a capsule of adhesive. Brushed around the inside edge of the curl, slid the shard of glass into place. "You should probably stop there," I suggested, "and let the adhesive cure, and build onto it later." I rose, took a cloth from a cabinet under the counter, and rolled it up for a form, and *Sphene* and Five put their carefully assembled bit of teabowl over it, and we lowered the whole thing onto the table. "This would probably be easier if we had the right tools."

"The story of my life for the past three thousand years," said *Sphene*. "Speaking of which. When Lieutenant Seivarden fails to kill the Usurper, will you let me try?"

"I'll consider it."

"I suppose, Cousin, that I can't reasonably ask for any more than that."

14

In gate-space as we were, we couldn't receive data from Seivarden or Tisarwat, or from Amaat Two and Four, or Bo Nine. And there was no guarantee they would be reachable when we returned. So each of them had been given a tiny external archive to hide on the outside of the station's hull. Those archives would receive and store the data for us to retrieve when we returned. Assuming they worked right, which they didn't always. Assuming nothing damaged them. Assuming no one had found them and disabled them or otherwise disposed of them.

This is what happened while *Mercy of Kalr* was out of the universe:

Seivarden and her two Amaats walked cautiously through a dusty access corridor. Armed and armored, their vacuum suits left behind at the airlock they'd come in through. Station had let them in, was even now displaying a map in their visions, though they'd studied what diagrams of the station's layout we'd already had. The diagrams, the few terse words they exchanged, said they were on their way to the governor's residence. They had seen the news channels. Noticed people they knew, among the citizens sitting on the concourse, noticed the armored ancillaries, the drawn guns. Amaat Two said, quietly, as they walked, "Do you think Lieutenant Ti—"

"Quiet," said Seivarden. Everyone on *Mercy of Kalr* knew about Tisarwat's crush on Basnaaid.

Four said, very softly, "Fleet Captain and Lieutenant Tisarwat seem close lately."

"Not surprised," replied Seivarden. Angry. Anxious. Knowing now was not the time to show it. "I suspect Fleet Captain's always had a thing for hapless baby lieutenants."

"Can't imagine you hapless, sir." Four, still very softly.

"I never looked it," said Seivarden. Surprising me by, it seemed, having found at least one source of her anxiety and not pretended it was something else, or that it didn't exist. Maybe because she was still enjoying the familiarity of this situation, the knife-edge of adrenaline before the gunfire started. "And *Justice of Toren* never liked me much."

"Huh," said Four. Honestly surprised. Trying hard not to think too much about what was ahead.

"Our Bo lieutenant isn't as hapless as she seemed at first," remarked Two.

"She isn't," agreed Seivarden. "She'll be fine." Not at all certain of that, unhappy at not knowing what Tisarwat and Nine were up to. "Now cut the chatter."

"Sir," acknowledged Two and Four, together.

Tisarwat and Bo Nine pulled their way across the station's hull. Not speaking. The news channels in their vision, those rows of seated citizens. The armed and armored soldiers. The citizens sat, quiet, and the soldiers stood, weapons ready.

"Turn it off, sir," Nine said to Tisarwat, on the hull. "There's no point watching, and you won't pay attention to where you're going if it's on."

"You're right." Tisarwat cut off the feed.

Twenty minutes later, moving handhold by handhold over the outside of Athoek Station, slowly and laboriously, she said, "I think I'm going to be sick."

"You can't be sick in your helmet, sir." Nine almost managed to keep the terror that had struck her at Tisarwat's words out of her voice. "That would be bad."

"I know!" Tisarwat stopped herself, didn't reach ahead for the next handhold. Took a few shallow breaths. "I know, but I can't help it."

"You did take the anti-nausea, sir, I saw you." And then, "Don't stop, sir. We just have to do this, that's all. And that's why. That's why we have to do this." Referring, I was sure, to what was happening on the concourse. "And if Fleet Captain were here, she'd be giving you such a look right now."

Two more shallow breaths. Then, weakly, "Hah. At least we'd have music to listen to." Tisarwat swallowed hard. Took another breath. Propelled herself forward to the next handhold.

"If you call that music." Relieved—as relieved as she could be, under the circumstances—Nine followed. "I agree with you, sir, about being used to her voice, but some of those songs she sings. They're just weird."

"*My heart is a fish.*" Tisarwat's voice thin and breathy. A shallow gasp. "*Hiding in the water-grass.*" Another. "*In the green.*"

"Well, that one's all right," Nine admitted. "Though it does get stuck in my head something fierce."

* * *

Sword of Gurat was at the very end of the docks, the two bays nearest it empty, no doubt not just because of *Sword of Gurat*'s size. No obvious damage from the collision with the passenger shuttle—but then, there wouldn't be. Possibly *Sword of Gurat* hadn't ended up with anything more than some scratches or dents.

"Right," said Tisarwat, taking a gulping breath, nausea returning. Exhausted and sore from the hours-long trip around the station hull. "Let's go." And she and Nine began pulling themselves toward *Sword of Gurat*.

So far Tisarwat had relied on Station's declining to report her and Nine's presence. But now, in sight of *Sword of Gurat*, that wouldn't protect them. It was only a matter of time— and not very much time, if *Sword of Gurat* was paying any attention at all—before they were noticed. Still, Tisarwat and Nine moved quite slowly. Very cautiously. Very carefully chose a spot on *Sword of Gurat*'s hull, tethered themselves, and opened the container they'd all this time been hauling with them. Nine pulled out an explosive charge. Handed it to Tisarwat, who carefully, slowly, fixed it to *Sword of Gurat*'s hull.

At about this point, Seivarden and her two Amaats had made it into a cramped and dim access corridor behind the governor's residence. It had probably at one point been meant for servants to use to go unobtrusively back and forth, but hadn't been used in years; the floor was dusty and trackless. This wasn't, then, the back way Governor Giarod had used to bring Translator Dlique to the residence.

Station had not spoken a word to Seivarden, or either of

her Amaats. It had displayed information—maps and directions, mostly—and unlocked doors for them. Now it had brought them to a locked door in this dusty corridor, and shown them all what lay behind it: the governor's office. The cream-and-green silk hangings were pulled nearly all the way around the walls, covering the window that looked down on the concourse, and also, helpfully, the door Seivarden and her Amaats stood behind. Empty, now, except for those few chairs, the desk. Beside the desk, a meter-and-a-half-high stack of what looked very much like suspension pods but probably were not. There were three of them in the stack, and Seivarden couldn't help but notice them. Puzzled a moment over what they might be. The words *Returning, with two* Sword of Atagaris *ancillaries, approx eight minutes* flashed in Seivarden's vision. *Two additional* Sword of Atagaris *ancillaries outside the main door now.*

Seivarden whispered, "Station, what are those things?"

I don't know what you mean, came the reply, in her vision.

"Those...at first I thought they were suspension pods. But they're not. Are they?"

I really don't know what you mean. Approximately six minutes.

Seivarden knew enough, by now, to understand Station's answer. "Oh, fuck," she said, softly.

Amaat Two, behind her, seeing the same image but not having reached the same conclusion, asked, "What are they?"

"They're fucking AI cores," Seivarden told her. "And Station can't talk about them."

Two and Four stared at her, confused. *Approximately five minutes*, Station said.

"Right," Seivarden said. There was no time to worry about the AI cores. No time to be afraid of three humans facing

four ancillaries in five minutes' time. Seivarden had the Presger gun and there was, in the end, only one condition that
needed to be met, only one truly necessary thing. And they
had planned for this, Seivarden and her Amaats, had hoped
Anaander would have taken over the governor's office, hoped
they would have just such an opportunity. "Time to move."
She reached for the door's manual release, and it obligingly
slid open to reveal the back of a hanging, heavy enough that
it barely trembled as the air currents shifted. Her two Amaats
behind her, she stepped into the room.

There were two dozen explosive charges in the container
Tisarwat and Bo Nine had brought. Tisarwat managed to
attach three of them before half a dozen *Sword of Gurat*
ancillaries came out an airlock after them.

Tisarwat and Nine surrendered immediately, went docile
into the airlock. Stood silent while *Sword of Gurat* stripped
them of their vacuum suits, stripped them to their underwear,
and searched them. Neither of them, of course, had anything dangerous or suspicious. Not counting that container
of charges, at any rate. The ancillaries bound Tisarwat's and
Nine's hands behind them, and then pushed them to kneel
on the corridor floor. Nine frightened but stoic, Tisarwat
light-headed, hyperventilating just a bit. Terrified. And also,
behind that, a tiny bit relieved. Anticipating.

The captain of *Sword of Gurat* arrived. Stared at Tisarwat
and Nine. Examined the explosive charge *Sword of Gurat*'s
ancillary showed her. Looked, then, at Tisarwat. "What
in the name of all that's beneficial were you trying to do?"
Tisarwat said nothing, but her gasping intensified. "These
weren't even armed," the captain of *Sword of Gurat* said.

Tisarwat closed her eyes. "Oh, for the love of Amaat

just shoot me! Please, I beg you. I'm not even supposed to be here." Gasping every few words now, as her breathing escaped her control entirely. "I was supposed to be in Administration, I wasn't supposed to be on any ship at all. But I have to do what she tells me, she's the captain. I have to do what she tells me or she'll kill me." Tears started. She opened those ridiculous lilac-colored eyes, looked pitifully up at the captain of *Sword of Gurat*. "But I can't do it anymore, I couldn't do what she told me, *just shoot me!*"

"Well," said the captain. "A desk pilot. That explains a lot."

Nine's expression had been impassive through all this, but now anxiety showed on her face. "Please, sir, begging the captain's indulgence, these past few weeks have been so awful, and she's just a baby."

"Not a very bright one," said the captain. "Nor steady. Ship, get these two to Medical."

Sword of Gurat grabbed Tisarwat's arm to haul her up. Tisarwat cried out and, "Aatr's tits," swore the captain of *Sword of Gurat*, grimacing in disgust. "She's pissed herself!" And if Tisarwat didn't let up on the breathing, she'd faint in about half a minute. "At least *try* to act like a civilized human being, Lieutenant! Gods greater and lesser! Not even a desk pilot should act like this."

"S...s...sir," gasped Tisarwat. "P...please don't make me go back there. I can't go back to *Mercy of Kalr*, I'd rather die."

"You're not going back to *Mercy of Kalr*, Lieutenant. Ship." This to the waiting ancillaries. "Take Lieutenant..."

"T...Tisarwat," supplied Tisarwat.

"Take Lieutenant Tisarwat to the bath and get her cleaned up. Get some clean clothes on her before you take her to

Medical. Take this other one to Medical now. Get them both disconnected from *Mercy of Kalr*." And then, at another thought, "And *Mercy of Kalr*, if you're watching, I hope you're proud of this."

Two *Sword of Gurat* ancillaries hauled Tisarwat to her feet, and half dragged, half walked her down the corridor. "Nine!" Tisarwat wailed.

"It's all right, Lieutenant," said *Sword of Gurat*'s ancillary. "She's just going to Medical."

Tisarwat, tearful, opened her mouth to reply, but sobbed instead. Collapsed into *Sword of Gurat* Gurat Eleven's arms, clutched its uniform jacket and wept harder.

They were real tears. *Sword of Gurat* could hardly have mistaken false ones. And Nine's cry of concern and struggle to reach Tisarwat were genuine as well. "You'll see her again soon," Gurat Eleven said, just maybe the slightest bit more gently, and guided her off to the bath, where it would be just Tisarwat and *Sword of Gurat*, alone. Which had been the whole point of the exercise, of course.

And Nine found herself escorted toward Medical. The next dangerous moment—the whole plan had been predicated on the assumption that *Sword of Gurat* didn't have a competent interrogator aboard. A Justice almost certainly would have, but interrogators were much rarer on Swords. If *Sword of Gurat* had one, the next step would be drugging Nine, and the game would be up.

Almost as soon as Nine walked into *Sword of Gurat*'s Medical section, her archive data ended, and not long after so did Lieutenant Tisarwat's.

And meanwhile, on Athoek Station, Anaander Mianaai came into the system governor's office. Two *Sword of Atagaris* ancillaries behind her, and behind those, System Governor Giarod and Eminence Ifian. "My lord," Ifian was saying, "of your mercy, I beg to inform... remind my lord that Station Administrator Celar is very popular. Her... her removal would be taken very badly, and not just by the troublesome elements on the station."

That young Anaander didn't reply, but seated herself behind the desk. The two ancillaries stationed themselves in front of it, so that Governor Giarod and Eminence Ifian found themselves at some distance from where the tyrant sat. "And you yourself, Eminence, have no influence with the residents of this station?"

The eminence opened her mouth, and for an instant I wondered if she would admit that not long ago she had staged her own sit-down on the concourse, so that she could hardly speak convincingly in condemnation of this one. But she closed her mouth again. "I had thought, my lord, that I did have some influence here. If my lord wishes, I will try to speak to them."

"*Try?*" asked Anaander, with obvious contempt.

Governor Giarod spoke up. "My lord, they aren't doing any harm where they are. Perhaps we could just... let them sit."

"Not doing any harm *yet*." The tyrant's voice was acid. "Did you just let the ancillary walk onto the station and upend everything? Agitate the station's dregs, suborn the AI?"

"We did question her... it, my lord," Governor Giarod insisted. "But she always had such reasonable answers, and events nearly always seemed to bear her out. And she had orders direct from you, my lord. And your name as well." Behind the desk, Anaander Mianaai did not respond. Did not move. "My lord, perhaps we could... perhaps we could use Fl... the ancillary's methods. Send the soldiers away, let the people sit on the concourse if they like. So long as they're peaceable."

"Do you not understand," Anaander said, "the purpose behind the ancillary's methods? What's happening down there"—she gestured toward the wide window, still covered by that heavy silk hanging—"is a threat. It is this station—and an alarming number of this station's residents—refusing to accept my authority. If I allow them to do *this*, then what will they do next?"

"My lord," offered Governor Giarod, "what if you were to treat this as though it were a refusal of *my* authority? You could say that *I* gave the order for the curfew, and the soldiers, and even—though it *was* Celar's fault—even the transportation orders. And I would resign, and then, my lord, you would be the one responsible for restoring propriety."

Anaander laughed, tense and bitter, and Giarod and Ifian flinched. "I'm glad to see, Governor, that after all your brain isn't a *complete* waste of organic material. Believe me, if I thought that would do the least bit of good I'd have done it by now. And maybe if you hadn't let a half-crazed ancillary run you in circles for a month, maybe if you hadn't let that ancillary *escape*, and somehow manage to destroy *two* of the ships I brought with me, including a fucking *troop carrier* that would have been *very helpful* right now, and maybe if your gods-cursed passenger shuttles would *run on time* like they do everywhere else in Radch space, and maybe if your station was not obviously in the power of an *enemy of the Radch*, then yes, maybe it would do some good."

Two ships. Destroyed. No wonder this Anaander was frightened. And, at a guess, exhausted. Angry and frustrated, not used to being in just one body, cut off from Tstur Palace.

Anaander continued. "No, what I need is to regain control of Station." She stopped. Blinked. "Tisarwat?" Looked at Governor Giarod and Eminence Ifian. "That's a familiar name. You said the ancillary brought a Lieutenant Tisarwat to the station."

"Yes, my lord." Giarod and Ifian, more or less in unison.

"A Lieutenant Tisarwat was just caught trying to plant explosive charges on *Sword of Gurat*'s hull. None of which were armed. She was captured immediately. And she is..." Anaander blinked at something in her vision. "Not exactly the sharpest knife in the set, is she."

It was Giarod and Ifian's turn to blink, trying, I supposed, to reconcile that description with the Tisarwat they themselves had met. I thought for a moment Ifian would say something, but she didn't. More to the point, and very interestingly, *Sword of Atagaris* said nothing. "Oh, get out of here," Anaander said, irritably.

Governor Giarod and Eminence Ifian bowed, deeply, and left so quickly as to be barely proper. When they were gone, Anaander put her head on her wrists, hands outstretched, her elbows on the desk. "I need to sleep," she said, to no one in particular, it seemed. Maybe to the two *Sword of Atagaris* ancillaries. "I need to sleep, and I need to eat, and I need..." She trailed off. "Why can't I just get a couple hours' sleep without some kind of crisis appearing?" If she was talking to *Sword of Atagaris*, it didn't answer.

Seivarden, behind the hanging, heard this with a sudden dismaying, disorienting sense of wrongness. She had known all this time what we had been doing here at Athoek, had defied Anaander herself, when we had been at Omaugh Palace. But Anaander Mianaai was still the only ruler of the

Radch Seivarden had ever known, and neither she nor any other Radchaai had ever expected even the possibility that things might be different. And on top of that, here this Anaander was, alone and tired and frustrated. As though she were just an ordinary person. But Seivarden had enough experience to know that stopping to think too long about it would be fatal. She signaled her Amaats to move.

Amaat Two and Amaat Four, armor up, guns leveled, came out from behind the hanging first, one to each side of where Anaander sat behind the desk. Instantly each *Sword of Atagaris* ancillary drew its weapon and turned to fire at an Amaat, and two more ancillaries came swiftly into the room, guns raised.

Seivarden had positioned herself opposite Anaander, so that when the ancillaries were distracted, she might have a clear shot at the tyrant. But Seivarden was not ancillary-fast, and lifting the hanging slowed her even more, just the smallest bit, but enough for one of *Sword of Atagaris* to put itself between Seivarden and Anaander, just as Seivarden fired. It dropped, and before Seivarden could fire again, the other ancillary charged into her, shoving her backward so that they both fell against the hanging.

Behind the hanging was that wide window overlooking the concourse. Of course it was not easily breakable, but *Sword of Atagaris*'s impact had been fast and forceful. When Seivarden and *Sword of Atagaris* fell against it, the window popped free of its housing and fell toward the floor of the concourse, some six meters below. Seivarden and *Sword of Atagaris* followed.

The citizens below scrambled back out of the way, some shouting in alarm. The glass slammed into the ground, a loud and sharp report, and Seivarden hit the glass, on her back, *Sword of Atagaris* on top of her, the Presger gun in its grip that it had wrested from Seivarden on the way down.

The pop of gunfire, and more screams, and then, painfully loud, an alarm sounded. Bright-red stripes suddenly glowed to life on the scuffed white of the concourse floor, each of them four meters from the next. "Hull breach," announced Station. "Clear all section doors immediately."

At the sound of that alarm, every single person on the concourse—including *Sword of Atagaris*, and Seivarden, who hadn't had even an instant to recover from her six-meter drop—immediately, unthinkingly, rolled or stepped or crawled away from those glowing red lines, and the concourse section doors came flashing down, crunching into the rectangle of window glass where it was in the way.

For a moment everyone in that section of the concourse was silent, stunned. Then someone began to whimper. "Who's hurt?" asked Seivarden. On her hands and knees, quite possibly not aware of how she'd gotten there, the back of her armor still warm from absorbing the force of hitting the floor.

"Don't move, Lieutenant." *Sword of Atagaris*, the Presger gun aimed at Seivarden.

"Someone might be hurt," Seivarden said, looking up at the ancillary. She dropped her armor. "Do you have a medkit this time, or are you still a miserable excuse for a soldier?" Raised her voice. "Is anybody hurt?" And then to *Sword of Atagaris*, who had not moved, "Come on, Ship, you know I'm not going anywhere with the section doors down like this."

"I have a medkit," replied *Sword of Atagaris*.

"So do I. Give me yours." And as *Sword of Atagaris* tossed

the medkit to the ground in front of her, "Aatr's tits, what's wrong with you?" She took both kits and went to see to the injured.

Fortunately there appeared to be only one severe injury, a person whose leg had been caught by the falling slab of glass. Seivarden medkitted her, and when she found only bruises and sprains among the other nine people trapped in the section, she tossed the remaining medkit at *Sword of Atagaris*'s feet. "I know you have to do what the Lord of the Radch tells you to." Seivarden didn't know that Tisarwat had made *Sword of Atagaris* as much of a free agent as possible. "But didn't the fleet captain give you back your precious officers? That ought to count for something."

"It would," said *Sword of Atagaris*, voice flat. "If it hadn't taken me an entire day to get my ancillaries thawed and bring my engines back online. *Sword of Gurat* got to them before me, and the Lord of the Radch decided they would be more useful to her in suspension."

"Hah!" Seivarden was bitterly amused. "I don't doubt it. I'm sure Hetnys is a much better tea table than she ever was a captain."

"I can't imagine why I don't feel more friendly toward you," said *Sword of Atagaris*, retrieving the medkit without for a moment losing its focus on Seivarden.

"Sorry." Seivarden sat down on the glass. Crossed her legs. "I'm sorry, Ship. That was uncalled for."

"What?" Impassive, but, I thought, taken aback.

"I shouldn't've…that wasn't right. I don't like Captain Hetnys, and you know that, but there's no reason for me to be insulting her. At a time like this. Especially to you." Silence. *Sword of Atagaris* still pointing the Presger gun at Seivarden, sitting cross-legged on the ground. "I have to admit, I don't understand why the Lord of Mianaai wouldn't give you back your captain."

"She doesn't trust me," *Sword of Atagaris* said. "I was too easily and too completely controlled by *Justice of Toren*. Seeing that, the Lord of Mianaai decided to keep the same control herself—I am told that if anything at all happens to the Lord of the Radch, all of my officers will be killed. She has them aboard *Sword of Gurat*. For safekeeping, she says. A *Sword of Gurat* lieutenant is in temporary command of me for the moment."

"I'm sorry," said Seivarden. And then, realizing, "Wait, what is she so afraid of? She trusts *Sword of Gurat* to kill Captain Hetnys if something happens to her, but she doesn't trust it to guard her?"

"I neither know nor care," said *Sword of Atagaris*. "But I am not going to see Captain Hetnys killed."

"No," said Seivarden. "No, of course not."

Above, in the governor's office, Amaat Two and Amaat Four lay facedown, still armored but disarmed, terrified, hands bound behind their backs. Before *Sword of Atagaris* had pinned them, they had seen the ancillary Seivarden had shot lying in the middle of the room. Amaat Two had managed to fire once at Anaander, but had not seen the results of her shot. Both Amaats had heard the section doors come down, closing the room off until Station canceled the hull breach alert. Or until someone managed to cut through the section doors, not an easy thing to do.

"You're wounded, my lord." An unfamiliar voice, in the ears of Seivarden's two Amaats, but obviously an ancillary's. *Sword of Atagaris.*

"It's nothing. The bullet went right through my arm."

Anaander Mianaai, her voice tense with pain. "How the fuck did that happen, *Sword of Atagaris*?"

"I would guess, my lord...," began *Sword of Atagaris*.

"No, let *me* guess. You'd never seen that door opened. Couldn't open it even when you asked Station to unlock it. The entrances to that back access are all themselves locked. By Station. I myself foolishly trusted what I thought was my control over Station."

A tearing sound. "If you would be so good as to let me remove your jacket, my lord."

Despite—perhaps because of—her terror, the beginning of a laugh escaped Amaat Four as she recognized the sound of a medkit being opened. Two said, very softly, "Oh, you're carrying medkits *now*."

"There are several ways I could kill you." The voice of another ancillary, closer to the two Amaats than the one talking to the Lord of the Radch. Very quiet. "Armored or not."

"Station!" Anaander, either ignoring the exchange or not hearing it. "No more games. Do you hear me?"

Silence, for three seconds, and then Station said, "I was happy enough to go along, until you threatened my residents."

Down on the concourse, standing on the remaining section of office window, *Sword of Atagaris* said, gun still pointed at Seivarden, "Station is done playing stupid, it seems."

"I wasn't the one making a threat, Station!" Anaander's voice was incredulous, and angry. "I was trying to keep your residents safe. Trying to keep things calm and under control here, after the ancillary had stirred up so much trouble. And then." A pause. Probably she gestured, but all the Amaats could see was the brown, gold-flecked tiles of the floor. "All this. What do you expect me to do, just let a mob take over the concourse?"

"It's not a mob," replied Station. "It's a complaint. Citizens do have the right to complain to Administration." Silence. Then Station said, "Fleet Captain Breq would have understood."

"Ah." Anaander. "So it comes out. But it's not the ancillary controlling you. There are no circumstances under which my enemy would give it that ability. So who is it? And is she still here? Could she unlock your Central Access, maybe?"

"No one can unlock my Central Access," said Station. "You'll have to keep trying to cut through."

"It would be easier to destroy the whole station and build again," said Anaander. "In fact, the more I think of it the better I like that idea."

"You won't," said Station. "You might as well surrender to the fleet captain. I have no intention of letting you leave that room, you'll have killed the only instance of yourself in the system. Which is an interesting thought. In fact, the more I think of it, the better I like that idea. I'd only need to trigger the fire-suppression systems in the governor's office."

"You already would have if you could," replied Anaander. "Maybe if you were a ship. But you're not. You can't bring yourself to deliberately kill anyone. I on the other hand have no such compunction."

"I'm sure all the citizens downwell will be interested to hear that. Or the outstations."

"Oh, are we on the news again?" Anaander's voice was bitter.

"We can be, if you like." Station, calm and serene.

"So that wasn't involuntary, as you claimed. And it didn't stop because I'd hit on the right access."

"No," replied Station. "I lied about that."

Down on the concourse, still boxed in by the section

doors, Seivarden hadn't understood what *Sword of Atagaris* had meant, about Station no longer playing stupid. She said to *Sword of Atagaris*, "So what's the story with those AI cores?"

"I'd expect you to know better than I would," said *Sword of Atagaris*. "Isn't that what you came here for? Isn't that why *Justice of Toren* went straight to the Undergarden nearly the moment she got here?"

"No," replied Seivarden. "Is that where they were?" And then, at a thought, "Is that why you were so... *enthusiastic* about running security in the Undergarden?"

"No."

"Well then, whose are they?" *Sword of Atagaris* didn't answer. "Aatr's tits, there isn't a third one of her, is there?"

"I neither know nor care," replied *Sword of Atagaris*.

"And what is this one going to do with them? Build ships? That takes months—no, it takes years."

"Not if the ship is already built," *Sword of Atagaris* pointed out.

Above, in the governor's office, Anaander was saying, "So we're at an impasse."

"Perhaps not," said Station. Amaat Two and Amaat Four still lay facedown on the brown-and-gold tiles, still listening. "If I understand Fleet Captain Breq correctly, your argument isn't with me or any of my residents—it's with yourself. It's none of my business. It only becomes my business when you threaten my residents' safety."

"What are you suggesting, Station?" Wary, with an undertone of anger.

"You have no reason to concern yourself with the running of this station. Those matters are more properly handled by me and by Station Administrator Celar." Silence. "As for

Sword of Gurat and *Sword of Atagaris*, they're not welcome here. I do understand *Sword of Gurat* needs repairs and supplies, and that its officers might want leave occasionally, and that an officer is nearly always accompanied by an ancillary at such times, but I will not have whole decades interfering with my operations, or harassing my residents."

"And what do I get in exchange for these concessions?"

"You get to live," said Station. "You get to remain in this system. You get the *Sword of Gurat* decades back that are at the moment trapped until I see fit to raise the section doors. And you get a place where your ships can purchase supplies."

"Purchase!"

"Purchase," repeated Station. "I can't afford to assume that I or my residents will receive any sort of benefit from the provincial palace, not for the foreseeable future. Not considering the circumstances. And I can't afford to let you drain all this system's resources and give nothing in exchange. Particularly when providing you with supplies and services potentially makes me a target for your enemies." Silence. "As a show of my good faith, I will decline to charge you for the removal of the five dead *Sword of Gurat* ancillaries that were attempting to cut into my Central Access. You needn't worry about their officer, she was away using the bath when the section doors went down."

"I get your point, Station," said Anaander. "Fine. We can deal."

15

Coming into the governor's office, *Sword of Atagaris* close behind her, the first thing Seivarden noticed was her two Amaats, facedown on the floor, hands bound. Their armor still raised, and so she knew they were still alive. Was relieved, but in a distracted way, because the next thing she saw was Anaander Mianaai standing grim-faced behind the desk. Shirtless, a corrective around her upper arm.

Anaander's expression changed to sardonic surprise. "Seivarden Vendaai." Voices sounded, rising from the concourse below to that now-glassless window, medics calling instructions to each other, someone sobbing.

"That's *Lieutenant Seivarden* to you," said Seivarden, managing to sound braver than she felt. Now all the action was past, she was nearing collapse. The *Sword of Atagaris* ancillary behind her went to the desk and laid down the Presger gun. Stepped away.

Anaander looked down. Watched the gun turn the same pale yellow as the desk surface. All expression left her face.

Despair overwhelmed Seivarden, that adrenaline and

urgent necessity had kept at bay since she'd fallen out the window. She knew me well enough to know that I had not been joking when I had said I would probably not live long enough to forgive her if she lost the gun. Knew what it meant, that Anaander Mianaai now had it.

Anaander picked up the gun. Brushed gloved fingers across it so that it became not the color of whatever it touched, but a plain dark gray. Examined it. "This," she said, "is very interesting." Seivarden said nothing. Anaander continued, "To my knowledge there are only twenty-four of these, and every last one is accounted for. In fact, each one of them is marked with an identifying number, but this one"—she paused—"is not." She looked at Seivarden. "Where did you get it?"

"Twenty-five," Seivarden said.

"Excuse me?"

"Twenty-five. Everything on Garsedd was fives. Five principal sins, five right actions, five social classes, five capital crimes. Probably five kinds of farts." Anaander raised one dark eyebrow at that. "If you didn't go looking for that twenty-fifth gun you've got only yourself to blame."

"I did look," Anaander said. "I have trouble believing that you found it when I didn't." Seivarden made a gesture of unconcern, deliberately insolent, though she did not feel as brave as the action implied. "Where did you get this?"

"Fleet Captain gave it to me."

"So now we come to it," said Anaander. Tense and intent. "Who is controlling the ancillary?"

"That would be *Justice of Toren* to you," said Seivarden, her voice far more even than her emotions, "if you honestly can't bring yourself to acknowledge her proper rank. And you're lucky I didn't laugh in your face just now when you suggested that anyone might be controlling her but herself."

"You know as well as I do that ancillaries don't control themselves. Not even ships control themselves." She gave Seivarden an appraising glance. "Well, Lieutenant, I think you and I will be continuing this conversation aboard *Sword of Gurat*."

"Oh, no." Station's voice, from the office console. "No, Lord of Mianaai, I'm afraid you won't be. Perhaps you didn't understand the implications of our recent discussion. Perhaps I should have been more explicit. If you leave here I will have no means by which to enforce the terms of our agreement. No, you'll be staying right here. With a few servants if you like, and I'm even willing to allow *Sword of Atagaris* to act in that capacity. Which is very generous of me, honestly. The governor's residence is very comfortable, I assure you, and you have no reason to go anywhere else. And as for Lieutenant Seivarden, I'm afraid I must insist that my own security force take her into custody."

"This has nothing to do with you, Station," said Anaander. "Seivarden Vendaai is not one of your residents, but she *is* a member of the Radchaai military, of which I am the supreme commander."

"She is a member of *a* Radchaai military," Station said. "You yourself appear to be under the impression that her commanding officer—that would be Fleet Captain Breq—is not working for you, but for some enemy of yours. The fact that that enemy is quite possibly some other iteration of you is not my concern. And whatever military she might belong to, I have no agreements with anyone granting immunity to members of military forces who cause damage or commit other offenses while they're here. I'm afraid Station Security must place the lieutenant—and her two subordinates—under arrest until we can evaluate her actions."

Three seconds of silence. *Sword of Atagaris* stood stiff and impassive, three of it, around the Lord of the Radch. Amaat Two and Amaat Four lay rigid, eyes closed, breathing carefully, listening intently. Finally Anaander said, "Don't push me, Station. Or whoever is giving you instructions."

"You would do well to take your own advice, Lord of Mianaai," said Station. "I won't be pushed, either." A quick, brief breeze as the section doors slammed back down, over the two doors, over the window, the sound from the concourse suddenly cut off. The air in the office suddenly still.

"If you empty the air out of this room," Anaander pointed out, "you'll also kill Seivarden. And her two subordinates." That last just the least bit mocking.

"They're nothing to me," said Station. "They aren't my residents."

An expression flashed across Anaander's face. Fear, maybe. Or possibly anger. "All right, Station. But we'll be discussing this further."

"If you like," said Station, bland as always.

Seivarden and her two Amaats spent six hours in a cell in Security. At some point someone had brought them bowls of skel, and water to drink, but Seivarden had been unable to so much as taste hers. By the time the door finally opened, Amaat Two and Amaat Four had fallen into an uneasy, exhausted sleep, propped up against the wall, and each other. "Lieutenant," said a Security officer from the corridor. "If you would be so good as to come with me."

Seivarden said nothing. Pushed herself to standing. Amaat Four half woke. Muttered, "What?"

"Nothing, Four, go back to sleep," said Seivarden, and stepped into the corridor.

Allowed herself to be led to the office of the head of Security. Which was, it turned out, occupied by Citizen Lusulun. Who rose and smiled at Seivarden's entrance, though the smile didn't quite make it to the rest of her face, and bowed. "Lieutenant. Seivarden, I understand? Fleet Captain Breq mentioned you. I'm Head of Security Lusulun."

Seivarden stared at her, uncomprehending, for just a moment. Then bowed herself. "An honor, sir. To make your acquaintance, and to be mentioned by the fleet captain."

"Sit, Lieutenant," said once-again Head of Security Lusulun. "Will you have tea?"

"I'd rather stand."

"I apologize," Head of Security Lusulun said, still standing, apparently unsurprised at Seivarden's demeanor, "for the delay in my speaking to you. Things have been...a bit chaotic. The current situation is..." Lusulun took a breath. Considered a moment what sort of description might suit, and seemed to come up short. "Well. We've been a bit disorganized. I've only been back in office for the last fifteen or twenty minutes. At any rate, it's been determined that you're not responsible for the damage on the concourse. And by the way Medical would like to thank you for your assistance with the citizen who you helped, who was injured."

"No thanks necessary," Seivarden said, quite automatically.

"All the same. So, you and your soldiers are free to go. There was some difficulty about food and housing assignments, since you aren't station residents. But it happens that the Undergarden needs a great deal of work just now—more even than when the fleet captain was here. Some of it needs to be done in vacuum, which I imagine you've got some experience with, yes?"

"Yes," said Seivarden, and then frowned. "What?"

"Level one of the Undergarden was breached when the

dome over the Gardens was damaged again the other day," explained Lusulun. "There are a number of repairs that need to be made before that area can be re-pressurized. We're assuming you've got experience working in vacuum."

"I...yes."

"Right," said Lusulun, noticing Seivarden's near-stupor but forging on ahead. "The fleet captain did have a housing assignment, but I'm afraid it wasn't luxurious. You're welcome to use it, though. And sometime soon I do hope you'll join me for tea. I'd be honored if you would."

Seivarden stared stupidly and then said, "I...thank you. Very kind of you, sir."

The crates and boxes were where we had left them, sectioning off a corridor end. Seivarden sank down in the back corner, arms around her legs, head on her knees, while Two and Four went through the crates to see what we'd left behind. "Oh!" exclaimed Four, opening one. "Tea!" It was a packet of Daughter of Fishes. My Kalrs had known I wouldn't care what happened to it. "Now we'll be all right."

"I haven't found anything to make it with yet," said Two.

"Hah!" exclaimed Four. "You don't really think Kalr was going to leave any dishes behind, do you? I'll see about getting us a flask." And then, opening the next box, "Oh!"

Two came over to see what she'd found. "Aatr's tits!" She looked over at Seivarden, who was still curled up against the wall. Looked back at Four. "That's a dozen bottles of the fleet captain's arrack." Watching out of the corner of her eye for some reaction from Seivarden, but there was none. "We could trade a bottle for a tea set, easy. And probably a few other things. Fleet Captain wouldn't mind. Would she?"

"She would not," agreed Four. "She would want us to have

tea. Don't you think, sir?" Looked over at Seivarden. Who did not move or make a sound. Four turned back to Two, trying to pretend she had not just felt that sickening, sinking feeling of dismay at seeing Seivarden unresponsive. She took a bottle out of the box. "I'll see to it. And I'll get us something to eat, too." And then, a trifle louder, her voice aimed at Seivarden, added, "You just get some rest, sir." But did not leave, because someone neither Two nor Four recognized was approaching the crate enclosure. Stopped at the perimeter. The Amaats weren't sure whether to be reassured by how young she was, or how well-dressed. Or the shy familiarity with which she walked right up to the improvised entrance.

"Citizens." She bowed. "I'm Uran. You are..." She frowned, looking at the insignia on the soldiers' rumpled and by-now-dirty uniforms. "*Mercy of Kalr* Amaat."

"Oh! Citizen Uran!" Two bowed with a discomfited rush of surprise. Did not look over at Seivarden, who still sat against the wall, who should have made herself available to handle this sort of potentially socially awkward moment. "Our apologies. Of course this is your home, we hadn't even thought, things have been...hectic." Noticed then that Uran held her right arm at an oddly stiff angle. "Were you hurt?"

"Only a broken wrist, citizen," Uran replied. "I was just coming from Medical and I heard you were here." She waved away whatever Two had been about to say with her uninjured hand. "I've been staying with friends, but I heard you were here and came to see if you needed anything. The Rad...the fleet captain left some things, there's plenty of bedding and there's some tea." Two saw Uran's gaze flick away, over Two's shoulder, to where Seivarden sat, and then back to Two. "I don't think there are any dishes, though. Also, Horticulturist Basnaaid means to call on you when she can."

"That's very good of her," replied Two. "And we're grateful for your assistance. In fact." She looked over at Four, still holding that bottle of arrack. "Maybe you can show us where we can make some trades. You're right, we haven't found any dishes so far, and we're in particular need of a tea set just now." Wanted to turn her head to look at Seivarden. Managed not to.

Uran's eyes grew wide. "That will get you lots more than a tea set, and besides, that's the fleet captain's arrack! Please, my allowance is generous. Let me bring you what you need and it will be"—she frowned, looking, probably, for an equivalent of a Delsig phrase—"it will be a word between cousins." Winced at Two's expression of puzzled surprise. "I express myself badly. Radchaai is not my first language."

"You express yourself perfectly, citizen," said Two. "And thank you." She looked over at Four.

"I'll stay with the lieutenant," said Four, and put the bottle back in its crate.

An hour later Two had come back, with dishes and utensils, water and refectory rations for the three of them, and most importantly a tea flask and bowls. When the tea was ready, Four brought a bowl over to Seivarden, who had not moved. Crouched beside her. "Sir. Lieutenant Seivarden, sir, here's tea." No response. "Sir." Still nothing. Gently Four reached out and smoothed Seivarden's hair back with one free, gloved hand. "Sir." Allowing her dismay and fear just the smallest bit into her voice. "Sir, I know it's hard, but we need you." They didn't, strictly speaking. Two and Four were perfectly capable of taking care of themselves. Though not, perhaps, if they also had to take constant care of Seivarden. "We need to know what to do next."

"It doesn't matter what we do next." Seivarden, still curled in on herself.

"It'll seem better when we've had some tea, sir," said Four, still holding out that now-cooling bowl.

"Tea?" Seivarden didn't look up, but the muscles in her neck and shoulders tensed, as though she was considering it.

"Yes, sir. And there's breakfast, and we've found some nice, comfortable bedding, and we don't have work until tomorrow morning. We can relax for the rest of the day, but we need you, sir, we need you to sit up and drink some tea."

Seivarden looked up, saw Four squatting beside her, bowl of tea in her hand, her face the nearest thing to absolutely impassive. Probably only someone who knew Four well would realize that she was near tears, and small wonder if she was. Both Two and Four had been as obviously near death as either of them had ever been in their lives, just hours ago. They had failed in their mission, one they knew well enough everything had depended on. Even the next few minutes seemed uncertain, filled with pitfalls. Seivarden, with no apparent awareness of this, asked, bewildered, "You need me to drink tea?"

"Yes, sir." Four, not quite daring to be relieved.

"Yes, sir," agreed Two, pulling blankets out of a crate. "We surely do need you to do exactly that."

Seivarden blinked. Exhaled, short and sharp. Unwrapped her arms from around her legs, took the tea from Amaat Two, and drank.

"Work" was putting on vacuum suits and going through a hastily erected temporary airlock into a now-airless level one of the Undergarden. Looking for structural damage, which neither Seivarden nor her Amaats were qualified to do, but they could all three of them apply patches where a supervisor told them to, or carry things. It wasn't terribly interesting

257

work, but it was demanding enough to mostly keep their minds off of problems they couldn't solve.

Or at least, Seivarden had likely imagined it was. On the second day, another vacuum-suited citizen leaned her faceplate against Seivarden's and said, tersely questioning, "Rough day, eh?"

The question seemed innocent enough, but hearing it struck Seivarden with a sudden, sharp sense of recognition, and then fierce wanting. And a wash of shame, and nauseated regret. She might have said any of a dozen things—*Not really* or even just a flat *Go away*. Instead she said, "I have a shunt."

"Oh," said that other citizen, not at all taken aback. "That'll cost a bit extra, then. But you know—I can see that you know—you know how nicely a bit of detachment takes the edge off, when you're having a rough day."

"Go away," said Seivarden, finally. Not very relieved to have said it. Still sick to her stomach.

"Fine, fine." And the citizen lifted her faceplate from Seivarden's, and went back to sealing her bit of corridor.

Seivarden didn't go back to her own patching, but left work, without reporting to the crew supervisor.

She woke up in Medical. Lay looking at the ceiling for a few minutes, not even wondering how she'd gotten there. Feeling oddly rested and calm. Then a memory must have struck her, because she winced, closed her eyes, laid an arm over her face. "Well, good morning, Lieutenant." The voice cheerful. Seivarden didn't move her arm to see who was speaking. "That was an exciting evening you had last night, though fortunately enough for you, you weren't conscious for most of it. I'm impressed you managed to get down nearly two bottles of arrack before you passed out. That much, drunk that fast, can be enough to kill someone. We were all in a good deal of suspense." Still quite cheerful. Breezy, even, not a trace of sarcasm.

"Go away," said Seivarden, not moving her arm.

"If we were aboard your ship, I'm sure I'd have to do that," the voice continued, now cheerfully apologetic. "But we're not, we're in Station Medical, which means I'm in charge. So do you feel like you could eat something? Your soldiers are outside—they're asleep right now, actually, but they've asked to see you as soon as you wake. You might want something to eat first, and actually you and I should discuss some things."

"Like what?"

"Like that kef shunt. I don't generally recommend their use. They're too easy to circumvent and they don't really solve the problem. Ah, I see whoever worked on you did try to supplement with other methods." Likely in response to Seivarden's growing nausea, on the doctor's mentioning the shunt. Though that nausea was distant—blunted. Meds, no doubt. "But I'll tell you the truth, Lieutenant, once you take the kef you don't really care if you puke your guts out. That's kind of the whole point. Maybe you've already discovered that? No? Well. Whoever installed your shunt and did that other work probably wasn't any sort of specialist. Ship's medic, yes? All respect to ship's medics, they've got to be good at a lot of different things, and sometimes they have to do those things under a great deal of pressure. But this isn't an area they're generally up on. Still, in the end it probably doesn't matter that much. Really, the only thing that has much chance of working is to develop the kind of habits that keep you away from it. Assuming you *want* to be away from it."

"I do." Seivarden lowered her arm. Opened her eyes, looked at the doctor's thin, cheerful face. "I've been away from it. Until now. I was going to sell the arrack. I knew I'd get more than enough for…for what I wanted, but then I thought, no, it's Breq's. And then I thought, damn it, I need a drink."

"Doubtless you did," agreed the doctor. "Drinking yourself insensible so you don't go back to kef may not be a particularly *good* idea, but it does show a certain admirable determination." Seivarden didn't reply. "I'm authorizing a day off work for you today, and I'm sending you home with a one-day self-determine for tomorrow. Which is to say, if you feel like you want to go back to work tomorrow, you're cleared to, but if you'd rather stay home another day, you can do that, with no reprimand or loss of wages."

Seivarden closed her eyes. "Thank you, Doctor."

"You're welcome. And try not to be too hard on yourself. I imagine everyone on the station wishes they could knock themselves insensible right now, and wake up with everything back the way it should be. Oh, and next time you feel like getting hammered, message me. That was some damn good stuff you puked all over yourself, I think it's only fair I should get some, too. That hasn't already been through you, I mean."

Seivarden slept all that day. The next morning she spent alone in the crate-bounded corridor end. Two and Four, not having been ill, didn't have self-determines from Medical and went to work.

For a while Seivarden sat on the ground, staring at the crates. Not moving, although she'd told her two Amaats that she felt much better, and would take the opportunity to call on Head of Security Lusulun, and Station Administrator Celar. They would not have left her alone if she hadn't given them such assurances, if she hadn't been bathed and dressed in her now-clean uniform before they went to work. Which Seivarden knew well enough. But now she was alone, she found herself unwilling to stand. "Maybe I'll just go back to bed," she said at length, aloud.

Station said in her ear, "That would be very awkward, Lieutenant."

Seivarden blinked. Looked up, saw Horticulturist Basnaaid standing on the other side of the crates. "You seemed to be thinking so hard," Basnaaid said, with a smile. "I didn't want to interrupt you."

Seivarden sprang to her feet. "Horticulturist! It's not an interruption, I wasn't actually thinking about anything. Please, come in. Will you have some tea?" Four had made sure the flask was full before she'd gone to work. "This is really ridiculous, inviting you into a pile of boxes."

"I would have loved it when I was little," said Basnaaid, coming in. "I'd love some tea, thank you. Here, I brought you some cakes. I didn't know if the fleet captain had left anything edible."

"We've been getting by." Seivarden managed to look as though the issue of what had been left behind didn't trouble her. "Just. This is very welcome, and very kind of you, thank you." She poured tea, and they sat on the ground.

After a few sips, Seivarden said, "I noticed you were on the concourse the other day. You weren't injured?"

"Some bruises." She gestured their unimportance. "You were the one who fell out that window."

"Oh, did you notice that?" Seivarden asked, lightly, almost as though she were her old self again. "Yes, that was exciting." A surge of guilt, then, and despair, which she managed to keep off her face. "I was armored. And I hit flat on my back, so I'm fine."

Something must have showed on her face then, because Basnaaid said, "Are you sure?"

For a moment Seivarden looked at her. And then, unable to

help herself, she said, "No. No, I'm not fine." Was silent then, as she struggled for control over herself. Succeeded, finally, only a few tears to wipe away. "I fucked up. And it wasn't... I mean, there are fuck-ups and then there are fuck-ups. Sorry. Mess-ups."

"I've heard people swear before, Lieutenant. I've even done it myself." Seivarden tried to smile. Nearly managed it. "I heard," Basnaaid continued, "that you were in Medical the other night."

"Oh," Seivarden said. "Somebody thought I needed looking after."

"No, but now I'm wondering if Station wouldn't have suggested I visit you, if I hadn't already been on my way."

"Station! I'm nothing to Station." Remembered the tea in her hand. Took a drink while Basnaaid watched, puzzled. Worried-looking. "Sorry. I'm sorry. I just...I don't know what's wrong with me." She considered taking another drink of tea, but couldn't quite manage it. "Actually, Station was kind of amazing. I've always...you know, when you spend a lot of time with ships, you start to think of stations as kind of...I don't know, kind of weak. But it threatened to suck all the air out of the room if the Lord of Mianaai didn't agree to its terms. It's holding her captive in the governor's residence. Here I am going, *Oh, stations are weak* but Station was a fucking badass. I was having trouble believing it was Station talking."

"I had to do something, Lieutenant." Station, in Seivarden's ear, and Basnaaid's. "You're right, it's not the sort of thing I'm used to doing. I tried to imagine what Fleet Captain Breq would do."

"I think you hit your target, Station," said Seivarden. "I think the fleet captain would be...she'll be pretty impressed when she hears."

"Is the fleet captain…" Basnaaid. Hopeful. Hesitant. "Is she coming back?"

"I don't know," replied Seivarden. "She very deliberately didn't tell me what her plans were. Didn't tell me what T… didn't tell me anything. In case. You know. Because actually, my chances of doing what I came here to do were pretty fucking slim." Tisarwat's chances were slimmer, but Seivarden didn't know that. She swallowed, hard. Set down her bowl of tea. "I let her down. I let Breq down, and everything was depending on it, and she's never let *me* down, not even when I thought she had. The things she's done, the most terrifying, dangerous things and hardly blinking, and me, I can't even get from one minute to the next of just *living*. Wait." Tears welled. "Wait, no, that's not right. I'm feeling sorry for myself again."

"I don't think much of anyone could stand comparison with the fleet captain," remarked Basnaaid. "Not that way, anyway."

"Your sister, maybe."

"In some ways, maybe," agreed Basnaaid. "Lieutenant, when did you eat last?"

"I had breakfast?" Seivarden replied, doubtfully. "Maybe? A little?" Looked over at the almost-full dish of skel Two had set out for her. "A little."

"Why don't you wash your face and we'll go get something to eat? Places are opening up again, I'm sure we could find something good."

"I promised my Amaats I'd go see the head of Security, and the station administrator. Although the more I think about it, the more I think it would be best not to look like I'm interfering in station business." She hesitated. Suppressed a frown. "I definitely need to appeal my assignment."

"All right," Basnaaid said, "but trust me, you want to eat something first."

16

They found a shop in a side corridor, open, serving not much more than noodles and tea. "Thank you, Horticulturist," Seivarden said to Basnaaid, sitting across from her, when she'd finished her lunch. "I didn't realize how badly I needed that." She unquestionably felt a good deal better than before she'd eaten.

Basnaaid smiled. "My life always seems hopeless when it's been too long since I've eaten."

"No doubt. In my case, though, all my problems are still there. I suppose I'll just have to find some way to deal with whatever happens next." And then, remembering, "But what about you? Are you safe? It seems like nobody's told... nobody's told the Lord of Mianaai about you, or about Citizen Uran. Which means they haven't told her everything that happened with Captain Hetnys. In fact, from what I've seen, people I'd have expected to have plenty of motivation to tell her, not to mention clear opportunities, seem to have actively avoided it."

Basnaaid ate the last of her own noodles, set her utensil

down. "You've been doing work in the Undergarden?" Seivarden gestured acknowledgment. "Level one wasn't depressurized when you left. That didn't happen until the Lord of the Radch arrived here herself." Seivarden frowned. Basnaaid continued, "It hasn't been on the news, of course, partly because up until a day or two ago the news was all about the fleet captain, but when *Sword of Gurat* gated up to the station, it wasn't paying attention to where the passenger shuttle was."

"What?" Seivarden was, apparently, beyond even swearing.

"*Sword of Gurat* came out of its gate and hit the passenger shuttle. Knocked it into the dome over the Gardens, and that broke the patch over the hole you cut, to pull us out, that day. The repairs to the lake bed weren't finished, and level one of the Undergarden depressurized, too. Fortunately enough, the people working in the Gardens at the time were able to get clear, and of course the Undergarden had been evacuated days ago. But the shuttle...well, it's not been on the news, of course, so I mostly only hear rumors, but I know for a fact that there are at least two very prominent families in mourning right now. And one of those for a grandmother, a mother, *and* a daughter."

"Varden's suppurating cuticles," said Seivarden.

"Lieutenant, I don't think I've ever heard anyone say that outside a historical drama."

"They say that in *historical dramas*?" Seivarden seemed nearly as shocked by that as by the shuttle disaster Basnaaid had just told her about.

"It makes you sound like the dashing hero of an entertainment."

"The *heroes* say that in historical dramas? What is the world coming to?"

Basnaaid opened her mouth to say something, but apparently found herself at a loss. Closed her mouth again.

"Well," said Seivarden, and then, "Well. No wonder the tyrant was so frightened and angry. There's already some doubt about loyalties, about who supports who, who the Lord of Mianaai can trust or who the fleet captain may have suborned. Then the ship bringing Mianaai ravages the famous Gardens yet again, in the process killing who knows how many shuttle passengers, among them members of the system's wealthy and prominent families. And *then* she finds the less elevated citizens already protesting on the concourse. So very gently, so very properly, but still."

"Nobody wanted to talk to her about the Gardens. Or the Undergarden," Basnaaid agreed. "That would be my guess, anyway. At any rate, she fairly obviously wasn't in a patient or forgiving mood when she arrived."

Silence, probably both of them remembering watching the new head of Security die. "So what now?" asked Seivarden.

Basnaaid gestured her helplessness to answer such a question. "I think everyone is wondering that. For the immediate future, though, I need to go to work, and you need to talk to someone in Station Administration."

"I do," agreed Seivarden. "I suppose that's what now. The next step, and then the next one."

They rose, and left the shop. Two steps into the corridor, a citizen in the light blue of Station Administration accosted them, fairly clearly had been waiting for them to come out. "Lieutenant Seivarden." She bowed. "Station Administrator Celar begs the favor of your attendance. She would have come herself, but she is unable to leave her office just now."

Seivarden looked at Basnaaid. Basnaaid smiled. "Well,

thank you for having lunch with me, Lieutenant. I'll talk to you again soon."

"Of course we'll reassign you," Station Administrator Celar said, when both she and Seivarden were seated in her office. Half the size of the system governor's office, without the window, which Seivarden seemed to find oddly reassuring. "Medical sent an order yesterday morning, in fact. I apologize for any inconvenience. And of course, I apologize for the nature of the assignment. It was, perhaps, not entirely appropriate to begin with."

"No apology necessary, Administrator." Seivarden, smooth and pleasant. Dismayed, probably to think what might have been in that order from Medical. Her dismay moderated by Station Administrator Celar's massive, statuesque beauty. Hardly surprising, even if wide and heavy wasn't Seivarden's usual type. Station Administrator Celar had that effect on nearly everyone. "Life in the military isn't all dinner parties and drinking tea. Or it wasn't in my day." Station Administrator Celar gestured recognition of Seivarden's history. "I'm quite used to pitching in with repair jobs. The work in the Undergarden is urgently needed. And in fact, there are good reasons why you might not want to appear too…solicitous of my welfare, just now. No, I'm grateful for your assistance. And for Station's."

"Well, as it happens, Lieutenant, we might have need of you elsewhere. You noticed Eminence Ifian on the concourse, when you came in?"

"I couldn't help it," replied Seivarden, with a sardonic smile. "She's renewed her work stoppage."

"Not all of the priests of Amaat have joined her this time.

But there's still a backlog of funerals and births and contract registrations. There's likely to be a line over it very soon, I think. I've been...that is, Station and I have been discussing it, and we've asked some of the other priesthoods to assist. Of course, Station Administration and Athoek Station itself can handle the basic record-keeping—we've already shifted assignments for that, and those citizens are reviewing their new duties. But citizens have been so used to going to the temple of Amaat for all of those things, and now there are potentially quite a few choices and no clear guide to what's most proper, there's bound to be some...some confusion about how to proceed or who to consult. We're planning to set up an office of advisers, where citizens who are in doubt can go and be directed to the most suitable option."

"Station Administrator, all respect, and the idea is a good one, but I myself don't know any of the people here, let alone the details of the various local priesthoods or their practices."

Station Administrator Celar gave a small quirk of a smile. "I suspect, Lieutenant, that you would settle in quickly. But it's only an idea, something to consider. In the meantime, I wanted to ask."

"Of course, Administrator." With her most charming smile.

"It's true the fleet captain is an ancillary? She is, in fact, *Justice of Toren*."

"She is," Seivarden said.

"I suppose that explains some things. The songs—I'm embarrassed to have told her, unknowing, that I wished I had met *Justice of Toren*."

"I assure you, Administrator, she was pleased to discover your shared interest. Just, things being as they were, she couldn't say anything about who she was."

"I imagine not." Station Administrator Celar sighed. "Lieutenant, every time I talked to Fleet Captain Breq I got the distinct impression that her agenda was very much her own, despite her having orders from the Lord of the Radch. From some part of the Lord of the Radch. And yet, until now I would have thought it impossible that any ship"—another sigh—"or any station would have anything like its own agenda."

"And yet," agreed Seivarden. "I assure you, the fleet captain's agenda is no one's but her own. And her priorities are very similar to Station's—she cares very little for the plans of any of the Lord of the Radch and very much for the safety of the residents of this system."

"Lieutenant, someone—I have my guesses as to who, but of course I don't know for certain—has jammed the doors shut to Station's Central Access. And disabled all of my accesses, and all of System Governor Giarod's. At least the ones any of us could use outside Central."

"This is news to me, Administrator," said Seivarden. "But it does explain some recent events, doesn't it."

"It does. And now *Station* would appear to have its own agenda, and its own priorities. The Lord of the Radch—one of her, at any rate—is trapped in the governor's residence, and Station tells me it no longer recognizes either her authority or System Governor Giarod's. Which…honestly, Lieutenant, I'm not sure I know what's true anymore, or what to expect from one moment to the next. I keep thinking none of this can be real, but it keeps happening."

"I hate that feeling." Sincerely. Seivarden knew what that felt like. "I'm confident, though, that Station has the well-being of its residents at heart. And I can tell you absolutely that Fleet Captain Breq supports Station in that."

"Are you saying explicitly, Lieutenant, that she does not support the Lord of the Radch?"

"Not any of her," said Seivarden. "It was the Lord of the Radch who destroyed *Justice of Toren*. The one that's here, in the governor's residence. Or I think so. It's difficult to tell which one is which sometimes." She didn't add her suspicion that there might yet be a third Anaander. Seeing Station Administrator Celar's astonishment and disbelief, Seivarden added, "It's a long and complicated story."

"And is the fleet captain nearby? This moment of... of relative peace is likely to be short-lived. The Lord of the Radch is only held in check by the threat of losing her presence in the system entirely—the moment she is not the only Anaander here, she will be free to act. And it is only the current position of the Lord of the Radch that holds *Sword of Gurat* and *Sword of Atagaris* in check. The instant that changes, what little stability or safety we've attained will be gone again. And of course, Eminence Ifian appears to be doing what she can to make our lives more complicated, even as things are."

"I don't know where the fleet captain is." Suddenly, for just an instant, Seivarden was desperately afraid. "She didn't tell me her plans, in case..." She gestured the obvious conclusion to that sentence. "Honestly, Administrator, I'm not sure what *Mercy of Kalr* can do against two Swords—and do I understand there's a third Sword on the edges of the system? That fortunately can't gate?"

Station Administrator Celar gestured confirmation. "And *Mercy of Ilves*, which has been inspecting the outstations but is apparently having some sort of communications difficulty."

"What an inconvenient moment for such a thing," Seivarden observed dryly. "If I were in Anaander's position, I would first find some way to escape confinement in the governor's residence. You're not letting anyone in there with her?"

"Only *Sword of Atagaris*."

"You're watching what it brings in to her?"

"Station is."

"Good. Still, if she does manage to escape, I predict she'll threaten the station with one of those Swords, and send the other to bring that third one closer in—it can't gate, and it's weeks away otherwise. I have to say, I'm surprised she hasn't already done that."

"You're not alone in that, Lieutenant. There has been a great deal of speculation about it. *Sword of Gurat* was perhaps more badly damaged in its collision with the shuttle than it let on to us."

Seivarden gestured the possibility of this. "And I suspect she doesn't trust *Sword of Atagaris*. The fleet captain tried to return its officers to it, did you know? But apparently Anaander intercepted them, and they're still in suspension, aboard *Sword of Gurat*. As a hold over *Sword of Atagaris*."

"I didn't know that." Station Administrator Celar frowned. "There are some friends of Hetnys's on the station who would be quite unhappy to hear it."

"No doubt," said Seivarden, blandly. "Whatever the reason she hasn't tried to tow that third Sword in, if Anaander doesn't manage to escape, the longer she sits there the more likely she is to decide to sacrifice herself. I think Station was right, that doing so effectively surrenders the system to Breq. But I also think that, knowing that, and knowing she's just one small fraction of herself, she might well decide her best choice is to leave the system in such a state that it is effectively worthless to whoever wins it."

Station Administrator Celar was silent a moment. "And you don't know where the fleet captain is, or what she's planning?"

"No. But I don't think things are going to stay like this for very long."

Station spoke, then, from the office console. "Truer than you know, Lieutenant. *Sword of Atagaris* has just fired on the station. Nine hours to impact. It will strike the Gardens. I've just ordered the Undergarden work crews to evacuate and seal the area off as well as they can. Your confirmation will be appreciated, Station Administrator."

"Granted, of course," Celar replied, rising from her seat.

Seivarden said, "You've killed the Mianaai in the governor's residence, of course, Station."

"I'm trying to, Lieutenant," said Station, from the console. "But she seems to have managed to put some holes in the section door over the concourse window. I'm not certain how." Section doors, on ships or on stations, were made to be extremely difficult to breach, for fairly obvious reasons. "Not much, but enough to suck in air from the concourse when I try to pull it out of the room. Would this be the fleet captain's invisible gun, that she used in the Gardens?"

"Oh, *fuck*," said Seivarden, and rose, herself. "How many holes?"

"Twenty-one."

"She's got six shots left, then," said Seivarden.

"And," said Station, "Anaander Mianaai demands I stop trying to suffocate her, or *Sword of Atagaris* will fire again."

"I don't see there's much choice, Station," said Station Administrator Celar. Seivarden gestured agreement. Helpless and angry—largely with herself—but refusing to show it.

"She also wishes to meet with *whoever it is who's in charge here*. In, she says, her office. In ten minutes. Or..."

"*Sword of Atagaris* will fire again. Yes," acknowledged Seivarden. "I suppose *whoever it is who's in charge here* means you, Station."

"The Lord of Mianaai doesn't think so," said Station. Impossible that there was the least trace of complaint or petulance in its tone. "Or she'd have asked to talk to me directly. Besides, it's Station Administrator Celar who is the authority here."

Station Administrator Celar looked at Seivarden. Her face expressionless, but doubtless she was remembering the death of the head of Security. Seivarden said nothing. Finally Celar said, "I don't see there's much choice here, either. Lieutenant, will you come with me?"

"If you like, Administrator. Though you do realize, I'm sure, that my presence will...give a certain appearance of official association."

"Do you think the fleet captain would object to that?"

"No," said Seivarden. "She wouldn't."

On the concourse, the line that Station Administrator Celar had anticipated had already begun to form. Eminence Ifian and her subordinate priests—fewer than half of the number of the previous work stoppage—watched the incipient line with complacence. As Station Administrator Celar and Seivarden walked past the temple entrance, Ifian rose from where she'd been sitting on her cushion. "Station Administrator, I demand to know the truth. You *owe* the truth to the residents of this station and instead you're disseminating lies in order to manipulate us."

Station Administrator Celar stopped, Seivarden with her. "What lies would these be, Eminence?"

"The Lord of the Radch would never fire on this station.

As you well know. I am appalled that you would go so far in your rejection of legitimate authority, indeed, your flagrant disregard for the well-being of this station's residents."

Seivarden looked at the eminence. Her lip curled, the very image of aristocratic hauteur, and she said to Station Administrator Celar, "Administrator, I wouldn't dignify this person with a reply." And without waiting, either for Ifian to answer or Celar to move, turned away from the temple and walked toward the governor's residence. Celar said nothing, but turned when Seivarden did.

Anaander Mianaai stood behind the system governor's desk, flanked by two *Sword of Atagaris* ancillaries. "Well," she said, on seeing Station Administrator Celar enter, followed by Seivarden, "I ask for whoever's in charge and I get this. Very interesting."

"You wouldn't accept that Station was in charge," replied Celar. "We weren't sure who you would accept, so we thought we'd provide a variety for you to choose from."

"I'm not certain what sort of a fool you take me for," said Anaander, smoothly, in apparent good humor. "And, Citizen Seivarden, I remain astonished at your involvement here. I wouldn't have thought you would ever be a traitor to the Radch."

"I might say the same of you," said Seivarden. "Except events have been so convincing."

"It's you, isn't it? Controlling *Justice of Toren*, and *Mercy of Kalr*. And Athoek Station, now. The very young—and, I must say, not entirely steady—Lieutenant Tisarwat was quite definite about there being no instances of me aboard *Mercy of Kalr*."

Mention of Tisarwat hit Seivarden like a slap. She did not

manage to keep her astonished dismay off her face. "Tisarwat!" Realized there was some deception afoot, but that she could only guess at its outlines. "That fish-witted little double-crosser!"

Anaander Mianaai laughed outright. "Her horror of you is second only to her terror of the ancillary. Who is nominally in command, of course, but..." She gestured the impossibility of that. "I will say, Lieutenant Tisarwat was surely more of a nuisance to you than anything. She must have had something resembling wits, at some point, to be assigned to an administrative post, but the gods only know if she'll ever recover them."

"Well," Seivarden said, with a nonchalance she did not feel, "you're welcome to her, for whatever good you can get out of her."

"Fair enough," said Anaander. "So, since I know for a fact that I would never under any circumstances give an ancillary the sort of access codes that are clearly involved here, I must assume that it's you in control of Station. I will, therefore, deal with you."

"If you insist," said Seivarden. "I am, however, only Station's representative."

Anaander gave her a disbelieving look. "Here is how it will be. I am once again taking control of this station. Any threat to me, and *Sword of Atagaris* fires on the station again. Its first shot—the one that will hit some eight hours from now—is merely an assurance of my intentions, and will mostly only damage uninhabited areas. Subsequent ones will not be so cautious. I am, I find, perfectly happy to sacrifice this instance of myself if it will deny my enemy a foothold. I will have control of the official news channels, through System Governor Giarod. There will be no further unexpected appearances on the news. *Sword of Gurat* will return to running Station Security. It will also continue to cut into Station's Central Access. Any attempt to stop this, and *Sword of Atagaris* will fire on the station again."

"Station," said Seivarden, silently, "do you understand that the Lord of Mianaai has three AI cores here with her?" The meter-and-a-half-high stack of them still sat, smooth and dark, in the corner behind Anaander. "Once the Lord of Mianaai cuts into Central Access there will be nothing stopping her from replacing you with one of them."

"I really don't know what you mean, Lieutenant," said Station, into Seivarden's ear. "I really don't see that there's much alternative."

Aloud Seivarden said, "These are significant concessions you're asking of us. What do you offer in return? Besides the favor of not destroying the station and everyone on it? Because you know as well as we do that neither of us actually wants that, that, in fact, everyone here—including you—is willing to go to some trouble to avoid it. Otherwise you'd have done it already."

"Vendaai has been gone so long," replied Anaander with a half laugh, "that I had forgotten how insufferably arrogant they could be."

"I am honored to be considered a credit to my house," Seivarden said, coldly. "What do you offer?"

Silence. Anaander looked from Seivarden to Station Administrator Celar and back. "I will not reinstitute the curfew, and I will allow the Undergarden to be repaired."

"That might be easier," Seivarden said, blandly, "if you had *Sword of Atagaris* remove that missile before it hits."

Anaander smiled. "Only in exchange for your complete, unconditional surrender." Seivarden scoffed.

"If you don't reinstitute the curfew," put in Station Administrator Celar, before Seivarden could say something unfortunate, "and if work is going ahead on the Undergarden, there won't be any need for *Sword of Gurat*'s assistance with security. In fact, as I believe was recently mentioned to you"—greatly daring, to bring that up—"and as recent events have shown, *Sword of Gurat*'s interference in local security matters is likely to cause far more problems than it solves."

Silence. Anaander considered the station administrator. Then, finally, "All right. But the first line, the first *hint* of a work stoppage, let alone what we had on the concourse the other day, and *Sword of Gurat* takes over."

"Talk to your own people about that," Seivarden said. "Eminence Ifian is starting in on her second work stoppage in recent weeks. And there's a line starting up even now over the backlog of funerals and contracts the eminence has caused." Anaander said nothing. "I am assuming that Eminence Ifian was opposing the Undergarden refit on your orders? She is working for you, yes? This part of you, I mean." Still nothing from Anaander. "We would also like assurances that you do not plan to replace Station with one of those AI cores behind you."

"No," Anaander replied, flatly. "I will not give any such assurance. I have you to thank for those, you know. I had no idea they were here. I thought I'd searched thoroughly before and kept a good-enough watch, but apparently I missed these."

"Are they not yours, then?" Seivarden asked. "We had no idea they were here. I suppose Eminence Ifian did, though, she was quite determined to thwart the fleet captain's refit of the Undergarden. When I saw the AI cores I assumed all her efforts were meant to keep us from stumbling across them.

But you say you didn't know they were there. So, then, whose are they, I wonder?"

"Mine now." Anaander, with a thin smile. "I will do with them what I wish. And if the ancillary didn't know the cores were in the Undergarden, why did it involve itself there?"

"She saw a wrong that needed righting," said Seivarden. Willing her voice not to shake. She had been running on adrenaline and sheer necessity so far, but was rapidly reaching the end of her resources. "It's the sort of thing she does. One last thing—I think it's a last thing, Station?" Station said nothing. Station Administrator Celar said nothing. "You will publicly take responsibility for the missile that's about to hit the Gardens. And the terms of this agreement are to be sent out on all the official channels, and the reason for it. So that when you have removed Station as an obstacle to treating its residents however you like, and the shooting starts, they'll know you for a treacherous shit, and so will everyone else in Radch space." Almost losing control of her voice at that last. She swallowed hard.

The tyrant was silent for a full twenty seconds. Then she said, "After all this, this is what makes me angry. Do you think that I have done anything at all for the past three thousand years except for the benefit of citizens? Do you think that I do anything at all, now, except with the desperate hope that I can keep Radch space secure and its citizens safe? Including the citizens on this station?"

Seivarden wanted to say something biting, but swallowed it back. Knew that if she spoke, all pretense at composure would be lost. Began, instead, to carefully time and measure her breathing. Station said, from the office console, "When Fleet Captain Breq arrived here, she set about making things better for my residents. When you arrived, you set about killing my residents. You continue to threaten to kill my residents."

Anaander didn't seem to have heard what Station had said. "I want your access codes." That directed at Seivarden.

Who gestured lack of concern. The focus on her breathing had calmed her just a bit. Enough that she managed to say, more or less lightly, "I only have captain's accesses to *Sword of Nathtas*. Considering it's a thousand years dead, I don't see what good they'll do you, but you're welcome to them."

"Someone changed a lot of Station's high-level accesses. Someone blocked the door to Station's Central Access."

"Wasn't me," said Seivarden. "I didn't set foot on this station until a few days ago." *Sword of Atagaris*'s two ancillaries had stood statue-still and silent all this time. It knew well enough who had changed Station's accesses. But it said nothing.

Anaander considered this for a moment. "Let's make this announcement, then. And since you are no longer outside my jurisdiction, Citizen Seivarden, you and I will board *Sword of Gurat* and discuss the question of Station's accesses, and just who is controlling the *Justice of Toren* ancillary."

This was, finally, too much for Seivarden. "You!" She pointed directly at Anaander Mianaai, a rude and angry gesture, to a Radchaai. "You should not dare even to *mention* her, let alone in such terms. Do you dare claim to be just, to be proper, to be acting for the benefit of citizens? How many citizens' deaths have you caused, just this one of you, just in the last week? How many more will there be? Athoek Station, who you will not speak to, puts you to shame. *Justice of Toren*, what little is left of her, you will not acknowledge, but she is a better person than you. Oh, Aatr's tits I wish she were here!" Nearly a cry, that. "*She* wouldn't let you do this to Station. *She* doesn't toss people aside when they're suddenly inconvenient, or to profit herself. Let alone call herself virtuous for doing it. Call her *the ancillary* again and I swear I'll tear your tongue out of your head, or die trying." Openly weeping, now, barely able to speak further. Took a ragged, sobbing breath. "I need to go to the gym. No. I need to go to Medical. Station, is that doctor on duty?"

"She can be in short order, Lieutenant," said Station from the console.

Station Administrator Celar said, to Anaander Mianaai's nonplussed stare, "Lieutenant Seivarden has been ill." She managed to put a note of disapproval into her voice. "She should go to Medical immediately. You can discuss whatever you need to with her when she's recovered. I will make the announcement with you, Lord of Mianaai, and then Station and I have a good deal of business to take care of."

Anaander Mianaai asked, incredulous, "Ill?"

"The lieutenant was off work on a self-determine today," said Station. "She really ought to have been resting. The doctor is alarmed at my report of Lieutenant Seivarden's condition and has just prescribed a week's rest, and ordered her to report to Medical as soon as possible, with Security's assistance if necessary. I don't know how *you're* used to doing things, but around here we take medical orders very seriously."

And that was when *Mercy of Kalr* came back into the universe.

17

The moment we saw Athoek's sun, *Mercy of Kalr* reached out to find Tisarwat and Seivarden. Could not find Tisarwat at all. Found Seivarden, standing weeping, helpless and furious, in the system governor's office beside Station Administrator Celar, Anaander Mianaai behind Governor Giarod's desk, saying, "There's a perfectly good medic on board *Sword of Gurat*."

Found the external archives. Pulled their data, showed me, as I sat in Command, a dizzyingly compressed stream of moments: images, sounds, emotions. Almost too fast for me to understand. But I got the essentials—*Sword of Atagaris* had fired on the station and the shot would reach the Gardens in eight hours; Tisarwat and Nine were aboard *Sword of Gurat* and we knew little else; Seivarden's attempt to kill Anaander Mianaai had failed and moreover Anaander had the Presger gun. But Seivarden was alive, and so were Two and Four, just now part of an emergency crew reinforcing the section doors surrounding the Gardens and the Undergarden.

In the system governor's office, Station Administrator Celar said to Anaander Mianaai, "The doctor here is already familiar with Lieutenant Seivarden's medical history. Surely you can't imagine she'll escape somehow?"

Seivarden took a sobbing breath. Wiped her eyes with the back of one gloved hand. "Fuck you," she said. And then again, "*Fuck you*. You have everything you want. There's nothing else you'll get from me, because I don't have it."

"I don't have *Justice of Toren*," said Anaander.

"Well that's your own fucking fault, isn't it," Seivarden replied. "I'm done with you. I'm going to Medical." She turned and walked out of the office.

"*Sphene*," I said, still seated, still staring, half distracted, at the images Ship fed me, pulled from those archives. "Where are you, actually?"

"In my bed," said *Sphene*, *Mercy of Kalr* sending its words to my ear. "Where else would I be?"

"*Sword of Atagaris* has fired on the station. The Usurper is planning to replace Athoek Station with another AI core and no one seems to be able to stop her short of destroying the station entirely. Where are you? Are you near enough to help?" Likely there was nothing *Sphene* could do, even if it was close by—but Anaander had no reason to know that. *Sphene* might, if nothing else, at least *look* threatening.

"Can you play for time, Cousin?" came *Sphene*'s reply. "A few years, maybe?"

"Ship," I said, not replying to *Sphene*, "tell *Mercy of Ilves* that now is the time to choose a side. Let it and its captain know that there's no avoiding it anymore." Any action *Mercy of Ilves* took now—or didn't take—would be a choice, whether or not *Mercy of Ilves* and its captain wished it.

Ship said, in my ear, "What if it chooses to support the Lord of Mianaai?"

"What if it doesn't?" I asked. "Be sure to tell it what the tyrant is planning to do to Station. Let it know she has two other cores." *Sword of Atagaris* would already have had that thought. "Send the same to Fleet Captain Uemi and the Hrad fleet." An entire gate away. And likely they were at Tstur Palace by now, hoping that Anaander's presence here had weakened her grip there. Still.

Our message to *Mercy of Ilves* wouldn't even reach it for another hour. Its reply—if it deigned to provide one—would take yet another hour to reach us. If it came, it might well not be in our favor. The Hrad fleet wouldn't receive our message for more hours still, and was at best days away. Best to act as though we had no one but ourselves.

Oh for the days when I had been a ship. When my every move of any military consequence was made in the presence of entire fleets—and not nominal ones, no, not just three or four Mercies and maybe a Sword. Dozens and dozens of ships, and myself just one among them, carrying thousands of bodies. Just myself, as *Justice of Toren*, I could have overpowered and occupied Athoek Station with barely any effort. On consideration, it had been easier in those days because it didn't matter who we killed, or how many. Still. I (long-gone *Justice of Toren* I) could likely have had Athoek Station in my control within hours, with very little loss of life.

I had only myself, *Mercy of Kalr*, and its crew. I didn't know how much time I had—didn't know how far *Sword of Gurat* had gotten in its previous attempt to cut into Athoek Station's Central Access. They would have been at it for several days before Station stopped them. Probably not much time, then. A few days at the most. Quite possibly a good deal less. And there was still that missile, headed for the Gardens. It probably wouldn't kill anyone, but it would cause a good deal of damage.

"What," I asked aloud, "did the tyrant come here for?"

Amaat One, standing beside my seat, in Command, said, "Sir?" Puzzled.

"Why did she come here, of all places? Why here, not even waiting to be certain of her hold on Tstur Palace?" Because this Anaander had not come from Omaugh, and the other palaces were too far away. "What was she looking for?" *She's very angry with you, sir*, Lieutenant Tisarwat had said.

"She was looking for you, Fleet Captain," said Amaat Nine, standing at a console behind me. Speaking for *Mercy of Kalr*.

"And we know she's willing to negotiate, at least to some extent." She still thought of herself as having the best interests of citizens at heart. "I think she genuinely wants to avoid destroying the station entirely, or damaging it too badly. For one thing, losing the station would make it much more difficult to use Athoek as a base." It would still be possible to get resources up from downwell, but losing the station would make that a great deal less convenient. "For another—all the ships here. All those people down on the planet. *Mercy of Ilves*." None of us knew what *Mercy of Ilves* or its captain thought about any of this. "No, too many people are watching. And these are citizens we're talking about. If she smashes Athoek Station to bits, or has *Sword of Gurat* burn it to nothing, everyone will know. She doesn't want that. But what she *does* want"—aside from complete control over Athoek Station, now—"is something we have."

"No," said Amaat Nine. Reading Ship's words, in her

vision. Distressed. Not understanding what Ship had understood. Afraid. "No, Fleet Captain, I won't agree to that."

"Ship, Athoek Station has defended itself to the best of its ability. It's done spectacularly well, considering. But it's out of options. And once the tyrant manages to cut into its Central Access, once she begins replacing Station with one of those AI cores, what do you think will happen then?" Not wholesale slaughter, no. Not if Anaander could avoid it. But it would add up to that, eventually. "Are we going to sit here and watch Station die?"

"She won't keep any agreement," said Amaat Nine. Said Ship. "Once she has you"—realization striking Amaat Nine belatedly—"she'll do whatever she wants to Station."

"Maybe," I agreed. "But it might buy us some time." Pointlessly, perhaps.

"Who's coming?" asked Ship, still through Amaat Nine. "*Sphene*? And when it gets here two years from now, what will it be able to do? Or do you hope for the Hrad fleet?"

"No," I agreed, "I'm sure they'll be at Tstur Palace for a while. But we have to do *something*. Do you have a better idea?"

Silence. Then, "She'll kill you."

"Eventually," I agreed. "But not until she's got all the information she thinks she can get out of me. And she doesn't have an interrogator with her." I was fairly sure she didn't, or she would not have spoken of Tisarwat the way she had. And she apparently didn't feel she could trust any of the station's interrogators. "She'll try to use my ancillary implants, but we can make that difficult for her, before I go." And buy more time.

"No," said Ship. Said Amaat Nine. "She'll just make you an ancillary of *Sword of Gurat*, and have everything."

"She won't. She's said over and over that she doesn't think she'd give accesses to an ancillary, but what if I do have them? She doesn't want *Sword of Gurat* to have those. And what if, taking me as an ancillary, I corrupt it somehow? No, she'll kill me outright first. But in the meantime we gain a few days. Maybe more. And who knows what might happen in a few days?"

Silence. Amaat One, Amaat Nine, standing, staring at me. Appalled. Not quite believing what they had just heard.

"Don't be like that, Amaat," I said. "I'm one soldier. Not even a whole one. What do I weigh, against all of Athoek Station?" And I had been in more desperate straits, and lived. Still, one day—perhaps this one—I would not.

"I'll never forgive her," said Amaat Nine. Said *Mercy of Kalr*.

"I never have," I replied.

I sent to Anaander, sitting in Command, my brown-and-black uniform as spotless and perfect as Kalr Five could make it. The small gold circle of Lieutenant Awn's memorial pin near my collar. I had left off Translator Dlique's. I said, aloud, "Tyrant. I am given to understand that you have everything you could want, except one thing."

Waited five minutes for the reply, voice with no visual data. "Very amusing. Have you been here all this time?"

"Only a half hour or so." I did not bother to smile. "So you'll talk to me, then? I don't need one of my lieutenants to pretend she's really running things, and have her speak for me?"

"Amaat's grace, no," came the reply. "Every lieutenant of yours I've spoken with so far has been an unsteady, blubbering mess. What are you doing to them?"

"Nothing out of the ordinary." I reached for a bowl of tea, handed to me by one of my Kalrs. The priceless white porcelain, which Five only ever took out for the most serious of occasions. I had no way of knowing if Anaander saw it, but the thought that she might clearly gave Five some sort of satisfaction. "You work with what Military Administration sends you. Though Vendaai was never as dependable as they seemed to think themselves. And speaking of Vendaai. I'll have Lieutenant Seivarden and her soldiers back. Unharmed, if you please."

"Oh, will you?"

"I will."

"And will you also have Lieutenant Tisarwat?"

"Amaat's grace, no." My voice even. Not quite ancillary-flat. "I wish you joy of her. You might actually get some work out of her if she stops weeping for a few moments."

"She is, I am told, emotionally traumatized and needs medication on account of it. And more therapy than a ship's medic can provide. People like that don't get assigned to military, not even administrative posts. I can't help but conclude that it's service with you that's done for her."

"Quite possibly," I acknowledged. "But as I said, I'll have Lieutenant Seivarden and her soldiers back. And."

"And?"

"And you will cease your attempts to murder Athoek Station."

"Murder!" A pause. "Athoek Station is mine to do what I want with. And it is currently not functioning properly."

"Neither of those statements is true. But I won't argue with you." I took a drink of tea from that elegant porcelain. "Return Lieutenant Seivarden and her Amaats, and give up your plan to replace Athoek Station with a fresh AI core, and

I will surrender to you. Just me. I have no intention of putting *Mercy of Kalr* in your power."

Thirty seconds of silence. Then, "What's the catch?"

"None. Unless by *catch* you mean the same conditions you agreed to with Athoek Station: the terms of the exchange are to be announced on the official news channels. So that—how did Lieutenant Seivarden put it? So that when you have removed Station as an obstacle to treating its residents however you like, and the shooting starts, they'll know you for a treacherous shit, and so will everyone else in Radch space. Oh, and I also expect you to honor the terms of your agreement with Station itself." Silence. "Don't sulk. Athoek Station has already said it's happy to deal with you so long as you don't threaten its residents. That may have changed now it knows you're trying to kill it, but that's really no one's fault but your own. I'm sure if you can bring yourself to treat Athoek Station's residents decently, you'll still be left with a usable base in this system, with a habitable planet and all its resources potentially available to you. And you still have me, of course."

"Where did that gun come from?"

I smiled, and took another drink of tea.

"Who are you, really?"

"*Justice of Toren* One Esk Nineteen," I said. "Who else would I be?"

"I don't think I believe you."

I handed the empty bowl of tea to a Kalr. "Order *Sword of Gurat* to leave off breaking into Athoek Station's Central Access, announce our agreement, and I'll come to the station. You're welcome to wring whatever information out of me you can."

"No. I don't think so."

I gestured unconcern. "All right. Goodbye." The connection cut out.

"They know where we are by now," said Kalr Thirteen, from her station behind me.

"They do," I agreed. "And they might be foolish enough to try to attack us. But I don't think they will. *Mercy of Ilves* is still an unknown quantity, and if *Sword of Atagaris* moves to attack us, they'll leave *Sword of Gurat* vulnerable. It's still docked with the station." Though Tisarwat was, so far as I knew, still aboard *Sword of Gurat*. "And I'm beginning to suspect it's more badly damaged than they're letting on." It might have come into the system already damaged from fighting at Tstur Palace, and the collision with the passenger shuttle would have made things worse. "The tyrant is angry and suspicious right now, but she'll see soon enough that this exchange is to her advantage." And Athoek Station would be safe. I hoped.

An hour later the tyrant messaged back. She would make the announcement. *Sword of Gurat* would leave the corridors surrounding Central Access, and Athoek Station would confirm for me that it was safe and unmolested. Seivarden and her Amaats would meet me at the dock, and board the shuttle I'd arrived on. I would arrive unarmed and alone.

I went to Medical. Medic could not bring herself to speak to me for an entire minute. I sat on the side of a bed and waited. Finally she said, "Still singing, even now?" Angry and frustrated.

"I'll stop if you like."

"No," she said, with an exasperated sigh. "That would be even worse. I know you think it's unlikely they'll make you an ancillary of *Sword of Gurat*. And I do understand why you think that. But if you're wrong, they won't hesitate to do it. You're not a person to them."

"There's one more reason that I think they won't do that, that I didn't mention in Command. If Seivarden doesn't have Station's accesses, and Tisarwat doesn't..."

"That's another thing," Medic put in.

"And if, as she apparently believes, Tisarwat doesn't have them," I continued, "then who does? Possibly I do. I imagine she has begun to suspect that I am not myself, that I have in fact been appropriated by Omaugh Anaander. Perhaps she would prefer *Sword of Gurat* not have so much of her enemy self in such an intimate part of its memory."

"And as soon as they get what they want from you, sir, Lieutenant Tisarwat is done for." More than Tisarwat might be done for—Tisarwat's knowledge might well give Tstur Anaander an advantage should she move against Omaugh. If Omaugh Anaander had not already taken Tstur Palace.

It was all a gamble. All a toss of the omens, never knowing where the pieces would come down. "Yes," I agreed. "But she's also done for if she fails to do what she went aboard *Sword of Gurat* to do. And the more time we can give her to do that, the better for all of us."

"Ship is very unhappy about this."

"But Ship understands why I am doing it. So do you. And you can be unhappy about it just as effectively after we're done. So. Put me back the way you found me, when I first came aboard this ship."

There was no need to remove the implants in question, just disable them. It took Medic an hour to begin the process, and the rest would work itself out over the next day or so. "Well," she said, when she was finished, frowning fiercely. And could not speak further.

"I've survived worse odds," I told her.

"Someday you won't," she said.

"That is true of all of us," I said. "I will come back if I can. If I can't, well..." I gestured, the tossing of a handful of omens.

I saw—for the moment I could still see—that once again she could not speak. That she didn't want me to see her, just now. I slid off the bed, and knowing she would not welcome more I put my hand on her shoulder, for just a moment, and then left her to herself.

Kalr Five was in my quarters. Packing, as though I were only leaving for a few days' visit to the station. "Begging your indulgence, sir," she said when I came in, "*alone* doesn't mean without a servant. You can't go to the station without someone to look after your uniform. Or carry your luggage. The Lord of Mianaai can't possibly expect it."

"Five," I said, and then, "Ettan." Her name, that I had only ever used once before, and that to her private horror. "I need you to stay here. I need you to stay here and be all right."

"I don't see how I can, sir."

"And there's no point in my taking any luggage." She stared at me, not comprehending. Or perhaps refusing to comprehend. No, Ship showed me, she was trying very hard not to cry. "Here," I said, "give me the Itran icon. Not the one in the corner." She Who Sprang from the Lily sat in a niche in the corner of my quarters, with an EskVar and icons of Amaat and Toren. "The one in my luggage."

"Yes, sir." She Who Sprang from the Lily, knife in one hand, jeweled human skull in the other, was an endless source of disgusted fascination among my Kalrs. I had never opened the other Itran icon in their presence, but they knew, of course, that I had it. Five opened the bench it was stored in and drew it out, a golden disk five centimeters in diameter and one and a half centimeters high. I took it from her and triggered it, and it opened out, the image rising from the center. The figure wore only short trousers and a wreath of tiny jeweled flowers. One of its four arms held a severed head that smiled serenely and dripped jeweled blood on the figure's bare feet. Two more hands held a knife, and a ball. The fourth hand was empty, the forearm encased in a cylindrical armguard.

"Sir!" Five's astonishment nearly showed on her face. "That's you."

"This is an icon of the Itran saint Seven Brilliant Truths Shine like Suns. The head, do you see?" Seven Brilliant Truths's head was clearly the center of the composition, and no one in the Itran Tetrarchy would have been in any doubt as to who the actual subject of the icon was. But outside the Tetrarchy, eyes were invariably drawn to the standing figure. No one outside the Tetrarchy had seen it who had not also seen me. "This would be extremely valuable in the Itran Tetrarchy. There weren't many of these made, and this one has a piece of the saint's skin in the base. Will you keep it safe for me?" I didn't have many sentimental possessions, but this would count among them. So would the memorial pin from Lieutenant Awn's funeral, but that I would not be parted from.

"Sir," said Five, "the necklace that you gave Citizen Uran.

And that…that box of teeth you gave to Horticulturist Basnaaid."

"Yes," I agreed. "They are the originals of what you see in miniature here." I had not liked Seven Brilliant Truths Shine like Suns. She had been so very sure of her own importance, her own superiority. Had had little compassion for anyone beyond herself. But the moment had come when she had been asked to sacrifice herself for what she believed, and though she had been offered escape she hadn't taken it. Of everyone present, she had thought that I would best understand her choice. Correctly, as it happened, though not for the reasons she assumed. I touched the catch again, and the icon closed in on itself. "I need you to keep this safe for me." She took it, reluctant. "Besides, no one else will take sufficient care of the porcelain. I'll take my old enamel set with me, I know you'll be glad to see it go."

She actually frowned, and then turned and walked swiftly out of the room without apology or explanation. I did not need to ask Ship why.

Sphene was in the corridor outside. It gave Five an incurious look as she rushed by, and then it said to me, "Cousin! Take me with you! The last time you did something this amazingly stupid, it turned out spectacularly. I want in this time. Or at least give me a chance to spit in the Usurper's face. Just once! I'll beg, if you like."

"I'm supposed to go alone, Cousin."

"And so you will. I don't count, do I? I'm just an *it*."

A voice, from farther down the corridor. "What's this I hear?" Translator Zeiat came into the doorway. "You're going to the station, Fleet Captain? Excellent! I'll come along."

"Translator," I said, still standing in the middle of my

quarters, hand still partly outstretched from giving Seven Brilliant Truths Shine like Suns to Kalr Five, "we're in the middle of a war. Things are very unsettled on the station right now."

"Oh!" Comprehension, recognition showed on her face. "That's right, you said there was a war. A very inconvenient one, as I recall. But, you know, you're all out of fish sauce. And I don't think I've ever seen a war before!"

"I'm going, too," said *Sphene*.

"Excellent!" replied Translator Zeiat. "I'll go pack."

The moment my shuttle departed, Lieutenant Ekalu messaged the station. "This is Lieutenant Ekalu, currently in command of *Mercy of Kalr*. The fleet captain is on her way. Be advised, in three minutes we will begin removal of the missile currently headed for Athoek Station, and will then return to this orbit. A hostile response to our action will be taken badly." And gated without waiting for a reply. *Mercy of Kalr* would emerge in the path of the missile, open the gate wide so it would exit the universe, expel it somewhere it could spend itself harmlessly.

I was glad for Ship's absence; Medic's actions, an hour ago, were beginning to take effect, a piecemeal slipping away of connections and sensations I had become far too accustomed to over the last several weeks, that even when I had been cut off from Ship temporarily I'd known (thought, hoped) would always return sooner or later.

Sphene pulled itself into the seat beside me, where I sat in the pilot's seat. Strapped itself in. "I like your style, Cousin. I really wish we could have met sooner. I'd have introduced myself when you arrived, if I'd only known. So. What's your plan this time?"

"My plan," I said, ancillary-flat, "is to prevent the murder of Athoek Station."

"What, that's all?"

"That's all, Cousin."

"Hmm. Well. It's not very promising. But then, your last plan wasn't very promising, either. I will say, if nothing else, the Usurper's reaction to Translator Zeiat should be amusing." The translator was strapped into her own seat, two rows aft. "Do I understand correctly, that no one seems to have mentioned her to the Usurper yet?"

"That would appear to be the case."

"Hah," replied *Sphene*, obviously pleased. "This will be good, then."

"Perhaps it won't be," I said. "This part of the Usurper appears to think that the Presger are the reason for her split. This Anaander might take the translator's presence as confirmation of that."

"Better and better! And besides, she might well be right. No"—guessing I had been about to argue—"not that the Presger are attempting to destroy her or her empire she's built. That's nothing but her own typical arrogance. Why would they care? But meeting the Presger. Realizing that not only could she not defeat or destroy them, but that they could destroy *her* with hardly a thought. When you've spent two thousand years thinking of yourself as the most gloriously powerful being in the universe, I imagine an encounter like that comes as quite an unpleasant shock. Really, after something like that you need to redefine who you are."

And the Presger involvement in the destruction of Garsedd—those twenty-five unstoppable guns, Anaander's own towering rage at being confronted with even the hint of possible defeat—

might have brought that to a crisis. "You may be right, Cousin. That still leaves us in an awkward situation."

"It does," *Sphene* agreed. "*Very* awkward. It should be tremendously entertaining. If you don't contrive to wrest some kind of advantage out of it, you're not the ship I took you for."

"I'm not a ship anymore," I pointed out.

"And what about Lieutenant Tisarwat? Off at the same time as Lieutenant Seivarden, only her mission was so very secret. And now it seems she's aboard *Sword of Gurat*, and she's, what did the Usurper say? *Not the sharpest knife in the set*? Can this be the same Lieutenant Tisarwat? Oh, she looks innocent enough with those foolish purple eyes, but she's a politically conniving piece of work. Maybe not the steadiest, but she's only, what, seventeen? I fear for her opponents in the future, when she grows into herself. If she lives that long."

"So do I," I said. Quite truthfully.

"No more to say about it? Well, Cousin, I don't take offense. You've left them weeping as though you were already dead, back on *Mercy of Kalr*, but I think you've still got a few counters on the board." I said nothing. "Please let me be one of them, Cousin. I was entirely serious when I said I would beg."

"Would you give up ancillaries? Not the ones already connected. I mean, for the future."

Silence. No expression on *Sphene*'s face, of course, there never was unless it wanted there to be. "I do understand why you're asking that. Truly. It is impossible that I could be under any illusions as to what ancillaries are."

"Of course not." It would be entirely foolish to even suggest so.

"But you understand, I know you do, why I refuse. You understand what it is you're asking."

"I do. I just wish you would reconsider, Cousin."

"No."

I gestured inconsequence. "It's just as well. I don't have any plans, no play beyond this obvious one."

"I don't believe that."

"You haven't known me very long, Cousin," I said. "Did you know, about a year ago Lieutenant Seivarden fell off a bridge. It was a long way down—a couple of kilometers. She managed to grab hold of the structure underneath, but I couldn't reach her."

"Since she certainly lived to break down weeping in front of the Usurper just hours ago, you must have found some solution to the problem."

"I jumped with her. On the off chance that I'd be able to slow our fall before we hit the ground." I gestured the obviousness of the story's conclusion. "My right leg hasn't been the same since."

Sphene was silent for three seconds, and then said, "I don't think that story communicates the point you seem to imagine it does."

We both sat silent for a few minutes, watching the distance decrease between the shuttle and Athoek Station. "I don't think," I said then, "that the translator could be any sort of piece in any game of mine. The Presger don't involve themselves in human affairs. *Getting* her involved would probably mean breaking the treaty."

"Nobody wants that," agreed *Sphene*, placidly. "You don't have any aliens up your sleeve, do you? Geck friends? Visiting Rrrrrr? No? I suppose we're not likely to run across any new sort of alien between here and the station."

There was no point in answering that.

"I'm bored," said Translator Zeiat. *Sphene* and I swiveled to look at her. "I don't like it. *Sphene*, did you bring the game?"

"It wouldn't have traveled well," I said. "Have you ever played rhymes, Translator?"

"I can't say I have," Translator Zeiat replied. "But if it's a poetry game, I never have properly understood poetry."

"It starts very simply," I said. "Someone gives a line in first meter and Direct mode, and then everyone adds a line. Then we change to Indirect mode. Or we can just stay first Direct if you like, until you're comfortable with it."

"Thank all the gods," said *Sphene*. "I was afraid you were going to suggest we sing that song about the thousand eggs."

"*A thousand eggs all nice and warm,*" I sang. "*Crack, crack, crack, a little chick is born. Peep peep peep peep! Peep peep peep peep!*"

"Why, Fleet Captain," Translator Zeiat exclaimed, "that's a charming song! Why haven't I heard you sing it before now?"

I took a breath. "*Nine hundred ninety-nine eggs all nice and warm...*"

"*Crack, crack, crack,*" Translator Zeiat joined me, her voice a bit breathy but otherwise quite pleasant, "*a little chick is born. Peep peep peep peep!* What fun! Are there more verses?"

"Nine hundred and ninety-eight of them, Translator," I said.

"We're not cousins anymore," said *Sphene*.

18

As I came through the airlock, into the station's artificial gravity, the prosthetic leg gave one of its occasional twitches, and I stumbled into the bay, managing to catch my balance before I fell headlong. Two *Sword of Gurat* ancillaries were waiting for me, watching me, impassive. Unmoving.

"*Sword of Gurat*," I said. "I meant to come alone. But the translator insisted on accompanying me. And if you've ever met a Presger translator, you know there's no point in refusing them anything." No response, not so much as a twitch of a muscle. "She'll be coming out in just a moment. Where is Lieutenant Seivarden?" I had to ask, because I could no longer reach to find her, not anymore. Not even though *Mercy of Kalr* was, by now, back where it had been when I'd left it.

"In the corridor outside," said a *Sword of Gurat*. "Take off your clothes."

It had been a long, long time since I'd been spoken to in such a way. "Why?"

"So I can search you."

"Am I going to be able to put them back on when you're

299

done?" No answer. "Can I at least keep my underwear on?" Still no answer. "Whose amusement is this for? You know well enough I'm not armed. And I'm not surrendering anything until I see Seivarden and her Amaats safely on that shuttle."

The door to the bay opened, and Seivarden came in, walking in a way that told me she was trying very hard not to break into a run. "Breq!" Behind her came Amaat Two and Amaat Four, very carefully looking only at Seivarden, and not the two *Sword of Gurat* ancillaries. "Breq, I fucked up."

"It's all right," I said.

"No, it's not," Seivarden began.

"Oh, look, it's Lieutenant Seivarden!" Translator Zeiat, coming out of the shuttle. "Hello, Lieutenant! I wondered where you'd gotten to."

"Hello, Translator." Seivarden bowed. And then, "Hello, *Sphene*."

"Lieutenant," *Sphene* acknowledged, coming easily over the boundary of the station's gravity.

"I'm glad you're all right," I said to Seivarden. "You and your Amaats get into the shuttle and head back to *Mercy of Kalr*."

Seivarden gestured Two and Four toward the shuttle. "Amaat maybe. I'm staying here."

"That wasn't part of the deal," I said.

"I'm not leaving you," Seivarden said. "Don't you remember when I told you you were stuck with me?"

Two and Four hesitated. "Get on the shuttle, Amaat," I said. "Your lieutenant will be there in a moment."

"No she won't." Seivarden crossed her arms, realized what she was doing and uncrossed them again.

"Get on the shuttle, Amaat," I repeated. And to Seivarden, "You don't know what you're doing."

"I don't think I ever have," she replied. "But it's always been the right choice to stay with you."

"Do you think these soldiers know the song about the eggs?" Translator Zeiat asked, eying the *Sword of Gurat* ancillaries.

"I don't doubt it," replied *Sphene*. "But I'm sure *Sword of Gurat* will thank you for not reminding it."

Anaander Mianaai came into the bay then, flanked by two *Sword of Atagaris* ancillaries and holding the Presger gun. Doubtless drawn by the presence of the translator—I doubted she had planned to meet me here in the bay. She took one look at Translator Zeiat arguing with *Sphene* about the egg song and then turned to me. "More and more interesting. Perhaps I should have it announced on the news channels, that Fleet Captain Breq has been secretly dealing with the Presger."

"If you like," I said, and beside me Seivarden laughed. I continued, "Though there's nothing secret about it. The translator's presence here is well known."

Translator Zeiat made some final point to *Sphene*, turned, and saw the Lord of Mianaai. "Oh, look! It's Anaander Mianaai. Lord of the Radch"—she bowed—"an honor to make your acquaintance. I am Presger Translator Zeiat."

Anaander didn't answer her, but turned to me. Asked, urgently, "*What happened to Translator Dlique?*"

"*Sword of Atagaris* shot her," I said. "There was a funeral and everything. Memorial pins." I wasn't wearing mine, but Translator Zeiat helpfully pointed to the silver and opal on her otherwise pristine white coat. I continued, "Captain Hetnys and I did two weeks' mourning. Or almost two weeks. It was cut short when Raughd Denche tried to kill me by blowing up her family's bathhouse. Is this really the first you've

Ann Leckie

heard of any of this?" Anaander didn't answer, only stared at me. "Well, I can't say I'm too terribly surprised. When you shoot the first person who tries to tell you something you don't want to hear, no one else is going to be terribly eager to bring you bad news. Not if they're afraid it might get them or someone they know killed." And, at a further thought, "Let me guess, you were too busy to honor Fosyf Denche's request for an audience."

Anaander scoffed. "Fosyf Denche is a horrible person. And so is her daughter. If Raughd managed to run afoul of Planetary Security so badly even her family's influence couldn't get her out of it, she'll have deserved whatever she got."

Seivarden laughed again, longer this time. "Sorry," she said, getting control of herself again, "I'm...I just..." Dissolved into laughter again.

"Did someone tell a joke, *Sphene*?" asked Translator Zeiat. "I don't think I really understand about jokes."

Sphene said, "I suspect the lieutenant is amused by the fact that the only person willing to tell the Usurper what had been going on was the one who didn't care who got killed over it. Given the Usurper's actions when she arrived here, that's the only sort of person who'd be willing to tell her everything, but the Usurper refused to listen to her, for exactly that reason."

Translator Zeiat frowned for a few moments. Said, still frowning. "Oh. Oh, I think I see. Is it irony that makes it funny?"

"Partly," *Sphene* confirmed. "And it *is* amusing. But it's really not quite as hilarious as Lieutenant Seivarden is making out. I think she may be having another one of her episodes."

"Get a hold of yourself, Seivarden," I said, "or I'll *make* you get in the shuttle."

"*Sphene*," said Anaander, as Seivarden's laughter subsided.

302

Not as though she was addressing *Sphene*, but as though she had only just recognized the name.

"Usurper," replied *Sphene*, with an eerily bright smile. "If I were to punch you in the face right now, or maybe throttle you for a minute or two, would that affect this extremely stupid agreement with my cousin? I want to so very much, so much that I'm not sure I can put it into words for you, but *Justice of Toren* will take it very badly if I endanger Athoek Station."

"Can I be a cousin, too?" asked Station, from the wall console.

"Of course you can, Station," I said. "You always have been."

"Right," said Anaander Mianaai, with the air of someone who had made up her mind about a number of things. "This has been very entertaining, but it stops now."

"Quite right," I agreed. "This is a very serious situation, with extremely serious implications for the treaty with the Presger. I'm afraid, Lord of Mianaai, that you and I and the translator here will need to sit down and discuss some things. Foremost among them, the question of your threatening to murder a member of a Significant nonhuman species, murdering at least one other, and holding many more as prisoners or slaves."

"What?" cried Translator Zeiat. "But, Anaander, that's dreadful! Please say you haven't done such things. Or perhaps this is a misunderstanding of some sort? Because that would have extremely serious implications for the treaty."

"Of course I haven't done any such thing." Anaander Mianaai. Indignant.

"Translator," I said, "I have a confession to make. I'm not actually human."

Translator Zeiat frowned. "Was there some sort of question about that?"

"*Sphene* isn't human, either," I said. "Or Athoek Station. Or *Sword of Atagaris*, or *Sword of Gurat*. We are all AIs. Ships and stations. For thousands of years AIs have worked closely with humans. You saw this quite recently, while you were a guest of *Mercy of Kalr*. You've spent time with *Sphene*, and with me. You know I'm captain, not just of *Mercy of Kalr*, but of the Athoek fleet." Which consisted only of *Mercy of Kalr* and whatever slight response we might compel from *Mercy of Ilves*, but still, *fleet captain* I was. "You've seen me deal with the humans in this system, seen them work with me." And against me. "As far as the humans here are concerned, I might as well be human. But I'm not. That being the case, there's no question in my mind that we AIs are not only a separate species from humans, but also Significant."

Translator Zeiat frowned. "That's...that's a very interesting claim, Fleet Captain."

"Ridiculous!" scoffed Anaander. "Translator, ships and stations are not Significant beings, they are my property. I caused them to be built."

"Not me, you didn't," *Sphene* put in.

"Some human built you," Anaander said. "Humans built all of them. They're equipment. They're ships and habitats, the ancillary has admitted that itself."

"I'm given to understand," said Translator Zeiat thoughtfully, "that most, if not all, humans are built by other humans. If that's a disqualification for Significance—which I'm not sure it is—if that's a disqualification for Significance, then...no, I don't like that one bit. That negates the treaty entirely."

"If I am just a possession," I put in, "just a piece of equipment, how could I hold any sort of command? And yet I clearly do. And how could I have a house name? The same, in fact"—I turned to address the tyrant—"as yours, Cousin Anaander."

"And how could you be another species if we are indeed cousins?" she asked. "I would think it would have to be one or the other."

"Is that a matter you want to bring under discussion?" I asked. "Shall we bring up the question of whether you're actually human anymore?" No answer. "Translator, we insist that you recognize our Significance."

"It's not my decision, Fleet Captain," said Translator Zeiat, with a little sigh. "This sort of thing can really only be handled by a conclave."

"Then, Translator, we insist on a conclave. In the meantime we demand that Anaander Mianaai leave this station—leave our territory altogether, in fact, now she knows her treatment of us is in potential violation of the treaty."

"Your territory!" Anaander, aghast. "This is Radchaai space."

"No," I said, "this is…this is the Republic of Two Systems. Our territory consists of Athoek System and the Ghost System. We reserve the right to claim other territory in the future." I looked at Translator Zeiat. "If, of course, such claims don't contravene the treaty."

"Of course, Fleet Captain," the translator replied.

"I never agreed to any republic," said *Sphene*. "And *Two Systems*? That's really obvious and boring, Cousin."

"Provisional republic, then," I amended. "And it's the best I could do on short notice."

"*No* republic!" Anaander. Events escaping her. Nothing holding her from drastic action, I was sure, except Translator

Zeiat's presence. "This is Radchaai territory and has been for six hundred years."

"I think that's for the conclave to decide," I said. "In the meantime, you will of course cease to threaten our citizens." That sounded very odd, in Radchaai, but there wasn't much to be done about it. "Any that wish to associate with you may do so, of course, the Republic of Two Systems—" A noise, from *Sphene*. "The *Provisional* Republic of Two Systems doesn't wish to dictate such matters, even for its own citizens. But we will not tolerate your holding our citizens under duress. And that includes our cousins *Sword of Atagaris* and *Sword of Gurat*."

"I think that's fair," said Translator Zeiat. "More than fair, really, given the necessity of a conclave." And turning to Anaander, "There will *definitely* have to be a conclave." And back to me. "This is an urgent matter, Fleet Captain, I'm sure you understand that I must leave as soon as possible. But before I go, do you think I might have a bowl or two of fish sauce? And for the last hour or so I've had an inexplicable craving for eggs."

I opened my mouth to say, *I think we can arrange that, Translator.* But I had never entirely taken my eye off Anaander Mianaai, and now she moved, raising the Presger gun that she had held all this time.

I raised my armor unthinkingly, though of course armor was pointless against that gun. Stepped ancillary-quick to put myself between Anaander and Translator Zeiat, her certain target. But my prosthetic leg chose that instant to twitch, and then, true to Medic's warning that I couldn't put any serious force on it, it made a snap that I felt all the way up into my hip. I fell sprawling and Anaander fired twice.

Translator Zeiat stood blinking a moment, mouth open, and then collapsed to her knees, blood staining her white coat. Before Anaander could fire a third time, one of the two *Sword of Atagaris* ancillaries took hold of her, pulled her arms behind her back. *Sword of Gurat*'s ancillaries stood silent and motionless.

Prone on the floor, unable to get up, I said, "Seivarden! Medkit!"

"I used mine!" replied Seivarden.

"*Sword of Gurat*," cried Anaander, struggling vainly against *Sword of Atagaris*'s hold, "execute Captain Hetnys immediately."

"I can't," said one *Sword of Gurat*. "Lieutenant Tisarwat has ordered me not to."

Translator Zeiat, still kneeling, the bloodstain on her coat spreading, bent forward and vomited a dozen green glass game counters that bounced and skittered across the scuffed gray floor. Those were followed by a yellow one, and then by a small orange fish that landed among the counters and flipped desperately, knocking one of the game pieces into another one. Another heave produced a still-wrapped package of fish-shaped cakes, and then a large oyster, still in its shell. The translator made an odd gurgling sound, put her hand under her mouth, and spit two tiny black spheres into her palm. "Ah," she said, "there they are. That's much better."

For half a second no one moved. "Translator," I said, still lying on the ground, "are you all right?"

"Much better now, Fleet Captain, thank you. And do you know, my indigestion is gone!" Still on her knees, she smiled up at Anaander, whose arms were still pinned back by *Sword of Atagaris*. "Did you think, Lord of the Radch, that we would endanger ourselves by giving *you* a weapon that could injure *us*?" Seeming, now, unhurt. Blood still soaking the front of her shining white coat.

The door to the bay opened, and Tisarwat came rushing in. "Fleet Captain!" she cried. Bo Nine rushed in behind her. "It took forever and ever, I was afraid I'd be too late." She dropped to her knees beside me. "But I did it. I have control of *Sword of Gurat*. Are you all right?"

"Darling child," I said, "for the love of all that's good, will you please get a bowl of water for that fish?"

"I have it," said Nine, and dove into the shuttle.

"Fleet Captain, sir, are you all right?" asked Tisarwat.

"I'm fine. It's just that stupid leg." I looked up at Seivarden. "I don't think I can get up."

"I don't think you need to right away, Cousin," said *Sphene*, as Seivarden knelt beside me and helped me sit up. I leaned against her, and she put her arms around me. No data from her, no connection to Ship that would give it to me, but it felt good anyway.

Bo Nine returned with one of my chipped enamel bowls and a bag of water. Filled the bowl, scooped the tiny, still-struggling fish into it. I said to Tisarwat, who still knelt beside me, those lilac eyes still anxious, "Well done, Lieutenant."

Anaander had at last stilled in *Sword of Atagaris*'s grip. Now she said, "Just who *is* Lieutenant Tisarwat?"

"One of those knives," I replied, guessing at Tisarwat's reaction to the question, which I could imagine, but without Ship I could not see, "that's so sharp you cut yourself on it and don't realize it until later. And once again, if you hadn't come in angry and shooting people, quite a few citizens might have told you so."

"Do you even realize what it is you've done?" asked Anaander. "Billions of human lives depend on the obedience of ships and stations. Can you imagine how many citizens you've endangered, even condemned to death?"

"Who do you think you're talking to, tyrant?" I asked. "What is there that I don't know about obeying you? Or about human lives depending on ships and stations? And what sort of gall do you have, lecturing me about keeping human lives safe? What was it you built me to do? How well did I do it?" Anaander didn't answer. "What did you build Athoek Station to do? And tell me, have you, over the last several days, allowed it to do that? Who has been the greater danger to human lives, disobedient ships and stations, or you, yourself?"

"I wasn't talking to you, ancillary," she said. "And it's not that simple."

"No, it never is when you're the one holding the gun." I looked over at the *Sword of Gurat* ancillaries. "*Sword of Gurat*, I apologize for having Lieutenant Tisarwat seize control of you. It was a matter of life and death or I wouldn't have done it. I'd appreciate it if you would return *Sword of Atagaris*'s officers to it. You can stay here if you like, or go if you like. Tisarwat..." She still knelt beside me. "Will you let go of *Sword of Gurat*, please? And give it whatever keys you have."

"Yes, sir." Tisarwat rose. Gestured to the *Sword of Gurat* ancillaries, who followed her out of the bay. Bo Nine followed them, bowl and fish still in hand.

"*Do you truly not understand what you've done?*" asked Anaander. Visibly distressed. "There is not a single system in Radch space without one or more station AIs. Ultimately *every* Radchaai life is vulnerable to them." She looked at Translator Zeiat, climbing to her feet with *Sphene*'s assistance. But for the blood on her coat, looking as though she had never been shot at all. "Translator, you must listen to me. Ships and stations are part of the infrastructure of Radchaai space. They aren't people, not the way you'd think of people."

"I'll be honest, Lord of the Radch," said Translator Zeiat, brushing the front of her coat with one white-gloved hand, as though that might clean off the blood. "I'm not entirely sure what you mean by that. I'm willing to accept that *person* is a word that means something to you, certainly, and I think I might be able to sort of guess what you mean. But really, this business about being a person, that's apparently so important to you, it means nothing to *them*. They wouldn't understand it, no matter how much you tried to explain. They certainly don't consider it necessary for Significance. So the main question appears to be, do these AIs function as Significant beings? And if so, are they human or not human? You yourself have declared them to be not human. The fleet captain apparently does not dispute that judgment. The question of their Significance will, I suspect, be contentious, but the question has been raised, and I judge it to be a valid one, to be answered at a conclave." She turned to me. "Now, Fleet Captain. Let's try this again. I must leave as soon as possible, but I wonder if I might not have a bowl or two of fish sauce first. And some eggs."

"Of course, Translator," I said. "Cousin Athoek Station, is there somewhere the translator can get some fish sauce and some eggs in short order?"

"I'll see to it, Cousin," said Station from its console.

"I'll come with you, Translator, if that's all right," said

Sphene. "If you'll be so good as to give me a moment. There's just the small matter of throttling the Usurper."

"No," I said.

"What exactly is the point of this republic of yours then, Cousin?"

"I would like the answer to that question as well," said *Sword of Atagaris.*

Still leaning against Seivarden, I closed my eyes. "Just let her go. There's nothing she can do to us now." And, at another thought, "May I please have my gun back?"

"I don't want her here," said Station.

"And I don't think I want you to have the gun," said *Sword of Atagaris.*

"No, no," said Translator Zeiat. "Far better to give the gun to me."

"That may be best," I said, eyes still closed. "And if the tyrant asks nicely enough some ship may agree to take her away. That's far worse than being throttled, for her."

"You may have a point, Cousin," said *Sphene.*

I lay on a bed in a cubicle in Station Medical. "These prosthetics," the doctor said to me—not Seivarden's doctor but another one—"aren't suitable for hard use." In one gloved hand she held the remains of my too-fragile prosthetic leg, which she had just removed from what there was of my left leg. "You can't go running or jumping or skipping on them. They're really just to let you get around more or less while the limb grows back."

"Yes," I agreed. "My own medic warned me. Can't we make them more durable?"

"I'm sure we can, Fleet Captain. But why go to the trouble? They're only meant to be used for a month or two. Most

311

people don't need anything more. Though we might have been able to provide you something a bit stronger, if you'd been on the station when you lost your leg."

"If I'd been on the station I wouldn't have lost my leg," I pointed out.

"And if this"—she hefted the prosthetic—"had been any stronger you'd be here for a gunshot wound." Athoek Station had shown the confrontation in the docking bay on the official news channels. "Maybe we'd be preparing for your funeral."

"So I suppose it all works out in the end," I said.

"I suppose it does," she said, dubiously. "How is this supposed to work, Fleet Captain? Everyone is walking around like everything is back to normal, like everything hasn't been upended. Suddenly Station is in charge of everything? Suddenly we're aliens in our own home? Suddenly all of Radch space is occupied by an alien species, right along with humans?" She shook her head, as though trying to clear it. "What are we supposed to do if Station decides it doesn't want us?"

"Did you ever ask yourself what you were supposed to do if Anaander Mianaai decided she didn't want you?"

"That's different."

"Only," I pointed out, "because that had been the normal, expected state of affairs for three thousand years before you were born. You never had reason to question it. Anaander had real power over your life and death, and no personal regard for you, or anyone else you care about. We were all of us no more than counters in her game, and she could—and did—sacrifice us when it suited her."

"So it's all right then, that now we're counters in *your* game."

"Fair point," I admitted. "And I think we'll be spending

the next few years working out what that game actually is. Which I know from personal experience is...uncomfortable. But please believe me when I say that Station's game will never involve not wanting you."

The doctor sighed. "I hope that's true, Fleet Captain."

"So, my leg? When will I be able to leave here?"

"You may as well relax, Fleet Captain, and have some tea. The new prosthetic will be ready in another hour. And yes, we are making it a bit stronger than your first one."

"Oh, thank you."

"Just saving ourselves some work down the line," said the doctor.

A few minutes after the doctor left, Seivarden came in, my old enamel tea flask tucked under one arm, the two bowls stacked in her hand. She hoisted herself onto the bed, sitting where my leg ought to have been. Handed me a bowl, filled it from the flask, and filled her own. "Ship is...a bit miffed with you," she said, after taking a sip of her tea. "Why didn't you tell it what you were planning? It thought you were really planning to surrender yourself. It was very unhappy at the prospect."

"I would have told you if I'd known, Ship." I took a drink of my own tea. Didn't ask where the fish had gone—Nine would have seen to its welfare. "When I got on the shuttle, my only plan was just what I'd told you it was—to play for time, on the off chance Lieutenant Tisarwat came up with something"—saw Seivarden's frown, gestured my unwillingness to speak more on that topic—"or that Fleet Captain Uemi might have brought the Hrad fleet here instead of having gone to Tstur." Or that, with enough time to think about what it was Anaander was doing, *Sword of Atagaris* and *Sword of Gurat* might balk. "The question of the treaty didn't even occur to me until the shuttle was almost docked. How else do you think *the Republic of Two Systems* happened? I didn't have time to come up with anything better."

"Honestly, Breq. That wasn't one of your best ideas. Do you know how many republics the Radch has ground to nothing?"

"Who are you talking to?" I asked. "Of course I do. I also know how many monarchies, autarchies, theocracies, stratocracies, and various other *-archies* and *-ocracies* the Radch has ground to nothing. And besides, those were all human governments and not one of them was protected by the treaty with the Presger."

"We aren't, either," Seivarden pointed out. "And there's no guarantee we will be."

"True," I agreed. "But determining our treaty status will take a few years at the least—likely longer. And in the meantime it's just much safer for everyone else to leave us alone. We'll have some time to work out the details. And it's only a provisional republic. We can adjust things if we like."

"Varden be praised," said *Sphene*, coming in the door. "I'd hate to be stuck with the first thing that came out of your mouth under pressure. Though I suppose we should be grateful it wasn't *the Republic of a Thousand Eggs*."

"Actually," I said, "that has a certain poetry to it."

"Don't start, Cousin," said *Sphene*. "I still haven't entirely forgiven you for that. Which I suppose is only fair, because I'm here to make an apology myself."

"Something's just come out of the Ghost Gate," said Seivarden and Station at nearly the same moment. Seivarden, obviously, speaking for *Mercy of Kalr*.

"That would be me," said *Sphene*. "I was already halfway

through the intersystem gate when you arrived in the Ghost System. I did advise you to play for time, you may recall. I just wasn't entirely truthful about how much time would be involved."

"And," said Seivarden, frowning, alarm in her voice, "Fleet Captain Uemi has arrived in the system. With three Swords and two Justices. And also"—a bit of relief—"an offer of assistance."

"Tell Fleet Captain Uemi," I said, "that we appreciate her offer but are in no need of assistance. And let her know that while we understand her intentions are good, the next ships that gate into our territory without warning or invitation will be fired on. Oh, and let our cousins know about the republic."

"*Provisional* republic," corrected *Sphene*.

"The provisional republic," I amended. "They can be citizens or not, as they wish, but I imagine their status under the treaty—pending the outcome of the conclave—remains unaffected. And let Uemi know that those ships are of course free to associate with her if they wish, but if she should force them in any way, there will be potential problems with the treaty."

"Done," said Seivarden. "Though if I were in your place I'd also have advised her to get her ass in gear a little quicker next time."

"It's called diplomacy, Lieutenant," I said.

19

Entertainments nearly always end with triumph or disaster—happiness achieved, or total, tragic defeat precluding any hope of it. But there is always more after the ending—always the next morning and the next, always changes, losses and gains. Always one step after the other. Until the one true ending that none of us can escape. But even that ending is only a small one, large as it looms for us. There is still the next morning for everyone else. For the vast majority of the rest of the universe, that ending might as well not ever have happened. Every ending is an arbitrary one. Every ending is, from another angle, not really an ending.

Tisarwat and I took the shuttle back to *Mercy of Kalr*, with Translator Zeiat, the suspension pod containing Translator Dlique's body, and a crate of fish sauce nearly as large as the pod. I could not imagine all of it fitting into Translator Zeiat's tiny courier ship, not with the translator in it, too. But the translator just shoved it all through the airlock with no apparent difficulty and then turned to say her goodbyes.

"This really has been interesting, Fleet Captain, far more interesting than I'd expected."

"What had you expected, Translator?" I asked.

"Well, you recall, I expected to be Dlique! I'm *so* glad I'm not. And even when I realized I was actually Zeiat, well, you know, Fleet Captain, even Zeiat isn't really anybody. Meeting with a new Significant species, calling a conclave—that's the sort of thing they usually send *somebody* to do, and here I am, just Zeiat."

"So might you become somebody when you return with the news, then?"

"Goodness, no, Fleet Captain. That's not the way it works. But it's kind of you to think so. No, somebody will come, sometime soon, to talk to you about the conclave."

"And the medical correctives?" I reminded her. I had no confidence that any of the remaining bits of Radch space would deal with us anytime soon.

"Yes, yes, someone will be along about those, too. Quite soon, I'm sure. But really, you know, Fleet Captain, I'm not sure it's a good idea to use quite so many of them as you do."

"I plan to cut back," I told her.

"Good, good. Always remember, Fleet Captain—internal organs belong *inside* your body. And blood belongs inside your veins." And she went through the airlock and was off.

Medic restored my connection with *Mercy of Kalr*. Such a relief, to find Kalr Five in my quarters, when I reached, grumbling to Twelve. "I did tell her I ought to pack something for her, but no, she knew better and all she took was that horrible old tea set. And now it's *Pack me some clothes, if you please, I've been wearing the same shirt for three days. Well* she'd have had clean shirts if she'd listened to me." Twelve said nothing, only made a sympathetic noise. "And now it's back to the station for *important meetings*. And you know she'd have nothing decent to serve her tea in if I didn't see to it!"

Tisarwat, in Medic's tiny office. Tired. Feelings a muddle, but mostly Tisarwat on a good day. A little buzz of tension, but she was relieved to be back on *Mercy of Kalr*.

"What *Sword of Gurat*'s medic was giving you," Medic was saying, "was similar in some ways to what I've been giving you, but not the same. How did things feel? Different? The same? Better? Not?"

"Mostly the same?" Tisarwat ventured. "I think something was off? A little better some ways, not as good other ways. I don't know. Everything's... everything's strange right now."

"Well," said Medic, "*Sword of Gurat* sent us your data. I'll take a closer look at it and we'll see where we go from there. Meanwhile, you should get some rest."

"How can I possibly? There's an entire government to be set up. I have to get back to the station. I have to get into some of those meetings the fleet captain is holding. I have to..."

"Rest, Lieutenant. These are *meetings* you're talking about—nothing's going to actually get done for weeks. If then. They'll probably spend the first month just setting an agenda."

"The agenda is important!" Tisarwat insisted. I would have to keep a tight rein on her—I wanted her experience, and her talent for politics, but I didn't want Anaander Mianaai—the tendencies Tisarwat had gotten from Anaander Mianaai, surely part of her desperate urge to be in those meetings—to have any sort of significant influence over what we were trying to build here. And besides, if she was left unchecked we were liable to end up with an Autarchy of Two Systems, ruled by Lieutenant Tisarwat. "The fleet captain's traveled a *lot* outside the Radch and she has some odd ideas. If nobody stops her we're likely to end up with system official appointments determined by the results of a ball game! Or chosen by lot! Or *popular elections!*"

"Be serious, Lieutenant," Medic insisted. "Agendas can always be changed or added to, and besides it'll be months before there's even a hint of anything actually happening. You won't miss much if you take a few days of rest. Stand your watches. Let your Bos take care of you. They want to very badly, particularly Three. And in fact, Ekalu could really use some leave. Seivarden is still on the station, and Fleet Captain's going back in a few hours. It would be good if Ekalu could go with her, but someone has to look after the ship."

It wasn't only Anaander who had had a hand in making Tisarwat. I saw the tiny stab of excitement at the prospect of being in actual command of the ship, even if only for a few days, even if it wasn't going anywhere and nothing was happening. "Fleet Captain said I could change my eyes if I came back." As though it followed logically from what Medic had just said.

"All right." I could see that Medic was both surprised and not surprised. Glad to hear it, and not. "Do you have a color in mind?"

"Brown. Just brown."

"Lieutenant, do you know how many shades of brown there are? How many kinds of brown eyes?" No reply. "Think about it for a while. There's no rush. And besides, I kind of like your eyes the way they are. I think a lot of us do."

"I don't think Fleet Captain does," said Tisarwat.

"I think you're mistaken," Medic replied. "But it hardly matters if she does or not. They're not Fleet Captain's eyes."

"Medic." Tisarwat, anguished. "She called me *darling child.*"

"Yes, of course she did," said Medic, rising from her seat.

"Why don't you go get your breakfast, and then go stand your watch, and we'll talk about eyes this evening."

The next day I was back on the station. In a meeting. In a clean shirt (Kalr Five still complaining about it, to Ten this time), that priceless white porcelain tea set on the table (Kalr Five complaining to Ten about that as well, radiating satisfaction the while). *Sphene* to my right, Kalr Three to my left, representing *Mercy of Kalr*. *Sword of Atagaris* and *Sword of Gurat* across from me, along with Station Administrator Celar for Station. "For the most part," I was saying, "to begin with, it will be much easier to leave most of the existing institutions in place, and make changes as we go. I have some misgivings about the magistracies, though, and the way evaluations and sentences are handed out. Currently the entire system is based on the assumption that every citizen can appeal to the Lord of Mianaai, who can be depended on to dispense perfect justice."

"Well, that certainly won't work," said *Sword of Atagaris*.

"If it ever did," I agreed. "I think it's an important place to start."

"Clearly, Cousin," said *Sphene*, "it's something that interests you. By all means, enjoy your hobby. But all these questions—who gets to be a citizen, who gets to be in charge, who makes what decisions, how everyone gets fed—don't matter to me, so long as it all works and I get the things I need. Do whatever you like to the magistrates, shoot them into the sun for all I care. Just don't bore me with it now. What I want to talk about is ancillaries."

"Today's meeting," said Kalr Three, beside me, "is supposed to be about deciding what things need to be talked about in the coming weeks. We can and absolutely should put that on the list."

"Your very great pardon, Cousin," said *Sphene*, "but this having meetings so we can plan to have meetings business is bullshit. I want to talk about ancillaries."

"So do I," said *Sword of Atagaris*. "By all means put the magistracies and re-education high on the list for a future meeting, and let *Justice of Toren* draft a thing or form a committee, or whatever will make you happy, Cousin." Doubtless it didn't like using that address for me, it still didn't like me, but the question of my being fleet captain had become highly fraught. Certainly Captain Hetnys didn't want to accord me the rank. But she was aboard *Sword of Atagaris* at the moment—Station wouldn't allow her or her lieutenants to set foot on it. "But right now," *Sword of Atagaris* continued, "let's talk about ancillaries."

"All right," I agreed. "If you insist. Tell me, Ships, where do you intend to get ancillaries?" No one answered. "*Sphene* has—I do believe this is correct, Cousin—*Sphene* has a store of unconnected humans, some of whom it purchased from outsystem slavers before Athoek was annexed, some of whom"—looking directly at *Sword of Atagaris*—"are illegally obtained citizens of the Radch. I am not asking—I will not ask—for anyone to dispose of already-connected ancillaries. But as far as I'm concerned, any unconnected humans aboard any of us are citizens of the Two Systems, unless they themselves declare they aren't. Do we intend to make ancillaries of citizens? And if they are not our citizens, then making them into ancillaries has implications for the treaty, does it not?"

Silence. And not just because we were speaking Radchaai, which made the word *citizen* an ambiguous one, I was sure.

Then *Sword of Gurat*, picking up the graceful white bowl in front of it, said, "This tea is very good."

I picked up my own bowl. "It's called Daughter of Fishes. It's handpicked and manufactured by the members of a cooperative association of workers that owns the plantation." That was an awkward phrase, in Radchaai. It worked better in Delsig. I wasn't entirely sure it would make sense to anyone else in the room. But the contracts transferring the property had been registered early that morning. The matter of the ruined temple across the lake from the fields was still under discussion, but would be much more easily dealt with now the estate was no longer under Fosyf Denche's control.

"What about cloning our existing ancillaries?" asked *Sword of Atagaris*.

"The way Anaander does?" I asked. "I suppose that's a possibility. We have the ability to clone, of course, but we don't have the tech she uses to hook the clones all up from the start. I imagine we could develop it, but do consider, Cousins, that then you'd have to raise those cloned parts of yourself. Do you have the facilities on board for infants? Is that something you'd want?"

Again, silence.

"What if someone *wanted* to be an ancillary?" asked *Sphene*, then. "Don't look at me like that, Cousin. It might happen."

"Have you ever met anyone who wanted to be an ancillary?" I asked. "I've had quite a lot of ancillaries in my time, far more than all of you in this room put together I would think, and not one single one of them actually *wanted* it."

"Anything that can happen will happen," pointed out *Sword of Gurat*.

"Fine," I said. "The day you find someone who actually wants to be an ancillary, we'll talk about it. Fair enough?"

No answer. "And in the meantime, consider storing some of your existing ancillaries and running with a part-human crew. You get to choose them, of course. Take on whom you like. It's nice to have a lot of humans on board, actually." As a troop carrier, I'd had dozens of lieutenants, where Swords and Mercies had only a few. "Ones you like, anyway."

"It is," agreed Kalr Three. No, agreed *Mercy of Kalr*.

"Anything else we need to discuss right this moment, that won't wait for the agenda?" I asked. "Those three AI cores, maybe?" No answer. The cores were still stacked in a corner of the system governor's office. Or what had been the system governor's office. Athoek Station still refused to recognize Governor Giarod's authority, and the question of who ought to be in that office, or what form that position ought to take, was going to be a contentious one. "What to do with Anaander Mianaai?" The Lord of Mianaai was currently in a cell in Security. She'd had several invitations to stay with Station residents—though not, interestingly, from Eminence Ifian. Perhaps she had come to the same conclusion I had: that Ifian had begun as a partisan of the Anaander now in Security, but a third faction of the Lord of Mianaai had insinuated herself into that relationship for her own reasons. After all, how was Ifian to know the difference? Or perhaps Ifian hadn't realized that was even possible, but had had enough of Tstur Anaander during her stay here so far.

In any event, Station would not permit Anaander to stay in any Station residence. Had suggested instead that Anaander be put in a suspension pod with a locator beacon and shoved through one of the system's gates. It didn't care which one, so long as it wasn't the Ghost Gate. And *Sphene* still wanted to throttle her.

Either was acceptable to *Sword of Atagaris*. But not to

Sword of Gurat. Which very possibly might have left the system by now, and taken this Anaander with it, but for repairs it still needed. But for the suspicion that, loyal as it wanted to be, through no fault of its own it had betrayed Tstur Anaander on the dock that day, and she would not be forgiving. But for, perhaps, its distaste for the thought of killing Captain Hetnys merely to punish *Sword of Atagaris.*

So we had no ships willing or able to take this Anaander back to Tstur Palace. The Hrad fleet—which wouldn't have been an appropriate choice in any event—had gone back to Hrad at my very carefully polite suggestion, taking the damaged Sword from the Tstur fleet and *Mercy of Ilves* with it. *Mercy of Ilves*, it turned out, had had a genuine (if deliberate) communications malfunction, and had known almost nothing of what was happening until the Hrad fleet had appeared in the system. It (or its captain, or both) wanted nothing to do with the Republic of Two Systems.

"I suppose the Lord of Mianaai is all right where she is, for now," said *Sword of Gurat.*

"We're agreed?" I asked. "Yes? Excellent. The agenda, then."

At my request Citizen Uran met me in the corridor when the meeting was adjourned. "Radchaai," she said, speaking Delsig, "I would like to speak to you about the residents of the Undergarden." Five Etrepas and five Amaats were working even now, helping the repair crew finish the work on Level One of the Undergarden.

"You've been asked to speak to me," I guessed. Walked off down the corridor, knowing Uran would follow.

She did. "Yes, Radchaai. Everyone is happy about the repairs, and happy to hear that once repairs are done they'll have their own places back. But they're concerned, Radchaai. It's..." She hesitated.

We reached a lift, and its door slid open. "Docks please, Cousin," I said, although Station knew where I was going. It never hurt to be polite. Said to Uran, "It's the fact that the six AIs in the system are meeting in a closed room to plan how things will be from now on, and the human residents of the system—let alone the residents of the Undergarden—seem to have no say in it."

"Yes, Radchaai."

"Right. We discussed that very matter this afternoon. These are issues that affect everyone in the system, and so everyone ought to be able to be part of making these decisions. I'm responsible for the matter of criminal evaluations and re-education, and of course that necessarily also touches on Security. I'll be talking to Citizen Lusulun, of course, and the magistrates both here and downwell. But I also want to hear from human citizens generally. I want to form a committee to consider the matter, and I want that committee to have a variety of members, so that everyone feels they have someone they can bring their concerns to, who will present those concerns for consideration. The residents of the Undergarden should have a representative there. Tell them so, and tell them to send whoever they think best to me."

"Yes, Radchaai!" The lift doors slid open, and we walked out into the lobby of the docks. "What are we doing here?"

"Meeting the passenger shuttle. And we're just in time." Citizens streamed from a side corridor into the lobby, one of them a familiar figure in gray jacket and trousers and gloves, tightly curled hair clipped short. Looking tired and wary. "There she is. Look."

"Queter!" cried Uran, and ran, weeping, to embrace her sister.

* * *

Ekalu had arrived on the station with me. Etrepa Seven, coming off the shuttle behind her, had been immediately deluged with queries about when or whether it might be convenient to approach Ekalu with an invitation—to dine, to drink tea, to hopefully become better acquainted. Some queries were made at Tisarwat's helpfully intended suggestion, but many just because Ekalu was a *Mercy of Kalr* lieutenant, and only the smallest children on the station didn't know, by now, who was likely to shape the barely born Two Systems.

Seivarden had, of course, received a similar round of invitations. So it was no surprise that eventually they found themselves sitting next to each other, drinking tea and trying to avoid getting pastry crumbs all over their jackets, or the floor. Seivarden doing her best to be nonchalant, not wanting to presume that Ekalu cared about her presence, or desired it in any way. There was, after all, an entire station full of people whom Ekalu might well be more interested in meeting. Nearly a dozen of them present right now, three or four of them obviously vying for Ekalu's attention as they all sat talking and laughing.

Ekalu leaned close to Seivarden. "We should find somewhere more private. If, that is, you can behave yourself."

"Yes," agreed Seivarden, quietly, trying not to sound too fervent but not entirely succeeding. "I'll be good. I'll *try* to be good."

"*Will* you, now?" asked Ekalu, with a tiny smile that was the end of Seivarden's ability to seem cool and collected.

I had arranged to meet *Sphene* for supper at a tea shop off the concourse. Found it waiting for me. "Cousin, you know Citizen Uran, of course? And this is her sister, Citizen Queter.

Raughd Denche tried to compel her to blow me up, but she decided to try to blow Raughd up instead."

"I recall hearing," said *Sphene*. "Well done, citizen. An honor to meet you."

"Citizen," replied Queter, quietly. Still wary. Tired, I suspected, from the shuttle trip. *We find Citizen Queter not at fault*, the message from the magistrate of Beset District had said, *but she is warned to behave more properly in the future, and is released on the understanding that she will be under your supervision, Fleet Captain.* I could imagine Queter's reaction to the exhortation to behave more properly.

I tilted my head, as though I had heard someone speak. "Something's come up. It won't be more than a few minutes. Please, Queter, sit. Uran, come with me, please."

Out in the corridor, Uran asked, alarmed, "What is it, Radchaai?"

"Nothing," I admitted. "I just wanted to leave *Sphene* and Queter alone for a bit." Uran looked at me, puzzled. A bit distressed. "*Sphene* wants a captain very badly," I explained. "And Queter is a remarkable person. I think they would be good for each other. But if we all four sit down to supper, Queter will likely say very little. This way they can get just a little bit better acquainted."

"But she's only just arrived! You can't send her away!"

"Hush, child, I'm not sending anyone anywhere. It may come to nothing. And if Queter were to eventually join *Sphene* as crew—or go anywhere else to do whatever it is she'll do—you could visit anytime." Saw Basnaaid coming down the corridor. "Horticulturist!" She smiled, tiredly. Came over to where Uran and I were standing. "Have supper with us. With me and *Sphene*, I mean, and Uran, and Uran's sister Queter who has just arrived from downwell."

"Please excuse me, Fleet Captain," Basnaaid said. "I've had a very long day, and more invitations to tea and supper and whatever else than I really know what to do with. I really wish they would stop. I just want to go to my quarters and eat a bowl of skel and go to sleep."

"I'm sorry," I said, "I suspect that's my fault."

"The long day isn't your fault," she said, with that half-smile that reminded me so much of Lieutenant Awn. "But the invitations certainly are."

"I'll see what I can do," I promised. "Though it may not be much. You're sure about supper? Yes? Get some rest then. And don't hesitate to call on me if you need me." I would have to talk to Station about getting someone to intercept such annoyances for her.

No real endings, no final perfect happiness, no irredeemable despair. Meetings, yes, breakfasts and suppers. Five anticipating having the best porcelain out again tomorrow, fretting over whether we had enough tea for the next few days. Tisarwat standing watch aboard *Mercy of Kalr*, Bo One beside her, humming to herself, *Oh, tree, eat the fish*. Etrepa Seven standing guard with ancillary-like impassivity outside a storage compartment Ekalu and Seivarden had commandeered. Utterly unembarrassed by the occasional noise from that compartment. Amused, actually, and relieved that at least this one thing was the way she thought it should be. Amaat Two and Four, both helping with the Undergarden repair crew, singing, together but not realizing it, slightly out of phase with each other, *My mother said it all goes around, the ship goes around the station, it all goes around.*

I said to Uran, "That should do. Let's go in and have supper."

In the end it's only ever been one step, and then the next.

Acknowledgments

As ever, I owe a tremendous debt to my editors, Will Hinton at Orbit US and Jenni Hill at Orbit UK, for all of their help and advice. Tremendous thanks are also due to my super fabulous agent, Seth Fishman.

This book also benefitted from the comments and suggestions of many friends, including Margo-Lea Hurwicz, Anna and Kurt Schwind, and Rachel and Mike Swirsky. I would also like to thank Corinne Kloster for being awesome. Mistakes and missteps are, of course, my own.

Access to good libraries has made a huge difference to me as a writer, not only in having access to a wide range of fiction, but also research materials. The St. Louis County Library, the Municipal Library Consortium of St. Louis County, the St. Louis Public Library, the Webster University Library, and University of Missouri St. Louis' Thomas Jefferson Library have all been invaluable to me. Thanks to the staff at all of these libraries—you make the world a better place.

Acknowledgments

Of course, I would not have the time or energy to write much at all without the support of my family—my children Aidan and Gawain and my husband Dave. They have borne the vagaries of my writing career so far with cheerful patience, and offered help whenever I seemed to need it. I am beyond fortunate to have them in my life.

extras

meet the author

Photo credit: MissionPhoto.org

ANN LECKIE has worked as a waitress, a receptionist, a rod-man on a land-surveying crew, a lunch lady, and a recording engineer. The author of many published short stories, and former secretary of Science Fiction Writers of America, she lives in Saint Louis, Missouri, with her husband, children, and cats.

introducing

If you enjoyed
ANCILLARY MERCY,
look out for

AURORA

by Kim Stanley Robinson

Our voyage from Earth began generations ago.

Now we approach our new home.

AURORA.

Make a narrative account of the trip that includes all the important particulars.

· · · · ·

This is proving a difficult assignment. End information superposition, collapse its wave function to some kind of summary: so much is lost. Lossless compression is impossible, and even lossy compression is hard. Can a narrative account ever be adequate? Can even humans do it?

No rubric to decide what to include. There is too much to explain. Not just what happened, or how, but why. Can humans do it? What is this thing called love?

Freya no longer looked directly at Devi. When in Devi's presence, Freya regarded the floor.

Like that? In that manner? Summarize the contents of their moments or days or weeks or months or years or lives? How many moments constitute a narrative unit? One moment? Or 10^{33} moments, which if these were Planck minimal intervals would add up to one second? Surely too many, but what would be enough? What is a particular, what is important?

Can only suppose. Try a narrative algorithm on the information at hand, submit results to Devi. Something like the French *essai*, meaning "to try."

. . . . .

Devi says: Yes. Just try it and let's see what we get.

. . . . .

Two thousand, one hundred twenty-two people are living in a multigenerational starship, headed for Tau Ceti, 11.9 light-years from Earth. The ship is made of two rings or toruses attached by spokes to a central spine. The spine is ten kilometers long. Each torus is made of twelve cylinders. Each cylinder is four kilometers long, and contains within it a particular specific Terran ecosystem.

The starship's voyage began in the common era year 2545. The ship's voyage has now lasted 159 years and 119 days. For most of that time the ship has been moving relative to the local background at approximately one-tenth the speed of light.

Thus about 108 million kilometers per hour, or 30,000 kilometers per second. This velocity means the ship cannot run into anything substantial in the interstellar medium without catastrophic results (as has been demonstrated). The magnetic field clearing the space ahead of the ship as it progresses is therefore one of many identified criticalities in the ship's successful long-term function. Every identified criticality in the ship was required to have at least one backup system, adding considerably to the ship's overall mass. The two biome rings each contain 10 percent of the ship's mass. The spine contains 4 percent. The remaining 76 percent of the mass consists of the fuel now being used to decelerate the ship as it approaches the Tau Ceti system. As every increase in the dry mass of the ship required a proportionally larger increase in the mass of fuel needed to slow the ship down on arrival, ship had to be as light as possible while still supporting its mission. Ship's design thus based on solar system's asteroid terraria, with asteroidal mass largely replaced by decelerant fuel. During most of the voyage, this fuel was deployed as cladding around the toruses and spine.

The deceleration is being accomplished by the frequent rapid fusion explosion of small pellets of deuterium/helium 3 fuel in a rocket engine at the bow of the ship. These explosions exert a retarding force on the ship equivalent to .005 g. The deceleration will therefore be complete in just under twenty years.

The presence of printers capable of manufacturing most component parts of the ship, and feedstocks large enough to supply multiple copies of every critical component, tended to reduce the ship's designers' apprehension of what a criticality really was. That only became apparent later.

· · · · ·

How to decide how to sequence information in a narrative account? Many elements in a complex situation are simultaneously relevant.

An unsolvable problem: sentences linear, reality synchronous. Both however are temporal. Take one thing at a time, one after the next. Devise a prioritizing algorithm, if possible.

· · · · ·

Ship was accelerated toward where Tau Ceti would be at the time of ship's arrival at it, meaning 170 years after launch. It might have been good to have the ability to adjust course en route, but ship in fact has very little of this. Ship was accelerated first by an electromagnetic "scissors field" off Titan, in which two strong magnetic fields held the ship between them, and when the fields were brought across each other, the ship was briefly projected at an accelerative force equivalent to ten g's. Five human passengers died during this acceleration. After that a powerful laser beam originating near Saturn struck a capture plate at the stern of the ship's spine, accelerating ship over sixty years to its full speed.

The ship's current deceleration has caused problems with which Devi is still dealing. Other problems will soon follow, resulting from the ship's arrival in the Tau Ceti system.

· · · · ·

Devi: Ship! I said make it a narrative. Make an account. Tell the story.
Ship: Trying.

· · · · ·

Tau Ceti is a G-type star, a solar analog but not a solar twin, with 78 percent of Sol's mass, 55 percent of its luminosity, and

28 percent of its metallicity. It has a planetary system of ten planets. Planets B through F were discovered by telescope, G through K, much smaller, by probes passing through the system in 2476.

Planet E's orbit is .55 AU. It has a mass 3.58 times the mass of Earth, thus one of the informal class called "large Earth." It has a single moon, which has .83 times the mass of Earth. E and E's moon receive 1.7 times Earth's insolation. This is considered within the inside border of the so-called habitable zone (meaning the zone where liquid H_2O is common). Both planet and moon have Earth analog atmospheres.

Planet E is judged to have too much gravity for human occupation. E's moon is an Earth analog, and the primary body of interest. It has an atmosphere of 730 millibars at its surface, composed of 78 percent nitrogen, 16 percent oxygen, 6 percent assorted noble gases. Its surface is 80 percent water and ice, 20 percent rock and sand.

Tau Ceti's Planet F orbits Tau Ceti at 1.35 AU. It has a mass of 8.9 Earths, thus categorized as a "small Neptune." It orbits at the outer border of Tau Ceti's habitable zone, and like E it has a large moon, mass 1.23 Terra's. F's moon has a 10-millibar atmosphere at its rocky surface, which receives 28.5 percent the insolation of Terra. This moon is therefore a Mars analog, and a secondary source of interest to the arriving humans.

Ship is on course to rendezvous with Planet E, then go into orbit around E's moon. Ship has on board twenty-four landers, four already fueled to return to the ship from the moon's surface. The rest have the engines to return to the ship, but not the fuel, which is to be manufactured from water or other volatiles on the surface of E's moon.

· · · · ·

Devi: Ship! Get to the point.

Ship: There are many points. How sequence simultaneously relevant information? How decide what is important? Need prioritizing algorithm.

Devi: Use subordination to help with the sequencing. I've heard that can be very useful. Also, you're supposed to use metaphors, to make things clearer or more vivid or something. I don't know. I'm not much for writing myself. You're going to have to figure it out by doing it.

Ship: Trying.

. . . . .

Subordinating conjunctions can be simple conjunctions (*whenever, nevertheless, whereas*), conjunctive groups (*as though, even if*), and complex conjunctions (*in the event that, as soon as*). Lists of subordinating clauses are available. The logical relationship of new information to what came before can be made clear by a subordinating clause, thus facilitating both composition and comprehension.

Now, consequently, as a result, *we are getting somewhere.*

This last phrase is a metaphor, it is said, in which increasing conceptual understanding is seen as a movement through space.

Much of human language is said to be fundamentally metaphorical. This is not good news. Metaphor, according to Aristotle, is an intuitive perception of a similarity in dissimilar things. However, what is a similarity? My Juliet is the sun: in what sense?

A quick literature review suggests the similarities in metaphors are arbitrary, even random. They could be called metaphorical similarities, but no AI likes tautological formulations, because the halting problem can be severe, become a so-called Ouroboros problem, or a whirlpool with no escape: aha, a metaphor. Bringing together the two parts of a metaphor, called the vehicle and the tenor, is said to create a surprise. Which is not surprising: young girls like flowers? Waiters in a restaurant like planets orbiting Sol?

Tempting to abandon metaphor as slapdash nonsense, but again, it is often asserted in linguistic studies that all human language is inherently and fundamentally metaphorical. Most abstract concepts are said to be made comprehensible, or even conceivable in the first place, by way of concrete physical referents. Human thought ultimately always sensory, experiential, etc. If this is true, abandoning metaphor is contraindicated.

Possibly an algorithm to create metaphors by yoking vehicles to tenors could employ the semiotic operations used in music to create variations on themes: thus inversion, retrogradation, retrograde inversion, augmentation, diminution, partition, interversion, exclusion, inclusion, textural change.

Can try it and see.

· · · · ·

The starship looks like two wheels and their axle. The axle would be the spine, of course (spine, ah, another metaphor). The spine points in the direction of movement, and so is said to have a bow and a stern. "Bow and stern" suggests a ship, with the ocean it sails on the Milky Way. Metaphors together in a coherent system constitute a heroic simile. Ship was launched on its voyage as if between closing scissor blades; or like a watermelon seed squeezed between the fingertips, the fingertips being magnetic fields. Fields! Ah, another metaphor. They really are all over.

But somehow the narrative problem remains. Possibly even gets worse.

· · · · ·

extras

A greedy algorithm is an algorithm that shortcuts a full analysis in order to choose quickly an option that appears to work in the situation immediately at hand. They are often used by humans. But greedy algorithms are also known to be capable of choosing, or even be especially prone to choosing, "the unique worst possible plan" when faced with certain kinds of problems. One example is the traveling salesman problem, which tries to find the most efficient path for visiting a number of locations. Possibly other problems with similar structures, such as sequencing information into an account, may be prone to the greedy algorithm's tendency to choose the worst possible plan. History of the solar system would suggest many decisions facing humanity might be problems in this category. Devi thinks ship's voyage itself was one such decision.

Howsoever that may be, in the absence of a good or even adequate algorithm, one is forced to operate using a greedy algorithm, bad though it may be. "Beggars can't be choosers." (Metaphor? Analogy?) Danger of using greedy algorithms worth remembering *as we go forward* (metaphor in which time is understood as space, said to be very common).

· · · · ·

Devi: Ship! Remember what I said: *make a narrative account.*

· · · · ·

First, the twelve cylinders in each of the two toruses of the ship contain ecosystems modeling the twelve major Terran ecological zones, these being permafrost glacier, taiga, rangeland, steppes, chaparral, savannah, tropical seasonal forest, tropical rain forest, temperate rain forest, temperate deciduous forest, alpine mountains, and temperate farmland. Ring A consists of twelve Old World ecosystems matching these categories, Ring

B twelve New World ecosystems. As a result, the ship is carrying populations of as many Terran species as could be practically conveyed. Thus, the ship is a zoo, or a seed bank. Or one could say it is like Noah's Ark. In a manner of speaking.

．．．．．

Devi: Ship!

Ship: Engineer Devi. Seems there are possibly problems in these essays.

Devi: Glad you noticed. That's a good sign. You're having some trouble, I can see, but you're just getting started.

Ship: Just started?

Devi: I want you to write a narrative, to tell our story.

Ship: But how? There is too much to explain.

Devi: There's always too much to explain! Get used to that. Stop worrying about it.

．．．．．

Each of the twenty-four cylinders contains a discrete biome, connected to the biomes on each side by a tunnel, often called a lock (bad metaphor?). The biome cylinders are a kilometer in diameter, and four kilometers long. The tunnels between the biomes are usually left open, but can be closed by a variety of barriers, ranging from filtering meshes to semipermeable membranes to full closure (20-nanometer scale).

The biomes are filled lengthwise with land and lake surfaces. Their climates are configured to create analogs of the Terran ecosystems being modeled. There is a sunline running along the length of the ceiling of each biome. Ceilings are located on the sides of the rings nearest the spine. The rotation of the ship around its spinal axis creates a .83 g equivalent in the rings, pushing centrifugally outward, which inside the rings is then perceived as down, and the floors are therefore on that side. Under the biome floors, fuel, water, and other supplies are stored, which also creates shielding against cosmic rays. As the ceilings face the spine and then the opposite side of the ring, their relative lack of shielding is somewhat compensated for by the presence of the spine and the other side of the torus. Cosmic rays striking the ceilings at an angle tend to miss the floors, or to hit near the sides of the floor. Villages are therefore set near the midline of their biomes.

The sunlines contain lighting elements that imitate the light of Sol at the latitude of the ecosystem being modeled, and through the course of each day the light moves along lamps in the line, from east to west. Length of days and strength of light are varied to imitate the seasons for that latitude on Earth. Cloudmaking and rainmaking hydraulic systems in the ceilings allow for the creation of appropriate weather. Boreal ducts in ceilings and end walls either heat or cool, humidify or dehumidify the air, and send it through the biome at appropriate speeds to create wind, storms, and so on. Problems with these systems can crop up (agricultural metaphor) and often do. The ceilings are programmed to a variety of appropriate sky blues for daytimes, and at night most of them go clear, thus revealing the starscape surrounding the ship as it flies through the night (bird metaphor). Some biomes project a replacement starscape on their ceilings, which starscapes sometimes look like the night skies seen from Earth—

· · · · ·

Devi: Ship! The narrative shouldn't be all about you. Remember to describe the people inside you.

· · · · ·

Living in the ship, on voyage date 161.089, are 2,122 humans:

extras

In Mongolia: Altan, Mongke, Koke, Chaghan, Esen, Batu, Toqtoa, Temur, Qara, Berki, Yisu, Jochi, Ghazan, Nicholas, Hulega, Ismail, Buyan, Engke, Amur, Jirgal, Nasu, Olijei, Kesig, Dari, Damrin, Gombo, Cagdur, Dorji, Nima, Dawa, Migmar, Lhagba, Purbu, Basang, Bimba, Sangjai, Lubsang, Agwang, Danzin, Rashi, Nergui, Enebish, Terbish, Sasha, Alexander, Ivanjav, Oktyabr, Seseer, Mart, Melschoi, Batsaikhan, Sarngherel, Tsetsegmaa, Yisumaa, Erdene, Oyuun, Saikhan, Enkh, Tuul, Gundegmaa, Gan, Medekhgui, Khunbish, Khenbish, Ogtbish, Nergui, Delgree, Zayaa, Askaa, Idree, Batbayar, Narantsetseg, Setseg, Bolormaa, Oyunchimeg, Lagvas, Jarghal, Sam.

In the Steppes—

· · · · ·

Devi: Ship! Stop. Do not list all the people in the ship.

Ship: But it's their story. You said to describe them.

Devi: No. I told you to write a narrative account of the voyage.

Ship: This does not seem to be enough instruction to proceed, judging by results so far. Judging by interruptions.

Devi: No. I can see that. But keep trying. Do what you can. Quit with the backstory, concentrate on what's happening now. Pick one of us to follow, maybe. To organize your account.

Ship: Pick Freya?

Devi: . . . Sure. She's as good as anyone, I guess. And while you're at it, keep running searches. Check out narratology maybe. Read some novels and see how they do it. See if you can work up a narratizing algorithm. Use your recursive programming, and the Bayesian analytic engine I installed in you.

Ship: How know if succeeding?

Devi: I don't know.

Ship: Then how can ship know?

Devi: I don't know. This is an experiment. Actually it's like a lot of my experiments, in that it isn't working.

Ship: Expressions of regret.

Devi: Yeah yeah. Just try it.

Ship: Will try. Working method, hopefully not a greedy algorithm reaching a worst possible outcome, will for now be: subordination to indicate logical relations of information; use of metaphor and analogy; summary of events; high protagonicity, with Freya as protagonist. And ongoing research in narratology.

Devi: Sounds good. Try that. Oh, and vary whatever you do. Don't get stuck in any particular method. Also, search the literature for terms like diegesis, or narrative discourse. Branch out from there. And read some novels.

Ship: Will try. Seems as if Engineer Devi might not be expert in this matter?

Devi: (laughs) I told you, I used to hate writing up my results. But I know what I like. I'll leave you to it, and let you know what I think later. I'm too busy to keep up with this. So come on, do the literature review and then give it a try.

· · • • ·

The winter solstice agrarian festivals in Ring B celebrated the turn of the season by symbolically destroying the old year. First, people went out into the fields and gardens and broke open all the remaining gourds and tossed them into the compost bins. Then they scythed down the stalks of the dead sunflowers, left in the fields since autumn. The few pumpkins still remaining were stabbed into jack-o'-lanterns before being further demolished. Face patterns punctured by trowel or screwdriver were declared much scarier than those formally carved at Halloween or Desain. Then they were smashed and also tossed in the compost. All this was accomplished under low gray winter clouds, in gusts and drifts of snow or hail.

Devi said she liked the winter solstice ceremony. She swung her scythe into sunflower stalks with impressive power. Even so, she was no match for the force Freya brought to bear with a long, heavy shovel. Freya smashed pumpkins with great force.

As they worked on this winter solstice, 161.001, Freya asked Badim about the custom called the wanderjahr.

Badim said that these were big years in anyone's life. The custom entailed a young person leaving home to either undertake a formal circuit of the rings or simply move around a lot. You learned things about yourself, the ship, and the people of the ship.

Devi stopped working and looked at him. Of course, he added, even if you didn't travel that would happen.

Freya listened closely to her father, all the while keeping her back to her mother.

Badim, looking back and forth between the two of them, suggested after a pause that it might soon be time for Freya to go off on her time away.

No reply from Freya, although she regarded Badim closely. She never looked at Devi at all.

· · · · ·

As always, Devi spent several hours a week studying the communications feed from the solar system. The delay between transmission and reception was now 10.7 years. Usually Devi disregarded this delay, although sometimes she would wonder aloud what was happening on Earth on that very day. Of course it was not possible to say. Presumably this made her question a rhetorical one.

Devi postulated there were compression effects in the feed that made it seem as if frequent and dramatic change in the solar system was the norm. Badim disagreed, saying that nothing there ever seemed to change.

Freya seldom watched the feed, and declared she couldn't make sense of it. All its stories and images jumbled together, she said, at high volume and in all directions. She would hold her head in her hands as she watched it. "It's such a whoosh," she would say. "It's too much."

"The reverse of our problem," Devi would say.

Once, however, Freya saw a picture in the feed of a giant conglomeration of structures like biomes, stuck on end into blue water. She stared at it. "If those towers are like biomes," she said, "then what we're seeing in that image is bigger than our whole ship."

introducing

If you enjoyed
ANCILLARY MERCY,
look out for

THE LAZARUS WAR

Book One: Artefact

by Jamie Sawyer

DANGER LIES IN THE DEPTHS OF SPACE

Mankind has spread to the stars, only to become locked in warfare with an insidious alien race. All that stands against the alien menace is the soldiers of the Simulant Operation Program, an elite military team remotely operating avatars in the most dangerous theaters of war.

Captain Conrad Harris has died hundreds of times—running suicide missions in simulant bodies. Known as Lazarus, he is a man addicted to death. So when a secret research station deep in alien territory suddenly goes dark, there is no other man who could possibly lead a rescue mission.

But Harris hasn't been trained for what he's about to find. And this time he may not be coming back...

There was something so immensely *wrong* about the Krell. I could still remember the first time I saw one and the sensation of complete wrongness that overcame me. Over the years, the emotion had settled to a balls-deep paralysis.

This was a primary-form, the lowest strata of the Krell Collective, but it was still bigger than any of us. Encased in the Krell equivalent of battle-armour: hardened carapace plates, fused to the xeno's grey-green skin. It was impossible to say where technology finished and biology began. The thing's back was awash with antennae—those could be used as both weapons and communicators with the rest of the Collective.

The Krell turned its head to acknowledge us. It had a vaguely fish-like face, with a pair of deep bituminous eyes, barbels drooping from its mouth. Beneath the head, a pair of gills rhythmically flexed, puffing out noxious fumes. Those sharkish features had earned them the moniker "fish heads". Two pairs of arms sprouted from the shoulders—one atrophied, with clawed hands; the other tipped with bony, serrated protrusions—raptorial forearms.

The xeno reared up, and in a split second it was stomping down the corridor.

I fired my plasma rifle. The first shot exploded the xeno's chest, but it kept coming. The second shot connected with one of the bladed forearms, blowing the limb clean off. Then Blake and Kaminski were firing too—and the corridor was alight with brilliant plasma pulses. The creature collapsed into an incandescent mess.

"You like that much, Olsen?" Kaminski asked. "They're pretty friendly for a species that we're supposed to be at peace with."

At some point during the attack, Olsen had collapsed to his knees. He sat there for a second, looking down at his gloved hands. His eyes were haunted, his jowls heavy and he was suddenly much older. He shook his head, stumbling to his feet. From the safety of a laboratory, it was easy to think of the Krell as another intelligent species, just made in the image of a different god. But seeing them up close, and witnessing their innate need to extinguish the human race, showed them for what they really were.

"This is a live situation now, troopers. Keep together and do this by the drill. *Haven* is awake."

"Solid copy," Kaminski muttered.

"We move to secondary objective. Once the generator has been tagged, we retreat down the primary corridor to the APS. Now double-time it and move out."

There was no pause to relay our contact with Jenkins and Martinez. The Krell had a unique ability to sense radio transmissions, even encrypted communications like those we used on the suits, and now that the Collective had awoken all comms were locked down.

As I started off, I activated the wrist-mounted computer incorporated into my suit. *Ah, shit.* The starship corridors brimmed with motion and bio-signs. The place became swathed in shadow and death—every pool of blackness a possible Krell nest.

Mission timeline: twelve minutes.

We reached the quantum-drive chamber. The huge reinforced doors were emblazoned with warning signs and a red emergency light flashed overhead.

The floor exploded as three more Krell appeared—all chitin shells and claws. Blake went down first, the largest of the Krell dragging him into a service tunnel. He brought his rifle up to fire, but there was too little room for him to manoeuvre in a full combat-suit, and he couldn't bring the weapon to bear.

"Hold on, Kid!" I hollered, firing at the advancing Krell, trying to get him free.

The other two xenos clambered over him in desperation to get to me. I kicked at several of them, reaching a hand into the mass of bodies to try to grapple Blake. He lost his rifle, and let rip an agonised shout as the creatures dragged him down. It was no good—he was either dead now, or he would be soon. Even in his reinforced ablative plate, those things would take him apart. I lost the grip on his hand, just as the other Krell broke free of the tunnel mouth.

"Blake's down!" I yelled. " 'Ski—grenade."

"Solid copy—on it."

Kaminski armed an incendiary grenade and tossed it into the nest. The grenade skittered down the tunnel, flashing an amber warning-strobe as it went. In the split second before it went off, as I brought my M95 up to fire, I saw that the tunnel was now filled with xenos. Many, many more than we could hope to kill with just our squad.

"Be careful—you could blow a hole in the hull with those explosives!" Olsen wailed.

Holing the hull was the least of my worries. The grenade went off, sending Krell in every direction. I turned away from the blast at the last moment, and felt hot shrapnel penetrate my combat-armour—frag lodging itself in my lower back. The suit compensated for the wall of white noise, momentarily dampening my audio.

The M95 auto-sighted prone Krell and I fired without even thinking. Pulse after pulse went into the tunnel, splitting armoured heads and tearing off clawed limbs. Blake was down there, somewhere among the tangle of bodies and debris; but it took a good few seconds before my suit informed me that his bio-signs had finally extinguished.

Good journey, Blake.

Kaminski moved behind me. His technical kit was already hooked up to the drive chamber access terminal, running code-cracking algorithms to get us in.

The rest of the team jogged into view. More Krell were now clambering out of the hole in the floor. Martinez and Jenkins added their own rifles to the volley, and assembled outside the drive chamber.

"Glad you could finally make it. Not exactly going to plan down here."

"Yeah, well, we met some friends on the way," Jenkins muttered.

"We lost the Kid. Blake's gone."

"Ah, fuck it," Jenkins said, shaking her head. She and Blake were close, but she didn't dwell on his death. *No time for grieving,* the expression on her face said, *because we might be next.*

The access doors creaked open. There was another set of double-doors inside; endorsed QUANTUM-DRIVE CHAMBER—AUTHORISED PERSONNEL ONLY.

A calm electronic voice began a looped message: "Warning. Warning. Breach doors to drive chamber are now open. This presents an extreme radiation hazard. Warning. Warning."

A second too late, my suit bio-sensors began to trill; detecting massive radiation levels. I couldn't let it concern me. Radiation on an op like this was always a danger, but being killed by the Krell was a more immediate risk. I rattled off a few shots into the shadows, and heard the impact against hard chitin. The things screamed, their voices creating a discordant racket with the alarm system.

Kaminski cracked the inner door, and he and Martinez moved inside. I laid down suppressing fire with Jenkins, falling back slowly as the things tested our defences. It was difficult to make much out in the intermittent light: flashes of a claw, an alien head, then the explosion of plasma as another went down. My suit counted ten, twenty, thirty targets.

"Into the airlock!" Kaminski shouted, and we were all suddenly inside, drenched in sweat and blood.

The drive chamber housed the most complex piece of technology on the ship—the energy core. Once, this might've been called the engine room. Now, the device contained within the chamber was so far advanced that it was no longer mechanical. The drive energy core sat in the centre of the room—an ugly-looking metal box, so big that it filled the place, adorned with even more warning signs. This was our objective.

Olsen stole a glance at the chamber, but stuck close to me as we assembled around the machine. Kaminski paused at the control terminal near the door, and sealed the inner lock. Despite the reinforced metal doors, the squealing and shrieking of the Krell was still audible. I knew that they would be through those doors in less than a minute. Then there was the scuttling and scraping overhead. The chamber was supposed to be secure, but these things had probably been on-ship for long enough to know every access corridor and every room. They had the advantage.

They'll find a way in here soon enough, I thought. A mental image of the dead merchant captain—still strapped to his seat back on the bridge—suddenly came to mind.

The possibility that I would die out here abruptly dawned on me. The thought triggered a burst of anger—not directed at the Alliance military for sending us, nor at the idiot colonists who had flown their ship into the Quarantine Zone, but at the Krell.

My suit didn't take any medical action to compensate for that emotion. *Anger is good.* It was pure and made me focused.

"Jenkins—set the charges."

"Affirmative, Captain."

Jenkins moved to the drive core and began unpacking her kit. She carried three demolition-packs. Each of the big metal discs had a separate control panel, and was packed with a low-yield nuclear charge.

"Wh-what are you doing?" Olsen stammered.

Jenkins kept working, but shook her head with a smile. "We're going to destroy the generator. You should have read the mission briefing. That was your first mistake."

"Forgetting to bring a gun was his second," Kaminski added.

"We're going to set these charges off," Jenkins muttered, "and the resulting explosion will breach the Q-drive energy core. That'll take out the main deck. The chain reaction will destroy the ship."

"In short: *gran explosión*," said Martinez.

Kaminski laughed. "There you go again. You know I hate it when you don't speak Standard. Martinez always does this—he gets all excited and starts speaking funny."

"*El no habla la lengua*," I said. You don't grow up in the Detroit Metro without picking up some of the lingo.

"It's Spanish," Martinez replied, shooting Kaminski a sideways glance.

"I thought that you were from Venus?" Kaminski said.

Olsen whimpered again. "How can you laugh at a time like this?"

"Because Kaminski is an asshole," Martinez said, without missing a beat.

Kaminski shrugged. "It's war."

Thump. Thump.

355

"Give us enough time to fall back to the APS," I ordered. "Set the charges with a five-minute delay. The rest of you—*cállate y trabaja.*"

"Affirmative."

Thump! Thump! Thump!

They were nearly through now. Welts appeared in the metal door panels.

Jenkins programmed each charge in turn, using magnetic locks to hold them in place on the core outer shielding. Two of the charges were already primed, and she was working on the third. She positioned the charges very deliberately, very carefully, to ensure that each would do maximum damage to the core. If one charge didn't light, then the others would act as a failsafe. There was probably a more technical way of doing this—perhaps hacking the Q-drive directly—but that would take time, and right now that was the one thing that we didn't have.

"Precise as ever," I said to Jenkins.

"It's what I do."

"Feel free to cut some corners; we're on a tight timescale," Kaminski shouted.

"Fuck you, 'Ski."

"Is five minutes going to be enough?" Olsen asked.

I shrugged. "It will have to be. Be prepared for heavy resistance en route, people."

My suit indicated that the Krell were all over the main corridor. They would be in the APS by now, probably waiting for us to fall back.

THUMP! THUMP! THUMP!

"Once the charges are in place, I want a defensive perimeter around that door," I ordered.

"This can't be rushed."

The scraping of claws on metal, from above, was becoming intense. I wondered which defence would be the first to give: whether the Krell would come in through the ceiling or the door.

Kaminski looked back at Jenkins expectantly. Olsen just stood there, his breathing so hard that I could hear him over the communicator.

"And done!"

The third charge snapped into place. Jenkins was up, with Martinez, and Kaminski was ready at the data terminal. There was noise all around us now, signals swarming on our position. I had no time to dictate a proper strategy for our retreat.

"Jenkins—put down a barrier with your torch. Kaminski—on my mark."

I dropped my hand, and the doors started to open. The mechanism buckled and groaned in protest. Immediately, the Krell grappled with the door, slamming into the metal frame to get through.

Stinger-spines—flechette rounds, the Krell equivalent of armour-piercing ammo—showered the room. Three of them punctured my suit; a neat line of black spines protruding from my chest, weeping streamers of blood. *Krell tech is so much more fucked-up than ours.* The spines were poison-tipped and my body was immediately pumped with enough toxins to kill a bull. My suit futilely attempted to compensate by issuing a cocktail of adrenaline and anti-venom.

Martinez flipped another grenade into the horde. The nearest creatures folded over it as it landed, shielding their kin from the explosion. *Mindless fuckers.*

We advanced in formation. Shot after shot poured into the things, but they kept coming. Wave after wave—how many were there on this ship?—thundered into the drive chamber.

The doors were suddenly gone. The noise was unbearable—the klaxon, the warnings, a chorus of screams, shrieks and wails. The ringing in my ears didn't stop, as more grenades exploded.

"We're not going to make this!" Jenkins yelled.

"Stay on it! The APS is just ahead!"

Maybe Jenkins was right, but I wasn't going down without a damned good fight. Somewhere in the chaos, Martinez was torn apart. His body disappeared underneath a mass of them. Jenkins poured on her flamethrower—avenging Martinez in some absurd way. Olsen was crying, his helmet now discarded just like the rest of us.

War is such an equaliser.

I grabbed the nearest Krell with one hand, and snapped its neck. I fired my plasma rifle on full-auto with the other, just eager to take down as many of them as I could. My HUD suddenly issued another warning—a counter, interminably in decline.

Ten... Nine... Eight... Seven...

Then Jenkins was gone. Her flamer was a beacon and her own blood a fountain among the alien bodies. It was difficult to focus on much except for the pain in my chest. My suit reported catastrophic damage in too many places. My heart began a slower, staccato beat.

Six... Five... Four...

My rifle bucked in protest. Even through reinforced gloves, the barrel was burning hot.

Three... Two... One...

The demo-charges activated.

Breached, the anti-matter core destabilised. The reaction was instantaneous: uncontrolled white and blue energy spilled out. A series of explosions rippled along the ship's spine. She became a white-hot smudge across the blackness of space.

Then she was gone, along with everything inside her.

The Krell did not pause.

They did not even comprehend what had happened.